TRANSPLANT

TRANSPLANT

▼

S.R.Maxeiner, Jr.

We writers have to stick together, don't we! Best wishes Kanny

[signature]

Writers Club Press
San Jose New York Lincoln Shanghai

Transplant

Writers Club Press
an imprint of iUniverse.com, Inc.

For information address:
iUniverse.com, Inc.
5220 S 16th, Ste. 200
Lincoln, NE 68512
www.iuniverse.com

Although this story is true to the dramatic historical events of 1985 it is a work of fiction. No character is drawn from any real person.

ISBN: 0-595-18707-2

Printed in the United States of America

To those of us who dare to recognize the chance for our own sudden death, who care enough to talk about our own organs and sign our donor cards, this book is dedicated.

Without sacrifice there is no resurreection. Nothing grows and blooms save by giving.

Andre Gide

Results are what you expect, and consequences are what you get.
a schoolgirl definition, Ladies' Home Journal

ACKNOWLEDGEMENTS

I am indebted to members of the Writers' Groups of Sanibel and Captiva, especially those of my own Group One. They are the midwives to this book. They have watched it grow, spanked its bottom to make it breathe, and encouraged me to send it on its way.

The cover art is the work of Joan B. Bitzer.

PART ONE

---▼---

ADVENT

Brilliant beams from the multiplex operating light fell into the great cavity of open left chest; even the inclined heads and moving hands of the surgeons caused no shadow. Under Dr. Sandor Brovek's careful eye, the preserved lobe of lung lay compressed and airless, softly speckled in pink and gray. With every beat of the patient's heart, the stainless steel handles of the last long clamp leapt in his assistant's fingers. One critical step remained. He had still to place a row of sutures across the amputated stump of the lower lobe bronchus, and seal it air-tight.

But his eyes went to the clock, where even as he looked the long hand twitched off another minute toward his deadline. Right now, he thought, the Regents will be arriving, greeting each other in their plush board room, smiling, sipping from the University's expensive porcelain coffee cups, and eying the long walnut table for pecking position. He drew a deep breath. At ten o'clock I've got to be there, hat in hand, for their decision. I'd better hurry.

He turned back to his patient, set the clock and the regents out of his mind, and slowed his hand in his constant demand for precision. The stitches went in, the clamp came off, the knots went down. He gathered the long threads together like a ponytail in his brawny fingers, and watched Desmond's long scissors snip the strands away.

"Irrigate," he said.

Desmond tipped a pitcher of warm saline and flooded the chest. The anesthetist squeezed her airway bag, and the remaining lung, the precious left upper lobe he had labored to save, inflated like an outsized pink marshmallow. No bubbles arose from the sutured bronchus, no wisp of red from ligated vessels. All closures tested snug and airtight.

There's some time saved, he thought. He stepped back from his circle of assistants, shrugged the gown from his massive shoulders and shot his size-nine latex gloves like a pair of rubber bands into a bucket under the scrub sink.

"Close it up, Des, I've got to run," he said, and powered his way out of the O.R.

*   *   *

Seated now at the foot of the Regents' glistening walnut table, Brovek was grateful for the extra minutes that his good surgery had given him. He had dumped his hospital scrubs, showered and dressed in a fresh shirt, a new tie, his best gray suit. Still, even feeling natty, he was as jumpy as a schoolboy. Today was decision day, and the stakes were high.

Owen Durshaw presided from a leather chair at the head of the table. Light falling from the window behind him made a halo of his silver hair. The other members sat in apparently random order along each side, seven men freshly shaved and lotioned, three women newly coifed. Before them water glasses gleamed in two neat rows.

"Now, Dr. Brovek." After a brief introduction of the surgeon, Durshaw set to business, frowning across his half-rim glasses. "The Board has struggled with your proposal. Some members support it. Still, the idea of a major building program at this time remains—ah—controversial."

Brovek blotted his forehead. "Any bold new idea probably should be controversial, Mr. Durshaw." He paused. "That is, until its wisdom is defined."

But it was defined, damn it. In previous sessions with the regents he had hawked his twin proposals as coolly as any salesman. He had flourished his facts and his opinions with a spark and push that were the product of his own need; the proposal, as ambitious as it was for the university, was also his own last grasp at glory.

Durshaw stared at Brovek. "Review for the Board how you can even imagine that we should expand at such great scope and expense."

My God, Brovek thought, I've spent five meetings already before these guys, with slides and charts and outside experts, and now he says Review it. He's like a damned internist, he always wants one more test. He forced a half smile to his face.

"Eight years ago your timely expansion unleashed our cardiovascular surgical service. It has grown magnificently. Today the facility is fully utilized; as you know, the Heart Institute is jammed. Now, 1984, suddenly, research has given us another major break-through, and a whole new opportunity. But we have no space to exploit it."

Durshaw lifted his hand, and Brovek paused.

"Susannah?" The chairman called upon Regent Politon, seated at Brovek's right. Administrator of the University Hospital, her fiery red hair fell in bangs over close-set eyes that stared coldly at the surgical chief.

"Space is tight, Owen, no argument there."

Durshaw's hand returned to the table, his frown directed again at Brovek,

"We have a one-time-in-history opportunity," Brovek repeated. His nerves jangled against Durshaw's stop-and-go style. "Any way you measure it, this new development rivals heart surgery—in numbers, in dollars, in scientific challenge. We are as ready for it as almost any surgical center in this country. If we seize the day, our university can achieve national leadership. If we delay, we will be too small and we will lose what little we have. It is vital that we make our move."

He paused, took a sip from his water glass. Tiny ripples trembled on its surface.

"You are talking, we all know, about the transplantation of human organs." Durshaw's voice droned out of four pedantic decades. "But some of us are not sure about this break-through; what is it?"

Brovek's heart pounded. If Durshaw had decided to say No, he wouldn't want to review the facts! So screw him, let him have all the tests he wants. He drew a deep breath and spoke with confidence.

"For about seventy years, surgeons have been able to hook up organs in alien bodies—no challenge in doing that—you just sew the blood vessels together. But always the alien body develops an immune response against the transplant and destroys it."

He folded his hands into his lap, out of Durshaw's sight.

"Gradually ways were found to suppress that immune response. They were good enough for some modest success with kidney transplants, but we couldn't count on them for vital organs. If the immune suppression was strong enough to protect the transplant it was liable to kill the patient. Until now, transplant surgery has been a program of desperation, justified by its value in research."

"And now?" Durshaw prodded.

"Now we have a break-through. Research has given us a new drug called Cyclosporin-A. It suppresses the immune response without harming the patient. Gentlemen, this drug takes the cork out of the bottle."

He felt Politon's glare.

"And ladies," he amended. "Today transplants are busting out of the research lab into practical clinical use. Tomorrow they will be the cutting edge of medicine. And not just kidneys." He heard his voice going faster. Higher. Louder. He tried to hold it back. "Not just kidneys, but hearts, lungs, livers. All the vital organs. Who knows how far we can go? Maybe pancreas, with a cure for diabetes."

Durshaw's thin hand fluttered again. His gaze circled the long table and came to rest at Brovek's left, on the Dean of the medical school. The Board's invited medical expert. He offered the Chairman a confirmatory nod. Brovek saw the moving head mirrored in the table's polished surface. At the far end, Durshaw's reflection held a water glass balanced on its forehead. Brovek's laugh burst from his throat, and he smothered it, coughing into his hand. Tension drained from his shoulders and arms; his fingers went loose.

"Our next question concerns magnitude, Dr. Brovek. We find it difficult to believe we should build a whole new unit of our hospital because of one procedure."

He was sure now that the Board was voting Yes, and he wished Durshaw would quit dinking around. He wrestled his mind away from his other worry, his dark second proposal, to spit out the required response.

"Mr. Chairman, the transplant business is not 'one procedure;' it is a whole new universe of surgical care. It is inevitable, and it is big. This university can grow with it into national rank. But as we stand today we are too cramped, we're stuck in second class." He choked back his rising impatience. "It is your choice: Either hitch your wagon to the star, or park it in the barn."

Durshaw jerked upright. His eyes flared, and circled the faces again, his eyebrows soliciting comments. Susannah Politon shook her bangs and clucked softly. Brovek had smelled victory before; had he blown it now?

No one spoke.

Durshaw scowled at Brovek and cleared his throat. "The Board has already voted in executive session. We favor a compromise position. We approve your proposal in principle, but make it subject to certain conditions."

That sounded okay, depending on the conditions. Brovek pushed his water glass aside and fingered the spiral-bound note pad provided at his place. "Yes, sir," he said.

"First: in addition to all your regular duties as Professor and Chairman of Surgery, you will chair the Building Committee."

He would be in charge? That was a plus—more than he hoped for.

"No problem," he said.

"And your first goal," Durshaw thumped the table with a bony forefinger, "is to find a suitable site."

Brovek smiled. That was a reasonable priority; he was already searching. In fact he already knew where he wanted to build his spanking new Transplant Institute. On a hilltop a mile away, a marble jewel set against the city's skyline.

"And further," Durshaw continued from on high, "that 'suitable site' must be in direct connection to the present hospital and integrated with its support facilities. We will not approve a satellite location. Understood?"

Brovek's heart sank. There was nothing available—even possible—at the present campus. There was no way.

Faces turned toward him. The Dean looked glum, as if he understood. Politon smirked, as if she relished this obstacle to her own expansion.

"Yes, Mr. Durshaw, I understand. And I hope, sir, that you also understand that possible sites are few. Your restriction may be too narrow for the plan to go through."

Durshaw glared at him. "I must tell you, Professor, that support for your proposal is less than unanimous. What we have elaborated here is a compromise, and you will have to live with it."

Well, it was a limited success, and a lot better than a turndown. He would have to tackle it, have to face Durshaw's heightened challenge. There had to be a way. His juices flowed.

"I welcome the opportunity, Mr. Chairman. A well founded transplant program will bring great credit to this university, and I congratulate the Board for your courage and foresight. I will do my best."

Durshaw poured two fingers of bottled water from his decanter, and consulted his agenda. When he looked up, Brovek still sat at the foot of the table.

"Something more, Dr. Brovek?"

"I wonder, sir, whether the Board has reached a decision on my other suggestion, about the structure of the transplant program?"

A couple of chairs shifted on the carpet; somebody coughed. Politon poured water in her glass and thumped the pitcher back on the table. Durshaw spoke like a schoolmaster to a slow child.

"You requested, I believe, that all transplant surgery be brought under your department, specifically including kidney transplants that now fall to the Department of Urology. Correct?"

"In essence, correct."

"Here again we have had to strive for a compromise position. Frankly, some members think your suggestion smacks of a power grab."

"That is not…" Brovek started to say 'my motive, sir.' Durshaw's hand cut him off.

"Our decision is left pending. Before we decide anything else, we will see whether you can come up with that 'suitable site.'" He hissed the two words like a magic formula, and glared at Brovek. "Now, is that all?"

*   *   *

That's not nearly all, Brovek thought, as he squeezed his bulk into the elevator and rode it down to the street. He had greater problems than Durshaw even dreamed of. But his spirits soared. He had the Regents' green light, and better yet, he had the driver's seat. Against all the obstacles he could see ahead, he was ready to roll. The elevator doors opened and he moved on out.

He danced a two-step half way across University Avenue. The first snow of late November had disappeared, but lingering patches of ice warned him to contain himself. He settled his big frame into the rhythm of his usual purposeful strides, chanting as he went.

What goes first? Find the site!
What comes after? Build it right!

He groped for the next line. It fell behind his pace, and he gave it up.

He sailed along the sidewalk, weightless, unstoppable. He felt like the halfback he had been years ago when he broke a tackle and saw open field ahead. He knew he could score. He came to the corporate headquarters building that stood across the street from his hospital. His image reflected from its marble facade, and he stretched tall and smoothed his hair. He looked pretty natty in his best suit, and he didn't even have to suck in his belly. Not much, anyway.

He looked like a guy who could handle the future, who could make big things happen. Like a Transplant Institute. His academic and scientific program would grow to national rank. His little surgical department, now so obscure, would soar to prominence. And he himself, in this last decade that he had left for leadership, would earn his place of honor in surgical history. Face it, Sandor, he told himself; that's what you really want, more than anything else in the world!

The fall air, crisp in his throat, made him glad he was walking. Yellow leaves that were scattered on the pavement skidded in the wind, and he danced from one foot to the other, kicking at them. He came to the corner and cut across into the tiny parking lot under his second-floor office windows. His black Lincoln was parked there, and he slowed, dragging his hand across the shiny hood. He wished he had bought a brighter color—yellow maybe, like the leaves. Not red, though, like—

He slammed to a stop. By God, look at that. In the shadow of his car, as if it were hiding, sat Grover Iverson's tiny red Porsche.

Red, like stolen kidneys.

He banged a heavy fist against his own black fender. That bastard Iverson. His dirty traffic was the reason for Brovek's "grab for power." Okay, so he had asked the Regents to put him in charge of all organ transplants. But his proposal had nothing to do with power or vanity—hell, he didn't even want Iverson's damn kidneys. What he wanted was to protect his beloved university.

The Regents had no idea how close they were to scandal. Brovek still lacked actual proof, but his observations had convinced him that Iverson ran a personal black market in kidney grafts. His waiting list for donor organs was a life-and-death lottery, with Iverson selling some of the winning tickets. A scam like that could explode just like—again he banged his big fist on the fender—like that. And if it did—hell, **when** it did—the fallout would smear everybody. Not just Iverson. A scandal like that could destroy the entire medical school.

He kicked at a leaf lying between the cars, and ground it under his heel.

But he was in a box. If he tried to expose Iverson's mischief, even only to the Dean, the whole world would know it. You can't cork a stink.

So he tried another route, putting himself in charge of all transplants. Durshaw called it a power grab. A reasonable thought, given his ignorance. Brovek shook his head. He was willing to absorb that personal calumny in order not to blow a public whistle. If the Board gave him what he asked for, he could take Iverson on in private and set him straight.

And relish doing it.

But there was more to it than authority. There was also the little matter of a building site.

He leaned his backside against his Lincoln, and ticked off the limits of his double obligation. He had the go-ahead for his new hospital, but Durshaw's definition of a "suitable site" made it damn near impossible. And then he had stuck kidney transplants behind the same obstacle. He stared down frowning at the red hood of Iverson's Porsche.

Thanks to Durshaw, finding the building site was the total game, and Brovek had to play it. His own dreams rode there. And Iverson's scam. Double or nothing.

He shoved himself up from his roost, and scowled his way to the doctors' entrance. At least his goal was definite. If that "suitable site" existed at all, he must find it; and if it didn't exist he must conjure it up. Whatever he had to do to get that site, he would do. Buy it, or steal it, or kill for it.

It all boiled down to that.

          *   *   *

Brovek didn't rest. He pored over his notes on the hospital's neighbors, studied city maps, gazed frowning into space. After two days he had identified a site. It was his only chance, and he settled to it with surgical precision. It was necessary, therefore it was possible.

And he found just the man to lead the chase.

Now he sat in his jumbled office with the old fox Horace Potts. His new friend's quiet manner and conservative dress belied his reputation: shrewd.

Through his window Brovek looked out at his parking lot and that damn red Porsche of Iverson's. He tapped a folded city map lightly against his finger tips, and his voice rumbled up from the recesses of his chest.

"I'll show you once more, Horace. There's only one place we can go."

Gently he opened the map's accordion pleats. The stiff paper crackled as he spread it across his cluttered desk. A bronze paper weight and a stack of surgical journals lifted the map's streets into impossible artificial hills. His desk lamp cast a yellow glow on the jumbled symbols of downtown, and the shadow of his pointing finger hovered over the single city block occupied by University Hospital. For Brovek that city block seemed a prison. The "suitable site" that the Board of Regents demanded, contiguous to the existing hospital, just wasn't there. On every side, labeled buildings surrounded his campus with solid walls against his dreams of expansion.

He stared down as if the force of his will could bring Potts to see the one possible hiatus in the confining brick. Every site was blocked, each for its own reason standing immune and impenetrable to his desire. Except one. Could Potts see it?

His finger stubbed into the map. Two of the blots bore a single label: St. Luke's Church and Rectory.

"There is our only chance," he rumbled. "We have to build it right there."

Horace Potts bent over the desk for a new look. He shook his head slowly. "That's the church, Sandy. That's already right there."

Brovek exhaled noisily and dropped his bulk into his swivel chair. "Damn it, there's something everywhere. Short of a good earthquake, there's nowhere else to look!"

Potts leaned his square bottom against the corner of Brovek's desk. The pink skin of his neck spilled out over a white broadcloth collar and a neatly tied foulard, and his blue eyes rested calmly on Brovek's red face.

"Let's just think it through, Sandy. What if there isn't any site for us? Let's not build right now."

Brovek measured his colleague. Potts was a cool-headed business man. But he couldn't know, couldn't understand, Brovek's feelings. Potts saw Brovek through parochial eyes, as professor of surgery, head of department, respected scientist, an eminence at national meetings.

Shit. Brovek knew who he really was. Head of a little department in a tiny medical school, with piddling numbers of cases in his published articles that kept him always in the back seat to the big boys. At his age he could never expect a new department, a better appointment elsewhere. He had ten years left to make his mark, maybe with luck fifteen. And the opportunity was dancing before him right where he was, right here at home, if only he could find a "suitable site."

Like a tired old schoolmaster he summoned his patience to go over the familiar ground all over again.

"Horace, I have told you and told you what the stakes are. Almost overnight the surgical transplantation of human organs has burst out of the research lab into real clinical possibility. We can take live organs out of dead people and put them into dying people and get living people. Last year we couldn't, this year we can. There are thousands of patients out there who are going to get it done, or die."

Potts did not move. "You have a modern surgery. Can't you use it?"

Brovek held firm to his temper. "We use it every day. To the hilt. The expansion we built eight years ago is crowded already. And I'm not talking about adding a few extra cases, Horace. I'm talking about a new research program, new facilities, a whole new hospital. If we don't do it full scale,

and now, the big institutions will have it all. Sooner or later the government will write rules and shut out anybody that's too small. And look at
the new opportunities for research. My God, it's like 1492 all over again."

"Watch your blood pressure, Sandy; mine's high enough for both of us."

He stood up and walked to Brovek's wall of books. Plaques of honorary
memberships and certificates of achievement attested to the professor's
credibility. He turned back to the desk.

"Okay. That's Step One: we need to expand. Now the question: why St.
Luke's?"

Brovek sat up. He felt rewarded for his restraint. "Because there's
nowhere else," he said softly. "Look at the map."

He circled the hospital campus, tapping the buildings with the tip of
his pen. "A corporate headquarters behind us—a big new building. Over
there, the heirs of these apartment buildings are in a legal fight that's
dragged on for years; there's no clear title. On this side the city has a
hold for more highway right of way. But right there in front of us sits old
St. Luke's with empty pews and one tired old priest. That's why St.
Luke's."

He watched Potts carefully. He had hand-picked this man for his
Building Committee. Thirty years of experience in real estate as an executive with Midwest Power, an active alumnus, unflappable, and as solid as
one of Brovek's knots. Potts would be the point man in going after St.
Luke's, but only if he was convinced. Clearly he was not.

"Did you know I went to school there?" Potts touched a fingertip to the
church. "I made my first communion at that altar rail. It was a big parish
in those days."

Brovek felt like a psychiatrist. "How do you feel about it now?" he
asked.

"Nostalgic, I guess. I'm not so sure I want to see it destroyed."

Brovek's patience was thin. "Balls, Horace. The best place for us is right
over that communion rail, and the necessary time is now."

Potts drew in his breath and slowly let it out again. He spoke softly. "There is the surgical mind at work. See the goal and shoot at it. Keep things simple."

Brovek poked his stubby finger under the map and slid his desk calendar into view. December 1984. "By this time next year," he said, "our crowded surgical suite will be doing cases that today you would call miracles. Then you'll understand. But we can't wait for you, Horace. You've got to believe right now, and start building. And the first thing you need to do is to buy St. Luke's."

Potts shrugged. "I don't even know that old priest over there. He probably thinks it's his church after all the years he's spent in it. But the building belongs to the Bishop, and I've known him since high school." A sudden smile brightened his face. "Do you know how bishops think? He'll probably tell me to call back in five hundred years."

Victories are won by inches, Brovek thought, and Potts had come an inch or two. "Not five months, even," he coaxed. "We need it now."

Potts rested his hand on the door knob and leaned his square shoulders against the jamb. "I tried to buy a church for the power company once," he said. "I remember about that. I'll check out a couple of things."

"What things?" Brovek asked.

"Well, there is no such thing as an offer the bishop can't refuse. If the church is not for sale, nobody is going to buy it. Nobody. That would be bad for us."

He nodded gently at Brovek.

"But if the church is for sale, then anybody can buy it. That sounds good, Sandy, but it might even be worse."

The door closed behind him.

Brovek gentled the map together again, its creases wearing thin, its edges frayed.

There was nothing more he could do right now. He sat down in his desk chair and rubbed his eyes. After a moment he snaked the new issue of

SG&O out of his stack of journals. He opened it at random, but he didn't read. He slumped over his folded arms; his eyes glazed.

Too many things hung fire. Expansion plans ate at him. He hated the dinking around trying to win Potts over to his side. And even if he did, Durshaw's site restriction might be too tough to lick. Damn him and his prissy ways.

And beyond all that the Iverson thing nagged at him. Iverson was a good scientist, a splendid operator. No question. But there were too many outsiders receiving kidney transplants. Too many people from out of state. Not enough patients from the local clinics. There could be only one explanation—Iverson had to be by-passing the normal allocation process, for hidden money. If that scandal broke it would wash Iverson away like leaves down a gutter. And the University Hospital and Brovek's dreams right along with him.

But he couldn't do anything about that now, and he had a department to run. He was overdue with his appointment of a new chief resident. Desmond's time was up and he was moving on to an appointment in Kansas. Not a single one of his other young men was ready—certainly not Pete for God's sake. The only candidate he had was female, and he didn't want her. But he couldn't stall any longer.

He fished around among his papers, and found the form. He filled it in, Doctor What's-her-name, Dana Garrison. Sounded like a man's name, anyway. And he scrawled his signature at the bottom.

Nothing against her personally—he just didn't want a woman in that job. It was too tough for women. They belonged in nursing, not in surgery, if they couldn't stay home.

And that made him think of Lotte, always at home nowadays. Another problem that he couldn't solve. Yesterday he had seen steam rising from the crack under her bathroom door, and found the water running in her tub, scalding hot and lapping out over the side. He splashed over and screwed down the tap, and then went looking for her. "Lotte?" he called.

"Here, Sandy." From downstairs. She was standing at the kitchen window, watering a cactus plant. He could not leave her alone any more.

And all the while his own needs went unmet. Managing without her warmth and comfort was getting tougher all the time. He sat home the long evenings reading his surgical journals, maybe playing Beethoven on his new compact disc machine, while Lotte clicked her knitting needles. What kind of life was that for a man? He was like a widower with a wife to care for. Maybe in academia people thought he was too old for a new appointment, a bigger department. But in his heart, in his desires, in his marriage, he was still a fairly young man.

Wasn't he?

PART TWO

▼

NEW YEAR'S DAY

The old priest sat alone in his kitchen, nestling in his hands his second steaming cup of fresh coffee. After his daily predawn mass in the dark old church, his bones were cold. The hot cup gave him the first creature comfort of his long day to come. He welcomed the caffeine pick-me-up as much as the liquid's heat against his fingers. His right knee hurt—it always did after genuflecting before an altar layered with frost. On this last day of 1984, the bare church and its empty pews lay on his heart like cold stones.

The coffee burned its hot trace down his gullet, and a touch of energy seeped into his limbs. He dunked his toast and slurped it into his mouth. Through the window he looked across the street, toward what he knew were the glass walls and steel mullions of University Hospital. But in the dull winter light of early morning his old eyes saw only a gray blur.

But his mind carried him past those walls. He knew well the polished passages and the chaste cubicles that sheltered the desperate souls he would attend this day. Over there, thank God, he could still exert his frail strength in a ministry that people needed.

He hoisted himself from his chair, limped to the closet and crammed a worn black fedora over his white thatch. In the tiny mirror that hung from a nail on the door, his eyebrows stuck out like cotton balls under his hat brim. His worn-thin winter coat felt heavy on his shoulders. But he knew he would need it, at his pace, even just for crossing the street. He did up his buttons and shuffled outside to the pedestrian crosswalk, his thoughts resting in his usual morning meditation.

Sure and there's not much left in the church. Only the sacraments. Not the people. Here in the hospital is about the only ministry I have left. Sick people still need me, maybe more now than ever. Funny. Hospital patients used to come in sick, like that fellow Potts the other day, and they usually get well and go home. But more and more nowadays they come in feeling pretty good. They don't get sick until they get their treatment, cancer, leukemia, whatever. And then they get sick. Like to die, sometimes. They're the ones that need somebody alongside, somebody to pull for them. Somebody like me.

He looked both ways on the empty street, and started across the paint-striped walkway.

I can pray for them. And just listen to them, too, while those radical treatments push them down, down to the very edge sometimes. Artificial breathing. Artificial feeding. Artificial everything, it looks like. Maybe I don't make much difference, but sure the Holy Spirit says to try.

The fingers of the wind crept up under his coattail and pushed him along. He reached the far curb, climbed it, and appraised the concrete steps rising to the hospital's fancy entrance.

Curious how it goes. Sometimes it's just too hard for them to try to get well. At least, that's what they tell me, sometimes. They haven't any more fight. They want to give up, but the machines won't let them. So they hang on, and then they feel ungrateful, or disloyal or something, so they can't just let go and die. So they don't. I ought to write a book.

He rubbed his aching knee and looked high up at the lettered arch of stone over the doorway:

TEACHING—RESEARCH—CARING

And I'd put that motto in the book, too, because it's wrong. It's caring should be the keystone.

The running irritation of it stiffened his back, and he hobbled up the stairs and through the portals to the tiny office the great hospital provided for chaplains.

*   *   *

He piled his coat and hat on a chair and rummaged in a file box. He selected a bundle of 3x5 index cards labeled "RC," and riffled through the patients' names and room numbers. These were the way points by which he would follow his rounds.

That fellow Potts on Station 21. That's the medical ward. Only a few days ago I anointed him in the Coronary Intensive Care Unit. He must be getting better. I'll go there first.

Mumbling to himself, Father O'Leary limped down the long hall, sorting his file cards into geographical order. Years ago the bishops had taken away his Latin mysteries, and he still missed them, their musical sonority, and the chant on high occasions. But even in English the sacraments were his spiritual granite. Communion was real, absolution worked, for those who believed.

He stepped into the familiar confines of Station 21, a long corridor of private rooms, then a short open ward with curtained beds and a central nurses' station. As a young priest in wards like this he had had only the sacraments to offer. And the old theology. "Offer it up," he used to say to suffering patients. "Offer up your pain." He shuddered. Those glib spiritual prescriptions were not enough.

No, I've learned to listen to people. Just listen. Be a human presence and let them grapple with their feelings. Lots of times they find peace that way, I can see it come over them, with very little assistance out of my clerical throat.

From the door of a small private room, he eyed the pink face and stocky body in the bed. He glanced over at the TV, flickering its commercial images.

"Do you remember me, Mr.Potts?"

Here I am, come to visit, and that mechanical tube goes right on with its chatter. People can't leave it—their eyes keep flicking at while it sells soap right through the Our Father. They'd watch it if the Pope himself marched in to make a visit. Even if he danced a jig—and this one might!

"Sure I remember you, Father O'Leary. You heard my confession and anointed me, and I thank you for that." Mr. Potts pointed to his bedside chair and—Glory be!—turned off the television. "And I want to talk to you about St. Luke's Church. Please sit down."

Father O'Leary chuckled, and lowered himself into the chair.

"It's too young in the day for a body to be tired, but sure a chair is always welcome. You didn't talk so brisk the other day, with your shortness of breath and your sweating pain. The Lord's healing powers are working in you, I see."

"That they are, Father, and I thank you for your part in it. I should be as fit as a fiddle string in a few days."

Father O'Leary's hands spread out toward Potts's face as if to smother the words.

"Ah, don't be after pushing the Lord for miracles now. The doctors know how long things take to heal, and they'll be bossing you about longer than that, I shouldn't wonder."

Potts lay back on his pillows and smiled.

"Well, I will surely follow their orders, Father. I've too much in my mind to do, to be foolish over a few days of doing it."

"Would it have anything to do with St. Luke's now?"

Potts looked at him sharply. He rolled up on his elbow to face the priest.

"Yes, Father, it would. Maybe you know, maybe you don't, that we are looking to expand this hospital. And I am the person charged to find the land."

The priest sat back against the hard chair. His blue eyes searched Potts's face.

"In my own simple way I thought you had done pretty big things already. Your little skyscraper here is only a year or two old, I'd say."

"Eight, Father. Eight years old. Half paid for. Full to the window sills with teaching and research. And patient care too, I am here to tell you. And we are growing. We need space, Father, lots more space."

Potts's face was growing red under his thinly fringed pink scalp. He lurched up, jammed his pillows further under his thick chest.

"We need space for more labs, and more offices, more operating rooms. Transplant surgery is a growth industry, Father; our transplant program alone could fill this building. We need space to grow."

Father O'Leary harbored a secret fear, and Potts's intensity triggered it. He was terrified of sitting there when some poor soul had a cardiac arrest. He dreamed about being caught beside a collapsed penitent, a stilled heart, with only his Holy Oils. Christ Himself would not put the sacrament ahead of resuscitation in those critical moments.

He smothered his thoughts, and tried to stem Potts's flood with light words.

"Well, now, Mr. Potts, I don't want you getting all worked up, don't you know. I think I'll just move along and see if I can find anybody that's sick around here today."

"Father, that new freeway cut your parish right in half. People on the other side find it easier to go to the Cathedral, and God knows there's room for them there. And on this side, your houses are disappearing to commercial buildings. I'm afraid St. Luke's is losing out. I don't want to hurt you, but aren't those the facts?"

Father O'Leary sat quiet, grieving, hoped it didn't show. Those were indeed the facts, rehearsed before him in his empty daily mass, and presented full dress in the Sunday collections. Or lack of them. He nodded.

"Yes, it is third and long for us over there, and we're behind in the score besides. But for now, Mr. Potts, let's just…"

"Father, when I get back on my feet, I want you to go with me to see the Bishop. I think St. Luke's is a very valuable property, even though it is a difficult church. There might be ways we could help each other."

Father O'Leary frowned, looked into his lap and examined his finger nails. Sure, and where would this kind of talk take us? What can I say? The bald truth will turn him up a few more notches, and I'd fear that. But I can't lie, either. If distraction fails, honesty is always best.

He hoisted himself to his feet, and extended his open hands over the twisted sheets. He spoke gently.

"My son, I want you to lie back now and get well. The power of the sacrament of anointing, which you received a few days ago, will continue to work in you and see you through this whole spell of illness. Cooperate with your doctors; and join me now in the prayer our Savior gave us. Our Father, Who art in heaven…"

He watched Horace Potts's face, redness fading, lines relaxing, as he recited the old rote, so profound and simple a prayer; "…but deliver us from evil."

He blessed his patient with the sign of the cross and turned to go.

"Father? Will you come?"

No escape. Don't be blunt, Kevin.

He turned again, poured his full heart into the other's eyes.

"Yes, Mr. Potts. I will be pleased to see the Bishop with you whenever you are able to go. And may he be favorably disposed to your cause. But honesty compels me to tell you…"

He hesitated.

"Tell me what, Father O'Leary?"

"I have already been to see the Bishop, with another party, with the same kind of a proposition."

*   *   *

Nurse Karen Sondergaard dabbed cool water over her cheeks, and discarded the wet Kleenex into a basket at her feet. A lock of blond hair hung down before her ear, and she tossed it back. The three-to-eleven shift on this last night of the year had been rough. She had moved ceaselessly in her sensible white oxfords, carrying medication, adjusting i.v. drips, answering lights. Only once or twice had she sat down, long enough to chart essential facts, and sneak in a rub of her aching foot.

Finally, mercifully, things had wound down. Visitors were gone now, and the ward was nearly dark. Soft lights along the baseboards cast gentle semicircles on the floor tiles. In their rows of beds and in their private alcoves her patients were either quiet or asleep.

All but one.

The doctors said Horace Potts was doing fine. His enzymes weren't bad; his heart damage was limited. But the doctors weren't here now, as she was, to watch him twist in bed, pull up his sheet and throw it back, look at her without seeing when she passed his bed. She knew it was hard for active men to downshift; they had to learn how to let things go, after a heart attack. But Mr. Potts wasn't just antsy; he was anxious.

She put her key to the locked cupboard and pulled out a medicine bottle. She would give him another sleeper. Whatever his anxiety might be, she thought, he didn't need it tonight.

She rattled two pink capsules into a paper cup—the kind that candies used to come in when her grade-school friends had birthday parties. She read the label once again: okay. She tucked the jar away and locked the cabinet, pinning the key to her starched pocket.

Mr. Potts still lay with his fists clenched, eyes staring. "Thank you, Nurse," he said, and dutifully swallowed the meds.

Karen was ready now to sign off and go home. It was always nice to see the lamps go dark and the station go quiet as the night hours came on. She would probably like three-to-eleven, except for going home in the dark. Alone. And in winter the nights so cold that even the mercury gave up hope.

At five minutes to eleven the night nurse puffed in, red-cheeked and wet-nosed, and stowed her parka in the nurses' locker.

"Hey, Pearl," Karen called. "Cold out there?

"Bitter," Pearl said. "I'm glad I work inside. Who's sick?"

"Nobody in trouble, I think. Keep your eye on Mr. Potts—he's still awake and fretting. I'm getting out of here."

Pearl hustled in behind her and sat down. "See you in the morning, Karen."

The blue eyes widened. "What…?"

She had forgotten. At seven a.m. she would take it all back again. She was snared in the nurse's plague: relief shift today, day shift tomorrow. Depart in the night for that quick trip to her cold bed, and hustle back before dawn.

"You know what I'd like to do just once in my life?" Karen threw it out like a challenge. "I'd like to stay out all night!"

Pearl snorted. "Sure you would," she said. "How'd ya keep warm, hey?"

"I'd drive around. I'd keep the heater on, turned up high, and I'd play the radio full blast, all polkas and schottisches."

"And show up in the morning dead on your feet. Gimme a break." Pearl disappeared into the bathroom.

Karen sighed and pulled on her pea coat.

And I'd stop in an all-night diner, too. Trade stories with the cook, or maybe a trucker. I'd smile invitingly at the motorcycle rider who'd be there, hunching his black leather shoulders over a lemon meringue. I'd drink all the coffee I wanted and in the morning I'd trot back to the hospital hot for nursing.

Hah. Dream on, pooped Viking. She knew fatigue would rule her roost, like it always did.

God, how she hated her galoshes!

She bent over and buckled them, and dropped down the stairs and out into the cold.

She scuffed her way across the ice-covered small court yard toward her room in the Annex. The dark shadows of the buildings jutted up around her as if they were the sky and the random lights of windows were the stars, where some one lay in worry or in pain. It was just the opposite of Prairie Falls, where her new-born brain had been imprinted with the universe. There she loved the way the sky drew a circle on the edge of the earth as if there were no more world beyond, and at night the stars lined God's umbrella.

She skidded on a patch of ice, and caught herself. Woops. She shook her head. After growing up in the country had she forgotten how to walk on ice?

It had been a long journey from that world into this one, but she couldn't see that she herself had changed very much. Weaned on fatigue and raised on hard work, she still carried that Prairie Falls baggage. And what had she accomplished? Was she happy? She wished she knew.

Why hadn't she been satisfied with her RN? It gave her a decent job. No, she had to earn the Bachelor's degree. Couldn't quit. And then what? Still duty bound, still imprinted with that old, cold work ethic she had to tackle graduate school. Postponed living for four more years—long lonely years of full nursing shifts and cramming in whatever segments of curriculum she could manage. "And look at me now," she said aloud into the night.

The words sent a stream of vapor into the still air, and she stopped walking. "Karen"…she breathed…. "Nurse"…she watched the steam…. "Master of Nursing Education"

They were not puff words—not like 'happy' or 'hopeful'—and not much happened. She took a deep breath and blew out a long streamer of frost. Keep walking, kid, get yourself home.

What was it all worth? Two weeks ago the gurus in academic robes had given her the diploma, and she hung it on her wall, next to the other one. "Be it known by these presents…"

Nuts. Her bones were still tired.

Her little apartment was pitch dark, but thank God it was warm. She flicked on the ceiling bulb and spread her pea coat over the back of a stick chair by the door. No point in hanging it up for just a couple of hours. She dumped her sloppy galoshes and lined them up on a folded newspaper alongside her nursing shoes under the chair. Her toes wriggled in white nylon against the wooden floor. She shucked off her uniform, balled it up and pitched its wilted starch in the direction of the closet. She wondered if she cared enough to brush her teeth.

On her hard cot her virginal sheet stretched hospital taut. Above the cot her diplomas stared down from the wall like two cold eyes. She bent to the horrid little clock ticking away on the bed stand. Six a.m. Set the alarm. Look at the hands. Two minutes after midnight!

"My God," she said, "I forgot. It's New Year's Eve."

She slumped down on the narrow bed. In the mirror opposite she faced her own image, a sober young face with lean planes and strong bones, and fine new lines of fatigue—of aging?—around her mouth. A thin strap hung off one shoulder.

Karen forced a smile. The other girl smiled. Pretty teeth—she should smile more often.

Well, it was New Year's Eve. A person should celebrate.

"Here's cheers," Karen said. She watched the words move on the other's lips. She watched the hand rise to match her own in an imaginary toast. "Happy New Year to you, Karen Sondergaard!"

And abruptly, without even knowing she would, she was weeping.

*　　　　　*　　　　　*

At seven-thirty on New Year's Day morning the doctors' lounge was deserted. Dr. Dana Garrison walked to the coffee pot and filled the day's first cup into a styrofoam cup. Ouch! It was too hot, and she set it down. She took her new pager from its wrappings and clipped it to her belt. It was a different model from the old squawker she had carried for years.

Less noise was the idea; instead of hailing her by name, the device would vibrate silently against her body. Another of many firsts for Dana Garrison on her first day as Chief Resident. Pete came in only a little late, shook a cup from the stack and filled it.

Warily they nodded greetings.

"Happy New Year, Pete," she said. "There are a couple of chest tubes to come out today. Check the films first, and if they're okay, pull the tubes. Right?"

She watched his reaction. Yesterday they had been peers in the surgical pyramid. Today she was his boss. Pete settled on the small of his back in the leather chair, cradled his cup in both hands and blew an "okay" across the steam. She hoped he would let their relationship remain a collegial one.

"I'll start rounds in ICU," she said. "You can catch up with me there."

She raised the coffee cup to her lips, and exactly then her new pager went off. The damn thing exploded against her belly with the shock force of a mugger's hand. She jerked up, and coffee sloshed out of her cup. With scalded fingers she groped for the shut-off button.

Pete doubled up in his chair. "Chief Resident's prerogative, Dana," he cackled. "You get the new silent pager, and look what happens."

Dana grabbed paper napkins and wiped her hands. "You'll get your turn, Pete, you'll see," she laughed.

Sure, she laughed. But she burned. After five years of slavery she had achieved the top rung and look what she got for it.

She pressed the speaker button and a tiny voice rasped, "Dr. Garrison, call Station 21."

Pete frowned. "21? That's the medical ward. Do we have anybody over there?"

"It's on the way to ICU," Dana said. "I'll find out."

"I'll catch up," Pete said.

Her first mission as chief resident. What would it bring?

She set off on winged heels that made no sound on the hospital floor. She grinned. Her flat rubber heels were part of the scrappy spirit she packed into her five-foot-one-inch frame. In seventh grade she'd been tall, but in ninth she watched her friends catch up and stretch on past her. She worried, and took supplements, and cried her eyes out. But by her senior year at Hanger High her pieces had fallen into place. Okay, she was small. But five-foot-one, she decided, would be tall enough provided she could always be clean, be neat, and be dominant.

Her quick strides over the black and white tiles carried her into the ell for Station 21, past half-open doors of private rooms and between the rows of curtained beds in the open ward.

At the nurses' station she stopped. "You paged?"

A nurse sat hunched over her desk. She was charting a blood pressure record, and she straightened up as if stung. "My God, Dr. Garrison, I didn't hear you come in."

"I was just outside. Trouble?"

"That's for you to say. I only suspect."

Dana had seen it before, this latent hostility. Behind the nurse's cool blue eyes and unsmiling words smoldered her resentment of another woman as physician: 'Yes, Doctor, I'll take your orders, but I don't have to like you.'

Dana said only. "I'm listening."

The nurse stood up and offered a chart. Her blond hair shone under her starched white cap with its single black-striped border. She was taller by a head than Dr. Garrison, and her eyes were cool, looking down.

"Mr. Potts was admitted here five days ago with a small MI. He did okay and came here from CICU yesterday. But today he has pain in his belly, his blood pressure is down twenty points, and I don't like the way he looks."

She tossed the words out defiantly. They both knew she should call the attending medical resident. Why had she called a surgeon? Especially an untried Chief Resident!

Quickly Dana skimmed the pages of the chart, picking at the essentials. MI, ECG, enzyme studies. All the usual stuff. The nurse had made herself vulnerable. Why?

Aha!

"The chart says he has an abdominal aortic aneurysm."

"That's why I called you directly, Dr. Garrison. Dr. Kanju didn't answer his page."

"He had no symptoms."

"He has them now."

That could mean trouble. Big trouble.

Dr. Garrison searched Karen Sondergaard's calm blue eyes. Vulnerable? More like heroic. "Good for you," she said. "Let's go look at him."

Mr. Potts lay curled up on his left side in a private world of pain. Everything was white, the walls, the sheet over his body; even his cheeks lacked color. Only the lines of pain around his eyes looked gray.

Her examining fingers were gentle, but they made him wince; and they signaled to her a sinister fullness deep in the left abdomen.

Potts tried to make light of his trouble. "It's the wrong side for appendicitis, Dr. Garrison. Don't try to sell me an operation for that."

She forced a smile. This man's situation was desperate. After five years of training, was she ready? Her first trial in the new job was going to be a bearcat.

"I'm glad you're thinking sharp, Mr. Potts. We need you to. We have to make some tough decisions, and make them right now. Do you know about your aneurysm?"

"Yes. They told me about it. A weak place in my biggest artery, they said. Like a bulge in an inner tube. But they said we shouldn't do anything about it right now."

Dana nodded. "That's because of your heart damage. You see, to repair it means putting you through anesthesia and surgery, and in the first weeks after a myocardial infarction that is especially dangerous. If we possibly can, we avoid surgery at such a time."

Potts's eyes were fixed on hers. His voice remained level. "I'm waiting for you to say 'But.'"

Her heart pounded, but she kept her eyes steady. "But…your aneurysm has started to leak. If we don't repair it right now, as an emergency, we cannot stop it from bleeding. Your operative risk is increased because of your heart damage. But your risk if we don't operate is a lot higher, like 99%. I think we should go to surgery just as fast as we can get you there."

Potts studied her. She looked across at the still figure of Miss Sondergaard, standing by the bed in silent support for both patient and doctor. Dana turned back to Mr. Potts and returned his gaze thoughtfully, unwavering. She didn't want to be nervous—it was his life that was in danger. She said nothing; there was nothing she could add to this bare and unrelenting script. Finally Potts spoke.

"You are just a girl, Dr. Garrison. I'm not used to that in a doctor. But you must be good to be here, and you are very definite. What choice do I have?"

"You're an intelligent man, Mr. Potts. You need what this hospital can offer, and right now I am it. Trust me."

Potts's eyes flicked over his stark room. The windows showed golden sun and white snow. The TV screen sat gray and blank. Neither of them would be watching the bowl games this afternoon. His eyes narrowed with a new pain, and sought out her face.

"I have to trust you, Dr. Garrison. Let's go for it."

At the nurses' desk, Dana recited crisp and urgent orders. "Keep trying to raise Dr. Kanju. After ten more minutes, call his attending staff doctor directly. I want the cardiologists in on this case all the way. Notify the Potts family. If they arrive before surgery, call me. If they do not, don't wait for them. Don't wait for anything. I want ten bottles of red blood cells ready, and two of them put into him within one hour. Get Dr. Pete over here to help. I want the anti-gravity suit applied now and inflated. You get started with these, while I write all my orders on the chart, and call my crew for the O.R."

Her voice gentled then, and lowered a pitch. "Miss Sondergaard, some-times we doctors forget how crucial a good nurse can be. I promise you I shall not. Not after today."

She turned to leave, but Sondergaard's question stopped her. "Dr. Garrison, you said '99%'. With aortic rupture they all die if you don't operate. What's the hedge?"

"That's 'just in case,'" she said flatly.

Her eyes looked up into Karen's.

"In case I have the wrong diagnosis."

*   *   *

From 33,000 feet, the real world looked even smaller in scale than the plastic models Martin Stern's people mocked up to demonstrate construc-tion projects. And simpler too. Martin Stern was not happy with his full-size world; it was screwed up.

He leaned his dark head against the window of his first-class seat, and mindlessly fingered the icy glass holding a very dry and very dull martini. Damn it all. This trip. His sick liver. Damn the new year which he wouldn't see the end of. And damn the doctors. They knew everything about his crazy disease that they called sclerosing cholangitis, except what caused it or how to fix it.

Four damn years he had put up with it. Had to learn new lessons all the time, as regular as paying bills, and every lesson worse than the last. First his damn gall bladder operation, then his damn diagnosis nobody ever heard of. It wasted him, made him sick, made him so damn weak. He lost Lila Mae because of that, and he didn't even care, that was the worst. And now at last the end was coming on, and he knew it even if the doctors all pussyfooted about it.

He wouldn't pussyfoot. He'd drive himself full bore as long as his strength held up. He had a deal in his sights right now that could turn into a sweet piece—if he could buy it right—across from University Hospital.

That place was drawing traffic from all over the world, and it was going to get bigger. A hotel and shopping center across the street would be a shoo-in. Maybe those doctors couldn't fix his damn liver, but they'd find out Martin Stern made a piece of change while they were trying.

Lila Mae. He was glad she was gone. She wasn't any good for a sick man. Didn't understand anything at all. He'd bought her to be his wife anyway; she didn't really want him. He always knew that. But he wanted her, classy young broad with the strong thighs and platinum head; he wanted her enough that he came up with what it took. And it was all right for a while, until he got sick. Until he couldn't physically dominate her any more. Pretty soon they both wanted out, and she didn't take him for much more than she had coming.

He watched the scale model world gradually growing larger as it skimmed by below his window. The city lay ahead, and then he could make out the city streets, toy cars scattered between gray lines of piled-up snow. He identified the First City Bank Tower—he had built it himself. But so what? He didn't even care any more.

Tomorrow he had to see his doctor at University Hospital, and then he would go again to see the damn bishop. He had a deal in mind the bishop couldn't refuse. He just had to get there without that old priest tagging along. Stern didn't like to let emotions mix into business deals. Somebody always got pinched that way. No, he meant to get to the bishop alone, and get his holy name on a contract, and the sooner the quicker.

He drained his glass and tossed it under his feet. He jammed his seat-back into the upright position and picked up the ends of his seat belt. "Why not," he said to himself, and buckled them together. "If I'm going to make one last deal, I've got to live that long."

*   *   *

Her knife sliced cleanly into Horace Potts's belly, full length, right down the middle. Dr. Garrison made it neat, but she made it swift. She knew that when she opened the belly wall she would release supporting pressure against the aneurysm—it might blow wide open.

"If it's there at all," she worried.

The abdominal cavity was clean. She wrapped the glistening loops of intestine and laid them aside. There in plain view behind the membrane of the belly cavity lay what she had felt—or thought she had felt—an hour ago. It was a mass of red and purple jelly, a quart or so of blood clot packed in there tight. Somewhere in the middle of it would be the aorta, like a rotting garden hose, leaking life's blood away, and maybe just about to explode.

In her own belly a hard ball of tension released its grip; she began to breathe again. This was what she came for, and she knew what to do.

She slid her hand into the belly cavity and upward as far as she could, to get above the rupture and above the clot. She had to stand on tiptoe and wished her arm were longer. By pushing backward against the spine, she was able to compress the aorta, and gain temporary control of the bleeding. Next she burrowed one finger, cautiously, aggressively, behind the aorta, working it between the vessel and the vertebrae, to make a tunnel for a clamp. Then she palmed the ratchet-lock handles of a stainless steel clamp as long as her forearm, and slipped its angled jaws across the aorta, before and behind. She closed the clamp, and those steel jaws shut down the aorta in a grasp as gentle and tough as a mother tiger's.

"Now," she said quietly to Pete, "is a good time to collect ourselves. We've shut off the bleeding. We can let anesthesia catch up."

Anesthesia was content. Blood volume had already been replaced, red cells dripping into veins in both arms. The cardiogram monitor showed a stable pulse. All the machinery was in place and working.

But a new voice said, "I can use some catch-up, Dana. Looks like you're well started."

"So far so good, Dr. Rudd. Thank you for coming."

She knew he would. Six feet and two inches of Ivy League polish, Lance Rudd was her attending surgeon, her immediate boss. He had backed her up on other critical occasions, often in the wee hours. Enough to earn her loyalty. Never intruding, he showed up "just to make sure you're okay, Dana." Her first gun-shot wound to the heart, only a year ago. "Just in case, on this first one."

Well, this case was a different kind of first for her. She had done separate parts of it before, from first cut of scalpel in one case to final adhesive tape in another. But those were just the surgical steps. Today this person named Horace Potts had put his life in her hands alone. She watched the handles of the aortic clamp as they surged against the rhyhmic pulse and pump of his damaged heart.

"We're okay, Dr. Garrison." The anesthesiologist nodded across the ether screen. Dr. Rudd, in new gown and gloves, elbowed in beside Pete.

"Trust me!" Her promise to Potts whispered in her ears. Her obligations settled on her like a mantle, and she squared her shoulders to fit it. Go to work.

They moved swiftly at the table. With the aorta now under control, Dr. Garrison cut into the clot. Gobs of the dark jelly spilled out and she grubbed up handfuls of it into a basin. Dr. Rudd sponged up more of the sticky mahogany goo with gauze, and Pete's sucker gurgled and rushed as air and old blood whistled up the tubing.

Next she cut into the aneurysm itself. Before that first clamp across the aorta, such a cut would have poured out Horace Potts's life, a gusher over her arms and down her gown and into her shoes. Now instead the color changed from bloody clot to the scabby yellow of the degenerated blood vessel. Without its coursing blood, the aneurysm was just a flabby bag, a sack of mushy debris and calcified shards like something dredged up from a tidal swamp.

"This junk always amazes me." Dr. Garrison said. "It doesn't seem like it's alive or even human. It's just boiler scale."

"Well, you've got the thing whipped now, Dana," Rudd said. "Let's sew in the graft so I can go home."

They worked smoothly together. They fitted a Y-shaped tube of woven Dacron against the cut-off end of aorta above and the two iliac arteries below, and began to sew. Dana was grateful for Dr. Rudd's manner. He never pushed in to do the operating himself. He just made it easy for her. She knew for her growth as a surgeon she had to venture into new depths. Rudd always let her test those deeper waters, but he was there with her to be sure she didn't step into disaster.

She didn't. They finished the graft and were ready to close the incision.

"Thanks, Dr. Rudd," Dana said. "I can finish up now, if you want to slip away."

She looked up to smile at him, and her heart froze. Over Rudd's shoulder loomed the giant figure and piercing black eyes of Dr. Sandor Brovek.

Where in the world had he come from? Sandor Oliver Brovek, Professor of Surgery, the terror of medical students, task-master of surgeons in training, the ruling brain and dominating personality of surgical research. In short, The Chief. What in the name of sense was he doing here?

Dana's pulse pounded.

Dr. Brovek stood on a platform and towered over Dr. Rudd. Under his twin lasers the young staff surgeon was shunted aside as if vaporized. Brovek's target was Dana.

"You are ready to close? I think I might have been called about this!"

Dana's mind raced. Called? The last resident who called Sandor Brovek on a holiday spent the next six months assigned to the TB Sanitarium. No one ever called the Chief at home. Why should this time be any different?

"Do you have any idea who your patient is, Doctor? Or his importance to this university and my—ah—that is, the university's transplant program? This is Horace Potts you are working on."

"I'm sorry, Dr. Brovek. I would have called you if I...."

"Did he have an aneurysm, Doctor? Did you find it? Was it leaking? Was all this rush strictly necessary?"

Dana Garrison iced her pulse. It was politics, and the Chief was mad.

Okay. Stay cool, Dana. Stay cool, and maybe survive. Slowly, clearly, she raised her voice to The Presence, making it be as calm as her eyes.

"Yes, sir. Yes on all four counts. We had every reason for quick action, and we took it."

Sandor Brovek was not appeased. His headgear and his mask could not contain his scowl, which burned over Dana Garrison like falling ash.

"What did the CT scan show, Doctor?"

He was boring in, and her own anger tried to flare. She forced it down. She had more urgent responsibility.

"With all due respect, Dr. Brovek, I still have surgery to finish for Mr. Potts, who is getting along smoothly so far. His case can be presented to Grand Rounds tomorrow; perhaps that would be a more suitable…"

Dr. Rudd prevented disaster after all. "Come on, Chief," he said. "Let's change clothes and I'll tell you all about this case. He's doing fine."

Dr. Brovek hovered on his platform for a long moment, unsatisfied. At last he stepped down and turned to follow Dr. Rudd. His words rolled back behind him and washed over Dana Garrison as she struggled to confine her attention to the small circle of brilliant light and the demanding task that still lay beneath her hands.

"Rudd, did you hear that?" Brovek said. "I want this case presented tomorrow for certain sure, and I intend to be there."

*   *   *

Sandor Brovek fretted and dreamed through the night, but awakened out of habit while his bedroom was still dark. Only the red digits of a clock radio on the table beside his telephone confirmed the routine 5:30 hour. His wife lay asleep beside him, her breathing gentle, her face buried in the pillow. He allowed his fingers to stray over her slender body, the curve of her hip, the warm round of her bare shoulder. For twenty-seven years his desires had found their match in Lotte, their mutual satisfactions flowing like a healing current through their marriage. Now the current had run dry.

He sat up and dropped his feet precisely into the fleece-lined slippers aligned on the woolen carpet. He padded into the bathroom, eased the door closed, and then turned on the light.

"Not at your best, Sandor," he murmured, blinking into the mirror. He ran one hand over his gray stubble and with the other twisted the faucet. Habitual morning odors of hot water and mentholated lather rose around him, and the soft scrape of razor strokes. His eyes narrowed as his mind shaped the day ahead. Grand Rounds came first, and he meant to check out that hen resident that jumped into Potts's aorta.

His stomach knotted. That was just one more obstruction raised up against his lust for his major transplant center. Things always went too slowly for his nature, all the plodding steps, winning Board approval, sweet-talking Horace Potts. But he had begun to taste progress. And then Potts's goddamn coronaries acted up and one of his own residents decided to throw gasoline on the fire.

Ouch! His razor dug in under his chin. He stamped a piece of toilet paper to the cut and held it while he turned his attention to Lotte. He laid out her clothes and wakened her. She could dress herself while he made breakfast.

Old habits died last. She perched like a duchess at the table in the kitchen, smiling at him over delicate sips of coffee. She had tied a splash of color at her throat—the silk scarf he had splurged for at Hermes on their last trip to Paris, not knowing what lay ahead.

"Do you operate today?" she asked. She had never lost the soft "r" of her Viennese childhood. "Opuhwate" was the way the word came out, and he never tired of it.

"Not today, love. It's Grand Rounds today."

"That's nice," she said, and nibbled her toast.

"Mrs. Kerry will be here soon," he said, reminding her. He checked the clock; Mrs. Kerry was running late again.

"I suppose you're going to operate today." Lotte touched the corner of her napkin to her fine lips.

He did not answer. The doorbell's brief warning ushered in a blast of wintry air followed by the portly Mrs. Kerry, breathing heavily and already pulling off her wraps. Brovek snatched his hat and coat and kissed his wife on the proffered cheek.

"Enjoy the day, Lotte," he said. "I'll be home tonight."

Her voice followed him into the garage, confiding to Mrs. Kerry. "He's needed at the hospital, you know. He has to operate."

He let the door snap shut behind him.

*   *   *

Wednesday morning, the second day of January 1985. Dana Garrison lugged a thick stack of x-rays into a nearly empty Keaton Amphitheater. She piled the films on the shelf of the view-box and clicked the switches to make sure the lights worked. She arranged her papers on the lectern, and stole a quick glance at the rows of seats rising in steep tiers before her, even now beginning to receive the early comers.

She loved this old hall, buried like a hidden gem in the ugly yellow brick box of what the medical students dubbed "Old U." The original hospital building adjoined the new steel and glass monument, inevitably called "New U," the two buildings connected back to back like grossly dissimilar Siamese twins. In Keaton, Dana had sat with her classmates, like other generations of medical students, and submitted to salvos of opportunity to learn her chosen profession. The hall had a lucky combination of good acoustics and bad seats which gave the advantage to the instructors and professors who lectured there. Over the years their repeated success became the tradition of learning that Dana thrived in, while Keaton Amphitheater earned its place in her heart.

But today was different. Today she would present her first Grand Rounds, and she expected fireworks.

For nearly a decade she had watched other Chief Residents at this podium. Three years ago Lance Rudd occupied the crucible. Now it was

her turn to present the week's surgical problems to the assembled gurus of
the department. Any lack on the part of the resident staff was fair game to
the wisdom of professorial hindsight. Overall, the purpose was educational:
interns and residents were required to attend. Nurses were generously
invited.

But today Dr. Brovek would have an unusual agenda; he would seek
Dana's scalp. She knew he was on high horse over Horace Potts—some
problem of his own that somehow had rubbed off on herself. Her heart
jumped. It was in his power to fire her. He didn't want a woman in her job
anyway.

But fire her over Horace Potts? Nuts! This first case of hers was no
blemish; it was a stunning success.

Still, Brovek was the only judge that counted; she had to be ready.

She left nothing to chance. She assigned the junior residents to present
their other cases. She checked for chalk at the blackboard. She flipped the
switches once more on the x-ray box. She tried to think of all the traps the
professor could lay for her, and made up triumphant answers. She leafed
through Horace Potts's chart one more time.

"Well," she told herself, "I'm as ready as I can get."

She sat down on a folding chair, her back against the wall of the pit,
and forced herself to relax. Her hands lay folded in her lap. She looked at
her smooth skin, her strong fingers, long for her stature. She reflected on
the skills those hands had already learned, what wonders they might still
come to do, if she could stay her course. She inspected the clean white
coat that covered her lap, and the dark edge of wool skirt below it that
formed a narrow ribbon across her knees. Tucked back out of her sight,
her feet rested on the terrazzo, primly crossed and encased—she grinned
at the thought— in her trade-mark rubber-soled flat shoes. She stood only
five-foot-one, but in her own estimation five-foot-one of Dana Garrison
was plenty. Let the old bastard come!

＊   ＊   ＊

Dr. Lance Rudd entered Keaton from the upper gallery level. He climbed carefully down the steep steps, down the series of terraces, curving rows of seats facing the bottom-level rostrum. He knew the room well from both sides of the lectern; today it seemed to him a coliseum more than a lecture hall, a mini-arena for a match between Christian and lion. Only this morning, he mused, the lion would be up in the seats.

He chose his usual place at the left end of the fourth row, knowing Dr. Brovek would station his formidable bulk front and center. Several assistants and students were already clustering their satellite positions on both sides and behind the emperor's chair. Dr. Brovek would also be ten minutes late.

Lance looked down at Dana, sitting quietly at the edge of the arena. He wished she would look up; he would like to make some gesture of encouragement to her. She had a tough menu for her first cook-out. But look at her! Her hair was brushed back, and her skin glowed pink and fresh. He wondered if she wore that same fragrance that attracted him yesterday. Beneath her white clinical coat he spied a lace collar peeking out over her sweater. Imagine going face to face with Sandor Brovek wearing a lace collar! He looked at her hands, relaxed and quiet on her lap.

Don't wait for old S.O.B., Dana, he breathed to himself. This conference is your presentation to the department, not a dance before the king.

As if he had given her a cue, Dr. Dana Garrison stood up, asked for attention, please, and began the conference. It was 7:31.

Lance Rudd sat back to listen. He was startled by the crowd of students in the seats behind him. He hadn't noticed any of them coming in.

*   *   *

Ten minutes later, Dr. Sandor Brovek entered Keaton Amphitheater directly through the professorial door onto the rostrum. He nodded at his target, his new Chief Resident. At least she had had the good sense to start on time.

He ascended one row of terraces and sat down in an empty place at the middle of the row. Just once, he thought, he would like to get there early enough to have somewhere else to sit. He knew he shouldn't be late all the time. But Lotte was so weak and dependent, he excused himself—he did pretty well to get here even this early. Well, he'd better see what this girl doctor had to say for herself.

At the moment she was allowing some mumbling girl student to present a very ordinary case; not much to think about there. He guessed he would never really favor women as physicians; he would just have to become resigned to them. They were cropping up in other departments; anesthesia had a bunch of them. Couldn't tell them from nurses. And now here was this one in surgery. Home turf. Well, now he was going to plumb her depth, see how good she was. He couldn't let his standards slip for any kind of case; but if she had goofed with Horace Potts!! The familiar churning set up in his belly again.

"...a ruptured aneurysm."

Brovek's attention snapped back to her—what was her name—Garrison. Take away her white coat and she could be his daughter. No, too small. Could she really be the dragon who put him down yesterday? Tactfully told him to go to hell? Oh, maybe he had it coming: she was still operating, after all. But she better damn well know what she was talking about today. He wanted answers.

He listened quietly while Mr. Horace Potts was reduced to an anonymous series of tissues and functions, trucked off to surgery, repaired, and carted back to bed. Staff asked a few ordinary questions—urine output, estimated total blood loss, amount replaced.

They're all talking about 'a case,' he thought, just a plain old surgical case. None of them knew that they had the future of this University's transplant program right under her bloody knife. Yesterday's panic flickered again.

"What did the CT scan show. I didn't hear you mention it." Sometimes when he spoke out, his voice surprised him. It rumbled in his chest, and he forgot how big it was. He intended to speak loud enough—he was the professor after all. And he wanted to set an example: young doctors always mumbled. He couldn't make out what they said at all, sometimes.

"…because we did no CT scan."

Period? Was that all she was going to say? Over the years he had found no better way to stampede a young doctor than to ask about a test he didn't do. It always worked. 'Gee, that report should be here somewhere.' 'Well, let's see, Dr. Brovek.' 'The lab had trouble that day.' He never yet heard one say he didn't think to do it, though that was generally the truth.

"Upon what basis did you establish the diagnosis of aneurysm, Dr. Garrison?"

"The aneurysm was discovered by the resident on physical examination at the time of admission, Dr. Brovek. By palpation. The diagnosis was concurred in by two other medical staff doctors."

"X-ray? Ultrasound?"

"No, sir. The patient's admission was because of a fresh MI. No studies were done on the aneurysm in that acute setting."

"'MI'? Say 'myocardial infarction', Doctor…So you acted on the unsubstantiated diagnostic impressions of physicians other than yourself?"

The concern that ate at him yesterday was justified; it beat at him in a critical crescendo. Too damn fast. Too much at stake. He burned Dana Garrison with his scowl. He watched her slow her pace against him, keep herself ramrod straight. She wasn't wounded yet.

"I did rely on the opinions of others, Dr. Brovek, as we all do. But I did not act on those opinions alone. I depended also on my own examination."

"Tell me exactly what findings allowed you to rush into surgery without any sort of objective imaging to verify even an aneurysm, much less one that's bleeding."

He watched her closely for some sign of panic. A tremor in her voice. Higher pitch. Stammering. He couldn't hear any. Icy control was what he saw. This young woman was under pressure; he had her full attention; but he saw no sign of uncertainty.

"Deep in the patient's left side, where his pain was located, he had tenderness and fullness. Not a mass, really, but not normal either."

She was tiny, this chief resident of his. She could have hidden behind the lectern, but she stood beside it, in full view, and engaged him directly in this battle of intentions. He folded his arms. The tiers of students around him emanated an intense stillness.

"Dr. Garrison, we know you did indeed find a ruptured aneurysm, and you did repair it. I won't ask you how you distinguished it from diverticulitis or from left kidney disease. You must know something I don't know."

His voice steamrollered past his own sarcasm.

"My interest in this case is the protection of standards in my department. I am interested in process here, so that patients are subjected to surgery for well-founded and logical reasons. I do not want them going to surgery on hunches."

Now he saw color in her cheeks! Could he touch her after all?

"Furthermore, Dr. Garrison, there is here a very special factor of risk. Do you know the figures on surgical mortality for patients with recent myocardial infarction? They are sky high. Do you think you should undertake that kind of risk when you have not even a proven diagnosis?"

His blade was squarely on mark now. When she faltered, he would thrust.

Her reply came promptly. Her voice was patient, confident. My God, did this dark-eyed girl still think she had ground to stand on?

"Dr. Brovek, your points are valid. I want to assure you I weighed the same issues yesterday. I believe in process. I believe in logic, not hunches. But sometimes a decision becomes a choice of likelihoods—odds, if you will. The selection of a dangerous course of action may still be best if it is the least dangerous. I considered the possibility of emergency CT scanning on a holiday morning. I knew that would take at least three hours before all was done and the radiologist could sign off on it. I was confident in the diagnosis because of the findings of four examiners, and because this patient was showing signs of blood loss. He felt dizzy when he sat up.

His skin was sallow and cold; his pulse was elevated; his blood pressure was down.

"Now as to risk. The most serious threat to his heart muscle would come from a period of shock as a result of blood loss. Anesthesia and surgery are bad enough. But shock is worse. All three would be intolerable. Therefore I made the judgment that the least risk for this patient at this time was to go to surgery as fast as we could go. I believe, sir, that was proper process, not hunch. Independent of that, I am happy to report that this patient so far is getting along very well."

Brovek leaned back in his front-row seat, quiet at last. He couldn't remember a lecture like that, directed at himself, since Lotte took sick. This had to be some kind of a woman doctor, he decided. Maybe Horace Potts would be all right after all.

He shifted in his seat, aware of renewed rustlings and whispers in the students around him. He rumbled over his shoulder.

"Dr. Rudd, do you have any comment on this case? I believe you attended the operation."

"Just to say, Dr. Brovek, that it was as well performed yesterday as it was defended today. I found Dr. Garrison's first case as Chief Resident to be very reassuring about the quality of your graduate training program."

The conference was over. Students and nurses in clinical coats and white uniforms chattered and jostled their way up the steep aisles to the exit doors. Dr. Brovek descended to the rostrum. He draped his heavy arm across the lectern, his eyes just inches from Dr. Garrison's. His voice was low, almost confidential.

"Dr. Garrison, one more question please. I would like to know just how you felt going in to that operation."

Her face turned up to him like an open flower.

"Dr. Brovek, I was worried sick."

"Good for you," he said quietly. "You should have been."

*   *   *

Far from Keaton Amphitheater, the doctors' lounge of University Hospital formed the hub of its medical world. From every corner of 'New U' the daily paths of migrating physicians wove changing patterns amid the aromas of tobacco smoke and coffee. Mumbles of conversation and short bursts of laughter arose from the soft retreats of leather chairs.

Harvey Kanju cradled a hot styrofoam cup in one hand, and leafed through the morning paper. Nothing interested him. Highway accidents over New Year's. Ohio State versus Southern Cal in the Rose Bowl this afternoon. Reagan versus Nakasone in L.A. Still more football. To no one in particular he grumbled aloud his irritation.

"Usual crap…Nothing in the paper today."

"Well that's better than what I got," said Barney Popper. "Look what I found in my box this morning." He waved a white paper in one hand, his summons to his annual refresher course in cardiopulmonary resuscitation. "I can't believe it's CPR time again. What a deep pain in the behind."

'Yeah," Harvey said. "I'm about due for it too, Barney. But you never know—you might need to use it. Any of us might."

'Not me," said Barney. "I don't get anywhere near emergencies except my own OBG patients."

"Why don't you just skip it then, Barney?" Grover Iverson stood behind Kanju's chair, tucking a cigarette daintily past his mustache.

Barney rolled his eyes. "And lose my staff privileges? Sure, Grover."

With his fancy voice and knife-crease slacks and red Porsche Targa, Grover Iverson was not Barney's type. And when he messed with female incontinence he intruded on Barney's turf.

"I don't see why I have to spend my free time pushing on that manikin and blowing on its ugly mouth with God knows who else that has the flu or worse."

"Afraid you'll get AIDS, Barney?" Harvey Kanju reentered the conversation. "I didn't think it was your mouth you had to worry about."

"Nothing funny about AIDS, Harve," Grover said. "Today's jokes aren't going to sound so funny tomorrow."

"'S'matter Grover? Afraid all those gay guys will flood your waiting room?"

Grover didn't smile. "There may be a lot more of them than you think, Barney. And women too. Look out!"

Barney took another caramel roll.

"Anybody reading this paper?" The new voice belonged to Walter Pugh, the surgical pathologist. Harvey remembered the young surgeons' taunt about his skill with the microscope. "Old Blind Pugh" they called him. Pugh took the newspaper from the table and disappeared into the doctors' bathroom.

Harvey Kanju sighed. Maybe the new ECG would be done on that fellow Potts. He crushed his empty cup into an ashtray, and set out for the surgical ICU.

*　　　　*　　　　*

The moment the conference ended, Karen Sondergaard slipped from her seat to exit the top of Keaton Amphitheater. She moved crisply in her starched whites, but she moved through a fog. Like distant strobe lights her white shoes flashed through the cloud in her eyes. Her heart pounded in her chest, and her moist palm dragged against the varnished handrail of the staircase. At the bottom step she paused, and leaned on the railing post to wait. After the brightness of the conference, the hallway was dim and obscure.

Why was she acting like this? Yesterday she took a risk when she broke out of channels and called Dr. Garrison. But that was for Horace Potts's sake. Now she was going out of channels again, and this time for herself. She didn't understand what drove her.

Her native reticence grated. The reproach of her grim Nordic mother hovered in her mind. But she needed to talk to Dana Garrison the way she wanted to breathe. Compulsion overrode her scruples, and her cheeks were flushed far beyond her swift descent of stairs.

The rostral door of the Amphitheater opened, and the massive shape of Dr. Brovek appeared. Karen shrank back, but he ignored her and cruised off toward his office. In her uniform, she was probably invisible to him. She tried to calm her heart. She counted its beats, willing them to slow.

The door opened again. In the light flooding through from the amphitheater, her silhouette revealed the tiny frame of Dana Garrison, a determined set to her head, strength in her square shoulders. Karen stepped down from the last stair.

"Dr. Garrison...Dana...it's me...Karen Sondergaard."

Dr. Garrison stopped. In the dimness Karen could see her eyes widen, flash white.

Karen scolded herself: she must have picked a bad time; maybe Dana was late for surgery; nurses shouldn't—she mustn't—it was all wrong. She didn't know what to do. She wanted to turn and run, to get away, to hide.

But Dana Garrison's voice was soft, and she began to laugh! "It's you!" she said. "Will you just look at the fine mess you got me in!"

Karen's chest uncoiled. Her ribs moved again, and she could breathe. She inhaled the fragrance of this private joke, this offered bond. She closed the circle.

"Dana, come to my apartment tonight, whenever you can break loose, and I'll cook up something simple. You have to eat somewhere, don't you?"

Dana said, "I sure do, Karen, some where and some time. But I can't leave the campus, you know. I'm stuck in these walls for six months, and this is only the second day. I have to stay within range of Bozo here." She patted the pager hanging on her belt.

Karen nodded. She offered Dana a slip of paper. Her fingers trembled. She couldn't remember writing her apartment number on it. "I'm just in the Annex. Maybe that's okay?"

Dana Garrison's steady fingers took the paper. Their eyes met.

"Are you lonely, Karen? I am, sometimes."

Karen's eyes began to sting. Lonely? Was that the name of the empty aching she had lived with for so long?

To feel lonely would be a weakness; she couldn't admit that. At least, she couldn't have, yesterday. But suddenly, in Dana's words, her emotion stood naked before her, and it was all right to call it by name. Her words tumbled softly out of her release.

"I worked four years for my Master's degree. My diploma has hung on my wall for two weeks, and there isn't a living soul who has seen it. Or wants to. Does that make me lonely?"

Dana touched her arm. Her hand was gentle. Karen's tension drained away, and Dana's words sang in her ears with the clarity of bells.

"You know I can't promise anything in this business. But if I can, I will come."

*   *   *

There were too many cross-currents in his life! They tore at him, and the pride he had to swallow at the conference was giving him heartburn. That tiny woman had rammed him again, and he knew it, and in his gut he didn't like it. And yet in his head he did like it. That spirit and that competence were what he looked for in his staff.

But the gut won. He stormed out of Keaton Amphitheater in a rage, damn near colliding with some nurse standing there like a spook in the dark. He clenched his fists and stalked away trying to decompress. He counted steps down the old corridor to the main hallway. His office lay in one direction so he turned the other. His shoes tapped a heavy rhythm— Left, Right, Son-of-a-Bitch, Cool-it-Brovek, Slow Down.

The light grew brighter and he found himself crossing onto the shiny tiles of New U. His shoes needed a shine—Lotte used to see to that. She didn't do it, but she made him do it. God, he shouldn't start looking tacky on top of all his other troubles.

Ahead of him lay the staff lounge, and beyond that the operating suite. Again he turned away, this time up the stairway to the main floor. He began to move more easily, hands relaxing, strides lengthening. The bright lobby greeted him, shiny marble, modern paintings on two walls—he couldn't see the value in those—a gift shop full of teddy bears. He pushed through the double set of over-size doors at the front entrance to the hospital, and ran directly into Susannah Politon. Her startled eyes screwed down to angry slits, and with both hands she shoved her large purse against his arm. With more force than really necessary, it seemed to him. More than just defensive.

"I'm sorry, Susannah!" he breathed. "Good morning to you."

"Yes, Dr. Brovek." She clipped the words. "Good morning indeed."

She swept through the door and Brovek let it close behind her.

He chuckled, and stepped out on the top step, breathing the frozen air, enjoying its sharp bite in his nose. From the curb a red Porsche pulled away with a squeal of rubber.

His gaze wandered across the street, and there stood the plot of land he lusted for. The dingy red brick parish house, paint peeling from its shutters. The tiny yard and empty playground covered with dirty snow. The silent church, its dark double doors closed against the world. 'Maybe nobody can buy it,' Horace had said. 'Maybe anybody can'—whatever he meant by that.

He stood looking across the street, his eyes drifting wide over the whole piece, his mind projecting the images of his dreams. In a tower to the left would be new research labs, gleaming tiers of animal cages, PhDs and graduate students and dieners, all elbow to elbow in quest of the secrets of immunity. On the right he imagined a hospital tower, a phalanx of operating rooms with nurses, technicians, doctors, the whole host of players needed to funnel transplantable organs into an expanding series of fine results. And out of it all would flow a stream of scientific papers he and his students would present before the national meetings to be published in the leading academic journals. His young surgeons would fan out to appointments in the nation's best transplant centers and universities. 'You trained under Sandor Brovek?' 'Oh, yes!'

"Good morning, Dr. Brovek."

The words wrenched him back to reality. The old priest came limping up the steps, puffing a cloud of steam the color of his eyebrows.

Brovek drew his own icy breath. There was nothing for him to say to this priest. All he could do was wait for Potts to deal, and he hated waiting. He wiped his lips with the back of his hand.

"Good morning, Father," he said, and held the heavy door while they passed inside.

*　　　　*　　　　*

To Grover Iverson the sad litany was all too familiar, intoned in hurt and anger by the series of uremics who sought out his Danish modern office for his drastic intercession. It began with diabetes, then insulin and its problems of control, probably too little with an episode of coma, or too much with attacks of hypoglycemic shock. Then, sooner or later, the decay. Maybe the eyes went bad, or the kidneys, or the legs and feet. His concern was the kidneys—he could do something about that.

"Deborah," he continued his discussion, "your only chance to get away from this dialysis that you hate so much is to get a new kidney by transplant."

Across his broad desk he watched the Buttner family, seated elbow to elbow in three leather chairs. The father's expensive jacket was skillfully tailored to his overweight frame. He spoke in a slow powerful drawl of modern industrial Georgia. The woman's suit was ultrasuede in a color that intensified her blue eyes, which burned steadily into Grover's own face. The patient was Deborah, their daughter, mid-thirties, attractive, except for clear skin that failed to glow.

"That's why we're here, Doctuh. Deborah is ready to try it."

Deborah's expression did not change. Her dark eyes were as steady as her mother's blues. He saw no surprise in them; not even interest. They were passive eyes, like a passenger on a bus. He made a guess.

"You have enlisted Deborah at other transplant centers as well, right?"

The big man chuckled without apology. "No stone unturned, Doctuh Iverson. We do have the means to—ah—favor her chances."

Grover winced. Favoritism on the transplant list might be his occasional practice, but it would be a dangerous reputation.

"There can be no compromise, sir, with the scientific necessities. Success in a kidney transplant absolutely requires a close tissue match between the kidney and the recipient."

He moved to regain control of the interview.

"That is why we look so hard for a living donor, usually a relative." He looked at them piercingly. "Perhaps a sibling. Or a parent."

At last Mrs. Buttner's eyes dropped from his face. The father was silent.

"For example, if Deborah had an identical twin...."

"We've been through all that." Buttner's words cut through like ice. "We are here to consider a cadaver graft, that's all."

"With a close tissue match."

"Of course. And the new drug. We want a success."

Grover placed his fingertips together, lightly, gracefully, across the front of his white clinical coat. He liked body language that portrayed skill, and finesse.

"That condition—a cadaver graft—puts Deborah in a rather large group of unfortunates for whom the supply of donor kidneys is very thin. I'm sure you all understand that."

Now it was the father's eyes that pierced.

"We need to talk about that," he said.

His drawl dripped industry and commerce. Grover kept fencing.

It was like foreplay, he thought. Like with Susannah, keeping her on edge, making her wonder whether tonight was the night.

"We'll keep Deborah's samples for matching to a donor," he said. "If her turn comes up with a suitable match, she will need to come back at once, ready to proceed."

"Exactly, Doctuh Iverson. I understand about the tissue match. That's a given. But I wonder if there is not some way to favor Deborah's turn coming up. I'd like to shade the odds, you know?"

And there it was. Grover fingered the clinical record on his desk, and beneath it her second folder—a credit report from Dun and Bradstreet, and the short form from his private investigator. He couldn't be too careful.

He leaned back in his leather chair. "I understand your concern," he said. "Actually, there is something you can do."

*   *   *

Martin Stern hung up his clothes in Dr. Lance Rudd's examining room. It was no better than last time, the same unrelieved harsh surfaces, glaring white walls, bare floor. The examining table of plastic and steel held one crackly strip of paper down its middle that he was supposed to sit on. The room was cold.

He had the system figured out. They made him wait there naked for the damn doctor just to put him one down so he wouldn't make trouble.

He stood and faced the full-length mirror. That maneuver wouldn't work with him. He felt just as good about himself standing there bare as he would have encased in his gabardine armor. He took in a deep breath, and contemplated the remains of Martin Stern. The scar on his belly wasn't too obvious, kind of like a beauty mark. But even with his deep breath, he stayed round like a ball through his middle. Fluid in his belly, they said. His hips were slender and his butt was flat. And his apparatus still looked like himself, even if it acted listless. His face darkened; that was the trouble: he was so tired. So damned pooped all the time. And he was turning yellow around the edges. He pulled down his lower lids and squinted at his eyes.

Well, that was why he was here. He took a paper gown and wrapped himself in it. He was never able to decide whether it should open in front or behind. Either way left problems. He sat down on the examining table, to warm it up, and to wait.

He didn't mind Dr. Rudd too much. The other doctors would always pussyfoot and not tell him anything. But Rudd was straight. He had laid it out for Stern after the gall bladder operation. More trouble, not just gall stones, he said. Something about ducts shriveling up. Stern couldn't believe it wasn't cancer. But when Rudd told him it was almost as bad, then he believed. Rudd said his liver was sick because the hollow tubes were turning into scar tissue; they couldn't carry the bile away any more. He called it "sclerosing cholangitis." When the liver finally quit, he'd be all through. And at every visit Dr. Rudd would tell him how much closer he was.

In his own opinion, this time he was pretty close.

"Well, I'm glad to see you again, Mr. Stern."

Rudd could be a pretty good-looking guy in his white coat, Stern thought, if he wasn't so fancy. Creased flannel pants, and loafers with tassels on them, for God's sake.

"Yeah, here I am again, like a penny with a bad liver. I think I'll trade it in for a new model."

"Good idea, Mr. Stern. Let's come back to that. Are you feeling about the same?"

"Everybody else, I say Yes. You, I tell. I get so tired I don't care any more. Lila Mae got bored with me and I don't even care. She's gone, and maybe I'm close. What do you think?"

Dr. Rudd grunted, examined, poked fingers, looked at some papers and grunted some more. Then he handed Martin Stern his clothes and waited for him to dress.

This was a new wrinkle, Stern thought. Usually he would pat my paper sheet and walk out.

He followed Rudd into the next room, softly carpeted, no windows. In the circle of light under a desk lamp Stern could see a litter of papers and books. Rudd sat down facing him, in the chair behind the desk. Nearly invisible on the wall behind him hung a series of diplomas and certificates proclaiming something undecipherable, but surely about the qualifications of Lancelot Motherwell Rudd, M.D.

He followed Rudd's gesture into a low chair in front of the desk. So what was cooking here, a hanging? a death notice? Rudd's manner was grave enough.

"Mr. Stern, in the past three months your liver has gone a long way downhill. That is why you feel so weak and tired. Your lab tests from today show pretty severe derangement in liver function. Do you understand what I am saying?"

Straight talk. Stern nodded. "Dr. Rudd, I am a very savvy guy in my circles. You don't have to draw a picture like the end of a rope for me to understand. So just tell me what's what. I've got irons in the fire."

"Okay. The end of the rope is exactly what I am talking about. The end for your liver. Until recently that meant the end for you too."

The entrepreneur in Stern heard the possible out at once. Cunning crept into his face.

"Enough already about the end of the rope. You got something else going on?"

Rudd nodded.

"There is a new possibility—a very difficult, very expensive possibility—for you to have a new life. It is working in Pittsburgh and a few other places, and we're ready to do it here. I am speaking of the chance of giving you a new liver."

Martin Stern sat back and stared at Dr. Rudd. He saw those long slender fingers rooting around his insides. Were they going to pull out his liver, for God's sake? Put in a new one? Whose business is that, where do they make new livers? Does his insurance cover a new liver? Maybe he can pull off that deal over at St. Luke's, after all. He can make a killing there with his hotel. Maybe even get Lila Mae back...To hell with Lila Mae.

To Dr. Rudd he said, simply, "When?"

Dr. Rudd smiled suddenly, a shy boyish grin. How did such an obvious person get to be such a big shot, Stern wondered.

"Well, Mr. Stern, we have to talk about many things before we can say when. You have to come to understand the risks and hazards of this treatment, the long course of follow-up after the new liver. And we have to consider the financing of this kind of care. It is extremely expensive."

"Not to worry. Building a skyscraper is expensive too, and some of the money might even rub off on a developer. I have a dollar or two, and what else is it good for since Lila Mae…"

He stopped. Rudd went on.

"There is also the matter of procedure. Where does a new liver come from? Who is going to get it? There are more people like you who need livers than we can possibly supply. These questions get very sticky, and they are not left to chance."

Stern pounced. "Not left to chance? Good! Raffles I don't like. Supply and demand, that I understand. That I can work on. I remember a few years ago when steel was hard to get…"

Rudd's look of astonishment cut him off. Rudd spoke into the silence.

"No, Mr. Stern, you don't understand. It can't work that way at all."

Can't work that way? Getting a liver is not a raffle, and it's not a market? What else is there? His thoughts tumbled. The flow of Rudd's words fell over him unheard. He shrugged, and spread his hands.

The soft light on the desktop left the walls in shadow; the array of diplomas hovered like ghosts. Why does he keep it so dark in here? Why can't they work to find a liver? Isn't Rudd his doctor, his partner? They should be a team to make a new liver happen. Improving the odds, how could it be such a bad thing?

He shook his head. "You lost me, Dr. Rudd. Go back again."

Rudd frowned and leaned forward, folding his arms on the desk. His clinical white sleeves reflected the light. His eyes bored into Stern.

"Finding a liver for you is not a market thing at all, not a buy-and-sell. It's not something you can go out and make happen. If there is to be a new liver for you, Mr. Stern, it will come as a pure gift, made by someone you will never even know, as a donation to save your life."

Stern sat back and watched Dr. Rudd's face. Earnest, and a touch angry, too. Transparent is what he is. You wonder what he thinks, look at him.

"A donation already? That's not so likely. But for that kind of a gift, what do I have to do? be a good boy?"

Rudd looked at his gold Rolex, leaned forward again over his arms. He raised his eyes to Stern's. His shallow smile came late to his lips and lasted too long. Angry, Stern thought. Tough.

"There is a formal process for selection, like a registry. Patients are selected to receive donor organs according to their seniority on the list, their urgency, and their likelihood for success. It is time to register your need, Mr. Stern, if you want to proceed. When a liver becomes available, someone else may be selected. But if you get the call, you will need to come in at once for the transplant."

Stern had heard enough. He spread his hands again, and waggled his fingers sideways, impatient.

"Don't waste your breath, Dr. Rudd. You show me a little chance I didn't know existed. What's to say? Sign me up. You want me to learn something, I learn it. You get a liver, I'll be here. What's my chance?"

Frown lines appeared in the boyish face. Now he's turning into a professor, Stern thought.

"If you can hold out," Rudd said, "and if we can put a liver in for you, you should have two chances out of three, or even three out of four, to celebrate an anniversary. And there's no limit after that. But there can be no promises, Mr. Stern, none at all, except that we will give you the best care we know how to give."

Martin Stern stared at this fountain of hope. He had no idea he could get odds like that. Yesterday they were zero. Today, three to one! His heart hammered in his chest. He wanted to leap to his feet, to shout, to hug this preppie genius. He was on a roll in a whole new game.

But what he did was to stand up slowly. Years of commercial pokering masked his face. He extended his hand to Dr. Rudd and outlined his contract.

"So, we've got a deal. Today I move into this city. My turn comes, I'll be here. With you in charge I don't worry, because I'm counting on you to make it happen. It's your job to take care of me, and mine to do what you say."

He felt his reserve slipping out of control. He dropped Rudd's fingers; his own two hands rubbed together.

"But now, if you will pardon a poor business man, there is one little call I have to make, and suddenly I want to make it today."

He strode out of Rudd's office. His pace was too fast, too bouncy; he knew his exuberance was showing. He guessed he didn't care.

*   *   *

When Sandor Brovek had pitched his proposals to the Board of Regents, he knew he was reaching beyond his own department. His attempt to consolidate all transplant surgery in his own department meant taking control of the kidney business from Iverson's Department of Urology. Hell, that was the whole point. But ordinary courtesy demanded that he inform Grover Iverson.

Brovek sat in his little second-floor office in Old U, his hand resting on his telephone. Iverson's number lay beside it, where Brovek had scrawled it a couple of weeks ago on a blank prescription pad.

Was the son of a bitch really selling kidneys? There just weren't enough local patients showing up for transplants, farmers and townsfolk from the University's own diabetes and dialysis clinics. These people were going without kidneys while Iverson's outsiders limoed in from the airport to take private rooms in the hospital and hire private nurses around the clock. How long could he get by with all that?

Just yesterday Brovek had closed his fingers around the phone and punched in Iverson's number. Then, just like all the other times, he hung up again before anyone answered. Colleague or no, convicted or no, Grover Iverson stuck in his gullet. So far he hadn't told him anything.

He drew a reluctant breath and started to punch in his colleague's number, and suddenly the problem came to a head. Grover Iverson marched in unannounced, all penny loafers and white front teeth.

"Good morning, Sandy. I hope you have a minute free."

"Yes, Grover, so I see."

He reached across his desk without rising, and touched the soft fingers Iverson extended. He pointed to his special chair.

"Sit down there," he said, and pushed a ragged pile of surgical journals to one side. "I have a few minutes."

An open sheaf of sketches of the St. Luke's property glared in the light, and he dropped his arm across it. Iverson seemed not to notice.

"I'll come right to the point. The Board of Regents minutes came out, and I see you got your approval. Why don't you tell me about it?"

"Nothing much to tell," he grunted. He would share none of his excitement with this man! "If we can find the site, we're okayed to build a transplant center. That's about it."

"And you are the one in charge?" Surrounding its brush of mustache, the urologist's urbane political face wore the alert, neutral expression that Brovek knew from staff meetings. Like a face on the TV news, it gave nothing away.

Brovek nodded. He too could be noncommittal.

"My Department of Urology is the only functioning transplant service in this university, Dr. Brovek. It's curious that I was left out of the discussion."

Brovek nodded again. Central control of all transplants was a core part of his proposal, and Iverson was the reason—he'd left the bastard out on purpose.

After a pause, he replied. "The new opportunities in transplants won't affect your operations very much. You'll just get better results. But the whole world will open up for us—hearts and lungs, livers, pancreas, maybe gut, you name it. Those are the areas for expansion, and they are all in my area of surgery."

He stopped. His mind flooded with ideas, with thrilling possibilities. But he'd choke before he shared them with this kidney merchant. He saw a glint in the other's eye.

"I think there is more to this than a building site, Sandy. Aren't you holding something back?"

Holding back? Of course he was. The idea of a single centralized transplant service was an explosive charge that was supposed to be secret. He could still hear Durshaw's voice against his back as he left the Regents' meeting: "Dr. Brovek's proposal for a Department of Transplantation, under himself as director, will not be reflected in the minutes."

He held himself neutral. "Apparently you have read the minutes, Dr. Iverson. Was there more?"

"You're damn right there's more." He lurched forward on the chair. "You're trying to steal my transplant business." The hot eyes, the scratchy voice reflected not a guess, no conjecture. Iverson knew the facts.

There was a leak, Brovek thought. Someone talked.

An image flashed into his mind—that morning after Grand Rounds when he went boiling through the hospital smack into Susannah Politon on the front steps; the red Porsche at the curb. It was Iverson's! Cozy! Susannah Politon coming to work with Grover Iverson, fresh from their breakfast bowls of Post Toasties and God knew what else.

So Politon was the leak! She would be a power in Iverson's camp, and no friend to Brovek.

He held himself rigid and tried to settle into his new insight. It was good to know where the winds blew.

"Stealing is an overstatement, Grover. Kidney transplants belong to you now"—he lingered over the possessive verb—"and you would still have them even in an integrated department."

Iverson shifted in his chair, twisting his spine around for an angle of repose. His scowl was unrelieved.

"Go for your building, Brovek," he said. "That helps everybody. But leave the integration shit to the Supreme Court. I'm doing all right in my own department."

I bet you are, Brovek thought. Aloud he said, "Last year your kidneys were the whole show. Next year transplants will be complex; they'll involve multiple organs and many surgeons. We'll need coordination of research, development of our own harvest and transplant teams, cooperation with ROPO in allocation of donor organs. These things demand a single department with central control."

Iverson hesitated, stroking his mustache with the tip of a finger. Then he flashed a winning smile. "Maybe you're right. Things change. Mind if I smoke?"

Brovek's eyes widened. He pressed back into his chair and its joints squeaked their complaint. He smelled a trap.

"I'd prefer you wait. I don't smoke myself, you know, and the odor lingers."

Iverson made no move to his pocket. "Just suppose," he went on, "that I like your idea. A centralized transplant program makes sense. I've been transplanting kidneys in my department for seven years now, with known results. Significant numbers, acceptable outcomes. I operate the dialysis program with Nephrology, and we run our own immune suppression post-op."

He smiled again, rather like a snake, Brovek thought.

"But what about your department, Dr. Brovek? Heart transplants? You've done none. Livers? Lungs? Zero! Those are just round numbers of course; but they're pretty close."

Acid dripped from his little joke. He leaned forward, elbows on his knees, watching Brovek's face.

Brovek said nothing. His work still lay ahead. He and Lance had developed their techniques in the animal lab; as an operating team they were slick. He had sent Lance off for extended visits to the leading transplant centers. All his staff studied the medical literature about immune suppression, and followed the chase in esoteric research journals. Hell, that's why he knew the future possibilities in transplants. He was ready and he knew it.

But his cases so far numbered exactly what Iverson said: zero. It was a weakness in his proposal that he had camouflaged from the Regents. Iverson had drawn blood here, and Brovek tried not to flinch.

Iverson's eyes drilled him from across the desk.

"So which one of us, Sandy, is better prepared to assume control of a transplant department? Clearly I am. And I will press that case to the Regents, if it becomes necessary. I have certain assets there, and I am confident I would prevail."

Brovek heard the confirmation: certain assets? Politon! The red-haired scarlet-lipped MBA had pushed her way up the hospital ladder to the top rung, and ridden the feminist wave to become a token woman on the Board. And some other kind of woman with Grover Iverson. The man had real power assembled in his camp.

Nothing Iverson said required a response, and Brovek made none. He sat impassive, as if he hadn't heard. But he was angry. He felt the familiar tension settle into his temples; his peripheral vision darkened so that he saw the leering face of Iverson in a tunnel of gray fog. He knew he must vent his tension before he lost control. He made his first thrust.

"Political combat would be a strange choice for you, Grover," he said, "considering your vulnerability."

"What's that supposed to mean?" Iverson sat up and shifted sideways on his chair.

"It means you walk far out on a long limb when you sell a kidney."

"You have no proof of that."

It was a defense, Brovek noted, not a denial.

"The records of your own dialysis clinic will show us which local patients languished without kidneys and died without transplants, while you put kidneys from local donors into wealthy clients from elsewhere."

Iverson smirked. "Remember tissue typing, Brovek. Those clients, as you call them, came in because they matched the kidneys that were available."

"I sure as hell hope they matched, or they're dead. But which of our local patients now dead would have matched those same kidneys? That's what I want to know. Whose chance for life did you take away when you took money from outside?"

Grover Iverson rose, trembling, teeth clenched. He kicked the chair aside.

"I guess you've just declared war, Brovek. But I don't have to fire a shot. You're already screwed."

He pointed a long finger at the sketch of St. Luke's, and sneered.

"You haven't found one square inch to build on. Without your fancy playhouse you won't get to first base—not with me, not with the Regents. In the transplant business, without that building, you are nothing but a wannabe. You are zilch."

He whirled out of the office, leaving the door standing open behind him and the hard truth spilled all over the floor.

Brovek watched him go, his shoulders slumping over his desk.

"Drop in any time, Grover," he whispered, "you son of a bitch."

*   *   *

Watching Stern's shoulders swagger away down the hall, Lance Rudd chuckled to himself. "So he remembers when steel was hard to get?" He checked the mirror, snugged up his neat Windsor knot and ran a pocket comb through his hair. "And a dollar or two rubbed off? I bet it did!"

He took up Stern's chart, and flicked off the light in his consulting room. He had plenty of time before his scheduled session with the medical students. New U's glistening hall led shortly into the dim corridor of Old U that brought him to his cubbyhole academic office. He filed the chart, checked with Estelle for messages and picked up his lecture notes. Savoring his leisure, he ambled along through the quiet old halls and dropped down the stairs to the warren of passages that led to Keaton. Still ahead of time, he pulled open the door to "the pit," the bottom rostral level of the lecture hall, and stepped inside.

Keaton Amphitheater was an old friend to Lance. This afternoon it slept in thick silence, like an empty church. He looked up at the tiers of empty seats, and his heart stirred. Echoes of lectures past whispered in his memory. The fragrance of learning. The thrill he felt here whenever some new concept took shape in his mind and found its place on the growing lattice of his knowledge.

From where he stood, two aisles passed up between the curving tiers of seats to a crosswalk above, connecting the main entry doors on each side. From the back wall, sunbeams slanted down through amber windows and flooded the seatbacks in yellow light. Hovering dust motes were transformed into speckles of gold. He hoped he could touch his own students' minds with light. He wanted them to love, as he had learned to love, the golden context in which float the basic facts of medicine.

Lance climbed to a seat in the first row, and sat down to wait.

His students would be coming to him from all parts of the campus—from pediatric bedsides, from electron microscopy, probably several from the library. Books, always books. It was Sir William Osler who compared patient care without books to sailing oceans without charts. Well, there were shiploads more of books today than Osler ever dreamed of, books awash on oceans of knowledge.

Lance remembered how things had been for him. The way they still were for students. They were just youngsters, struggling through relentless hours of work that ate up their energies, and left them with little reserve to deal with the other stresses of young lives—the challenges of growing up, of staying sane, of meeting expenses. Most of them had to borrow money. Lance himself, with all his Motherwell advantages, was still paying off the $63,000 he had owed at graduation.

And these kids, these neophyte doctors, with their leisure hours laid on the altars of scholarship, also had sex drives to struggle with. Their wild currents could never just run free. There was always a lecture or a lab to demand their time, or an all-night clerkship. Always they carried the onus and the guilt of unread books. They had to bottle up their free time like pills and parcel it out in small doses, an hour over coffee, an evening date once in a while. And then, exhausted, they might just fall asleep.

Sex was a challenge, all right. He didn't fight it any more. Long ago and for many reasons, he had decided to turn his back on sex.

He smiled to himself—that was a curious phrase.

Now here they came, spilling down the steps like otters, piling into seats, stacking their coats and spreading their notebooks on their laps. He had his own names for some of the characters. Here came Thomas, the class doubter: from the farthest, highest row he would make the keenest observations. Joan of Arc entered alone, her eyes on a distant star, her arms piled high with books. She must have carried every volume in the library by now. Finally, at the last possible moment, Romeo and Juliet, hand in hand.

Lance stepped down onto the rostral floor and spread his notes out on the podium. Probably he would not look at them again.

"Okay, students. Today we're talking about transplant surgery. Specifically, how to get live organs from cadaver donors. This field of care is younger than most of you, and changing faster too. Faster than anything else you will study. You'll have to chase it just to keep up."

He liked to start his lecture with a list, to trigger his students' Pavlovian pencils. The great Russian psychologist taught dogs to salivate at the sound of a bell. Rudd used phrases like 'three items…one is.' Like magic, student heads would bend over notebooks and student pencils begin to scratch.

"First we'll talk about permission to take organs for donation; then we'll decide what a cadaver donor is. And finally, what it is not."

He never felt cynical about his Pavlovian ploy. He used it for focus. He wanted to build a bond between his knowledge and their scholarship.

"The law defines who may give permission for the harvest of donor organs as the 'next of kin'. It gives us a complex list—lawyers wrote it—and it is in your printed notes. Surviving spouse, oldest child, whoever. Learn it. That person has the legal authority to give permission; no other person has it. Question: Is that person the only one we must consider?"

He waited. Students shuffled their feet on the terrazzo as they shifted their minds from 'receiving' into 'participatory' mode. Joan of Arc looked down her patrician nose and said, "Other kin?"

"Right," said Lance. "Legal permission is not enough. We must have the consent of every significant relative. In our practice here, if anybody in the cohort makes a sincere objection to harvesting organs, we will not do it. Why do you think we need to be so careful?"

Almost at once a voice said, "You'll get sued."

Lance shuddered. In the tricky waters of medicine, law suits were a constant whirlpool. They took people's eyes off their navigation of the main stream.

"Well, that is a constant specter. Fear of a law suit makes everybody pay attention to what's right. But hey, it doesn't determine what's right! Let's find a better answer."

No one volunteered. Lance continued.

"Donation of organs is voluntary. A man dies, and his widow agrees to the salvage of his organs. Primarily she sees it as a life-saving gift. But suppose she declines. If we still were to harvest those organs and ride rough-shod over her grief, we might gain an organ today. But her hostility, and by tomorrow the opposition of public opinion, would cost the whole program."

"Hold it, Dr. Rudd." Doubting Thomas leaned forward in his seat far above. The yellow windows left his face in shadow. "Do you give veto power to any Tom Dick or Harry relative? even if you have a legal okay? Suppose I've got a patient that needs that organ, and some cry-baby relative says No. I let my patient die? I don't think I could be so wimpy."

Lance nodded, and grinned at the invisible face.

"Maybe you couldn't. I couldn't either. So note the policy that rides up out of that conflict. Write it down! The doctor who uses an organ for transplant never takes care of a patient who might soon provide that organ. Repeat, never. If you are caught up in the care of a child who needs a liver, or a young mother dying of heart disease, you don't belong in the same universe as the motorcyclist with a head injury, a healthy liver, and a sound heart.

"Say it again. If you want an organ from a dying patient, you must never attend that patient as a doctor. You don't make any treatment decisions.

You don't declare death. You don't see relatives. You don't even exist for that family until the patient's own physician has declared death and secured consent to harvest. You pointed out the reason: we can't serve two masters."

Thomas was not satisfied. His face remained in shadow, but his words were clear. "In other words, the doctor that wants the organs can't ask for them; and whoever asks for them can't use them. That may not be a very good system, Dr. Rudd. No wonder there's a shortage of kidneys."

Rudd frowned. The student's point was right on the mark.

"This field is new; practices will change. Right now we are struggling to find the best ways to balance sensitivity and opportunity. Transplant surgery, right now in 1985, is just coming out of the research lab to become practical therapy. We are going to help patients we couldn't help before, and not only with kidneys. Hearts and livers are possible now; lungs are harder; pancreas and gut are farther away.

"But you are right about the shortage of donors. The sky is not the limit: donor organs are."

Joan of Arc lifted her face from her papers and squinted at Lance. "The government ought to do something about that," she said.

"They're beginning," Lance answered. "Congress passed the National Organ Transplant Act just last year, and we are expecting a report from a National Task Force soon. That may be some help."

"What about ROPO?"

Juliet's voice played the question like music.

"ROPO is the Regional Organ Procurement Organization—I'm glad you know about it. ROPO provides specialists in the art of asking. They step into these difficult situations and counsel, and ask, and get permission. They also help us to allocate organs to go where they are most likely to be successful. We rely heavily on ROPO."

Lance wondered if he could get Juliet to speak again. Her voice was liquid and hung heavy with possibility. Her smoldering eyes were incongruous with talk of cadavers. He went on.

"I want you to consider what happens when the body dies. Breathing stops. Circulation stops. Chemical processes break down and quit. But not all at once. Some tissues live longer than others. Examples?"

Juliet had an idea and he waited.

"I've heard that post-mortem Caesarean section can deliver a living baby."

He liked her example. Another student offered "skin and eyes."

"Yes," Lance said, "those are good examples. It is possible to recover skin or cornea from bodies even after refrigeration, and have those tissues survive transplantation. Cadaver skin is vital in the care of major burns today.

"But solid organs are different. Kidney, lung, liver and heart all have high energy requirements. When they lose circulation to bring oxygen and carry away carbon dioxide, they decay rapidly. For successful transplant, these organs must be harvested when the circulation is intact. So another question: if my blood is circulating, and my heart is beating, how can I be dead?"

He nodded to Juliet again, but she was silent. Romeo whispered to her, and she nudged him with her elbow, tipping her head at Lance.

Romeo stammered, aloud, "You are talking about b-b-brain death, I think. Isn't that a n-n-new law under the s-s-sun?"

"Exactly." Lance smiled. "Death has always been defined as a stopped heart. You were not dead until your heart quit beating. And that was fine once, it was good enough. But today we can keep a body breathing and the heart beating with no living brain in it, and we can go on for a cruel and inhuman length of time. If we could declare that patient to be dead on the basis of the brain being dead, we could do two desirable things."

Lance almost said "Romeo," but he only pointed to him.

"If he's d-dead we can h-h-harvest organs, and we can s-s-s-top treatment."

"Right on. The concept of brain death makes transplant surgery possible. And it has come hard-won after years of debate, new laws and judicial review."

Abruptly Lance pushed away from the lectern and marched to the edge of the pit. He seized the railing with both hands and swept his eyes up over the scatter of students above him. Let him touch their minds with unforgettable light!

"Now let's be clear about brain death! What it is, and what it is not. Fuzzy thinking here will lead you into trouble. Remember two words."

Pencils jumped into readiness.

"The words are: total; and irreversible."

He watched the pencils move.

"Total means all of the brain is dead. Not part of it. Not just the higher centers but the brain stem too. A person who breathes or rolls his eyes isn't dead even if he can do nothing else. Total means no reflexes—none. It means electrical silence on the electroencephalogram, a flat tracing. It means no blood circulating through the brain on angiogram."

He waited, until his broken rhythm brought the students' faces up from their notes. He wanted contact. Now he went on.

"What about 'irreversible'? That means that the findings of 'total' stay that way on repeat examination and are not going to change." He swept them with his eyes. "Can you think of a reason for change? a reason why a brain that seems dead might still recover?"

Juliet responded to his previous challenge, her voice dripping like honey. "Anesthesia, Dr. Rudd."

He smiled right back into her eyes. "Yes, anesthesia; and other drug intoxications too. There is too much of that nowadays." He looked around again. "One more cause? Very important?"

He stepped back from the rail and leaned on the small podium. No volunteers.

"A practical possibility for this time of year?"

Faces lit up. Several voices said together: "Hypothermia!"

"Correct. Never decide anything about a brain that is cold; wait for a day or two of normal body temperature."

Thomas shifted in his seat at the top of the hall. The sun was lower, and the windows darker. His face fixed upon Rudd like a mink looking into a chicken house, and his words probed for meat.

"You mentioned fuzzy thinking, Dr. Rudd. Can't you be more precise?"

Rudd loved this kid. Teaching was fun when students fought back. Yes, he could be precise about fuzzy.

"Where we must not be fuzzy is right here, talking about brain death. Fuzzy, for example, might let you retrieve organs from a person that is going to die anyway. Don't fall into that trap. Precision requires us to harvest only from a body that is already dead. The heart hasn't quit yet because of artificial support; but the brain is totally and forever dead. Okay?"

Thomas stared down at Rudd. "What about that girl in the newspapers—in coma for months and months. What about her?"

"Is she dead?"

"Might as well be."

"That you may decide only for yourself, not for some one else. Is she dead?"

"No."

"Exactly. And as long as she or any person lives, we are not donor candidates.

"But it's a tough and emotional issue. What she represents is called the 'vegetative state'. It carries hard questions: whether to start treatment; whether to stop it. But these are issues of the living. No matter how mindless or hopeless the patient may be, as long as the brain stem drives the breathing, he or she is alive. Not eligible for us even to think of as an organ donor. This is a critical distinction. Stay precise about it, and you'll keep organ transplantation on the right track."

It was a good place to stop. "Questions?"

The students agreed. Buzzing with sounds of release, they went rattling up the stairs, balancing their books and pulling on their coats. Romeo and Juliet tarried at the door, uniting the tips of their noses. They nibbled each other like two rabbits on one carrot, and then set off in opposite directions.

Lance sighed, watching them go. Lovers were everywhere, thank God. He wondered at this dewy-eyed pair, full of medical knowledge, steeped to saturation in a curriculum that included formal sexology and all its variations. And yet they seemed to be hearing, above it all, the serenades of Cyrano, and the songs of Elizabeth Barrett. He supposed he ought to feel inspired. For some reason, this afternoon, he felt only empty.

*   *   *

The short winter day left the church nearly dark. Faint rays from the western sky gave life to the stained-glass saints above the altar, and a few flickering votive lights set silent shadows to dancing in the apse.

Father O'Leary shuffled through the side door and approached his favorite place at the altar rail. He leaned on it heavily, taking his weight against his hands. His knees creaked down to the velvet cushion, and he moaned softly, his hurting mixed with relief. The sound lifted through the sanctuary like incense.

Isn't it strange, he mused. This old cushion is worn nearly bare where I kneel on it, and the knees of my trousers too. Each one worn off against the other. Where does it all go, one wonders.... Where does one's life go, for that matter, wearing away?...

"Well, Father in heaven, it was a long day and full. May you bring your healing power to all those sick and suffering people. And help this old priest remember to call the bishop tomorrow. He ought to be told there'll be another bidder for his church, so he don't decide something too soon, not knowing."

Gradually the old man released his daily care and settled into contemplation. He gazed up at the crucifix towering above him, the corpus sagging against its nails. There was a man reviled, rejected, humiliated by the world. But he rose above all that, and made his death a triumph, a victory for God's sake, and for us too, for all of us.

Father O'Leary's eyes rested on the shining red glass that held the vigil candle. Near it in the tabernacle lay the sacred host, consecrated by himself, the mystery of mysteries, the essence of the world's invisible God. He sighed. Reciting no prayer, he released himself into blankness. In simple wordless adoration, he knelt, content simply to exist in The Presence.

*   *   *

When three o'clock came at last, Karen Sondergaard dropped her duties on Station 21 and loped off to the grocery store. Humming a Norwegian folk tune that had a jazzy beat, she marched back to the Annex with brown paper bags cradled in each arm. She kicked off her galoshes and set to work in the kitchen. She chopped onions until her tears ran, and she kneaded the dicings, along with pepper and allspice, into the meatballs. She tossed sliced cukes and chunks of tomato into a bowl with shredded lettuce leaves and put the salad in the fridge.

Just after five she turned on the hot tap to the tub, and watched the water tumble and swirl, and turn to froth when she dripped in a cupful of bubble bath. She made the temp. as close to sauna rocks as she could stand, and lowered herself inch by inch into the brew. Fragrant steam caressed her lungs, and she sank down until the white foam closed over her shoulders and crackled in her ears. By six o'clock she was dry and dressed and looking for Dana Garrison.

Seven came. She paced around her tiny space, pulled at the coverlet on her narrow bed, set a pot of rice on to cook. She watched out the kitchen window where the snow-covered courtyard lay two stories below.

What had she started here? How did she have the gall to just push up to Dana Garrison the way she did this morning? She could never bridge the gulf between their roles. Dana, the doctor, gave orders. Nurse Karen obeyed them. Karen didn't know any doctor-nurse couples that were just friends. She knew of a few that made it with sex. In some strange visceral way, that thought disturbed her.

She decided that Dana wouldn't come. She turned off the stove, hung her dress in the closet, and pulled on her bathrobe. She started for the kitchen to make a peanut butter sandwich, when there was a knock at the door.

"You said 'Whenever I get through'?" Dana stood a couple of steps out in the hall. "Maybe it's too late?"

Karen had forgotten how small this doctor was. Her white coat hung an inch below her knees. One side pocket bulged with loose papers and a black notebook, and out of the other sagged the curled ends of her stethoscope. The coat's starch was gone for the day; maybe Dana's was too.

Karen swung the door wide. Her crimson robe, sashed at the waist, brushed the tops of her fluffy white slippers. Her blond hair was still tied back with a crimson ribbon. Her outfit was not what she had planned, but it would have to do.

"You must be beat. Come on in."

Dana nodded, tossed her coat on the stick chair by the door, and sagged into Karen's only stuffed chair.

"While I walked over here I counted my hours. I've been Chief Resident for almost two days, and one of those was a holiday, and I've notched up twenty-nine hours of work. I hope Bozo here will let me sit a spell." She patted the radio-pager clipped to her belt. "It's been a big day for him too."

Karen searched Dana's face. It was drawn with fatigue. A glass of something and a simple meal will do her good, she thought. She restored her assembly line in the kitchen and returned to set down a small plastic tray with two glasses of cider.

She felt stiff and awkward. What gall it took to invite the Chief Resident. Dana probably felt sorry for her. She tugged her bathrobe close at her neck, pulled a dining chair around and sat down next to Dana.

They eyed each other across the amber glasses, and took tentative little sips.

At last Karen said. "I'm glad I went to your conference this morning. I didn't know Dr. Brovek would be so tough."

Dana laughed. "He wanted to slay the dragon lady today. But he couldn't do it. Not in Round One, anyway."

Karen sat straight in the hard chair, appraising this doctor. Dana was setting out on the toughest job in the hospital, and yet, rumpled as she was, she had an air of grace. There was something crisp and dainty about her, a faint outdoorsy scent, her cheeks freshly scrubbed.

Abruptly Karen gathered herself and stood up. "Let me feed you something," she said.

Sitting opposite each other at Karen's tiny table, they nibbled at the salad in heavy silence. But steaming rice and fragrant meatballs with hot brown gravy brought appreciative sounds from Dana, and they began to talk about themselves. Where they came from. How they happened on University Hospital. Karen poured strong coffee into a pair of white pottery mugs, and they sipped slowly, relaxing into confidences, dipping into dreams.

"My dad was a doctor," Dana said. "He took me along on calls sometimes. I remember watching him put a farmer's hand back together after it got caught in a corn picker. I suppose he wanted me to be a doctor even then." She centered her mug on a paper napkin beside her plate.

"What does he think about your going into a tough specialty like surgery?"

Dana's eyes darkened. "He doesn't. The doctor's disease got him. He had a coronary at 58 and died in his sleep. I was in my first year of med. school."

Karen set her empty mug on the tiny table between them. "I'm sorry. I bet he'd be proud of you."

She watched Dana's dark eyes, saw the black pupils dilate.

"Oh I hope so! I've got to be good enough, Karen. As good as he was."

They sat for a few moments in silence. Karen felt as if she had turned over a stone. Finally she said, "My father died when I was eight. I hardly remember him. Except he was tall—at least to me he was. And unapproach-able. I don't know what he wanted for me."

"Different kinds of losses," Dana said. "None of them is easy. What did he do?"

Karen turned to the stove, and spoke over her shoulder.

"He was a Lutheran pastor, and he left my mother with four children and a tiny pension and a shack of a house out in the prairie. She still lives there, and she's like a hermit."

She stopped; she could feel the tears mounting. She kept her back to Dana until her eyes cleared, then she snatched up the coffee pot and came back to the table.

Dana was adjusting the salt and pepper shakers at the center of the table. She didn't look up. "But your mother would be there for you, I suppose, if you needed her. My mother died when I was little."

"I'm sorry," Karen said. She tipped the pot until coffee twisted out of the spout and swirled in the two heavy mugs. Fresh columns of steam rose over them.

"Enough of the sad stuff," Karen said. "Let's talk about something else." She thumped the pot on the table. "What about the men in your life?"

Dana's throaty laugh bubbled across the cup at her lips. "That's easy: there aren't any. In fact," she rose from her chair, settled her cup on the table, "there aren't going to be any. Not right now, anyway."

Karen jumped up and turned her one upholstered chair toward Dana.

"Sit here," she said, "and put your feet up. You sound pretty clear about it—no love life."

"Oh, I'm clear about it." She dropped onto the cushioned seat with a moan of pleasure. "You saw Dr. Brovek today. I think he let me in as a resident because I have a man's name. I bet he never read the form with the 'F' under 'Sex'." She laughed. "Seriously, though, he hates having a woman for his chief resident. He'd fire me tomorrow if he could find a way. I've got to be the best resident he's ever had, just to survive."

Karen knelt and lifted Dana's feet; she slid her own wooden chair under them. Dana's legs were well muscled and sheathed in nice flesh-colored pantyhose, not the dreary arctic white that she herself had to wear. Her shoes were sensible—flat heels despite her height.

Impulsively she said, "What's with the low shoes? Most girls wear something to make themselves taller."

Dana laughed. "That's my mark, my panache. Remember Cyrano's white plume? I haven't ever worn high heels."

"Never? I understand soft soles for the hospital. Saves your legs."

"And quiet too," Dana said. "Remember how I sneaked up on you the other morning?"

Karen chuckled, looking down at her new friend. "That was just yesterday, Dana." Her hands curled over the wooden chair back. "I always felt too tall, myself."

"That surely wasn't my problem! I about died in high school when all my friends grew past me. But when I was a junior I went to the Prom with the captain of the basketball team. Five-one against six-four. I felt so small I wore low heels to spite him, and he loved it. I've worn them ever since. Who needs to be tall?"

Again Karen felt awkward, fiddling with the chair, towering over Dana. "I'm going to do the dishes. Stay where you are."

There was little on the table to clear. She scraped the two plates into the sink and splashed hot suds over them.

Her heart sang. Too many nights she had stood here alone and dumped half her food in the garbage and swished the dishes with dead hands, just going through motions. Tonight things were different: the soap suds were fragrant, the glassware gleamed, and she found herself humming that old Norse folk melody.

She reached up to pull the little bead chain that turned off the light over the sink. Taut and slender, she felt alive again. Her skin tingled. Her belly sent messages. She turned. Just a couple of quiet steps in her fluffy slippers brought her to Dana's side, Dana, curled up there in the chair. Dana.

Karen knelt down beside her new friend. Dana Garrison was asleep in the sleep of exhaustion.

PART THREE

▼

VALENTINE'S DAY

Over her surgeon's hood and mask Dana had strapped on a magnifying loupe that now rode neatly before her eyes. It simplified her job to incise the femoral artery, clean its glistening wall of lingering wisps of tissue, and sew to it the open end of Gortex graft. She proceeded steadily with her tiny stitches, placing them precisely in the two edges, graft and artery, millimeter by millimeter. When the clamps came off, blood must flow smoothly through the new connection, out of the patient's groin into the long graft that still lay coiled beneath her hand. The groin connection was only the first half of the story.

Pete held her fine Dacron thread on light stretch as she placed each new stitch and pulled it snug. Its shimmering blue color played a synthetic contrast to the pink of the artery and the oyster color of the Gortex. The final stitch brought the last edges together, and she tied seven quick throws for a knot.

"Good, Pete," she said, as he put scissors to the extra thread.

Dana stood up and stretched, unhunching her shoulders and relaxing her arms. The procedure was going well; it would turn out all right.

And she wanted it to. The old man lying there under the drapes had won her heart. His name was Mr. Hargraves, and he was 85. At their first meeting in the Vascular Clinic, he said, "I cain't walk a block no more 'thout that hind laig crampin' up. I ain't been dancin' since harvest time."

"Do you like to dance?"

He grinned at her, his peg teeth stained brown.

"Fix me up, Doc, and I'll show you. I'll take you where there's fiddle music you kin stomp to."

And why not? Dana thought. His open approval of her person had fallen on her like warm rain.

She adjusted her clamps and tested the union for leakage. A tiny red fountain at one corner dwindled away, and the graft pounded against the clamp. She was satisfied. Now the second half.

She tunneled the tube of graft under the skin of the thigh, down past the level of blockage in the native artery, to reach the popliteal artery behind the knee. There she cleared the vessels and set them up for the second anastomosis.

Go dancing with Mr. Hargraves? The thought rubbed on her mind like an idea from another life. After six weeks of hard labor every day and most nights, the hospital walls had begun to close in around her. She was indentured to Dr. Brovek—as restricted until July as a medieval slave. But if this surgery let Mr. Hargraves dance again, why couldn't she dream of it herself?

Stop it, Dana. It isn't the dream of dancing that makes you stand over this man and cut holes in his arteries. Let him hope for fun; for you it is heavy responsibility.

She placed a clamp on the popliteal artery and excised a small oval of its wall for the new opening. She trimmed the end of the graft to fit and started the first stitch.

Always she strove for perfect technique, so healing could go forward without complication. But always in her mind hovered the non-technical risk that adheres to every surgical procedure. Infection. An accident of anesthesia. A bad artery in a leg could mean a bad artery somewhere else. The heart, or the brain. With or without her operation today, Mr. Hargraves could stroke out tonight. Maybe he would—it was always possible.

She shook her head. Negative thoughts were not her style.

The fine jaws of her needle holder seized and released the needle in regular cycles—seize, stitch, release; seize, pull through, release; seize and stitch again. She palmed the instrument, its looped handles hiding in her hand. Their ratchets opened and closed silently, obedient to the automatic actions of her slim fingers. Her left hand held a slender tissue forceps which danced counterpoint to the needle, holding first the weave of graft, then the leather of the artery, for passage of the stitch. And then holding the needle to be positioned anew. Rhythm. Precision. Satisfaction.

Hazard? stroke? failure? Again the corrosive thoughts intruded, and she tried to blot them out. Today was Valentine's Day. This sweet old man must dance again—she had set her heart on that.

She completed the suture, tested the union, and removed all clamps. The graft writhed with the thrust of her patient's pulse, blood coursing across her smooth suture lines and into the hungry arteries of his leg and foot. Good. He might dance again after all. Wasn't that what she wanted?

There was a grunting noise from behind her, a deep guttural sigh. When she turned, there was the rolling gait, the broad back that could only be Sandor Brovek, pushing through the swinging door out of her room.

Her face went hot.

"How long was he standing there, Pete?"

"Ten minutes, maybe." Pete smirked. He had seen the joke and watched her get caught out.

"Next time, let me know, man—ask to stamp his passport or something."

She passed him the needle holder. "You close the groin incision. I'll sew this one."

Sure, she thought, she wanted the best for Mr. Hargraves. Sure, she worried about complications. But cut the crap. She was just as intent on her own good record. She had to be flawless.

Brovek didn't want her. She knew that. He had waited and waited to name her as Chief Resident. He never greeted her with the collegial chuckle he sometimes granted to the male residents. He was tough on all of his people, but his squinty eye on her was palpable. She watched him at the weekly conferences. For one of the men, a complication would be a resident's occasional inevitable shortcoming. But for her? A female surgeon? Well, what could you expect? he'd say. The very idea is ridiculous! She could hear his comments as if he stood rumbling at her ear. She wanted desperately never to give him cause.

"What's the matter, Dana? You grumbling about something?"

"You wouldn't understand, Pete. It's nothing."

The hell it was nothing. New steel formed in her spine. Forget fun; forget dancing. Whatever effort it took, whatever sacrifice, she meant to succeed. For a critical half year her entire universe lay within the walls of University Hospital. Her spirit stiffened. She resolved anew to give it every beat of her heart.

*   *   *

The kidney lay in ice on the back table, shipped in from a contact in New England. Grover Iverson smiled behind his mask, and drew his scalpel across Deborah Buttner's abdomen.

It always paid to keep the big picture in mind, he thought. There were never enough organs to go around. Whether Deborah received her kidney today or went on waiting was fairly arbitrary. Why not fiddle the odds for her? He was just making the system work in his own favor. That was the American way, the free-enterprise system. It didn't hurt anybody.

It wasn't a moral question at all, was it?

Soft coils of intestine squirmed in the wound like empty sausage. He packed them safely away and sliced the membrane that still shielded the pelvic blood vessels.

In fact, he thought he was pretty clever. These were still early days in the transplant business. Tracking systems were—not loose, exactly—but, well, malleable. Like the description of fingerprints, tissue types were codified and easily communicated. Yesterday a kidney showed up on the donor network that fit Deborah. He jumped in with a plea for his mid-western transplant center, and the kidney was shipped in by air express. The rest was easy. A quick summons to the Buttners. A nice operation, done smoothly like this. He pinched a bleeder with his forceps and touched it with the electrocautery.

Postoperative care was straightforward; actually his resident staff managed it as a research study.

It was all so ideal: good surgery, good results, good research. He was his own king, free and clear—as long as he kept his own secret. He wanted no outside scrutiny of The Grover Research Foundation. "Remember that our 501c3 status is still pending, Mr. Buttner. If you try to claim your gift as a deduction, you'll only get yourself in trouble with the IRS!"

Neat.

Two pelvic blood vessels, artery and vein, were ready to be connected; the bladder was exposed and waiting; along the pelvic wall a pocket was developed for the new kidney to rest in.

He was fast, no doubt about that. Good scientist; good operator.

Good skier! Next week he'd be off to the Bugaboos, at the top of the Canadian Rockies. Fly up by helicopter, sail down by ski, knee deep in virgin powder. And it would all be paid for by the Grover Foundation's generous grant for medical research.

"Myrna," he smiled. "Please pass the kidney."

*   *   *

By mid-morning Karen Sondergaard's Norwegian blood clamored for coffee. The hum of voices along the polished corridor and the bustle of her nurses in and out of patient rooms went unheard. The spread of patients' charts across her desk blurred in her eyes. Her new duties still felt strange; she had not yet found the rhythm in her work that would allow an acceptable break. She palmed her starched skirt smooth against her long thighs and bent again over the charts, rigid against the coffee's siren song.

Only a few noons ago, in the cafeteria line, she had been tapped on her shoulder by a junior front-office type in spike heels and a mini skirt.

"Miss Sondergaard?" she whispered in a throaty voice.

"Yah?"

"When you finish your lunch, will you report please to the Administrator's office? Ms. Politon wants to see you."

Iced tea and egg salad went down in a mixture of guess and worry, and then she sat in a hard chair, heart pounding, looking at cold eyes and red bangs.

"I like to see a woman improve herself." Susannah Politon's accent smacked of East Coast and education. "Your graduate degree speaks well of you, and so do your peers."

"Thank you," Karen said. She knew the legends about this woman, a pioneer feminist, one of the first women to earn an Ivy League MBA. In the University community she had made a fast-track climb that Karen watched from afar.

Politon poked a long red fingernail at her ashtray, that was mounded with carmine butts. "I want you to take on Station 21 as Head Nurse. It's a salary position, better than you're doing now. I want a smooth operation. You run the personnel, no mistakes, happy troops. Interested?"

Karen's thoughts tumbled like flashing lights. No more night shift! A reward after all for her slavery in graduate school. And a real opportunity to make nursing better. Her words burst out.

"Yah, you bet." She could have bitten her tongue.

Now even the thought of her slip into Prairie Falls vernacular brought a hot flush creeping up her neck. She pushed the charts together in a neat stack. Her intent as head nurse would aim a lot higher than 'no mistakes, happy troops.' She wanted happy patients.

She looked down the ward where her newly assigned RN was making a bed. Ms. Marnie Bates, her untried lamb, fresh out of nursing school. Part of Karen's new job would be to teach Marnie the ways of Station 21. Karen's kind of Station 21. She watched the girl snap a sheet tight and pick up a pillow case.

A young nurse like Marnie faced so many traps, so many easy mistakes, starting out. She must learn to decipher doctors' crazy handwriting, order the right meds and give the right doses, follow the right schedule. Back rubs and bed baths and bed pans and exercise all became her job, and every move had to be recorded. Karen meant to be tough about this kind of discipline. It constituted the basics, the wheels and brakes of nursing.

She opened one of Marnie's charts—order sheet checked, med. record up to date, neatly written notes, all okay. A good start.

Coffee could wait. She drifted down the corridor and leaned on a door frame to watch Marnie at work. She wanted to see Marnie's way with a needle, her manner with a touch or a word. Often Karen felt bitter about the limitations of her profession, but she believed in its virtues. Others could toss off "TLC" like a trite expression, but for Karen care was nothing if it were not tender and loving. An aura of healing could arise from the gentle starch of nurses, from the fragrance of their concern. Some nurses produced it, some did not. Karen wondered if that quality would turn out to be something she could teach.

Marnie's youthful bloom filled out her crisp white uniform; she ought to be on a recruiting poster, Karen thought. Let's see how she'll look after a couple of bed baths.

A harsh voice broke into her thoughts. A man's voice.

"Nurse, you don't look busy; could you help me?"

Was he speaking to her? The man's impatient question sounded more like a command. She looked about and found him bending over her desk, writing on a chart. He threw the pen down, straightened, and frowned in Karen's direction.

He looked silly, she thought, for a well-built man. His feet were stuck into paper booties and his head was swathed in a hood like a bank robber. His white lab coat was too small; his bare forearms stuck out of the sleeves and his coat rode a couple of inches short of knee-length on his green cotton scrub suit. But she didn't dare giggle. Surgeons always took themselves too seriously, and this one, as she walked to the desk, was already showing a head of steam.

"I'm Dr. Rudd, nurse," he said. "I just saw your patient in 2110, the one with a ruptured appendix. You don't have anybody here that's sicker, I imagine, so take care of her. I want you to get these orders all done before we call her to surgery. Can you do that?"

Karen faced him. She stood almost as tall as he. Her blood surged, as scalding as the coffee she couldn't take time for. Would there never be, she wondered, a man who was gentle? who would look past her uniform into her gray eyes and see the woman there?

She kept her voice level. "I am the head nurse, Dr. Rudd. Yes, I can do that."

Watching him stride away, she felt grateful to her Nordic reserve. How many times in her life had it hidden her anger and saved her dignity? Her courtesy might be only a facade, but she believed every doctor deserved that much. Besides, if there were ever a confrontation, she knew who would lose.

She checked the orders he had written and set to work. There were wheels to turn: lab tests, i.v. antibiotics. And of course there was the order he wouldn't write, for the ingredient she would add on her own initiative: her understanding ear.

2110, indeed, she thought. Here came the hero, racing in to operate on this lady, and he couldn't even say her name.

*   *   *

After supper Dana elbowed Karen away from the sink and stole the Choreboy.

"My turn," she said. She pried a fingernail against a stubborn bit of lasagna stuck to Karen's baking dish.

Karen scowled. Her hair shone golden under the yellow bulb.

"You've been uppity all evening, Dana. You must have had a good day."

"Finest kind!" Dana agreed. "One darned good surgical case, and no other problems. I had all my work done before five o'clock, I soaked in a hot tub for twenty minutes, and even fell asleep in it. Valentine's Day was the best day so far."

Karen rubbed her dish towel over a plate that was already dry and said nothing.

"These suppers with you are a God-send too." Dana went on. "My only chance to relax with a friend. Everything else is business."

Karen bit off her words. "But you like your business. You're top dog in your business. You write your own ticket in your business." With each repetition her voice rose. She stared at Dana, and now her voice dropped to a whisper. "And I have to eat shit."

Her shoulders drooped. She put the plate down and twisted the dish towel between her hands.

Dana abandoned the lasagna pan. She hoisted her lean buttocks up on the counter, dangled her legs and wiped her hands on Karen's towel. "Tell me about it."

Karen gave up the towel and roosted on the step stool.

"It just all piles up on me, that's all. Except for you I have no friends. Nursing is all I've got. And it isn't enough. Not enough for me, and not enough for my patients. I can see things that would help them, and I can't make them happen. No nurse can. Doctors hurry with their patients and I'm not allowed to fill in, not the way they need."

Dana didn't stir. "What happened today?"

"Oh, one doctor gave me a hard time this morning. He was rough with me, and he wasn't all that good to his patient either. And that makes me mad."

Karen stretched to her full height, but gradually sagged down again like a leaky balloon. "And the truth is that's the only man I get to talk to all day. Or all night." Her voice dropped again; Dana strained to hear. "And the worst part is that I can't make things any different."

"But you're the head nurse now; you're in charge."

"It's no different. A nurse is just a nurse."

Dana watched the sad eyes, the quiet face. She was hearing no litany of grouch, just a simple inventory of heartache spilled out to a friend, to be shared, to be looked at. Dana struggled to be helpful.

"I thought you were a bundle of ice once," she said. "Do you remember what happened? You reached out to me—you offered me friendship. You made things different then. Different for both of us."

Karen raised a faint smile. "I was so lonely, Dana. I was driven. I even thought I was falling in love with you." She clasped her hands in her lap. "But the Lutherans won. I won't settle for less than a man."

Dana whooped. Her laughter echoed in the tiny kitchen.

"Hey, Karen, there is no way I am less than a man! I have to be twice times any man to be here at all!"

Karen flushed. She made an apologetic sound, but Dana ignored it.

"Which doctor gave you the hard time today?"

"Dr. Rudd, the pig. He was mean."

Dana was astonished. Gentle Lance? Her own constant support and mentor?

"What did he do, exactly?"

"He trampled over us on 21 and snatched a lady off to surgery when she hardly knew what was happening."

Dana nodded. "I heard him say he had to squeeze a consult in between surgeries today, and then add it on as an emergency. Karen, he must have been under pressure."

Karen snorted. "He could still treat me like a human being. And his patient like someone with feelings."

"Didn't he?"

"He told her he had to operate, otherwise she'd die. And then he left. He didn't tell her how long she'd wait, and he never told her she'd get well. She didn't know what to think. She was crying."

"Could you help?"

"Sure. All I had to do was listen to her for a few minutes, and answer her questions. She felt better."

Dana said nothing. Her legs swung slowly, her flat heels tapping a hollow rhythm against the cupboard door.

"Everybody's patients need to be listened to. You have no idea what feelings they have that you doctors never know. I wish I had the power to change the system, so patients had somebody to be on their side. Like a friend at court, or something."

"What are you talking about, another layer of care-givers?"

"If that's what it takes. Jesse Jackson talks about empowerment. That's what patients need, sometimes."

"Do you think you know how to do that?"

Karen glared at Dana. "I think I could find out in a hurry, if I had any authority. But I can't change the system. Nobody listens to nurses."

"You can make them listen to you, Karen. At least you can try!"

Bozo fired off his antic vibrations against Dana's groin. She clutched at him, poking frantic fingers at his off-button. She jumped down from the counter.

"Dr. Garrison," Bozo crackled. "Call Emergency Room."

Dana made a face, and shrugged at Karen.

"Figure out what you want to do," she said, "and go to the bosses. Sell your idea. Maybe it could turn into a whole new career. You can make a difference—but you've got to reach out!"

She lifted Karen's telephone and dialed the ER.

"And Karen," she spoke across her fingers on the mouthpiece, "give Dr. Rudd another chance. As men go, he's a good one."

PART FOUR

▼

CARNIVAL

"Please be careful, Danny!"

He winced. His mother always said that.

"I will, Ma," he hollered. At sixteen years old, he was a darned good rider. And pretty careful too. But he wished he could take off on his motorcycle and really go somewhere. He wanted to see things.

The door slammed behind him, cutting off her final words. "Wear your…" He knew. His helmet. But he'd left it at school. He'd pick it up and wear it home. She'd never know.

The last couple of weeks with no winter storms had left the roads in good shape, and Danny was hot to get out on them. Alone on his cycle, the cold wind in his face, he could feel like a king again—even if he was just heading for school to work on his science project.

He rolled his Honda out of the machine shed, the wheels crunching on the frozen gravel. He always kept his motorcycle gleaming and tuned up, ready to go. And today, after a week of warm weather for February, he was finally getting a chance to ride. He straddled the seat and kicked down on the starter. The engine coughed awake, and he waited while it warmed and smoothed into a low rumble.

He idled a circle around the yard. He skirted the edge of the barn, its doors closed against the winter cold. He threaded his way through a clutch of chickens scratching in the gravelly dirt, and past their coop where a rooster huffed feathers at him and backed away. He came around again to the machine shed. Through its open door he saw his father and two little brothers bending over into the big John Deere's insides. They straightened for a moment, and waved as he went by.

Going down the quarter mile of gravel to the county road he revved up a bit. When he reached the blacktop, it lay smooth and dry, and he goosed the cycle's throttle. The engine sang; he thrilled at the surge of power. The wind whipped his hair. Just a few more months and he'd buzz off to college. No more 4-H; no more calves and shitty boots. He'd study computers, and get a good job in the city. He dreamed about having Saturdays and Sundays off, no chores.

Today was Saturday. There wouldn't be many kids at school—maybe some of the guys at hockey practice. But Danny didn't care about hockey. His mind was full of his demonstration project: to make the school's new Macintosh draw curves in response to mathematical equations. He started with simple x's and y's, like analytical geometry. But then he tried to add formulas where the baselines changed. He was stuck; maybe he was in over his head. But this afternoon he had a new wrinkle he wanted to try.

The road was clear and he whizzed along all the way to town. He buzzed the curb in front of the drug store. Maybe some of his pals would be hanging around. He didn't see any, but he revved up a couple of backfires anyway. Wake them up a little! He cruised down Center Street, watching the road but still grabbing glances at his reflection in the store windows. Shiny bike, black leather jacket, his blond hair streaming back in the wind. At the Lutheran Church he turned and headed down the hill on Third Street, past the hospital, toward school.

Ahead of him a pick-up truck pulled out of somebody's driveway. It was loaded down on its springs with firewood, and it had to struggle to get up the hill. Just as Danny came near, a car darted out from behind the truck, into Danny's lane, coming up fast. Hey, trouble! Danny braked carefully, not too hard, and dodged into the driveway of the hospital. Plenty of room. No sweat.

Then he saw it. Dead ahead. Not ice. Sand. Loose sand somebody had spread all over the driveway, so nobody would skid. Danny's turn was too tight for sand, and there was no place he could go. His wheels began to slide, his cycle skewed around. He didn't have a chance. His wheels slammed into the curb, and Danny launched into the air. He saw the ground. He saw the sky. He saw the old elm tree coming at him. He saw nothing.

*   *   *

On Tuesday morning Jack Herold gave up trying to sleep. He rolled out of his bed in Old U, stepped barefoot to the dark window and lit a cigarette. They were trying to help, he knew that. They had given him this old hospital room to use while his wife was—what, dying? he forced himself to say it—in her bed in the Intensive Care Unit. God, she looked pathetic last night, pale and weak under the white sheet, with those oxygen prongs stuck in her nose.

He stubbed out his cigarette and pulled on his clothes, the same blue button-down, the same khaki slacks he had worn down to the hospital in Millicent's ambulance a couple of days ago. ICU was close by, in the New U, and he walked over there clinging to the faint hope that since they had not called him during the night, maybe she was better. Squinting under the Unit's bright lights, he tiptoed among the cubicles, with the softly soughing respirators, the blinking red eyes of monitors.

Millicent scared him. Cranked up on pillows, she lay inert in the bed. He watched her draw a few breaths, shallow, raspy. She did not respond when he took her hand, and held it. Her nails were blue, and her hand lay soft and limp in his palm, as if her bones had just melted away. He stood there, numb and unbelieving, while his allowed five minutes drifted by.

He had no place to go. He scuffed his way down a long hall. Through a window somewhere he watched the sky lighten. Then he wandered some more, and found himself again in Old U near his own temporary quarters. The room wasn't much—a bare tile floor, a porcelain wash basin with a chip by the drain, and a recycled hospital bed. He went in and lit a cigarette, and dragged on it, and stubbed it out in the sink. He threw his lanky frame down on the bed, folded his hands behind his neck, and closed his eyes. Images flashed through his mind as if a projectionist had gone mad. Fragment pictures; trouble pictures. Even as he grappled with one, another would thrust itself into his mind. Images of the past three weeks, Mil sick, Mil struggling for breath, a sea of problems, never progress, only more combers of disaster coming on. He felt beached, battered and helpless. Poor Millicent.

She was at the center of all his thoughts. Vibrant Mil, with her bubbling laugh and her joyous music. He loved to hear her sing—her gentle voice when she put the children to bed; her spark when somebody's party started to sag; her soul when somebody got married. One month ago she had sung the soprano solos at church. Now she was smothering, blue, gasping for every breath.

His eyes burned, and he turned his cheek against the pillow. He hadn't cried in years. Maybe it was time. Better now, alone, than later with Dr. Kanju, or Dr. Brovek.

The flu had started out to be so ordinary. It started with the kids, of course—they brought it home from school. Francine had just made it back to eighth grade when Eddie came home from sixth. Millicent took vacation time from work to care for the children, and then stayed home some more to take care of Jack. He had the flu so bad he took his first sick leave in ten years. And Mil got too tired; he could see that now. Guilt gnawed at him; somehow he should have made things different. For when the flu finally descended on Millicent it came with a fury. And she didn't get better.

She got worse. Mil went into the hospital near home. Aunt Maude came to manage the house—Mil's older sister that Jack never liked. He was grateful to her now. But Mil went down, every day another bump, like a ball rolling down stairs. He remembered how she first felt short of breath. The next day the doctor at home thought she had pneumonia. Then they found out she had heart failure. The next day Jack rode with her in the ambulance to University Hospital. Three horrible hours, and he held her hand all the way. It felt so limp and cold she might have been dead. Except that he could watch her, propped up on pillows, oxygen tubes in her nostrils, struggling to breathe.

And that wasn't bad enough. Here at the University, trouble really pulled out the stops. Dr. Kanju kept shaking his head as her tests grew steadily worse. Two days ago they said Mil's heart was just about destroyed. Myocarditis, they said: it would never recover.

Is there nothing we can do? No hope at all?

Well, there is one hope. One brand new possibility, just now coming into use. Maybe, if we could get a donor heart, we could transplant it into Millicent.

Would it work?

Yes, if she can live long enough. If a donor comes along. If the operation goes okay.

If, if, if. One never knows. Jack replayed his interview with Dr. Brovek. A giant of a man, but he seemed gentle. He tried to be hopeful. Jack's only good news was that his insurance would apply to a heart transplant. He didn't know; he'd read only about tonsils and appendix when he signed up for it.

'Mil needed a transplant,' the big man said. Okay.

'She couldn't last much longer without it.' Hell, he could see that—he didn't need a University doctor to tell him she's barely alive.

'Maybe there won't be a donor in time—there are never enough donor organs available.' Yes, Jack had read about that in the papers. How distant and comfortable he had been, and untouched, just a few weeks ago.

And then something stuck crosswise in his memory. Brovek had said No to an artificial heart. It was experimental, he said; he didn't believe in it. We just had to do the best we could. If no donor came in time, Millicent would die, Mr. Herold. Tragic.

Jack struggled with himself. He forced his mind to grapple with this worst-case scenario. Mil would die. He would go home, go back to work. But what about Francine and Eddy—Aunt Maude?—

Abruptly his swelling anger burned in his gut, too hot to contain, and boiled out in an anguished cry.

"Bull-shit she'll die!"

He surged up out of the bed, thrust his feet into his shoes. His courtesy room in Old U wasn't far from Brovek's office. He covered the distance in long strides, jerking the knot on his tie somewhere toward the front of his shirt. He jammed into the Professor's anteroom and confronted a flustered secretary.

"I have to see Dr. Brovek." His voice rose; it didn't quite break.

It was Brovek's own voice that answered him, rumbling out of the inner office.

"Please come in, Mr. Herold. Let's talk."

Jack Herold's coil spring was ratcheted down tight. One more twitch might send him slashing out of control. So he let his frustration boil out. In four terrible weeks, this was his first chance to strike back at fate, to uncoil, to make something happen. He strode up to Brovek's desk. He did not sit down.

"You bet we need to talk, Dr. Brovek." His voice was harsh, rigid. "My wife is damn near dead this morning. If your artificial heart is just experimental, then experiment on Millicent! And don't wait too long!"

His challenge was thrown, directly into the face of his only hope. He glared at the immovable mountain behind the cluttered plateau of his desk. Brovek's eyes were steady beneath the bushy brows, and his voice was soft.

"Millicent is critically ill. You are absolutely right. Her poor heart isn't going to sustain her much longer. She needs a transplant, and soon, if she is to have a chance to recover."

Jack grabbed the edge of Brovek's desk. "But we have no donor, Dr. Brovek. You told me you won't use an artificial heart. But I say you can't just let her die; you've got to do something...Francine and Eddy..."

His voice broke at last. "You've just got to keep her going."

Brovek was grave. "An artificial heart is no answer for her. These devices have serious problems still to be solved. We are going to do all we can for your wife; count on that. But short of an artificial heart."

Herold struggled for control. He knew he had to win this one. Brovek's face blurred before him. His arms felt stiff as broomsticks as he leaned across the desk.

"Look here," he said. "Today is Tuesday. Suppose she dies tomorrow, and then Thursday or Friday or next week you find a heart donor. I could never forgive you for holding back on the artificial heart, that little extra chance."

Brovek sat still in his chair, peering at Jack Herold across steepled fingers. He drew a deep breath and exhaled slowly, almost in a sigh.

"If a heart donor were to be found today, if we could go ahead with Mrs. Herold's transplant now, she would have a nearly 90% chance of survival. But suppose another person needs this heart also, a patient with only a 50% chance of success. Which patient should get the heart?"

Herold snorted, pulled his hands back and stood up straight.

"Hell, Dr. Brovek, I'm not the one to ask. Millicent should get it."

"Exactly, Mr. Herold. And I'm not the one to ask either. I say the scarce donor heart should go where it is most likely to survive, to the 90% patient, to Millicent. But do you know what ROPO might say? the organ procurement agency? They might say the 50% patient is more urgent because she is connected to an artificial heart."

Jack spread his hands again on the desk and bored in at the big man.

"Turn it around; maybe it's Millicent on the artificial heart, and she gets the transplant. 50:50 is a lot better than dead."

The steeple of Brovek's fingers collapsed. He leaned forward over his desk, looked straight into Jack Herold's eyes.

"I'm sorry. I have no right to ask you to look at any part of this problem beyond what your wife needs. Everything would be simpler if we had enough donor organs. As it is, we have a ton of questions about transplants—hard questions without good answers. But those are my problems, not yours."

Jack held his ground. "They are my problems when they affect Mil, Dr. Brovek. I mean it about the artificial heart. You be darn sure you don't wait too long."

His voice was harsh. He felt raw and desperate, and he wanted a promise, and with all his scratch and abrasion he expected Brovek to be angry.

The lines softened in Brovek's broad face. The great brows arched, and the professorial mouth played with its words as if it would not let them go.

"Now you are luring me into more indiscretion. I had a phone call this morning. We might have a donor for Millicent."

Jack gasped.

"I'm expecting to find out any minute." His mouth played with half a smile, but his eyes were serious. "May I presume you would want to proceed?"

Jack Herold was stunned. His world shifted beneath his feet. He stared at Brovek, the solemn face, the broad hands folded on the desk top. Once more he felt a surge of fear. But at once it transformed itself into something new, a strange fire in his chest. What was it—hope?

Brovek's phone rang one time. The surgeon's hand struck it like a snake.

"Brovek here...This morning?...I will have a crew there by noon...Thank you."

Herold's heart pounded in his ears. He watched Brovek replace the instrument. Again his vision blurred. In a fog he saw Brovek rise, and heard Brovek's voice.

"No more talk about artificial hearts, Mr. Herold. If all goes well, by sundown today your wife will have a new and healthy heart of her own."

Brovek reached across his desk, and Jack grasped his fingers in both trembling hands. Over their abandoned battleground their eyes met in renewed alliance. There were no more words. Jack Herold swept off to Millicent with a new message of hope, leaving Brovek to perform whatever incantations he might need to work his miracle.

*   *   *

The nose of the twin-engine Cessna Centurian pointed down at the tiny noodle of asphalt that would become Hangarville's municipal airport. Sitting in the copilot's seat, Dana Garrison gave up trying to puzzle out the dials and indicators. The few she could identify she still couldn't interpret. Only the altimeter was clear, and it was falling steadily. It passed 2,000 feet. She wondered whether it would go to zero at landing, or only 1,200 feet, which she knew was the elevation above sea level in her home town. Well, she was sure that Rusty knew....

Rusty. This had turned into a confusing day.

It had started smoothly, with her routine morning rounds. She saw her patients tended to and got the day's orders underway. She had a quick cup of coffee and changed into fresh scrubs for surgery. A good day lying ahead. But Dr. Brovek's peremptory message had shattered routines. "Come," it said. "Come now."

Oh God, she thought, what have I done? She paused only long enough to ask Lance Rudd to double up and oversee her resident's procedure. Then she raced over to Old U, and into the Chief's office. As soon as she saw his two-crease frown she relaxed. She could usually count four lines in his forehead when he was angry. His black eyes bored into her.

"Dr. Garrison," he said without preliminary, "we have the opportunity for a heart donor a couple hundred miles from here. The University aircraft is standing by to take a harvest team there, and I want you to go. Can you handle it?"

His question struck her like a blow to the stomach. She had to think fast. His question was real; her answer must be true. He had not asked whether she could displace her planned surgical case for something more urgent. Her career would forever be woven of such demands. She thought of Horace Potts: within an hour she had met him, examined his belly and thrown her own future into the stakes for his life.

But Brovek didn't ask whether she was willing; he asked if she was able. And hey! he must think she could handle it, or he would not have asked! She mustered her confidence.

"I'm familiar with all the techniques, Dr. Brovek, and I have assisted in a couple of harvests here. Yes, I can handle it. What about other organs?"

"No. Some youngster wiped out his brains on a motorcycle, and ruptured his bowel too. So his abdominal organs are not suitable. But Hangarville's a small town out there—we need to get right at it. The declaration of brain death was made just now, and I want to harvest as soon as we can. And this time the heart is going to stay right here, Dr. Garrison. No more shipping out. We need this heart for young Mrs. Herold, and she may not last the day without it."

Dana nodded. She knew Mrs. Herold, and she could see the fire in Brovek's eyes. But Hangarville? What an irony. She would face this challenge in her own home town!

"I'm on my way. What about the ice chest?"

"It will be at the airport. A technician will go with you. Good luck."

She snatched her trench coat on the way to a waiting taxi.

In his own overbearing way, Dr. Brovek had touched her. This assignment meant a big dose of trust in her, and she knew she would turn every screw to live up to it. As the taxi jolted and lurched along the icy streets to the air field, she rehearsed every step of the day ahead. First she would face the surgical challenge of removing the heart undamaged and intact. Then she would have to fight the ticking clock, the few critical hours—four, maybe—before the salvaged heart would fade away beyond recall. She resolved to collect her precious cargo and return it to the University within two hours. No one could reduce the travel time to less than that, and she would not allow another moment to be wasted. She grooved her mind to this goal; she would brook no distraction.

And then, as the speeding taxi deposited her almost at the door of the aircraft, she encountered Rusty.

"Hey, Doc," said a laughing baritone, "let's go break a heart."

Flippant words. She flared at them.

The man was crouched in the door of the plane, a cartoon of a pilot in brown leather and white scarf. His weathered face creased in a broad smile as he reached out to lift her through the door.

Flippant words, but she had urgent business. She took his hand and scrambled into the aircraft. A large box occupied the near seat, and a solemn young man in a scrub suit and overcoat sat opposite. Her support troop, as promised, but he wasn't much. Succeed or fail, she was alone now, to try to save one heart out of the two circles of hearts already grieving. She glared at the insensitive pilot, and unaccountably her anger vanished. His eyes were merry and free of guile. Almost innocent. The hard crust of her overwork cracked.

"Break your own heart, cowboy," she said. "Not mine."

"Name's Rusty, Doc." he said. He waved her forward into the copilot seat. "We've got over an hour's flight to Hangarville. I'll teach you to fly on the way out, and you teach me surgery on the way home. But we've got to make it chop-chop because the weather boys are cooking up trouble. Front coming in. Maybe a blizzard. I don't like the look of it. Let's go."

During all the chatter he had flicked easily through a series of switches, coaxed the big engines into life, and checked with the tower. He moved the aircraft to the runway and they were airborne.

The roaring engines drowned words. Dana fell back into her own thoughts, which refused to hold to the job at hand and settled again on her pilot. She watched Rusty's movements over the controls. He showed a good profile, strong nose, even features, rugged. He had the leathery skin that some redheads are lucky to get. Hair that matched it, tough and wiry, as thick as a scrub brush, and the color of copper. She remembered the flash of teeth and the green eyes that captured her with his first words. Watch out for this one, she thought.

Then she chided herself. Harvesting this heart today was her first big chance to convince Brovek that he could make a surgeon out of her. To be his Chief Resident demanded her total attention every day and every night. And this assignment today was a high hurdle all its own.

So cut it out, Dana. Don't sit here in an airplane and flutter like a schoolgirl!

The engines cut back and the plane settled in toward the runway at Hangarville. Dana watched the familiar farm fields of her own home town roll past under her window.

Rusty pointed to the sky. Clear, cold, unblemished blue. But at the western horizon the blue was smudged with gray, and wisps and streaks of thin cloud fingered toward the zenith.

"That front isn't too far away, Doc," he called. "Don't take all day. Don't get lost over there in the hospital."

Dana pressed her mind to her responsibilities. This was the town where she was born, the hospital where she saw her first surgical operation. Where she sat with her dying father just eight years ago, holding his cold fingers. She might even remember some of the people—a nurse or two, and—oh—maybe even the dead boy's family!

No, she would not get lost.

*   *   *

Barney Popper plowed into the doctors' lounge feeling smug. Even virtuous. Yesterday he had completed his refresher course in cardiopulmonary resuscitation, and today he could feel, resting in his thick wallet on his fat hip, his new CPR card.

He dropped his ex-athlete bulk into one of the recliner chairs. With a caramel roll in one hand and a cup of coffee in the other, he paid fastidious attention not to spill on his new Christmas jacket of camel-colored ultrasuede. Leaning sidewise over the chair arm, he bit off a large chunk of roll, chomped on it twice, and washed it down with tepid coffee. He grumbled. Coffee oughta be hot. The hospital oughta buy one of those new microwave ovens. But hell no, they won't do diddly for the medical staff.

He put the cup down and picked up the morning newspaper. Hey, here was something he'd thought about! The headline said they couldn't find enough donor organs. He already had an idea of his own about that. He plugged in the information from the newspaper, and sat and turned it all over in his mind, like a great salad. His idea was pretty far out, he probably oughta try it on somebody, and he was sitting in the best place. For ideas and opinions, the medical staff room was a regular trading post.

He spied Walter Pugh. No help there.

Who was that in the scrub suit? Old Rudd. He was in on that transplant stuff. He'd do.

"Rudd," he said in a conspiratorial tone, "is it really all that tough to find donors for liver transplants? I mean, people begging for livers on national TV and all?"

"Oh, hello, Barney."

No warmth, but enough courtesy. In Barney's book Rudd was a stuffed shirt, but he oughta answer.

"Sure it's tough. Some candidates die because there's no donor. We have a man on our wait list right now who isn't going to make it much longer, and we haven't any notion where to get a liver for him."

"But people die all the time here, hell, in all the hospitals. There ought to be lots of livers."

"Well, most of them are too old, or have cancer, or infection, or something. And the worst problem is for kids. That's what you saw on TV.

There aren't many kids dying, thank God, so there aren't many kid donors."

"Why can't you use adult donors for kids?"

"You can't put a pumpkin in a popcorn box. And nobody yet has thought of a way to make the pumpkin smaller."

Barney had steered the subject close to his target now. Elaborately casual, he picked at a fleck of caramel on his sleeve. His words dragged with indifference.

"Probably would be worth a lot of money if somebody could come up with little livers for kids, hey?"

"Yeh, I guess," said Rudd. He started away. But he looked back again at Barney Popper and sat down in an adjoining chair.

Walter Pugh looked on, as if he was listening.

"Here, Walter," said Barney. "I'm through with this section. You can have it."

Pugh came to a focus long enough to take the newspaper from Barney's hand. As if it triggered a reflex, he went off to his reading room.

Barney turned to Rudd, and read into his face some sign of interest. These academic types were always curious, if someone else got an idea.

"Well, I've been thinking that a fellow with a certain kind of laboratory could grow kid-size livers. Shouldn't be so hard. If the expenses were, like, you know, covered. Privately, sort of."

He waited. Rudd didn't move, and didn't say anything. Poker face.

"In my business," Barney went on, "we've got all kinds of women coming around that don't want their, you know, conception products any more. Never did, probably. So they want us to get rid of them. Usually at three, four months. But these gals are just like little laboratories, I mean, their plates are already incubating. All you have to do is wait a few weeks longer…"

He slowed his words—the idea might take some getting used to. He figured Rudd was a dressy dude who didn't plow his furrows very deep, but Barney didn't know how straight. He watched Rudd's eyes.

"I mean, these gals don't want anything except to get back to, you know, whatever they do every day. But some of them would be willing, I bet, to rent out for a few weeks, if they got something out of it, a fresh start like, you know?"

Barney sipped his coffee, and pretended not to watch Rudd's face. He oughta stop, but hell, so far Rudd hadn't given him a clue. One more try.

"I bet there's a few families would come up with it pretty good to get a liver for little Freddy, that nobody has to wait for somebody to die. D'you think so?"

He was uncomfortable with Rudd's silence. He didn't want to get too deep into a hole before he knew where Rudd stood. He waited, looking into the tepid dregs of his coffee.

Finally Rudd stood up, directly in front of Barney. His voice was low, but it was as hard as glass.

"Well, Barney, you are getting far out even for you. You want to let those plates incubate right in your laboratory, right? until they grow out a liver? until you have a seven-pound product of conception that nobody wants except somebody will pay for? Christ, Barney, it might even start to cry."

Barney put down his cup with a sigh. He tilted his bulk back in the recliner, and his feet rose up into Lance Rudd's face. His voice also was quiet, but it dripped venom.

"Oh, shit, Rudd, you talk just like those pro-lifers. You can't see an answer when it stares you in the face."

*   *   *

In a way she remembered them all. Hangarville was the community of her youth, and the Hovelund family were the sort of sturdy people who had patterned her growing-up world.

They filed into Dana's make-shift consulting room, shuffling and jostling each other on the yellow vinyl tile, pushing a couple of obstructing Naugahyde chairs out of the way. The room filled with their odors, of honest sweat, and grain dust, and the animal barn. Dana's heart swelled at the familiar fragrance. Shy, respectful, suffering, the Hovelunds hooked their thumbs on their clothing, or rested their hands on the chair backs, and looked at the floor.

Danny's mother was powerful and fat; giant orange poppies curved and bulged over her hips. His father was just a little short of scrawny. He wore no tie, and his buttoned-up shirt collar bobbed up and down with his Adam's apple. His jaw was set in the color of bronze, but his forehead shone milk-white like the skin of a child. Dana knew his bare head showed a special respect for the occasion—farmers like him kept their caps on all the time, except in bed or in church. She could see the missing cap sticking out of his bib overalls, its faded yellow letters spelling out something about Trojan Seeds.

There were four other persons. One was a weathered old woman like a rounded stone, Danny's grandmother. Three were siblings of the sacrificed boy, a teen-aged sister of nubile grace, and Danny's two younger brothers. Already the boys showed the permanent half-face sunburn of their father's fields.

She wished somebody would sit down in the arm chairs, but they all stood there facing her like a knot of sheep, by hip and elbow each one keeping contact with the others.

Dana's throat was tight. She could not trust her voice. "My name is Dr. Garrison," she said. "I have come here from University Hospital to…"

To what? To cut the heart out of your boy? She started again.

"I need to be sure you understand what we propose to do, and to answer any questions."

She tried to make eye contact, to find one person that she could reach. But they stood silent, unseeing, lost at the edges of new lives without Danny. She eyed the dead boy's parents and went on.

"This tragic accident for your son is the end for him. You know that legally and actually he is dead. There is nothing anyone can do that will bring him back…But his heart can be saved. We can transplant his living heart into another person. I have seen her at University Hospital; she is a young woman and the mother of two children. She is about to die because her own heart is giving out. This is her only chance. Do you understand?"

Danny's mother put her head down; her shoulders sagged in a rounded arch. For three days, Dana thought, this poor woman must have stood beside Danny, clinging to vain hope. Danny's sister rested her hands on her mother's shoulder and sobbed. The two young sons put their arms around the women; soundlessly they stood even closer than before. Danny's father looked at his wife. A long moment passed. At last he turned to Dana, his face blank, his voice flat.

"I don't see nothing good in this except what you say to do. So just go do it."

"Thank you, Mr. Hovelund. We will move as fast as we can, and I will not stay to see you after our operation here. So I do thank you now for your courage, and…and your…"

Whatever her words were to be, she could not say them. And the Hovelunds didn't need them. She left them huddled together but, with their decision made, beginning to release. In the hallway she rummaged for a Kleenex. Through the door she heard the man's voice again, Danny's father. Flat and unemotional. She understood what he was doing: trying to find something—anything—normal in his shattered world.

"Bernice," he said, "you think that could have been ol' Doc's girl?"

*   *   *

A good-looking chick, Rusty thought. Doc Garrison? Yes sir.

He expected only a short lay-over, but when it came to his aircraft he never cut corners. He ran through his routine for shutting it down, and drifted into the airport's dingy little office. A clerk in a green visor, a scrawny old guy who actually wore a garter on his sleeve, looked up from a dog-eared copy of Playboy.

"If you gonna fly outahere today, you better not set much." He tipped a can of Pepsi to his mouth. "Machine's over there." He pointed with the empty can and crushed it in his hand. "Weather comin', looks to me."

"Yeah," Rusty said. "Looks ominous."

"Well, except for the weather, nothin' ever happens around here, anyway. Welcome to Dullsville." He wiped his mouth on his gartered sleeve, belched softly and disappeared into a back room.

Rusty fed some quarters into the slot and selected a Dr. Pepper. There was a small table under the window, a flat top of scratchy wood set on thin legs. He set the Pepper down on it with his duffel, and dragged a wooden chair across the concrete floor.

He sat down and dug out his Sanford fine-point pen and a yellow legal pad. He scratched a doodle on the legal pad—yes, the pen worked—and gazed out the window. No place was ever dull if he could write, and here was a chance. Today he felt charged.

'Write what you know' was the old advice, and he had a lifetime of material to draw on. His thoughts wandered, and his pen hung idle in his fingers. It was a random path that had brought him to a country airstrip on a day when smart pilots would have stayed on the ground. A random college choice, determined by a baseball scholarship, summers here or there playing semi-pro. He parlayed that into a very unofficial flight school that got him his first license. For a couple of years he barnstormed Iowa county fairs in rickety old biplanes. Sold rides. Loved that. Did loops and rolls, even wing-walking. In his finale he always buzzed the grandstand, but after he nearly clipped a school bus on the infield, he grew up and entered Navy flight school. That short career ended in furious indignation and a spate of stories and articles about Viet Nam. He knew plenty he could write about.

His window looked out to the east, over the field's single runway. Still a clear blue sky. He was glad he couldn't see out toward the west. *Che sera, sera.* He popped the Pepper.

Some things couldn't be jiggered. They just happened. Like this chauffeur's job he had fallen into with the University. What he wanted was to teach. English lit. Creative writing. But when he applied to his alma mater, his B.A. cum laude wasn't enough. Not for the English Department. But the human relations person thought it, or he, was enough for her. He grinned. Drew a heart on the yellow paper. He dated her for a while, and she made him a proposition. The University was about to start up its own air service—a ferry for hospital patients, perks for high-flying professors and deans. Would he try that?

He would.

The good part was that the deans didn't fly every day, and his manuscript pages piled up in pregnant stacks. But there was a down side too. The rejection slips piled up nearly as fast, sheet after sheet, in unpregnant files. Writing was a lonely craft, and except for flying he hung out pretty much by himself. He'd had enough of meaningless women, of empty sex. His parents were dead, his sister far away in Oregon. His old buddies had spawned kids and dropped out of sight. Life was turning him into a loner, and he didn't like it.

Hah. Inspiration struck, and his pen went to work. *Dullsville,* he wrote. *Except for the weather, nothing ever happens here.* He grinned. Nothing except a kid dies, a glamourous lady-surgeon flies in from the big city, scrounges the kid's heart and packs it back to her airplane for a very iffy flight into the teeth of a blizzard.

He swigged the Pepper and wiped his lip. Nobody knows yet, he thought, how this story turns out.

*   *   *

At last the day came under Dana's command. The distraction, the confusion, the waiting were past. She strode into the operating suite, all sixty-one inches of her, the designated harvest surgeon, the only person present who was qualified to reap an intact and living heart from a dead boy.

The burly chief nurse pranced about her like an adjutant greeting a new general.

"Welcome, Dr. Garrison. I used to scrub for your father, and I remember when you used to come along too."

Dana smiled up at the looming woman. She warmed at the welcome. But she couldn't be 'ol' Doc's girl' today. It was her job to establish her own authority with this crew, her job to assure success. She spoke gently, but with precision, striving to project a confidence she did not feel.

"Yes, I remember too. I hope you will think I am worthy of his memory when we finish here."

She felt that was deft; she had drawn the point back to today. She touched each nurse with her eyes, as if she spoke to her alone.

"I want you to understand that this boy is dead. Legally, actually, dead. He doesn't look it, but he is. However, our procedure will be done exactly as if he were alive. We take all the usual care, especially for sterile technique. If you haven't operated on hearts here in Hangarville, just think of this like any open chest operation, and you'll get along fine. We will need special solutions and supplies for the heart itself, and my technician will supply those. Unless you have questions, we should get started."

Two nurses wheeled Danny Hovelund into the room, and lifted the cadaver-patient from the gurney to the operating table. The anesthesia nurse maintained his ventilation by hand, with regular squeezing of the oxygen bag. Dana watched as the nurse attached the mechanical ventilator to Danny's airway tube, and checked that his supporting fluids were running well through intravenous needles. She left the nurses to prepare the operating field, and joined Dr. Bockmun at the scrub sink.

"I appreciate your help, Dr. Bockmun," she said. Warm water streamed from the high faucet, and splashed on the white porcelain. With a black-bristled brush she worked slippery germicidal soap into a heavy yellow lather over her hands and arms. "You have put a lot of effort into this patient already."

Dr. Bockmun grunted through his mask. He assaulted his hairy right arm with brush and suds. "Yeah, right here in this room…Fixed his belly, but couldn't do much about his head."

"But if you hadn't done pretty heroic work for him, we couldn't salvage his heart today. That's a victory, in a way."

The two streams of water swirled layers of foam and gurgled down the drain.

"It may be easier for you to think of it as a victory. I knew Danny."

"I'm sorry," Dana said. "I didn't mean to be insensitive. But I think you can be proud, professionally at least, of a community hospital that performs right up to the technological minute. You recognized brain death and made organ salvage possible. I can tell you a lot of bigger hospitals strike out on that."

They kicked open the door into the operating room, and took sterile towels from the scrub nurse.

"The brain death part was right by the book," Dr. Bockmun said. "Danny didn't wake up. No reflexes. Pupils stayed dilated. The EEG was flat and the neurologist saw no change after 12 hours. So here you are."

It was an old story to Dana, but she welcomed the details in the declaration. She was about to pick up a scalpel and take a beating heart out of a warm human body that, for all she could tell, was alive. But it would not be when she was finished.

Well, it was no time for goose bumps.

Dana began exactly as she would for a coronary bypass operation. She sliced the skin down the middle of the breast bone, and split the bone with an oscillating saw. She opened the full length of the chest. The heart lay beneath her hands, in its sac of tough membranes, beating in regular sixteen-year-old vigor. She incised the membranes and exposed the raw muscle, clenching and relaxing and clenching again like a great fist. Two soft veins as big as garden hoses entered the right side of the heart, and one enormous artery came out on its way to the lungs.

Behind the heart and out of her view lay several veins returning from the lungs. At the top of the heart the aorta rose up and curled backward like a great throbbing serpent. These were the vessels she must control, divide and preserve. Within just a few hours their amputated ends might fit into place for Millicent Herold.

She worked carefully, dissecting extraneous tissues away from the vessel walls, until she could apply all the clamps. In a moment she would stop the heart with a paralyzing injection, close the clamps, and stop Danny's circulation forever. And at that instant the critical clock would begin to run for the severed heart, tolling the minutes of bloodless time, every tick costing the heart a bit of the strength it would need to kick in and drive the circulation in its new home.

Dana glanced at Dr. Bockmun. Ready? Good.

Her hands moved smoothly, casually, closing clamps, injecting the ice-cold paralyzing solution into the heart's own circulation. Danny's heart shuddered, twitched once or twice, and was still. Dr. Bockmun packed slush ice into the sac. Dana cut the vessels and irrigated the heart's open chambers with icy salt solution, washing away both unwanted blood cells and killing heat. She lifted Danny's heart out of its nest.

"Thanks, Dr. Bockmun. I hope you will close up the wound and see to Danny. I'll pack up the heart and start back to the University."

While she spoke, she placed the heart in a series of sterile bags, iced them down, and nestled the sacred package into the technician's box.

Dr. Bockmun bent to Danny's chest, armed with a large needle and heavy thread. A few coarse stitches would suffice—there was to be no healing.

"Go for it, Dr. Garrison," he said. "That was a slick job so far. Good luck with the rest of it."

Stripping off her gown and gloves, Dana only nodded. Danny's heart must survive the speeding minutes of its transfer time; only then could it become Millicent Herold's heart. She jerked her trench coat from its hanger, marshaled her technician and their precious box, and pressed forward to a waiting ambulance, and a gathering storm.

*　　　　　*　　　　　*

"Mizzoh, you are one tough broad."

She would never use that word for anyone else, but she called herself that once in a while, with a detached sense of affection. Twenty-four years of bossing the surgical suite at University Hospital had taught Maureen O'Hoolihan to be strong. Year around, clock around, she disposed her troops for action in the phalanx of operating rooms where the generals and the prima donnas could work only when she said Go. She had just said Stop.

She held the phone a foot from her ear. Dr. Popper's voice spouted out of the ear piece, and she waited for him to depressurize. She had learned over the years never to hang up on an angry surgeon; she knew she was tough; she could afford to be cool. Popper knew she was right, or would know when he simmered down. She would bounce somebody from the schedule for him, when the need was there, exactly the way she had just bounced him. After all, it wasn't Dr. Popper versus Dr. Brovek. The key was the urgency for Dr. Brovek's heart patient versus Dr. Popper's elective hysterectomy.

She sat at her utilitarian gray desk that she had squeezed into her glassed-in office at the hub of the O.R. suite. Three narrow chairs and her own vitality were all the space could hold. She scanned the schedule spread out on her desk, deciding on available rooms, planning her moves. The roar began to subside, and she moved the phone back to her ear.

"We can still start your case today in another room, Dr. Popper, maybe around four o'clock. Or would you prefer to reschedule for another day?"

The ear piece crackled some more, and they agreed on four o'clock.

"Thank you, Dr. Popper." She cradled the phone.

Now to the immediate needs. She notified the nurses and surgical techs about Dr. Popper's change of plans, and gave them new assignments.

"Gwen, we need you to stay late for Dr. Popper's case. Can you do it? He likes to have you scrub for him."

Gwen could. Gwen earned credits in Mizzoh's invisible ledger. Work them hard and reward them for it: that was her formula for a happy crew.

Next she caught Myrna Bates in the corridor. Dependable Myrna.

"Hey, Myrna, I need you for a special case at twelve-thirty. Take your lunch break now. I'll replace you in Room 4. Dr. Brovek has scheduled a heart transplant in 3, and you are in charge. I'll get some good help for you, okay?"

Okay must have been an understatement. Myrna loped off to lunch at a pace that said she would be back early. There are various kinds of rewards, thought Mizzoh. Trust and responsibility are trophies too.

She reviewed her staffing assignments. All in order. She checked again to notify anesthesia and the pump team. They were always ready nowadays; open heart procedures with the pump-oxygenator were becoming daily fare for her people.

She plopped her substantial behind on her chair, and clutched the desk to stop its squeaky wheels from sliding away with her. Or without her. She always wondered which it was going to be.

What had she forgotten? She checked the list once more, and—oh, damn! The Mardi Gras party! Wouldn't you know—plan a party and all hell breaks loose. Days ago she had reserved the nurses' lounge in Old U. She did it every year, and invited all the citizens of her domain, whatever their rank. Without distinction she offered to them all her store-bought cake and home-grown gratitude.

But now, on party night, she had extra crews working late, and on top of that the radio was talking about a blizzard blowing in. She flashed a picture of herself sitting at her party, all alone, crunching potato chips and listening to the wind howl outside.

Well, that was tonight; this was today. There were surgeons to care for, and here came one of them.

A high-pressure center moved toward her from the direction of the surgeons' dressing room. She knew what that meant. She powered out of her chair and cruised down the hall to meet Dr. Brovek head on. He was surrounded by students and residents. Her practiced eye checked them out, scrub suits, boots, hair covered, masks ready.

"Only scrubbers in here, Dr. Brovek. Any extras go up to the gallery."

"Hello, Mizzoh. Show them where to go, will you?"

She peeled four or five out of the crowd and set them into the stairway to a closed observation chamber looking down on Room 3. She grunted half-satisfaction. The less traffic, the less infection. Another way she had to be tough.

She looked through the window in to Room 3, and Myrna gave her a go-ahead nod. "We're ready when you are, Dr. B."

"Good," he said. "We will set up with the patient in the operating room, and we'll start as soon as Dr. Garrison hits the landing strip. She has left Hangarville, so it shouldn't be long."

Mizzoh stood by, appraising. A squad of anesthesia people appeared, buzzing around Millicent Herold's litter, pushing it along. They wheeled her into Room 3, lifted her to the table and checked her attachments: intravenous line in each arm, intraarterial blood pressure monitor at one wrist, a weave of electrocardiogram wires from her chest, an oxygen-measuring colorimeter on one ear lobe. They continued to assist her breathing. Her feeble heart couldn't push much blood around her body; the blood that did go had to carry all the oxygen it could. She was awake; but Mizzoh thought she looked mercifully unaware.

Sights and sounds of preparation surrounded Mizzoh like a bath. Dr. Brovek and three assistants splashed and rumbled at the scrub sink. Anesthesia folks murmured softly at Millicent's head, while Myrna scrubbed her patient's chest and daubed it with brown antiseptic. The scrub nurses set up their sterile tables, clicking and thumping instruments into orderly stacks, each kind in its appointed place. At last they rustled heavy green sheets over the surgical table and across the ether screen, covering the body of Millicent Herold. Only a central opening remained, an oval of pale and vulnerable flesh gleaming in a circle of light, like a sacrifice on some altar. And finally Dr. Brovek, the masked high priest in gown and gloves, led his cohort of acolytes to approach the table. Not to touch. Not yet. Only to wait.

To wait for a phone call, Mizzoh thought. To wait on a chain of untraceable messages, anonymous reports: 'the plane has landed', or 'they're on the way.' Messages that Dr. Brovek must translate at the proper time into: 'you can start.' He had to trust there would be no hitch, no confusion, no delay. To start this operation prematurely, she thought, or to wait too long: either way could lead to fatal error.

She watched Dr. Brovek's solid mass, broad and straight, waiting. She heard the slight sounds of Millicent Herold, stirring under all those drapes, waiting.

"Mizzoh," she thought to herself, "you are not the only one around here who has to be tough."

*   *   *

Wind howled through the first crack of the ambulance door as Dana and the technician clambered out onto the Hangarville tarmac with their box of life. She leaned into gale force; the wind whipped her hair and plastered her trench coat against her body. She pushed her way gratefully into the aircraft, and they secured the box with straps into the rear seat. Forewarned of her arrival, Rusty had the engines warmed, and he taxied at once to the runway for take-off.

"The front is on us, Doc," he shouted over the engines. "Another half hour and we'd have to be satisfied with a steak house right here in Hangarville." The plane bounced and jerked in a gust of wind. "We can make it off the ground okay. We'll race the front home, and if we beat it, no problem. If we don't, we can go on somewhere ahead of the front. Got it?"

Dana nodded. She buckled her seat belt and pulled it snug against the strange feelings stirring in her belly. Here in her first moment of released tension this man was shouldering his way again into her thoughts and commanding her mind. What was there in him, she wondered—and what in her?—to explain her fascination. There was more to it than a rough plane ride. She turned to watch him fly; she hoped he was good.

No other planes were abroad; only an urgent mission like hers could justify the risk. But she knew blizzards. Being marooned in the snow was part of growing up in Hangarville—schools closed, cars drifted in, her father trudging to the hospital in the dark of morning to care for his patients. She pictured Dr. Brovek's scowl if she got herself stuck in Hangarville with Danny's heart dying in her lap.

The plane rocked and bucked as it shot down the runway. It became airborne, lurched in a gust of wind, struggled, and rose. She watched as Rusty banked into their homeward bearing, grim with concentration. His face was set, his shoulders squared. He leaned forward in his seat, as if he blended every nerve and fiber into the sensations of his aircraft.

Heavy clouds grayed out the midday sun. Driving snow began to blot up the light, giving back the dark of evening.

The mission was not in her hands now, and she forced herself to relax. She turned away from Rusty and thought of her father and mother. They lay down there below, safe from the storm, side by side in Hangarville Cemetery. Come summer, after her training was ended in July, she would come back and visit the graves. What would her father have said about Dana's kind of surgery? To transplant a human heart! Never would he even have dreamed of it.

Her first visit to an operating room had been with her father. As a senior in high school, she had followed him on Career Day, and he had to do an emrgency appendectomy. She remembered how intensely his eyes had glinted over his surgical mask as he splashed at the scrub sink and lectured her about trust. As doctors, he said, we are asked to enter a crisis in our patient's life. Whatever we learn about our patient is private information.

We are privileged to share, but we are never entitled to divulge. We must never share it, nor even let anyone know we know. She hardly remembered the appendix—that image had blurred in a thousand others since.

But she did remember from that day her first view of the female generative tract. The tight little knob of womb. The Fallopian tubes pink and soft, wrapping their fern-like ends against the ovaries. The smooth and glistening tissues were beautiful! And each white ovary carried little bubbles of fluid that her father explained would pop out an egg each month. What she felt most that day was awe, at that delicate mechanism so full of mystery.

She glanced at Rusty, intent on his machine. He talked into his microphone, but she could hear nothing but the roar of wind and engines. His frown deepened. Her seat bucked beneath her and fell away again. She retreated to her thoughts, clinging to them like a lifeline.

She remembered her feelings so clearly because of what she saw the very next day. Again she watched an appendectomy, but this time the disease was different. The right Fallopian tube was infected, fiery red and swollen, dripping tears of ugly yellow pus over the cheek of its ovary. Why was that, Dad? She recalled his solemn answer, his eyes rising to meet hers over their masks. Careless sex with the wrong people, he said. And she had vowed to herself, right there in the operating room, that she would protect her own precious gift, and never screw it up.

The plane tossed like a leaf in the wind. Her body strained against the seat belt. She looked at Rusty, fright rising in her breast. His jaw clenched. But he turned for an instant and flashed a smile, white teeth, a dimple on his chin. Abruptly, unaccountably, she thought that at twenty-nine years of age another way to screw up her most precious gift would be never to use it at all.

Rusty beckoned to her and she leaned toward him.

"We haven't gained on this front," he shouted. "It's hitting home the same time we are. We can try landing by instruments with whatever visibility there is. But it's dangerous, Doc. What do you say?"

Dana fought down the panic thick in her throat. Mr. Hovelund's words echoed in her mind: 'Nothing good in this except what you say to do.'

She tried to think. They could fly ahead of the storm for a safe landing. The appeal of that lay heavy in her mouth. Then she thought of Millicent Herold, gasping for breath, being wheeled even now into the operating theater at the University, her family suspended in a mix of prayer and fear.

She looked back at the technician, questioning. He grinned, not knowing there was a decision to be made.

Rusty shouted again. "I'm just a fly-boy, Doc. I'll take risks if I have to. What do you say?"

Again she looked back at the box, the heart lying there in its dark nest, cold, paralyzed, but still full of promise. She shuddered. While she ran for a safe landing, the heart would ebb away, taking with it Mil Herold's only chance for life.

She looked out the window at the storm. She wondered if she was going to die. Unthinkable. She wasn't ready. Dying would be the wildest miscarriage of all her dreams and plans.

But it would not be meaningless, to die. This kind of mission was what her life was designed for. It would be meaningless to fail.

Finally she turned to her pilot. She had known him for a thousand years.

"Rusty," she said, faking confidence, "head for home. We've got to try."

Their eyes met, held to each other, searching deep. She knew that he was examining her, the set of her jaw, the mettle of her resolve. She folded her hands quietly into her lap, and sat back. Her part was played. He turned to the instruments and began their approach.

The plane lurched and bounced in the wind. Heavy plumes of snow coursed over Dana's side windows. She was tossed against her belt, and caught, pulled back and tossed again. She saw the altimeter needle falling as the plane descended into the invisible. Above the lighted instruments she could see through the windscreen only darkness, and somewhere far ahead one small floating blur of light.

The engine roar cut back; the plane sagged. She heard a loud crack as the wheels hit ground, and she felt the craft careen again into the air. She watched Rusty, hard on the controls, fighting for stability. The plane hit ground again, with less violence this time, and she saw a blur of light—the same one?—passing her window at a frightening speed. The engine noise dropped away and the wind screamed. The plane swerved and skidded sideways. It spun slowly, crazily, tipping up, hanging at a steep angle against the force of the wind. Dana hung by her seat belt. Were they turning over?

Gradually the seat came back under her, caught her sharply as the plane bounced down, rocked, and became still.

She checked the box; it sat safely strapped on the seat. The technician sat white-lipped and trembling, groping for his belt release. She looked at Rusty. He spoke quietly into his microphone, and then fell back in his bucket seat to let the tension drain out of his shoulders.

He turned to her, grinning, eyes dancing.

"It's midnight, Cinderella, and your coach is here."

Flashing red lights of the University ambulance pulsed the color of blood through the cockpit. She slipped out of her seat and helped the technician cradle their box out of the plane.

Down on the tarmac the wind slammed into her. Her eyes stung with the lash of icy snow as she peered at the plane. Inches of ice coated the wings. It stood at a rakish angle ten feet off the runway, tilted jauntily over a broken wheel. She followed the technician into the rear of the ambulance, with the heart of Danny Hovelund, heading for home.

As the great door of the vehicle swung shut behind her she glimpsed Rusty Waters, bareheaded in the storm, only his flight jacket against the cold. His hand was raised to her in farewell, or perhaps in benediction. The ambulance moved off, its siren awakening to pit its own scream against the wind.

Dana shivered, huddled small inside her flimsy coat. She rubbed her bare hands together. They were already numb with the cold. Somehow in the hustle she must have left her gloves on Rusty's airplane.

*   *   *

Over the intercom Mizzoh's voice blared like a trombone into his operating room.

"Dr. Brovek, the plane has landed, and they are leaving the airstrip. University Ambulance estimates twenty minutes with the weather the way it is."

He had no idea about the weather. He was buried with all these people in the basement O.R. of New U, no windows. What the hell did the weather have to do with anything? Not that it mattered; twenty minutes was close enough. He could begin.

He nodded to the anesthesiologist, who bent over his syringes and murmured a lullaby into Millicent Herold's left ear.

Probably he should have started a half hour ago. Brovek ragged himself, trying to sharpen his decision backwards. He had spent a lifetime guarding against risk; he needed to be sure the new heart would be here. With the induction of anesthesia and the first stroke of his scalpel he would tip his patient into her grave. Only if the new heart arrived and began to beat, could she rise again; there was no other way.

He watched over his drapes as the anesthesiologist injected, adjusted, checked monitors. Finally he looked up, found Brovek's eyes, and nodded. Brovek's right hand moved easily from Millicent's neck to her belly, and the length of the breast bone lay exposed. Deftly he controlled skin bleeders with electric cautery. His air-driven saw divided the bone, and spreaders opened the chest like a reluctant clam. He incised the tough membranes of pericardial sac, and looked at the sick heart. Flabby, dilated, pale, it had barely kept her alive and would do so no longer.

His first task was to connect the machine that would serve as heart and lungs for his patient while her own heart was gone. He punched a large tube into the aorta a few inches above the heart, and pulled up tight the heavy stitches surrounding it. He put a similar tube into each main vein, superior and inferior vena cava. From these veins he would drain the blood coming from the upper and lower halves of her body, run it away from the heart and into the machine. In its turn, the machine would pump blood between membranes which acted as lungs to add oxygen and remove carbon dioxide; then the machine would pump the blood back again into the aorta for recirculation through Millicent's body.

Brovek and Pete whizzed through this part of the procedure; it was standard technique for nearly all heart operations. Dissection of the great vessels for passage of clamps took little longer. The moment that he closed the clamps and started the machine, Millicent Herold would enjoy better heart-lung function than she had struggled with for the last four weeks. But the machine could be only temporary.

Mizzoh bustled through the door, an ice chest in her arms.

"Dr. Garrison made it through the storm; here is your heart!"

He was lightly irritated, like a gnat buzzing. What storm?

"Perfect timing, Mizzoh. Tell Dr. Garrison to scrub in here and see this thing through. And get that heart ready on the back table."

He watched Mizzoh only long enough to see her and Myrna open the outer bags of ice, and transfer the inner sterile bag to his nurse's instrument table. He turned back to his patient, closed clamps, and opened flow to the machine. The anesthesiologist ducked under the drapes, checking. The pump team worked smoothly over their complicated apparatus. All was in order, so far.

With a scissors he cut the aorta across, just above the heart. Then he divided the two venae cavae where they entered the heart. There was some back bleeding from the lungs, and he readjusted the clamp on the pulmonary artery. He sucked up the spilled blood, and amputated the pulmonary artery close to the heart. He could look right at the heart valves inside.

Now the heart was loose except for the several veins that came from the lungs. He did not even try to divide them all. He simply lopped off the wall of the atrium, the patch of heart muscle where the veins emptied together. He handed off the dead heart to go to the laboratory—Walter Pugh would be waiting—and was ready for the new one.

Careful hands passed the motionless organ, pale in an icy pan of saline slush. He fit it gently into the empty pericardial sac. New hands helped; Dr. Garrison had scrubbed in. He rumbled wordlessly, and began to implant the new heart.

He filleted the back wall so it would fit the atrial cuff he had just saved; he sewed it in. He joined the pulmonary artery stumps with a couple of stitches starting at the back and coming forward around each side to the front. He made the stitches lie smooth; turbulent blood flow across arterial joinings would lead to clots and complications. He wanted none of those. He irrigated the heart chambers, washing out the old paralyzing solution and all the air bubbles. Then he flicked his fingers gracefully and seated the last knot safely home.

"Halfway there, Dr. Garrison. It's a good-looking heart; you did a nice job."

She said, "Thanks for inviting me in for the implant. Makes a full circle."

He liked her attitude, damn her. "You've earned it," he said.

Their few words gave way to silent cooperation as they fit together and sewed the cuffs of right atrium from the two hearts. At last he looked down into the cuff of donor aorta. There was the aortic valve, and in two of its three leaflets lay the openings of the coronary arteries. They were open, and he flushed them with carefully balanced salt solution. When the aortic clamp came off, warm blood would flood into these arteries and bring new life to the dormant heart muscle. Again he ran a couple of stitches around to meet in front, and he tied the knot for the aorta.

The new heart was warming slowly all this time. One by one he tested the opening of clamps. Suture lines didn't leak; he took the clamps away. The heart chambers filled with blood. From the pulse of the pump machine, the coronary arteries writhed across the heart, and the cold muscle blushed bright red. Several seconds passed.

He watched the heart minutely. A few muscle fibers fluttered. Then others. A convulsive twitch. Suddenly the heavy-muscled ventricles came together like a great fist, squeezing themselves empty of blood. Then they relaxed, loosened, filling their chambers once more from the two atria.

A circle of attention closed around Brovek. Everyone watched for the magic to develop. The anesthesiologist, who never looked over the screen, was looking over the screen. Dana and Pete watched, rapt. Myrna stretched up on tiptoe. No one breathed.

Another contraction. Then another. Now a burst of regular beats. A rhythm.

"Danny's heart is beating again," Dr. Garrison whispered, barely audible.

But Brovek heard. "No, it's Millicent Herold's heart now. But it's beating. So far, so good."

Brovek clamped the tubes to the bypass machine. Could the heart sustain her circulation? He watched its action, getting stronger. He watched the anesthesiologist, who looked up from dials and gauges and nodded a Yes. Brovek waited. He hated waiting—it was always the hardest part of any procedure.

All the measurements stayed on track.

"Dr. Garrison, remove the bypass, will you? I'll help you with that, and leave you and Pete to close."

He watched her hands move, quiet, assured, no wasted motion. She cut a suture, applied a clamp, withdrew a tube, repaired the hole with a quick stitch or two. Neat.

He stepped back, relaxing. After doing dozens of these procedures in dogs, he had just completed his first human heart transplant, and he was exultant.

"Thank you, Myrna, and everyone. Thank you, Dr. Garrison. So far it is a good case."

"A wonderful case, Dr. Brovek. Like clockwork." Garrison's voice. A man wouldn't say that. He stripped off his gown and snapped his gloves away.

Clockwork?

Clockwork, he thought, is man-made. Or woman. Whichever. If a clock is made right it will run.

A heart-beat? That's different. It's more like a miracle.

*   *   *

She let the scalding water course down her back. The hot jets stung her skin like needles, gradually working their magic against the edges of her fatigue. The knots in her neck and shoulders began to loosen. Breathing deep of steam and the scent of thick lather, she worked shampoo into her dark hair. She tilted back under the spray, so that foamy suds streamed over her face and down her arms, and ran in a thick flood between her breasts.

As small as she was in stature, she was well-formed, and took pleasure in her neat body. She rubbed her hands in the hot slick over her flat belly, and replayed the day. The dangers of that harrowing flight through the storm, the decisions that fell to her, the stunning harvest and implant of Danny's heart. Most men would be done in after a day like this. But she was coming alive again; she felt cat-lean and resilient, and still ready for action. Not bad for five-foot-one, and the first day of her period.

She dressed quickly, grateful for her heavy hair with its short cut. A quick towel and a tug with a comb were all it needed. She touched her neck and ears with fragrance, and stepped into her low, cushioned shoes. She wished there was a decent mirror in this locker room; but she knew from practice that she was passable. She slipped on her white coat, and clipped Bozo to her belt. She pushed his little switch to make sure he was awake, and he vibrated busily against her waist. She grinned. He didn't feel quite like rapist fingers any more, but his attacks were still startling.

And now she was back in character: Dr. Dana Garrison, indestructible and in charge. Next stop, Recovery Room.

She entered, as always, squinting. Bright lights glared in the all-white facility, where a dozen or so patients on orderly rows of litters lay waking from anesthesia. Each stall had a curtain hanging from a track on the high ceiling, but every one was tied back, hanging in a fluted column out of harm's way. Above each litter a great square stalactite of chrome steel provided lines for suction and oxygen, and held hangers for bottles of fluid, blood and medications, from which a welter of tubes and hoses weaved their confusing colors over the white sheets. From the walls, winking red eyes and beeping electronics demanded attention to the monitors.

Looking about for Mrs. Herold, Dana evaded the usual jumble of traffic, litters pushing in and out, the scramble of nurses, doctors and technicians. She always thought the recovery room was a forbidding place—human gentleness had to make room for high stakes and high tech. Like a war zone.

Mrs. Herold checked out well. Stable vital signs. Steady pulse. Good cardiac output. Assisted ventilation via endotracheal tube. Kidneys working. Soon she would be ready for transfer to ICU.

Dana wrote a progress note and reviewed the orders Dr. Brovek had written.

Sweet old bear. He had done a number for her today. He had counted on her, and laid responsibilities on her. And she came through for him. For what she did today, she deserved stars. Even Dr. Brovek would have to give her credit. She was a woman doctor, but she had certainly measured up to his standards.

Hold it! The thought caught in her craw. She threw down the pen. Why was she thinking about his standards? What about her own?

Skill? Obvious. Judgment? Yes. Stamina? What she had done today would make an athlete cry, and she was still rolling. And she could give herself a plus for courage, too.

No one could ask for more than she had delivered this day, wrapped up neat and tied with a string. She had surely proved her worth, by anybody's standards. Even by Sandor Brovek's? Well, she'd have to see about that.

But how about Dana Garrison?

Abruptly she dropped the chart to the nurses' desk, out of her hands and out of her head. She swept her eyes around the glaring white cavern of the Recovery Room, this super-focus, high-tech, special-purpose micro-world. She knew every tube and wire in it. She understood every piece of machine that hummed or breathed, every blinking monitor eye. She was master here, not slave! It was she who set the checkpoints for every nurse's mind. It was she, Dana Garrison, who defined what was acceptable and red-lined the levels of alarm. All this technology existed for patients like Millicent Herold, struggling out of surgery and anesthesia to reenter the world. And Millicent Herold, with her pulsing transplanted heart, was alive in it because of Dana Garrison.

Her old perspectives shattered and fell around her feet. Dana Garrison, ingenue? wannabe? No more! Her sixty-one inches dominated this room. Suddenly its cold chrome and harsh light were not so hostile, after all. That high ceiling, and all the engineering under it, came easily within her reach.

Her pulses pounded in her breast.

Maybe there was more course to run in convincing Sandor Brovek of her excellence. But suddenly she knew, with the certainty of revelation, that this day she had won the biggest prize of all: she had convinced herself.

*   *   *

After his triumphant surgery, Brovek checked Mrs. Herold in the Recovery Room and changed happily into street clothes. Mrs. Kerry would stay with Lotte only until seven. Reality closed back over him. If he hurried, he could still make it home in time. He cut past his office in Old U on the way to his car. There was some kind of a low throb in the air and he slowed to puzzle at it, and it became the beat of music. Then he remembered Mizzoh's party.

Damn it. He wanted to go to Mizzoh's party. Today had been a land-mark in his career. A pivotal time. A dramatic example of what he could do in the future. He wanted to be with his troops. It wouldn't hurt Lotte to be alone for five minutes.

He turned toward the nurses' lounge and lengthened his stride. He reached the door to the party in a dead heat with Grover Iverson.

His gut knotted. Yeah. What he could do, in the future, *if*: if he could find a suitable site; if he could buy that church.

"After you, Sandor."

"You first, Grover."

Mock courtesy. Brovek let the bastard go in ahead of him.

They were the only two in street clothes. The others were in their scrub clothes, with caps awry and masks dangling from their necks. Their disarray was a good match for the tired room, with its shabby walls and slack draperies. The people held styrofoam cups of coffee or little round glasses of red punch. The happy din of their voices bubbled along like running water, through spikes of laughter and the steady bang of Mizzoh's music tape. He recognized Springsteen and "Born in the USA." With the big day done and everybody telling about the blizzard outside, the party was taking off.

He took a cup of coffee and wandered about, acknowledging the nods and Good Evenings that the boys and girls directed to Number One. There was no forgetting he was the Big Frog. But damn, it was a little pond.

He spied Myrna Bates near the punch bowl, talking with her hands. Red juice splashed in an arc out of her glass, and the slim nurse she was talking to dodged away with the grace of a young cat. The two women bent together, inspecting their clothes, and straightened up laughing. Myrna's green scrubs and the other's spotless white had stayed unblemished. Brovek was fascinated. Myrna was Myrna, sturdy and plain. But the other woman made his blood stir. Trim legs. Tiny waist. Full bust.

"You old goat," he said to himself, "you haven't looked at a nurse like that since first-year residency."

He had met the exotic Lotte that year. And that way, too, he remembered. He had dropped his cardboard cup full of coffee in the cafeteria line, and it splashed on her shoes. They always laughed about it over the years together. She said he did it on purpose; he said she would have sat with him anyway. Neither denied anything.

He walked over to speak to old Myrna—she deserved some credit for her good work today.

"Thanks, Dr. Brovek," she said. "It was my privilege to scrub with you on a case like that." She nodded at the other woman, who had knelt down to wipe up the spill, and rose to meet him, her hand dripping with red paper napkins. "This is my little sister, Marnie Bates. Marnie, Dr. Brovek."

He looked at glowing skin, a halo of dark hair, and a smile as broad as bright. A mischievous light danced in her eyes as if she were daring him to something. He thought of riding a bike, no hands. He groped for words, and mumbled "How d'you do."

Myrna went on talking, God bless her, and Brovek collected his wits. With a slight bow to both women he backed away, heart hammering.

Lotte's fires were out, gone cold in the ashes of her mind. His own fires, he knew, were only banked, smothered by his work and his consuming ambition. But this sudden leap of flame in response to a young Eve was too much. Leave her alone, you old fool, he thought. She's younger than your daughter!

Mizzoh put on another tape, and now out of the machine came the opening chords of "Camelot." He and Lotte had seen that show on their honeymoon in 1961, and they had made those songs their own. She would sing in her husky contralto about 'happy evah-aftahwing"; but he couldn't carry a tune. He liked to recite the lyrics to her, his voice rumbling, her head resting against his chest: "If ever I would leave you, it wouldn't be in autumn."

His heart filled with pain. He decided to go home. Beside the door was a tray where he could leave his cup.

And there she was, Myrna's sister—Marnie, was it?—her fistful of punch-wet napkins dropping onto the tray, squishing like a wad of bloody surgical sponges. She held her hands up toward his face, wiggling her fingers, grinning: "Stick-y stick-y, Dr. Brovek, I gotta go wash."

She turned away and he watched her hips swing until she was out of sight.

"If ever I would leave you…"

An infinite gulf lay between himself and that girl—a separation of age, of achievement, of expectation. He saw that all right, but he saw the flip side too, and it scared him. The barrier that kept his hot hands from those round buttocks was razor thin.

He shook himself, and looked around the room. Grover Iverson stood by the punch table dragging on a cigarette. Their eyes met and Iverson turned away.

The bastard had watched him with Marnie, Brovek figured. Then he grinned. If Iverson was here, Politon sure wouldn't be, and Brovek knew why.

He looked about for Mizzoh. She had some young man in tow by the other door. He decided he could thank her tomorrow. Surely Lotte was alone by now, and maybe he'd have to shovel the damned snow just to get into his garage.

He didn't. The electric door opener worked, and he jammed the Lincoln full bore through the drifts across his driveway and squealed to a stop inside. There was a piece of cold chicken in the fridge.

"Did you have a good day, Lotte?"

"Yes, dear."

"Did Mrs. Kerry leave any messages for me?"

"I don't think she did."

But on his desk, under the stack of today's mail, he found a sheet of paper penciled in with Mrs. Kerry's awkward hand: Call Horace Potts as soon as you get home.

*　　　　　　　　　*　　　　　　　　　*

Rusty slid the hanger door open just a crack, and the wind whipped hard crystals of snow into his eyes. Hell, he'd be crazy to go out in this blizzard just to hunt up a woman. He'd had plenty of women. He jerked the heavy door shut again. Was he crazy?

Maybe. All afternoon she had filled his thoughts. Sleek dark hair combed back from an intelligent face. In the chill gloom of the hangar her slight figure, wrapped tight in her trench coat, kept him company. He did his job; he checked the aircraft, every strut and bolt from nose cone to tail light. But he met her face at every step. Heard her voice.

One broken wheel? Hell, he was busted up worse than that, himself.

He went to work on the wheel. Jacked up the plane. Wrenched off the lugs. She must have been scared peeless. But she hadn't quit. She refused to give up her mission. He liked that.

He tightened the lugs on the new wheel. It was a bitch of a storm out there. It was no time to be flying. He should have hunkered down for a couple of days, and sure as hell he shouldn't have tried to land at U. City. But the flight was her mission, and he let her call it.

That's the moment he remembered. The way she weighed their chances, counted up the chips on both sides, and then made her decision. She had looked into his eyes, all the way down to the bottom of his well, and simply given him her trust. That was the moment that zapped him—his first real taste of a strong woman.

One taste wasn't enough. He wanted the whole meal.

He nudged the door open again. A blast of wind whipped his scarf against his face. He snugged it around his neck and tucked the ends inside his leather jacket. Sheltering behind the door, he pulled on his gloves and peeked out again at the storm. His car was a mound of snow, already half buried in a drift. A man would need sled dogs for weather like this! What the hell was he thinking about?

He'd had liaisons before—flyboys always did. But they fizzled. He'd about given up hope of ever finding richness, finding a woman that challenged him. And then today, here she was, this Doc Garrison. In his pocket he felt the bulge of her gloves that he had found in the Cessna. If she was even half of what she seemed!

He had to find her. Just a couple of miles through the biting wind would bring him to the hospital. He stepped out into the storm.

Snow crunched under his boots. The frigid wind bit his face and burned his ears. He hunched his shoulders and settled down to a steady pace.

Operating at Mach One this woman was. A surgeon on a mission. An honest-to-god fighting woman who could probably work up a sweat and not worry about it. Was this what he had been looking for? An equal partner who could stand tall beside him and thrill his mind? He had to know more.

He saw no one else trudging along in the storm. Through his slitted lids his eyes ran tears that he brushed away before they could freeze on his cheek. It was too late to turn back, but he would need shelter soon. His ears quit burning and became numb. His limbs grew wobbley and he knew the cold was taking his strength. He forced himself on until he found himself in a tiny parking lot beside the old hospital. Shivering, he strode across the ice, leapt up a couple of iron steps, and pulled open the hospital door. The warm ambience of the hallway enveloped him, and he paused there to rub his ears and let his shivers subside.

Was this woman really what he thought? He had seen her in a time of crisis, intent on her own purpose, and as independent as a she-lion. Yet with one sweep of her dark eyes she had taken him right into her life. God, he hadn't felt like that since Miss Price picked him out to clap erasers! And this Garrison was the only woman since Miss Price that saw her horizons more than about hip high.

Hip high? Hell, she was chasing the stars. Blizzard, hell. he'd go barefoot if he had to.

Now, how could he find her in the unmapped runways of this hospital? If the telephone operator was right, she was at some kind of party somewhere. Okay. He fingered her gloves in his pocket. They would be his ticket. He'd crashed parties with less.

*   *   *

After she left the Recovery Room, Dana's exhilaration faded fast. Her wings began to fold. She made evening rounds at a crawl, willing her mind to focus on one patient at a time, forcing her mouth to smile. Fatigue seeped like ground water through her body and settled in the low spots. Her arches ached and her back felt leaden. If only she could fall on her bed, nap for half an hour. After seven weeks of constant call, she was fed up with Bozo; his nagging messages had worn her down. She couldn't imagine how it would feel to sleep the night through.

But for a chief resident Mizzoh's party was a political must. That tough old nurse was the ramrod for whatever order and efficiency existed in the whirlwind of confusion that was the operating suite. Dana mustered her grit and pushed herself toward Old U.

She used to think the nurses' lounge looked pleasant, even inviting. But through tonight's eyes it looked as tired as she felt. The years had dulled the cream-colored plaster, and the burgundy drapes fell in a permanent droop. Mizzoh's party decorations—green candles, a few balloons, an assortment of Mardi gras masks—were sincere; it took more energy than she had left to see them as gay. On a boom box somewhere Madonna was belting out "Like a Virgin".

Dana scanned the crowd. Lance Rudd stood across the room by the coffee pot. At the food table, Barney Popper bulged his scrub suit with one more cookie going down. If Barney would color his suit red and hold his feet together, he'd look like a valentine. Myrna Bates talked to her beautiful sister Marnie, sober Myrna probably telling about her adventure in surgery today. Dana was surprised to see Dr. Brovek there—he usually went home to his wife. He was alone, but he was focused on the two nurses. Eavesdropping maybe? Dana was still searching for her hostess when the unmistakable bugle voice carried to her from yards away.

"Hey, Dr. Garrison, there's a gentleman here looking for you."

A gentleman? Green eyes and copper hair popped into her mind for the hundredth time today. Some compartment separate from her surgical chores had kept flicking pictures at her, like an irritable focus in the heart that triggers premature beats.

Mizzoh's broad shape cruised up to Dana, and close-hauled in her wake came Rusty Waters, jacket open, scarf trailing. Dana's mental images paled before his gleaming smile. How had she forgotten the furry sound of his voice?

"Hey, Doc, I wasn't sure you'd be here."

Renewed strength rushed into Dana's smile.

"I wouldn't miss this party for anything. Have you met Ms O'Hoolihan? Mizzoh, this is Rusty Waters, my—ah—my guardian angel. He drove the airplane today."

Mizzoh's eyes twinkled. "He told me about the storm, Dr. Garrison. Sounded like a close race right down to the wire."

Rusty drooped one eyelid at Dana and drawled his words. "Yeah, we figured if we didn't make it, you-all would just have more organs than you counted on."

"Not funny, Rusty," the tough lady grinned. "If you hadn't made it you would have creamed my operating schedule and destroyed my lovely party."

Dana laughed. "It is lovely, you are a dear to do it. Thanks for the Occasion."

Her cheeks burned. She wondered if Mizzoh heard the big "O" in her voice. Or if Rusty did. She turned to him.

"Well, Mr. Waters, you turned up here in pretty quick time. Should I be flattered?"

"Just being kind, Doc. I wouldn't want you to go through the blizzard without your gloves."

He pressed them into Dana's palm, and rested his hand there for a moment. Dana held her space, quiet and steady. Their eyes met. Her voice sounded husky.

"I should thank you for your successful flying today. That was a perfectly terrible landing; you must be proud of it."

He grinned, but his eyes did not waver. "It was a dandy, wasn't it? But the truth is I really cared that it come out right today…more than I have before…ever."

Dana withdrew her hand slowly and looked away. She stuffed her gloves into the pocket of her white coat. She heard the cue, and her heart quickened. She chose to divert it.

"Yes, Russell, you can be pleased about it because that precious heart functioned beautifully when we implanted it."

He peered at her with a mischievous grin. "Russell? Did you say 'Russell'? I haven't been called that since my mother died." Clearly his mind had not fastened on the outcome of anybody's surgery. "How did you know my name is Russell?"

Dana was caught like a kid out of school. Color flooded her cheeks. She tried: "Just a guess. Why else would anybody call you Rusty?"

His smile showed even more white teeth, and his eyes danced. He tapped his forefinger to his shock of copper hair, and waited for Dana's confession.

She was trapped. "It takes only five seconds to look you up in the University directory. 'Russell Waters, B.A. *cum laude*. Aviation Department.' That's all."

"Right on, Doc. And what else did you do to while away the long afternoon?"

Maybe a sandwich would level him down. She steered him toward the food table.

"Let's go somewhere to talk," he said. "Can you duck out to Chino's for a beer?"

Dana giggled. "You don't know about my sentence, do you? Six months at hard labor for trying to be a surgeon? Until today, I haven't been outside this hospital all year."

He stared at her. "Judas, Doc, that doesn't sound human. How long does that go on?"

"Until July. I've been in training for six years, building to this. It's climax time for me. It demands 100% and takes 110."

He chewed a bite of sandwich. "After that I suppose you can rejoin the human race. Is that right?"

Dana's throat grew tight. For months she had refused to think past this time of servitude to consider her future. She had no time for relationships. But just at this moment certain human relationships suddenly looked very attractive. She didn't know what to say, and a strange little voice inside was whispering Be careful, Dana, your answer might be important. She nibbled the corner of her sandwich. The bread tasted like sand in her mouth.

"I don't know the future, Rusty. I'll be ready to go out on my own after July, but that may not be an easy life either."

"I suppose you have to slave away for thirty years or something before you take care of Number One?"

She looked quickly at his leathery face. She saw no cynical crease, just the direct gaze of his eyes. She decided once again that his breezy manner was a screen he held up in front of his complete sincerity. She wanted to honor that; it was her own style as well.

"A surgical career isn't just a job, you know; it's a way of life."

"Exactly. And what do you hope for in your surgical career, Dr. Garrison? Let's say all your dreams come true."

Hope for? It was only an hour ago that she came to believe she truly belonged in this world of her dreams.

She studied his face, strong in its repose. His lips were moist. His eyes were steady on hers. She inhaled the sweet fragrance of him. She had known him nearly eight hours, and he was turning her world inside out. She had risked death with him and survived; now he asked her questions she dared not ask herself. What did she hope for? The answer arose unbidden; she spoke it as if she had never heard it before.

"I want to stay right here at University Hospital. To do surgery and research, and to teach." The strange words sounded presumptuous to her ear. "But whether I stay or not is up to them, you know, not to me."

The inquisitor became defender. His voice was intense.

"They'll want you. Nobody could help wanting you."

Dana turned hot cheeks away from his eyes. She threw her sandwich into a basket and groped for a reply.

"I hear rumors," she said. "If they expand the transplant program they'll need more bodies on the staff."

Rusty crowed, and rested his hand on her turned shoulder.

"If it's bodies they want, you're a shoo-in, Doc!" He pointed to the door. "Where can we go?"

She smiled. She remembered her high-school dances, slipping out onto the terrace with one young man or another, getting acquainted. She sobered. Maybe she had given up too much over the years, rejected too many opportunities.

"I have to go to ICU," she said. "A post-op check. Will you walk along that far?"

They slipped out of the lounge. She led the way down the dark corridor, past Keaton Amphitheater, and on toward New U. She strode along in her quiet, ground-eating gait, Rusty tagging behind. Ahead of them bright lights blossomed in the hallway, and the real world waited.

"Doc, hold up a minute."

He caught Dana's arm and turned her to face him. He grasped her hands, his hard calluses rough against her soft scrubbed skin.

"Straighten me out a little." he said. "I guess you don't have a man in your life—you don't have time. But I don't hear you say it will ever be any different. Will it?"

She watched him steadily. It was a fair question. Sometimes at night she would waken and wonder. Mostly she suppressed her desires in favor of hard work, and channeled her dreams into reasons to study. But the question needed to be answered, and he had thrown it right up to her.

"I don't know what I can say. Nobody ever asked me that before."

"Say Yes, Doc. Say 'Yes it will be different.' Say 'Yes, you'll have time for me.'"

Her throat tightened again. That feeling of import hung once more over her words. No subterfuge. She spoke in simple honesty.

"I can't say Yes I have time for you, Rusty. It wouldn't be fair. But I can't say No either. Not now. Not to you. I think I'm pretty mixed up."

"Okay," he said. "That's fair. Confused is better than bored. I'll try again. Can you squeeze a man into your life?"

Eight hours, going on nine. Today she had confirmed herself as a surgeon, she had touched the gold. But what a comic twist! In those same hours she had to wonder whether the price was too high.

He stood quiet, his hands holding hers without intruding on her space. Fatigue seeped into her body; her legs ached; her mind blurred. She tried to find the right words.

"I guess I just don't know. You'd have to help me find the answer. I could never ever give up my work. You'd have to learn what I do and who I am, and then we could see if there is enough of me left over to make you happy."

She watched his face, pale before her in the dim hallway. She wanted to take his head between her hands, stroke his wiry hair, make him understand.

His words were measured; he sounded stern. "Okay, Doc, it's worth a shot. But not next July. Now. If you can't escape this place for an hour once in a while, there's something wrong with it—or with you. Or maybe with me. So here's my number. You call me when you can, and I'll jump over here before you can hang up the phone."

He let her hands go and fished a card out of his pocket. She didn't take it.

Was her monastic commitment too extreme? She battled within herself. This beautiful man came along, and she trembled like a bitch in heat. But she was dedicated to surgery, wasn't she? Surely she was. But all of her? What about her precious gift?

She frowned in concentration; pulses throbbed in her ears.

Fatigue wiped away all her excuses.

She could not let him disappear. She knew with gut certainty that she wanted to know this man. So the decision was made, wasn't it? She took his card with the precision of a surgical maneuver, and dropped it alongside her gloves in the pocket of her white coat.

Her force began to flow again, into her confidence, into the cock of her head, into her strong hands which sought out Rusty's hands and held them.

"Okay, Rusty, you've got a deal. Somehow I'll make it work."

He moved to put his arms around her, but she held fast to his hands.

"One other condition. You can't call me Doc."

"What's the matter with Doc?"

"Just a hang-up I learned from my father. He hated it. 'Doc', he always said, 'is what you do to a horse's tail.'"

Rusty's teeth gleamed in the dark. "Then I'll call you Duck."

"My name is Dana."

He pulled his hands free and took her shoulders. "You can sign your checks Dana. Come to me as Duck."

Dana did not yield. He had forced her to a decision, but he must understand her terms.

"Back off, Russell. No quick fix here. If we come to that it will be in context and at the right time. Understood?"

The hall was too dark for her to see his expression. Had she driven him away after all?

He sighed. "Okay. Duck season isn't open. What we've got is just a pretty good way to get acquainted." He let his arms fall to his side. "But Cinderella, get this straight. I've been looking for you since the day I was born."

One after the other he had plucked her strings, and now they all sounded at once. She shivered with her pleasure, and raised her lips to his eager mouth. His arms went around her and they held each other close. In her own quick fire she pressed her body to his, unleashed and hungry, and then the bomb went off.

Explosively, Rusty tore his lips away. "Holy-God-what-is—"

He pushed Dana back like a hot rock. Clutching his groin with both hands he danced in front of her like a man betrayed.

Dana didn't know whether to laugh or cry, but laughter prevailed. It welled up out of her shoes, out of control, her shoulders shaking with it. She could hardly speak.

"Russell," she gasped, "that's your first lesson about me." She unclipped the black box from her belt. "Meet Bozo," she said, "my vibrating buddy, my radio-pager."

Bozo's chicken voice squawked through static: "Dr. Garrison, ICU, stat."

She grew serious. "I'm sorry, Rusty, really I am. But I have to go. And 'stat' means Now. Good night."

She feasted her eyes for another moment on a confused and angry little boy, and turned away. His words pursued her down the dark hall and into the light, and she took wing.

"You are one hell of a woman, Duck. I'll be back!"

And he too was laughing.

*   *   *

Horace Potts's inner storm matched the outer weather. He forgot his last shred of prudence for his own convalescence. Through the window of the cab he looked at blackness; even the whirling snow looked dark.

He paid the driver before he got out and kicked a trail in the snow up Brovek's sidewalk. He rattled the knocker and looked back from the stoop. The cab's red tail light faded in the falling snow, and his own tracks began to fill in and lose their sharp edges. Soon they would disappear, as if he had dropped here out of the air to wait on the doorstep.

Brovek didn't let him freeze.

"Horace, this must be something special to bring you out on a night like this. Please come in, come in!"

Brovek's home was like the man himself, solid and sensible, and full of heat. An airlock entryway kept the storm from blasting into sanctuary while Potts brushed snow from his trouser legs and shed his overshoes. He followed Brovek through the central hall into a warm brown library. Its walnut parquet floor supported a matched pair of Oriental rugs in rich reds and dark blues. Behind Brovek's mahogany desk and chair Potts saw shelves of books, and among them various plaques and pictures, diplomas, awards and honorary fellowships—countless badges of a long and illustrious academic career. Potts thought they looked much more personal here than the formal documents he remembered from the professor's office wall.

Brovek led him to a leather love seat before a stone fireplace, where a blazing fire radiated warmth and welcome. Two matching chairs were drawn up opposite, and in one Lotte sat with her knitting. She saw Horace, and rose to extend her long cool hand as if she were a duchess. She looked as regal and straight as a young tree. What a strange bunch of hurts this world can dish out, he thought, and kissed her cheek.

"Good evening, Horace." Her voice was rich and slightly accented. "Tell me how your dear Catherine is these days."

Potts was prepared. He spoke gently.

"Well, Lotte, you know Catherine passed away last year. And I do miss her."

Brovek's voice held authority, but he too was kind.

"Horace and I have some business to discuss, my dear."

He guided her to the love seat and placed her knitting on her lap. She sat obediently, her hands folded across the needles.

Brovek turned to Potts. "How about a spot of brandy on a winter night?"

Responding to the warmth, Potts settled deep into one of the soft chairs; its leather fragrance rose over him. Brovek sat in the other, his bulk swallowed up in its cushions. They swirled two fingers of golden Courvoisier in crystal snifters. Its essences rose into Potts's nostrils, adding its bite to the sweet pungency of wet oak, the split logs lying on the hearth, snow melting, running off. He breathed deeply, trying to let his tensions drain like the snow. Maybe he could pretend he didn't have problems.

"Well, Ho, it isn't good sense that brings you out on a night like this. What's afoot at the hospital?"

Potts nodded. He stared into the fire, wondering where to begin. His disappointment rankled. He needed to spit it out, to find some shred of salvage that he could still build on.

"I went to see the bishop today about St. Luke's. Father O'Leary and I went over just before this damn storm hit, and I wish we had stayed at home. The good news is that the bishop does want to decommission the church; he's already had it appraised for sale. And he would be delighted to see us expand our work here at University Hospital."

He sipped his brandy like a medication, and went on.

"The bad news is that somebody else with the same idea got there first. Somebody wants to build a hotel there, for God's sake."

Brovek nodded, looking through his glass at this new dimension.

"Well, the bishop can sell to anybody he wants. We may have to sweeten our offer."

"Worse than that." Potts's gloom mixed with anger; his words jerked out. "The bishop has already sold it. This person made the bishop an offer he couldn't refuse; he signed a sale contract six weeks ago."

Brovek stared at Potts.

"Big price?"

"Not out of sight, no. It's the option that's so unusual. This man came in with a certified check for one million dollars, and that was just for an option, for heaven's sake. Naturally it's applied to the purchase price if the option is exercised. But if it's not exercised, the bishop keeps the million bucks."

"And the bishop jumped at it, did he?"

Potts leaned forward over his knees. The damn chair was too low; it held him down.

"He had to jump at it—part of the deal. The offer was contingent on his signing that very day. So he did. Father O'Leary himself didn't know about it until the next day, when he called the bishop to tell him we wanted the property. And it was all over already."

Sandor Brovek lay back against his leather cushion and sucked his lip. He held the brandy glass against the firelight and swirled the glowing liquid. He wasn't seeing it, Potts thought; he was thinking furiously. Potts knew he would do that, knew suddenly why he had braved the blizzard outside. This gentle giant would find some kind of passage in any storm.

"Horace, are you sure of the facts?"

"Yes."

"And of the figures?"

"Yes."

"Such a large fraction down and not refundable? Maybe just to be left on the table?"

"The bishop told me himself."

The two men contemplated the licking flames. Potts hardly blinked. He was used up, spent, only seven weeks from his ordeal. He didn't know which way to run. He watched Brovek lean down and add a birch log to the fire. Its shreds of bark roared into flame and spewed hot light up the flue.

Brovek flared suddenly, like the fire. "There is nothing I would not do to get St. Luke's. Horace, it isn't our best chance, it's our only chance. That land has to be ours, and I don't care how we get it. Now, what about this man, whoever he is? Why should he throw money like that? What's his hurry? It sounds as if he has a weak spot somewhere. Find out what it is. I want him out of our way."

Potts nodded. It was a relief to let Brovek take the initiative. Investigate. Maybe something would turn up. At least it was something he could do. Later. After the storm. He let his tension go; the brandy worked its way with him at last; he felt mellow.

"The irony of it all is that this bugger made the deal while I was lying in the hospital. It was the very next day after your chief resident pulled my aorta out of the fire and saved my life."

Brovek grunted. "Oh, yes, that girl Garrison."

"'That girl'? Come on, Sandy, your chauvinism is showing. 'That girl' has to be a damn good surgeon. And I can tell you for sure she is a very fine physician."

Brovek searched Potts's face.

"You sound converted. Was there something specific?"

"Have you ever been cut on?"

Potts's eyes accused Brovek. How could he do all that cutting if he didn't really know what it was like?

"Well I have," Potts went on, "and not so long ago. Sandy, the hospital that you know, walking around with your minions in tow, is a different world from mine. Don't ever lie down in a hospital. The moment you're a patient, you're like prey. Equipment points right at you like a threat, but the people won't look you in the eye. They talk over your head. They say things just to move you through the program. And you know you have to go along because that's why you're there."

Potts wondered if he was blabbering. He had endured all his trials alone until now. And here were Brovek, and even Lotte—human ears in a moment of warmth. And the brandy…He swirled it in the crystal glass and inhaled its bite.

"Just once in a while, Sandy, it would be a great thing to have somebody in the white-coat crew stop and listen to you, as if you were a sentient human being. Even for just a few minutes…once in a while…"

Brovek's eyes were still fixed on him. "Garrison?" he prompted.

Potts gathered himself and shook his head.

"Garrison. That girl has learned to be human to her patients. I look back, I think there were a couple of things. She'd come in in her white coat with her stethoscope hanging around her neck, and do whatever she had to do. And then she'd listen to me. Even if I didn't say anything, she'd just stand there a few minutes, being there for me."

Brovek gave no perceptible reaction. "What's the second thing?"

Potts hesitated, watching Brovek's face.

"She touched me…laid on hands…. Oh, you can smile if you want to. But I was lying at the bottom of the trench, and I felt power flow through the hands of that vibrant young woman every time she laid them on my sore belly, or touched my arm."

Potts often found Brovek hard to read. The professor's grunt was noncommittal.

One further image pressed itself on Potts's mind. "Do you know what she did on my last visit at the clinic, when she discharged me? I was ready to go out the door, and she hugged me!"

Brovek erupted with laughter.

"Now who's being a chauvinist, Horace? If one of my male residents did that you'd throw him in jail."

The fire flickered. Lotte Brovek stirred in her chair. She seemed content to let the conversation flow around her, without demand. Brovek poured another finger of brandy into the glasses. He held his own lightly by the stem, without looking at it. His eyes danced impishly.

"Actually, Ho, I'm very high on that girl. She is doing good work for us. And today she played a very brave part in—guess what—a successful heart transplant."

Potts was caught short; he had no idea. Jubilation leapt into his throat.

"Sandor," he said, "your first! Congratulations!"

Brovek tossed off his brandy, smiling at his own game.

"It's too soon to say successful, I suppose. But it's a winner so far."

Abruptly he stood up, harshly intent, and scowled into Potts's face.

"Horace, we just have to get that church. Our transplant service could be the best thing in this entire university…better than…. Hell, it'll be bigger than the football team!"

They both laughed. Hope for their grand design floated on the brandy to the tops of their heads. Brovek led the way to the door, where Potts's cab had returned, tooting its horn. The two men shook hands, and Potts pulled on his overshoes.

"Sandy, I feel better. And I will see what I can find out about the mystery man. Good night."

Lotte stood beside her husband, tall and gracious, seeing him out.

"Good night, Horace," she said. "I am so sorry Catherine couldn't come."

▼

PART FIVE

LENT

The winter storm blustered on eastward, closing I-94 in drifting snow at Madison, glazing the streets of Chicago in slick ice. After three days, its trailing edges dwindled away at University City, the steel clouds tailing into wisps of white that coasted down a slackening wind.

High in the First City Bank Tower, isolated from the cold and the wind by the building's skin of heavy glass, Sandor Brovek gazed across the toes of his shoes toward the earth below. The city's blanket of fresh snow looked like a repeat of the white linen and gleaming silverware that graced his luncheon table; the undimmed brilliance of the winter sun in its infinite blue sky made him squint. A city truck the size of a child's toy etched a clean black roadway into the white surface; he imagined the rumble and scrape of its slanted plow blade. If he were running the city, he wouldn't hustle and bustle to restore its anxious commerce and its layers of grime. It was a pleasant change of pace the storm had forced on him, and he welcomed the leisurely chance for a planning session with Horace Potts.

The ritual for their meetings was unwritten, but even today they adhered to it: a light meal and airy conversation before they settled down to plot the future. Brovek turned back to the table and attacked his French onion soup, blowing a spoonful to cool it, and then sucking it into his mouth. Across the table, his companion did not share in Brovek's contentment. Potts sat rigid, his hands moving in jagged lines as he picked at his tuna salad—"Fridays in Lent, you know, Sandy," he had smiled apologetically. He toyed with his blush cabernet, twisting the stem of the glass one way and then the other.

Brovek wished there were more soup in his kettle and less cheese on top. He had a theory about onion soup: that chefs measure their Frenchness by the depth of the cheese. For Brovek's palate they overdid it by half.

He looked again at Potts, pushing a shred of lettuce around his plate. He was usually a solid, no-nonsense eater. There had to be a burr in his craw today. Brovek waited, his own anxiety mounting; soon enough they would talk.

He licked the tip of his index finger and stuck it against a blemish of poppy-seeds on the white linen. Call them dessert, he thought, and pulled in his belly, testing its weight against his belt. He licked his finger clean.

"Well, Horace, this is better weather than it was Tuesday night. You were a stout fellow to come out in that blizzard."

Horace Potts pushed his plate to one side.

Ordinarily he wouldn't do that either, Brovek thought. He was far too proper a gent. What could he have found out about St. Luke's?

Potts leaned forward, and engaged Brovek's eyes.

"You remember we decided to investigate that man. Well, I did."

He looked away again, squinting at the window, his pink face drawing lines Brovek had not seen before. "I have found out some things about him. He is vulnerable. We have a way to win...But...." He stopped.

Brovek waited. Potts's equivocal words did not yet match his turbulent demeanor.

"But?" he prompted.

Potts turned back, looked at Brovek's plate, at his chin, at something over his head. His words spurted out in uneven phrases.

"But the situation is awkward...I don't know how far we can go with it. I've turned it over...every way I can...I'm just confused. The stakes are so high. The game is so important to you...and to me...in both directions..."

"Hold it, Ho." Brovek folded his hands. "You're not making sense. Play that back from the beginning."

Potts sat back and took a fresh breath. "Yes. Maybe that will help." He leaned his elbows on the table, his gaze floating somewhere over Brovek's shoulder.

"You remember the option on St. Luke's. A million down, non-refundable, expiring after fifteen months. You said there is something different about a man who would make a deal like that. As if he didn't care about the money."

Brovek nodded; the meeting had begun. "I wondered if we could find out what makes him tick."

"Well, I found out, Sandy. He's dying."

Brovek felt a comfortable warmth across his shoulders, as the sun played against his dark worsted. He shaped a lazy smile at Potts. This did not sound like bad news to him.

"Dying?" he repeated.

"He'll never make it for fifteen months," Potts said. "He might as well have donated his money to the bishop and not messed us up with his bloody option."

Brovek prickled. Something was off track here. He watched Potts flick a tense hand at bread crumbs, scattering them across the white cloth.

"Then all we have to do is wait, isn't it? And pick up the property *post mortem suam...*" Then he thought of a hitch. "Can he sell or assign his option?"

"No," Potts said. "The option is personal and individual. Even his heirs have no interest in it. It dies when he does."

Brovek was still puzzled. "Then what is the problem, Ho? We have to spend nearly that long in planning anyway. And if we know we're going to get it…"

Potts's two hands stopped their fidgeting. His palms pressed against the table. For the first time he looked directly at Brovek's face.

"You are the problem, Sandy. You and your transplant program. This man is dying of liver disease, and he is at the top of your list for a liver transplant. If you fix him up, we lose St. Luke's."

Brovek didn't move. The roadblock came together in his mind, and all the rest of his world began to come apart. He took a deep breath, trying for control, exhaling slowly. His eyes darkened. Far away on the winter horizon a thin column of blue smoke rose straight into the air.

His thoughts tumbled in disarray. Each half-formed idea pushed into his mind and seized its place, only to dissolve at the attack of the next one…. An unknown man…blocking Brovek's destiny…but putting his life in Brovek's hands…the gleaming towers of his dreams falling to dust if he cures this man—who is he?…the curve of Marnie Bates's buttock (why that? why now?)…his integrity tempted to a fatal betrayal…and the Hippocratic oath: "I will do no harm".

But it would be so easy to fail! Successful results were always the last ones home, while risk lay in wait at every turn. He wouldn't even have to make a real mistake—just cut a corner, just wait too long. No one would know—no one except himself.

No. This was a new kind of game, and he didn't have the terms right. Waiting too long was the kind of legitimate treatment error that cropped up at Grand Rounds for analysis and education. But this new game was upside down; his goal would be to wait long enough. To stall. To intend that this man wither and die. The thought nauseated him.

And yet….

If he could not expand his transplant program, more people than this man would die. From lack of progress. From inadequate facilities. Patients would go off to bigger centers; other departments would grow, other professors win national reputation, while Brovek's own puddle would shrink and his voice wither.

"It is better for one man to die for the people," Pilate said. He thought of Grover Iverson, of priorities for sale. With kidneys, of course, it was easier; dialysis could stall people along, keep them alive, waiting for another chance. Grover could shrive his conscience on that.

But there could be no stalling with a liver. If a donor organ came along, if this man got his shot at salvation, his recovery would cost Brovek St. Luke's, his chance at Iverson, his dream of glory. His future.

He could see one good chance, one thing to hope for. Maybe, before a donor came along, this man would slide too far down hill. Brovek wouldn't have to gamble a donor organ on a lost cause; he could select instead a candidate with a better chance. Someone who hadn't bought St. Luke's!

Nobody could measure decisions like that one; no one could second-guess him. He was the ultimate authority, his own Supreme Court, his own high priest. Criteria or no, all decisions ultimately were arbitrary. From the heart of one person would emerge the final decree, and at University Hospital, for the liver, that person was Sandor Brovek.

It would be so easy…

He stirred. Horace Potts watched him intently.

"You are very patient with me. I was thinking."

Potts smiled.

"I think you went out the window and rode around the sky. But now you're back. Should we think about this for a few days?"

Brovek's brows pushed together, fanning three deep creases up from the bridge of his nose. His voice was low, conspiratorial.

"This question is between you and me, Horace. No one else must ever have even a hint of what we are discussing here."

He waited; Potts nodded faintly.

"Absolute secret. Agreed?"

"Agreed. I'll never speak of it."

"OK. We need that church, right?—it's our only chance. And he needs a liver; that's his only chance. One of us dies. Which is it going to be?"

Potts's frown almost matched Brovek's. He leaned on the table, almost whispered. "That's too simple. There are deeper values on both sides of the contract."

Brovek sat back. "And what are those, as if I didn't know?"

"On the patient's side, we're talking about trust—the trust he is giving to you, to your staff, and to this University. To your healing profession." Horace Potts fixed Brovek's eyes. "On your side we're talking about integrity—your own personal integrity." He smiled. "As if you didn't know."

A waiter appeared. He cleared the table, and brushed it clean; its cloth shone like the snow outside. The two men sat on, bound by unfinished business, by a vote not taken.

Brovek thought again of Marnie Bates, and how close he had come to a foolish act.

Horace diverted his tension into a new subject. "Tell me more about my favorite doctor, Sandy. How is she doing in her time of trial?"

Brovek welcomed a chance to think of something else. He leaned back expansively.

"Damn well, damn it, damn well. She should be looking ahead to career placement soon. And if we expand as we want, we'll need more staff. What do you think?"

Potts grinned. "You know what I think: she is tops. If you think so too, why don't you grab her?"

Brovek's tension released; his laugh came rumbling up from the caverns of his great chest. "I've thought of it, Ho, I really have. Fortunately, I thought twice!"

He wiped his face with his napkin. Potts waited for him to go on.

"Seriously. I have thought about it in the way you mean. And I keep wondering whether she would work out. We have to have somebody we can count on, you know. Can't have somebody in and out, maybe working, maybe not."

"Has she missed a day in five years?"

"No, not one. That is remarkable even among the men."

"Aha, Sandor! You see, you are worried specifically because she is a woman."

"Yes, I guess so. She has proven she is good. But she could get pregnant or married or something, and leave us stranded."

Potts marshaled his facts like a debater.

"80% of your residents are married, Sandy, and one of them is divorced. Half of them have kids."

Brovek rebutted. "But they weren't ever pregnant. They didn't moon around complaining of back aches, and they didn't take six weeks off when their babies came."

Potts's eyes flashed and his voice stabbed at Brovek.

"Maybe they should have! Some day you surgeons must answer for what your training programs do to your residents at home. To their wives and children. We ought to look at that question. For now I just ask you this: do you have a sick-leave policy?"

"Of course."

"Has it been tried?"

"Once or twice."

"Did it work?"

"Yes."

"Are you afraid Dana Garrison is an individual who would exploit you or abuse your policy?"

"No, I don't think so. I just don't want to take any chances."

Potts sat poised at the edge of his chair. His eyes were on Brovek like a snake's on a toad.

"Dr. Brovek, the most recent addition to your staff was Dr. Lance Rudd. How did you feel about taking chances with him? He has diabetes, doesn't he?"

Brovek started. His eyes widened as he looked at Potts. He wondered where he should defend his perimeter.

"Nobody is supposed to know that. Yes, he does. I thought about it—it could be a problem."

"But you hired him anyway. You took a chance. And he is good."

Potts sounded reasonable; he didn't push too hard. He went on.

"Don't you see that your judgment is clouded just by Dana's gender? Why else would you hire a man with diabetes, but turn down a healthy woman like her?"

Brovek made no answer. He drummed his fingers on the table cloth. He felt trapped. Slowly he began to smile.

"You will be pleased to know that Millicent Herold will probably go home in four or five days. Eight days post-op and home! I tell you this transplant business is no humbug. There is no possible way that woman could be alive today if it weren't for her new heart."

Brovek knew their agenda had changed; the tabled question demanded the floor. Potts spoke.

"Don't try to sell me on transplants. I'm convinced. Management gets simpler and better every day; your own residents tell me that. That drug of yours, whatever it is, works. The only question about the future is: are we going to be a part of it?"

Brovek had grappled with that problem all through their conversation; he had twisted it in and out without ever letting it surface. Now Potts had pulled away the lid, and Brovek's conviction poured out of him.

"Absolutely. We have to be part of it. We are a University center for research and training; we should be pioneers in transplant surgery. We can become a national center for transplants, and lead the way into that future you're talking about. But we have to expand to do it. Expansion is our destiny. We can't let anything stop us."

Anything? He wondered: what about a patient who trusted him? He trembled at how close he stood to the razor's edge.

"Now, Horace, what about this man at St. Luke's. What is his name?"

"Martin Stern."

"I have heard Rudd speak of him. The problem is: that property. We must have it and he's in our way. I think our direction is clear."

Brovek watched Potts squirm in discomfort, without sympathy. This decision was all Brovek's own to make.

"Our discussion today must remain absolutely secret—agreed?"

Potts's nod was barely perceptible.

"We may never have a shot at a liver donor before Stern dies. Understand?"

"Of course," Potts whispered.

"But if a donor comes along, then we will have a decision to make. Right?"

A small pulse was pounding in Potts's left temple. "That's when the chips come down," he said. "I want to know how you are going to play them."

Brovek stared at Potts; he made no answer. How could he decide? How could he know what he would do if his red phone rang? His hand fidgeted against the table, raising the white cloth into low ridges with his heavy palm.

"I'll have to play those chips when the time comes, Horace," he whispered. "I don't know right now what more I can say."

Potts pushed his chair back from the table. "I hoped you'd say more than that." Under his pink cheeks his jaw clenched in a firm line. His eyes were slits. "There's no leeway in my book; it's a moral thing."

Brovek hated painted corners. He rocketed forward out of his chair. The table rolled under the weight of his hands.

"Damn it, let it be! That's all the answer there is right now."

He glared at Horace Potts as if at an enemy. But Potts didn't flinch, and a corner of Brovek's mind called Foul! Potts was his friend, his ally, a key link to his ambition. Besides, he might be right.

He jammed restraint over his voice, and reached down into his boots to sound reasonable.

"Let's look at the bright side, Horace. Maybe, before this snow is gone, the bastard will check in his own chips."

"But won't it be too bad," Potts said softly, rising to face Brovek, "if he dies before you come to the right decision."

Brovek started for the elevator. Potts spoke to his back. "I'll pray for you, Sandy. For both of you, I guess."

"Yeah, do that." Brovek tossed the words over his shoulder.

Then he slowed, and when Potts caught up, he grasped his elbow and pulled him along.

"Cling to this, Horace," he said softly. "Martin Stern can't have much sand left in his glass, and I haven't a clue where a new liver might come from."

*   *   *

Martin Stern was pissed. Propped up in his hospital bed he glared at his horrid hospital lunch. *Chazzerai.*

Living at his hotel—waiting, maybe? who'd call it living!—he'd done everything they told him to do. Well, almost everything. But here he was, back in the slammer. Through February and early March he had roosted the days away in his $300 room, peeking under his cards at solitaire and drumming his fingers for a phone call that never came. Four times a day he glopped down the swill decreed by Dr. Rudd's dietitian, to the visible chagrin of the hotel's uppity French chef. Then on Saturday night he'd said to hell with it and had given in to a slab of rare prime rib au jus, and that did it. He knew they had hauled him back into the hospital, but what day was today? His memory was all blurred.

Anyhow here he was again, at the mercy of a Betty-Crocker dietitian who thought boiled rice was food. Boiled rice, for God's sake. He wrinkled his nose and pushed at his plate.

"How ya doin', Mr. Stern?" The young nurse was blonde, and well formed—he wished he could care. She fluffed his pillows and fussed with his i.v., and then she smiled right into his eyes and said, "Your're a good patient, Mr. Stern."

Martin Stern, who orders bankers around! Some kind of a big shot already, a regular tycoon. But now also I'm a good patient? This nurse, this young Lorelei, is giving me something to live up to?

He shoveled the rest of the swill into his mouth.

A good thing, too. He sure wouldn't put out for the dietitian. This morning she bobbed her fat smile over her clipboard and said, "Well, what shall we allow you today?" Then she scribbled a recipe—she even showed it to him—measured grams of protein, dabs of restricted fat, dull mouthfuls of carbohydrate. The food tasted like she recycled it out of her textbook. So why couldn't she leave the paste in it for flavor?

If he had his way, he probably wouldn't eat anything. He didn't care. The trays of food just marked notches on the day, and each day marked another damn notch in the dwindling of his life. He was pissing it away, wasting it in bed. Being a good patient, and for what? A new liver? He'd never get a new liver. He was going to die, and nobody cared. Hell, he didn't care himself any more, one way or the other.

Lorelei wiped his mouth with a wet cloth and cranked down the head of his bed. She fluffed his pillows again, patted his hand and carried away his lunch tray. He sank back, exhausted. Just from his effort to eat. He closed his eyes and tried to remember.

What day is it anyway? Three days I can count. Sunday I can count. Sunday I was too weak to fight and too mixed up to argue, and I got hauled in here. Yesterday was fog, and today I'm thinking again. So today is Tuesday? Wrong! Today is Friday. So what happened to Monday? Where did Tuesday go? Wednesday? That's the coma they talk about. Three days I lie here, not a man, not a person. Not Martin Stern. Just a lousy body, no brains at all. I should have died and had it over with. The sooner the quicker.

But I didn't. What else can I dredge up about Sunday? I remember lying like a lump on the stretcher. Then that rookie doctor came at me, the one with the pimple on her chin. She kept jabbing a needle into me, her face all screwed up, and then threaded it up one of those stringy veins I've got left in my arm. She looked like she was steering it with her tongue that she had stuck in her cheek.

Well, I'm still here. Maybe just for her sake I should try to stay alive for that miracle liver. Three damn months I'm on their transplant list, and every day I die a little bit. Maybe a little longer I should stick it out before I die all the way.

He turned on his side, and his belly shifted like a big bag of sea water.

He tried to recall something, anything at all, about those three lost days. Nothing appeared; nothing filled the void. Something hovered around the edges of his mind, but he couldn't capture an image. He dozed a while, and wakened, and whatever it was still floated over him like a dream. He had the sense of a human figure there, a figure that pressed at him, that nagged him with something he had to do. Something urgent. But he couldn't reach it. He was too tired to think.

He rested. He tried to sigh, but all that water in his belly pushed up into his lungs. Lying down flat like this I can't even take a deep breath. Like there's a load of books stacked on my chest.

Or something else? Yeah. Like having Lila Mae lying on me.

But that was different. She'd load on me, her soft body riding my breath. Hell, her weight on me made me strong, made me a tiger, not like this damn water in my belly.

But that was then and to hell with now. There's no point in living, not like this!

His eyes watered and stung. He wished he could cry, just bawl like a little kid, and then have everything be all right again. Then he could deal with things. Then he could pick up his option on that church, the only thing that he still had going for him. And then...

That's it! That's the urgent thing I gotta do. Cover my tracks!

At last the game came clear in his mind. In the building trade he lived by gossip. His motto was: take info in, give damn little out. And so two weeks ago he heard the talk on the street: University Hospital—his own ticket to health—wants to buy St. Luke's. They're steaming because they can't; the place is already sold to an unknown buyer.

Stern said nothing—he never showed his cards while the game was in play. But his pulses had hammered. New odds, new dangers.

Over the next days he played the scenario through, over and again, figuring the angles. Oh, he had his option tied up tight, no problem there. Yeah, as long as he was alive. But if the hospital found out their opponent was Stern, his game was done. They'd never find a liver for him. If Rudd knew, if Brovek knew.

The threat was clear, but he hadn't faced it. He was too weak.

But now I'm on the mend again, and that last piece of risk is on my list. Father O'Leary could finger me! The old priest knows about my first visit to the bishop. Hell, he went along and listened in. Until that old man is silenced, my odds need fixing.

He imagined what the doctors would say. *Stern bought the church? Hey, he's on our list for a transplant! Yeah, Rudd's patient. Well heh-heh, whadaya know? Poor old Martin Stern, waiting for a liver transplant.*

He could hear Brovek, *Sorry, old boy, we just can't seem to find a donor.* Or Rudd, *Bad news, Martin, you have gotten too sick for a transplant now.* Maybe a nurse would give the verdict, *Oops, Mr. Stern, we dropped your liver on the floor.*

And here he lay, helpless in their hospital. He screwed his eyes tight. All he could see was a jumble of negatives. He was lying alone in the pit, and nobody cared whether he lived or died. Except maybe his doctors, that probably hoped he would die.

God, there had to be somebody on his side! He threw back his sheet and bunched the pillow under his head.

Again that figure from his coma floated before him, out of reach, unreal. But he recognized it now; it was the priest himself. Had he been here? Or had he just conjured Father O'Leary up out of his urgency and confusion?

No matter. Father O'Leary was the focal spot of his danger, and yet his presence, real or imagined, brought a feeling of peace. Strange.

Stern opened his eyes. No vision now. There stood the priest himself.

"Hello, Mr. Stern, do you remember me? I'm Father O'Leary, and I'm surely glad to see the light in your eyes once more."

"What are you doing here, Father O'Leary? Who's watching your store?"

The priest's blue eyes twinkled beneath their cotton balls. His pink cheeks were brushed white with faint stubble.

"Oh, now, you know as well as anybody that I have more 'store' here in the hospital than I have across the street. I tend my flock wherever I can find them, Mr. Stern. And a few ailing souls besides, that I come to know in one way or the other."

"Yeah. Me, for example. Well, Father, I don't know why you're here, but I want to talk to you."

Stern stopped for breath. Even these few words winded him. He still felt foggy. But his vision of urgency drove him. Collect your thoughts, get it together, Martin. This has become a big part of the deal and you have to wrap it up right now. He raised a forearm and poked a yellow forefinger at the priest's chest.

"You are carrying a secret about me, Father. And it's got to stay a secret. About our visit to the bishop. Have you told anybody who I am?"

Father O'Leary pulled a stool close to the bed and perched on it as if he exposed his heart to the pointing finger. His eyes still twinkled, but his voice was grave.

"My son, I carry more secrets than I can remember. Many of them are sealed behind my lips forever and ever, world without end, amen. And I can't remember which ones are which. So I just never tell any of them. No, I have told no one here that you and I have seen the bishop. Nor will I."

Martin Stern sank down again, reassured. Father O'Leary continued.

"You are surely a better man today. Daily I stood here by your bedside, and heard no such desperate request. I wasn't sure you even saw me."

Stern's vision was not a dream, then. But still he was puzzled. He was used to attention only when somebody wanted something.

"Why do you spend your time on me, Father? I'm not one of your people."

"We all belong to each other, Mr. Stern. The way I see it is that the Lord chose to cross our paths in life, yours and mine, for purposes of His own. And then he put you in need, sick in my hospital, with nobody coming to share your fears. A man shouldn't have to walk a road like yours all alone, Mr. Stern. So I am thinking the Lord wants me to tag along with you, if you don't mind."

Stern gazed at the old man's eyes. If the old geezer was up to something, Stern was too tired to care. Let him come around, if he wants. I can keep tabs on him that way.

His gaze dropped indifferently, of its own weight, to empty air. "Tag along, Padre, be my guest. It isn't going to be much of a trip anyway."

"Discouraged, Mr. Stern?"

What a dumb question. Yes, I'm discouraged. For three months nothing happens except I get worse. I itch. I turn yellow. Every part of me gets smaller except my big belly sloshing around. Now even my brains are custard, sliding me in and out of fog. So who wants to know am I discouraged!

And the worst is I'm betrayed. Their damn system, if they have one, has forgotten Martin Stern. They get their chance and leave me to dangle.

Suddenly he wanted release; he wanted to dump the whole rotten story out on the ground and let it stink.

"A month ago, Father, I had a hunch. Just a gambler's feeling, you know? I was going to get a liver. So I got ready. I stayed by the phone. I quit smoking. I paid my bills. And then I read in the paper about a traffic accident. Some teen-age kid with a head injury was on a respirator. You know where? Right down the freeway at Midtown Hospital. And you know what happened to my liver? Nothing. She died."

He stopped for breath. Father O'Leary turned his good confessional ear to Martin Stern; the set of his shoulders and the cant of his body shutting out the world; he didn't stir.

Stern continued in short phrases, trying to breathe. "I asked Dr. Rudd. He found out. She died on the respirator…from her brains. She was an ideal…donor, Father, she was…my hunch…the liver I was waiting for. Trying to live long enough to get it. And you know why I didn't get it? Because nobody asked for it! Can you stand that, Father, they never even brought it up! They don't have a policy, they said. Christ, Father, aren't they doctors over there? Don't they care? I think I'll die with my liver and donate them my brains."

He lay back, desolate, panting, and stared toward the ceiling.

"I don't want somebody should die for me. I don't. But it happened. Next door almost. And still I got nothing. So I guess…I won't get anything…ever. I've been going down…the tube ever since…and look at me…I'm about to go…out the bottom."

He stopped. His chest heaved. He squeezed his eyes tight shut.

Father O'Leary's voice came husky, breathed right in Stern's ear. But it had an ordinary tone, as if he spoke of friends or neighbors.

"Mr. Stern, it is a great challenge in life to persevere, even when we think that hope has run out. Think of our forefather Abraham. Imagine his heavy heart when he climbed the mountain with Isaac, expecting to slaughter his own son as a sacrifice to Yahweh. But he persevered. He tried to do whatever God commanded him to do. Maybe that is what is important—to do what God commands us. Not so much the way the story turns out."

Stern lay still.

Fr. O'Leary said, "But in this case, we all know, Isaac was spared at the last moment by a ram provided by God.—a kind of donor, Mr. Stern—at the very last moment."

Martin Stern opened his eyes on the old priest. He smiled in spite of himself. He smiled to feel a surge of hope in his breast, a trace of vitality that he thought was gone.

"Father O'Leary, you put me in with company…I wouldn't dare to claim for myself. But maybe you're right…. Maybe there is a ram in a bush…that I haven't noticed just…down the hall somewhere. I guess we'll have to…wait and see."

*   *   *

Dana Garrison nearly scalded herself in the fragrant hot suds. She knew her alto croon would never make it in anybody's choir, but in a shower even she could sing. Her elbows banged dull thuds against the sides of the pinched shower stall, but not in rhythm with her song, as her high spirits bubbled out in approximate melody.

Her final operation of the day had left her on a high. The poor guy was about to lose a leg, probably above his knee. So she built a by-pass around his clogged artery and flooded new blood down to his cold foot. The big toe was mummified, dead. But now it could drop off and the stump would heal; he would still walk on his own foot.

She felt like a giant. Since the day she harvested Danny Hovelund's heart and contributed to Millicent Herold's salvage she had reveled in a flood of self-confidence. Her years of labor and sacrifice came to maturity that day. The disciplines of surgical science fell into place; they belonged to her now. Her judgments had begun to flow with assurance, and her scalpel took on new precision.

It's magic!! she sang, trying to remember the lyrics. No matter, she couldn't reach the high notes anyway. She put away the soap and gave herself to the sting of hot spray against her skin.

And her life, too, was a whole lot more fun, with Rusty Waters hanging around. When she tried him on the phone the first time, he popped up just as he said he would. And those few stolen moments with him felt right. She liked him. More each time. She wondered, would she ever have the nerve to call him twice on the same day?

She stepped from the shower and rubbed herself dry. The nurses' dressing room was a stingy facility that jammed her between a narrow bench and a row of steel lockers. The wall mirror was not much bigger than a legal pad. She stood on tiptoe and stretched and twisted around to see herself in it. She was glad she was alone. The posturing made her feel like a freak.

Once at night she had explored what everybody else called the surgeons' dressing room. Of course it had stand-up urinals, but it wasn't really any nicer. The same narrow bench on the bare tile floor, the same half-length lockers with the paint all chipped. But on the wall there was one good full-length mirror.

It was the semantics of locker rooms that galled her. *Surgeons* and *Nurses*. The terms rankled. She was a surgeon too, after all. Why didn't they label them for *Men* and *Women*?

To hell with that. The nubby towel was first class anyway, warm and fleecy. She felt fresh and clean, and her spirits sailed. She dressed quickly, skirt, blouse, white coat, low shoes. She added her touches of fragrance, and started out for the hospital's tea party.

Only three months after Karen Sondergaard's promotion to Head Nurse, Susannah Politon had picked her out again. A juicy and exciting new job. Dana was delighted for Karen, because in a strange way she had had a hand in it, because of a tiff during one of their dinners together.

"You doctors dictate too much. Like czars or something." Karen repeated her favorite theme.

Dana was sick of it. "Somebody has to be in charge, Karen, and the doctor is the one."

Karen poured her high-test Norwegian coffee into their cups.

"Come on, Dana, listen to me. You can be in charge without being bossy. It's a matter of respect. Patients need some say in what happens to them, and they should have more information. Doctors will still be number one."

"Who's got the time, Karen? I average eighteen-hour days as it is." Dana didn't want to get bitchy, but her words just popped out. "I don't get to work a shift and quit for the day."

Karen flared. "And you don't take orders, either. And you get respect. And all the money."

Her bitter tone hurt Dana. This argument had too many reruns, and each one dragged the two friends closer to the edge. She touched Karen's fingers.

"Let's go back to Go," she said. "Leave me out. Doctors can't play Twenty Questions so our patients can feel good. So who is there to give all this information?"

Karen laughed. "I thought you'd never ask! Nurses, Dana. Me. Do you know what an 'ombudsman' is?"

Dana knew it wasn't a disease. She shook her head.

"If the hospital employed me to represent your patient, I'd be his ombudsman. I'd help him through the maze; I'd be on his side."

"We're all on his side."

"But maybe he doesn't feel that way. Like Dr. Rudd's lady with the ruptured appendix. She needed a lot more than he gave her."

Dana nodded. "And you helped. I remember."

"There's a lot of that, Dana. It goes on all the time."

Dana took her cup to the sink and rinsed it. Her heart ached for her friend. Karen's acid view of doctors had some merit; but it was surely magnified by her terrible loneliness. Dana's own richness in the hands and heat of Rusty Waters had no counterpart in Karen's life.

Karen slumped over the table, twisting her cup back and forth. Dana's patience went down the drain.

"Okay, Karen, you've sung this song enough times. I don't want to hear it any more. Once upon a time you reached out to me, and we are friends because of it. So do it again. Go sell yourself to Susannah Politon. Maybe she'll buy this ombudsman idea. But until you've tried that, leave me out of your editorials."

Maybe she had been cruel that night. But she was glad. Karen had taken her fight to Politon, and Politon had bought it.

In the hallway she fell into step with Lance Rudd, emerging from the real doctors' dressing room.

"Hey, Lance, you better be going to the tea. Come with me."

Lance was not so bouncy.

"Oh, yeah, I forgot. What's it about, Dana?"

"It's about your transplant program; you ought to be interested. The new program for nursing education and patient advocacy. You told me the other day that you spend absurd amounts of time explaining basic information to patients. Now you're going to get help."

"I like that," Lance said. He trimmed his long strides to match Dana's. "In what shape does help come?"

Mary cocked her head at Lance, so tall beside her. She laughed; his question was more apt than he knew.

"I think you peeked at the answer, Dr. Rudd. Believe me, Karen Sondergaard's shape will present no barrier to staff cooperation."

She giggled again, thinking of cooperation. Susannah Politon probably took Karen's Master's degree as a sign of orthodoxy—some protection in her experiment, a sort of anchor to windward. Orthodoxy indeed! If Politon turned Karen loose she was going to get more than she bargained for.

They climbed the stairs from the surgery suite and entered the dingy corridor of Old U. Dana was glad that Lance, with his long legs, was in no hurry.

And speaking of orthodoxy! She peered up at her imperturbable colleague. He was so solid. What would it take to shake him up a little? In everybody's book he was the hospital's Most Eligible, but Dana thought he was also the Most Impervious. She knew that some of the nurses speculated about him. He was so good-looking. Why was he still single? One swinger insisted she wouldn't care if he was single or not if she ever got a chance at him.

She eyed Lance, cruising along beside her, smoothly dressed, solemn-faced. She'd love to find out what it would take to ruffle this guy. Would she dare set up a trap of some kind? What could it be?

"Karen is the head nurse on Station 21. She and I have become good friends in the past few weeks. You will like her. She has a Master's in Nursing Ed, a direct and honest manner, and very long legs."

He did not respond. She hoped he couldn't read her mind.

"Here we are, Lance; see if you can manage to smile."

With her pixie urge pulled back to a short leash, she led Lance into the nurses' lounge.

The reception was laid out quite simply. A long table held a white cloth, a large tea pot, a punch bowl and a scattering of cups. Two plates contained institutional cookies. Several persons wore civilian attire, their worsted suits and woolen skirts attesting to the administrative level of Karen's promotion. Standing tall beside Susannah Politon, Karen herself shone in a snow white uniform that looked double-starched. She had pinned a red rose at her shoulder.

Politon wore a heavy gold ring on her right hand, and she rapped it against the teapot, commanding silence. She described the new staff position she had created, the "patients' very own watch dog," and made extended self-laudatory remarks about progressive attitudes and patients'rights. At last, as the hum of contraband conversation became too strong for her, she introduced "our first Patient Advocate, Ms. Karen Sondergaard." Everyone applauded.

Dana dragged Lance after her into the cluster of folk gathering about the honoree. When their turn came, Dana hugged Karen, admired her red rose, and introduced Lance.

Karen's eyes were incredibly bright.

"Oh, yes. I have met Dr. Rudd."

Dana thought Lance's dutiful dour face made a poor contrast to Karen's glowing cheeks, and her pixy feelings slipped their leash. "Excuse me," she said. "I have to speak to Dr. Kanju." She stepped behind Lance and with her elbow jabbing into his kidney gave him a good shove toward Karen.

"What the…?"

But Dana moved away. She heard him try to recover, to come back to his stodgy role as Congratulating Surgeon. He stammered out a greeting to Karen—"Dana tells me you…" God, was the man shy? He sounded like Jimmy Stewart!

Intent on escape she stepped over to Harvey Kanju. Her mischief was leading her into strange waters. What on earth could she say to an internist?

"Hello, Harvey," she improvised. "I see you are losing a nurse."

*   *   *

What-the—! Lance protested Dana's shove, but she was gone, and he was face to face with—what's her name?—Ms Sondergaard. I ought to choke Dana for getting me into this, he thought. A bloody tea, for God's sake, and I'm stuck with the tea-ee.

Well, I have to be civil.

"Dana tells me you are going to solve some of my communication problems."

She turned directly to him and nodded. "I have some ideas, Dr. Rudd. Your transplant patients need lots of facts. But they have feelings too. I intend to help them, both with the facts and with their feelings."

Yeah. Whatever. How can I get out of here?

She's still talking. "Your attitude toward my work will make a huge difference."

Yes, I suppose it will. Dana was right about her legs, she's nearly my height. And wow! is she focused on me! Intense. Probably a nice girl, sincere. Wide-set blue eyes, blond hair. Scandinavian, I guess. But why in hell does she hold that teacup in front of her face. Probably has bad teeth.

"Well, in all honesty, Ms Sondergaard, I am eager to have you take on your new assignment. I'm all in favor of the 'facts' part. These patients need more teaching than I like to take time for. As for the 'feelings' part, I'm not so sure. Patients haven't much choice. They just have to go along with the program."

Whoa up, Lance. What did I say? Suddenly she's spewing fire. Yes I know Martin Stern. No I didn't know Father O'Leary had ever seen him. Cool it, lady, you're going to detonate.

These damn women nowadays, all this lib business. It's okay with Dana, she's a surgeon, she's all right. But this one, this nurse, wants to be partners? Nuts.

But when she drops that cup, she's gorgeous. Flawless teeth. A generous mouth. And boy is she giving me what-for with it. This female is a piece of work.

"The 'feelings part,' as you call it, is a hole in your program and you'd better fill it."

Whoever said blue eyes are cold eyes never saw these eyes. Okay, let's talk about her program. That's business. But God, those eyes! She's a princess, and I'm getting a hard on, and I don't need that.

The hell I don't. And maybe she's right about the program. Patients' feelings? What about mine? I want to meet her somewhere. God, I'll go anywhere. And ASAP.

"You might teach me a lot about feelings, Ms Sondergaard. I want to hear more about your—ah—desires. Your office, or mine?"

"I'll be glad to come to you, Dr. Rudd. I look forward to it."

Come to me. I like that. "How about tomorrow morning?"

"As early as you like."

*   *   *

Hey, catch this self-styled big-shot surgeon lurching into my space.

Karen stood her ground. He never would have come by himself. And I wouldn't care—except he's one of the doctors I'll have to deal with. Thanks to Dana for getting him here at all. Let's see what he says.

"Dana tells me you are going to solve some of my communication problems."

Would he even remember that day on 21? He was such a jerk. But up close like this he has nice eyes. Deep brown, steady. It's only courtesy, I suppose. He even looks bored. But how long has it been since a man spoke to me, just to me, like this?

"I have some ideas, Dr. Rudd. Your transplant patients need lots of facts. But they have feelings too. I intend to help them, both with the facts and with their feelings."

Holy joe he's a good-looking dude. Don't be bored, Lover Boy. Let me tell you my plans.

"Well, I'm pleased that you will have the chance. The administration is starting you off here as if they think you're important."

As if? By God, I am important. My mission is important. And if guys like you don't buy it, I'm dead.

"I think I'm important, too, Dr. Rudd; and I intend to make you agree." Easy, Karen. Butter him up a little. "Your attitude toward my work will make a huge difference." She contemplated him across her teacup. Here he is, my first challenge in the new job. I've got work to do on you, Dr. Rudd.

And why not? Maybe I'll like working on you.

"Well, in all honesty, Miss Sondergaard, I'm all in favor of the 'facts' part; these patients need more teaching than I like to take time for. So go to it. As for the 'feelings' part, I'm not so sure. Patients haven't much choice. They just have to go along with the program."

Oh you uppity bastard. You really tee me off. Well, stand back, Buster, Karen has big ammo here.

"Dr. Rudd, do you know Martin Stern?"

"Of course. He is my patient waiting for a liver transplant."

"Right on. He is fighting for his life, and you are desperate for a donor for him. But you have just told me in your own words where you fail him. And I tell you that if it were not for Father Kevin O'Leary's ministry to him, Martin Stern would be dead today. You'd have already lost your chance."

Look at him; he still doesn't get it. How can I make it any plainer?

"Are you listening to me, Dr. Rudd? The 'feelings part,' as you call it, is a hole in your program, and you'd better fill it."

Hey, that felt good! I just kissed off all my crummy years of kowtowing to doctors. And why not? I've got credentials too. An advanced degree. A special appointment. And more important, I'm right!

You, Dr. Rudd, with your big brown eyes, by God, I can stand up to you. I can slug it out with you, Queensbury Rules, or no rules at all.

Now what do you say to that?

"You might teach me a lot about feelings, Miss Sondergaard. I want to hear more about your—ah—desires. Your office or mine?"

Look at him light up. Okay, so we're going to meet. That's a good start for my—my what? What did he say—my *desires*?

Easy, Karen. This guy is turned on. To what? My program?

He's too hot for that. God, maybe to me?

Easy, Karen, nothing. Whatever lies ahead, I can't wait!

*   *   *

Lance spent a chaotic night. His life had been so settled and logical—okay, so stodgy—until yesterday. Until Karen. He tossed, sleepless, reviewing the old decisions he had made for his life. As a bad-gene childhood diabetic, he had found out the hard way that he couldn't fight the disease; he must learn to live with it. Live despite it. Early on he decided to stay single, and simply let his Motherwell genes lapse. He would make diabetes his life and his wife, his work and his mistress. He learned to follow a scrupulous regimen of diet and insulin. Studying the disease led him naturally into medical scholarship. By now a confirmed academic, he poured his energy into research. His other energies settled out of his life, unattended.

Was he happy? content? He never before asked the question.

But now Karen Sondergaard had shaken him up like a can of paint. When her cool Nordic beauty erupted in that scalding critique of his program she revealed a passionate soul that, God help him, ignited his own desires. Her generous mouth. The scent of that red rose.

At last he fell asleep, only to thrash in turmoil and awake in wild arousal.

At six a.m., robot-eyed, he shaved and dressed, measured out his breakfast calories and his insulin, laid the spoon and the needle by the edge of the sink, and set out for the hospital. The long walk settled him, and he centered himself in the morning's dull surgical procedure, grubbing out a tedious snake's nest of varicose veins. Two fat legs' worth. But just before ten o-clock he clipped shut the last incision, rolled on the big pressure bandages, and fell back into confusion. In raging ambivalence he dragged his eager steps back to Old U and his appointment with Karen Sondergaard.

He entered his tiny academic office, murmured an unconscious "Good morning" to Estelle, went on into his inner cubicle and closed the door. Karen was already there.

Cool and professional, she stood as he entered. Her rose from yesterday was pinned to her breast, still dewy, like her moist lips. His own appearance was no match for her. God, he was a mess. His paper boots stuck out of the legs of his scrub suit, and his white coat drooped. He snatched off the surgical mask dangling around his neck, and his cap flew off with it. He knew his hair would be sticking out in tufts.

Cool it, Lance. This is supposed to be a professional visit.

He squeezed past her in the tiny space and dropped into the chair behind his desk. Her eyes were unbelievably blue. He forced his brain. This appointment had some purpose, didn't it? something educational? He reached back for the words that stuck in his craw yesterday.

"Tell me, Ms. Sondergaard, about the hole in my program that needs filling."

Her eyes rested steadily on him, half smile and half mystery.

"Your program does marvelous things for your patients, Dr. Rudd. Frightening, marvelous things."

She folded herself into a chair.

"But when those people become your patients, they are frightened. You know what you are doing when you cut open their insides, but they don't. They need to understand."

"That's where we differ, isn't it? Patients just need to go along. Leave the driving to us."

Her eyes flickered in a different light, cooler, he thought, but even more intense. She leaned her elbows on his desk.

"Going along is the choice they make. You call it 'informed consent.' I'm talking about more than that. They also need comfort, confidence, peace of mind. You don't honor those items in your program."

Criticism rankled him. The lib thing again.

"What would you do different?"

Karen straightened against the back of her chair and ticked her ideas off on her fingers.

"Tell patients and their families what to expect, where they'll be, how long they'll wait. Visit with them. Answer questions. Be their champion in this alien hospital environment. Be their friend."

"Is that all?" Lance tried not to sound bitchy.

"That's the beginning. Another idea. You're starting organ transplants. If you are successful, people will come from miles away, and their relatives will have to hang around motels, isolated and miserable. Let's house them all together, in a community of support, to share the wins and losses."

"God, Karen, I can't do all that!"

"No, Dr. Rudd, you shouldn't have to. But your program should. Expand your team. Let me do it."

She sat straight upright. A T-square against her shoulders would fit her neck and head. She had a strong angular face, straight nose, steady eyes. He watched her, and didn't answer. Her cheeks colored. She folded her hands in her lap.

Finally he said, "That's a lot to think about."

"I suppose it is."

"We should meet again."

"I hope so."

He could not be in error now. There was sudden color in her cheek, even in the hollow of her neck.

Lance stood up. The tiny room hemmed them in. He squeezed past his desk; Karen stood to give him room, but she did not give way. Her face turned up to his, and her lips parted in a half smile. The heady scent of her red rose drew him in.

His arms encircled her body. She moved against him, yielding, slender, soft. She fit against him all the way to his toes, and he felt her arms around his shoulders, strong, clasping, as eager as his own. Their kiss was full, unhurried, passionate. It was a foretaste, and a mutual promise. His blood was up and in his mouth; he could taste his excitement.

Estelle's typewriter began to chatter on the other side of the door. Their arms dropped; their precious moment passed. Lance leaned back against his desk and sat on it; he dropped his hands on his thighs; he tried to come down.

"Well, Karen," he fumbled, "you said you could teach me something about emotions. Where do I sign up?"

Her voice caressed his ears.

"Actually it's a seminar, Dr. Rudd, and you are my only student."

Her cheeks were flushed; she was hot with excitement, just like himself.

"But Lance"—she switched her terms smoothly, and watched his eyes—"I want you to know that all of this is new to me. I mean, all of it. I haven't been ready for—explosions—like this," her blue eyes grew azure, "until now."

Oh God, Lance thought, I've never known a gift like this. She owes me nothing, and she offers me her open soul. Do I want this woman? Go for it! To hell with the consequences.

"Karen, come to me for dinner tonight. My little apartment is just a bachelor's pad, but I want you to come."

Heart pounding, he watched a cloud darken Karen's face. She seemed to shrink inside her starched white. Had he blown it? Her eyes went far away. Troubled. Even sad. Lance didn't breathe. Finally she took a long breath, exhaled slowly in a long soft sigh, and returned to him. She sat tall in the chair, her shoulders squared, and looked straight into his eyes.

"Thank you, Lance. I will."

*　　　　　*　　　　　*

"Reach out and touch someone," the ad voice said.

Father O'Leary stared at his 1974 Magnavox TV. The 19-inch screen looked blurry, but he could hear the message plain enough.

"It's me they're preaching to," he said aloud. He brushed broken crumbs of potato chips from his lap, limped over to the set and snapped it off. "Sure and I can't walk out so very well, but I guess I could reach out like the man says."

By the faint light of a gray winter afternoon filtering through dusty curtains, he groped his way through the hallway of his old house. He fingered around on the dark wainscoting until he found the wall switch. On his office desk a lamp began to shine. He sat down in his squeaky leather chair and pulled open a drawer. He slid that one shut again and tried another. In the telephone book he finally found his directions for long-distance dialing.

Finally he got it all together, the desk lamp pulled close, the phone book spread under his elbow, a magnifying glass in his left hand, the hand piece of the telephone tucked under his right ear, his right index finger poised over the circle of numbered holes on the dial. His eyes and his hand glass moved in unison, from book to dial and back again, one number at a time. One call to Directory Assistance. He penciled a number on the margin of his notes for next Sunday's homily, the Third Sunday of Lent. And at last he fingered in the eleven numbers for his seminary roommate, who might still be pastor at Assumption Church in Ottumwa.

"Billy? Kevin O'Leary here."

"Do you have the right number, Mr. O'Leary? This is the Church of the Assumption."

"Well I hope it is, young man. That's the number I dialed. Is Father Oliphant still pastor there? I want to speak to him."

"Billy?…Ah, yes, I think so…Let me check."

Father O'Leary chuckled. Some pink-cheeked assistant, he supposed. Sounded as if Assumption was doing better than St. Luke's. He'd expect that of Billy, too. He always had the flare. The alphabet was the only place where Kevin O'Leary was ever ahead of Billy Oliphant.

"Kevin, you old sinner, what brings you out of the woodwork? Are you in town? Can I see you?"

"No, Billy, I'm calling long distance. I need a favor."

"You got it. But don't hang up 'til you tell me about yourself."

The years of separation melted away in the familiar sound of Billy's voice. Kevin recalled the class where Billy argued with the rector about ethics, and how they had prayed the night away that Billy would not be dismissed. Billy teased Kevin for kicking a football through the chapel window, and laughed as he always did while Kevin tried to explain why the ball and the shards of glass all ended up on the lawn outside. And at last Kevin came to the point of his call.

"I want to find out how to reach a person who might live in your city."

While they talked, Father O'Leary put away the magnifying glass, and centered the lamp on his desk. He answered Billy's questions. He flipped the telephone book closed and shut it up in its drawer. They talked about the crowded masses at Assumption. He nudged the telephone base so it lined up with the edges of his blotter. A pencil found its way into his fingers, and soon he was drawing doodles on the margin of his sermon.

Finally Billy phrased the inevitable question.

"Well, since you ask, Billy, the truth is my little parish is cut up by a freeway and fading away. Like me. I think the bishop plans to absorb it into a couple of neighbors, don't you know, and I don't know what he'll do with me. Elephant's graveyard, I suppose."

The phone made denying noises which Father O'Leary interrupted. "No, I don't feel bad about it. I'll find some place to live, and there's plenty of priestly work to be doing around the hospital. That's sort of what the favor is about, you see, and I thank you again for whatever you can do. I'll wait to hear."

He gave his number once more—Billy seemed a little deaf, he thought. They exchanged goodbyes and God-blesses and he hung up the phone. He stared into the lamp.

Maybe what he was doing was meddling; maybe it would help. God knew. At least he was trying.

He chuckled. His situation wasn't all bad, in his empty little church. After supper tonight Billy had to go to a parish council meeting that threatened a fight about finances. But Kevin O'Leary would sit in his den and watch the National Geographic Special on PBS. They called it The Ballad of the Irish Horse, and it would show scenes of Dublin.

*   *   *

Karen lay pensive in her scented bath. Bubbles and suds moved over her skin like conflicting thoughts. When the water cooled she ran more hot from the faucet until her toes burned. At last she gathered herself; a brisk rub with the bath towel would settle her. She faced the mirror, stood up straight, and let the towel fall. She was too thin, she thought. Maybe too tall. But Lance was tall. She saw her bony shoulders and pointy hips. But she had enough muscle to fill out nice curves. She liked her legs well enough, smooth lines, long bones set on well through the joints. She had never coveted large breasts; she liked her own neat efficiency.

She pulled a brush through her heavy hair. It shone almost golden, and was still moist. It gave up a piney fragrance as she stroked it over her shoulders. She decided to leave it down, and just tie the long locks back behind her ears with a ribbon that would match her outfit, whatever that would be. Now, what should she choose?

She tugged herself into the tight designer jeans that she hadn't yet dared to wear. She turned before the mirror, and stretched like a ballerina. The fabric clung to her firm buttocks like a denim skin. She peeled the jeans off again.

She tried her one fancy party dress; it was too black. She had been nuts to buy it—pre-holiday crazy, she decided: why had she thought anybody would care what she wore under her rented academic robes when she walked up alone for her diploma?

She put on her favorite old stand-by, a full woolen skirt in royal blue, that cinched her narrow waist and fell in generous folds about her knees. She chose a short-sleeved white blouse that was shiny like silk. It bore a trim of lace around its collar, and it buttoned in the front.

She left the top button open, so that she could see the tiny gold cross on its fine chain, her gift on the morning of her confirmation. She remembered her mother bending to a stiff, unusual peck that almost missed her cheek, and the awkward handing over of the small white box from Hudson Jewelers in Minneapolis. It was the closest thing to an impractical, feminine thing her mother ever gave her.

That was years ago. Too many years.

She stared at the mirror, at a stranger there, a woman whose daring throbbed in the base of her neck, whose defiance rode in the toss of her head. She watched the stranger's hands rise to her breast, slip open the second button of her blouse, and fall to the third, and toy with it.

Karen turned away from the mirror and dropped her hands. Get real, girl, she thought. What you face now is a cold walk through the snow to Lance Rudd's apartment.

She slid her heavy coat from its hanger and pulled it on. Beside the door, like waiting totems, stood her hated galoshes. She felt as if her whole life had been spent in galoshes, first the ice and snow of Prairie Falls and now these wintry nights at University Hospital. She had lived her life in the cold. Fighting winter. Being alone. Definitely, it was time for a change.

*   *   *

Lance stumped back and forth, from his hot kitchen stove to the white cloth on the table he had set for two. His knives and forks refused to line up with the napkins, and he fiddled with them again. Through the window he looked down the snow-lined avenue toward University Hospital. A street light blinked on in the gathering darkness. Damn. He should have gone to pick her up—he hadn't even thought to offer. He wondered how many of his lonely ways he would have to change.

Maybe she wouldn't come. He remembered his impetuous invitation. Rash speech. And he saw her again, as she sat in his office chair and retreated somewhere into the far privacy of her mind, before she returned to him at last with her consent. Oh, she was going to come, all right.

But what about himself? When she had first raked him with the hot claws of her anger, he had hemorrhaged excitement. Now he needed to retreat, a chance to gather up his own rattled mind. What had he started here? Could he still pull back, still return to his celibate monotony? Ha! It was too late for pulling back—too late and too soon. Hot demand throbbed between his legs.

Her crazy ideas about the hospital were the beginning of it. He thought her new program was sophomoric, just what a woman would dream up. She would get patients all stirred up, questioning things, talking together, maybe even comparing their doctors. Trouble coming! But when he said so, she turned to fire. He pictured her as she stood transformed before him, and he felt again his own blood rise in answer. Well, he would sure as hell avoid that issue tonight. No hospital talk. Just kiss around it. Make a quick conquest, mount her early and send her home.

The idea died even as it formed. He had never been the man for that kind of action. If he was in a mess now, it wasn't for lust—well, not only for lust. He was in it for something he had seen in those blue eyes, something ageless and mystical, that he had shut out of his life and had almost forgotten.

And suddenly its force was out of its cage. He felt helpless before it, and it was knocking at his door.

*   *   *

The candles on the table between them burned down to flickering stubs. The warmth of this woman wrapped Lance in a spell. He clutched for his familiar detachment, but it refused to come. What he felt was a flooding sense of rightness, a rush of power.

The two sat in comfortable silence, enjoying their mutual reflection after—how long?—a candle's length of steady talk. Karen's hardy life in Prairie Falls, taking deer for winter meat or having none; working her way through nursing school and her advanced degree; her constant loneliness until her growing friendship with Dana Garrison.

Lance kept his one dark secret from Karen—he wasn't ready to bare his pancreas even to her. But he told everything else, and even found himself spilling old feelings about prep school and his mother's clan of Motherwells.

"You had it about as easy as I had it tough," Karen said. Her soft voice held no trace of bitterness.

"Yes. That bothers me sometimes."

"Does it? I'd have traded with you anywhere along the line. You don't need to feel guilty."

He chuckled. "I hadn't thought of 'guilty' before." He grew serious. "But I always feel—you know—obligated, I guess. Do it right—make a difference—help somebody. That's the good part about doing surgery, to help somebody."

She turned her face away. The candle flickered. Her fine profile was a portrait in pale ivory.

"Let's not get into that, Lance, not tonight."

It was a gentle rebuff, softly given. He didn't know what to say. He lifted his wine glass and sipped at it. It was empty. He set it down again.

She turned back to face him. Her long fingers turned the stem of her half-filled glass. A trace of a smile played on her lips. "There's more than one way to make a difference."

Her golden hair fell around her shoulders. The modest bun she wore beneath her nursing cap had given him no hint of such glory. He watched the candle light play over it and reflect from the oval of her face. Her richness staggered him. From her throat a tiny gold cross winked at him above shadows that deepened into the recesses of her blouse.

His hands trembled. He decanted the last drops of red wine into his own glass. Bits of black dregs swirled like shadows.

Lance raised his eyes to Karen, and found her staring at his face. Her blue eyes didn't waver.

His blood rose. He went to her, and she stood to meet him. She opened her arms, and at last they came together in the long embrace they had promised. Her open lips were moist against his mouth. His hands wandered over her body; he felt her solid strength, the lean curves of her flanks, her hips, her legs. She grasped his fingers.

"Oh Lance," she breathed, "we met just yesterday...I haven't had time...it takes a girl longer to..."

"It's okay, Karen," he whispered. It was the one clear thought he had had all day. "I came prepared."

Her body's last ounce of stiffness melted away in his arms. She clung to him, pliant, arching to his touch, leading him, and at last, urgently, demanding.

*   *   *

Lotte lay sleeping, curled on her side, her thin frame tucked up as if it followed her mind to a fetal position. The whisper of her soft breathing sounded as delicate as a child's. Sandor Brovek eased his bulk under the sheet. The bed groaned under his weight, but Lotte did not stir. He reached for the reading lamp. A film of dust covered his nightstand. He drew an X in it with his finger and snapped off the light.

His pillow curled about his head, and smelled stale, like old moisture left alone too long. He sighed. Lotte's house had always been immaculate, freshly scrubbed and crisp, and always with no effort that was visible to him. He had to depend on hired help now, and hired help alone just didn't cut it.

The pain of it all knotted in his chest, and a sting squinted his eyes. He turned on his side, his back toward hers, and stared into the darkness. The hall clock sounded a soft chime, half after something. If he listened for it, he could hear the clock working, the slow back-and-forth of its long brass pendulum in its ancient case. He felt Lotte's frail warmth, her lingering metabolism like the last remnant of their marriage. Her wit and fire were gone, and he must mourn; he was bereaved, but he was not free.

He counted over the necessary arrangements for her care—now a companion, later a nurse. How long could he keep her at home? How soon could he learn to live without her—without her automatic house, without the responses of her passion, without—the pain stabbed at him—the give and take of their communion, the insight she had always brought to his problems.

More and more he felt the need to tell her things, to talk over the issues of his life. She had always supplied wisdom and balance for the thorny questions of his domain. And no question had he ever found so thorny, so profound, as Martin Stern.

Now that was an apple with a worm at its core. The surgery of transplantation might have been invented for Stern, all those pioneers plodding ahead in a fidelity of hope through decades of embattled lives and failed kidneys, one barrier of ignorance after another succumbing to scientific achievement, until today, 1985. Now he could offer Martin Stern, in reasonable optimism, a real chance for recovery.

But if he did, and if Stern survived, Stern would smother the very program that had saved him. And smother Brovek with it.

He clenched his fists around the sheet, crumpled the corner of it into a tight ball. The faint odor of old laundry rose in his nostrils.

Critical mass, that's what a program needs. Every institution—his own, anyone's—has to show sufficient size, enough traffic. Lots of cases like Stern and Millicent Herold. Without that critical mass, the planners will choke the program out. The planners and the bureaucrats. They will control the flow of government dollars, the life blood of research. Before the powers get around to making too many rules, I must establish myself. Stern should be our first liver transplant. I need him and his good result. I need an answer to Iverson's taunt of zeros.

Yet Stern, alive, owns St. Luke's.

Brovek's teeth ground at the impasse. He thought of his Valium tablets, a few feet away, secreted in a bottle behind his shaving cream. Bad idea.

He listed his options. Maybe he could add up the good and the bad and see an answer to his dilemma. Like a brainstorming session, where anything was okay to think about. Lying alone and silent in the dark, he could think of anything he wanted. Anything at all.

The first idea bobbed up like an apple in a tub: kill Stern.

Find a donor liver, put it in, and make it fail. A knot left loose would do it. One false stitch in the union of the blood vessels could cause a fatal clot.

No. If one day he were to blaspheme the goddesses of healing, how could he ever again invoke their blessing?

Besides, Stern was Rudd's case; Rudd would be placing the stitches.

He wouldn't have to be so intentional anyway, to have Stern die. Liver transplants were new and dangerous. He and Rudd had done a dozen or so in the dog lab, staking out their own routes along the ways pioneered by Carrel and Eck and Mann, and in the modern era, by Starzl and others. They were ready.

But Stern would be their first human case. To get a success out of Stern would take all their skill and attention, and all their good luck as well. He wouldn't have to jiggle a stitch at all: Stern would probably get into trouble all by himself. They could let him die in some ordinary postoperative way, with infection, or rejection of the liver, nobody the wiser. Nobody guilty. Not really.

He groaned. Even this would not go down. He tossed on the bed, and turned, eyes staring toward the invisible ceiling. The clock chimed again, a single stroke. Was it one o'clock? or half past something? The top sheet pressed a tight box against his toes and he strained at it. It didn't yield, and he kicked it loose. Lotte stirred. He lay rigid, feeling caught, until the rhythm of her breathing returned.

No. To let Stern die is no answer. Transplant programs are not built on failures. I need Stern to blaze the way for other cases, other successes, that's the way we build a program. The flow of our human-interest stories will headline every newspaper throughout the upper Mississippi watershed. Cases will come to us because of our growing reputation. Our department will thrive.

Yet none of that can happen without a new hospital. If Stern has his transplant and dies, that's a poor start. But if he gets his liver and survives, we don't get St. Luke's, and the whole program dies.

He groaned.

Horace wants me to make a good decision about Stern. What the hell is that? Sorry, Horace. When the chips go down, there is nothing I will not consider to get St. Luke's. I just hope for the one good script I can think of: that Stern dies before a donor liver comes along. No one controls opportunity; that result would be blameless. I can stay intact, keep my program at the ready. There'll be plenty of patients coming along behind Stern, lots of opportunity in a new hospital.

Amen. Let Stern die in time.

He rolled over and placed a gentle hand on Lotte's hip. Before the clock chimed again, he was asleep.

▼

PART SIX

HOLY WEEK

All the next week, Lance buzzed through his days with fresh energy. The side-saddles of his mind burgeoned with the warmth and vigor of Karen Sondergaard. But every night decayed into emergency work—another ruptured aneurysm with Dana, an embolectomy for a patient of his own. Fatigue closed in, and his blood sugar teetered toward levels he didn't like. He enjoyed glimpses of Karen by day—she had taken to wearing a red rose pinned to her uniform as her personal mark—but he settled for the telephone at night. She always let it ring a second time before breathing her Hello.

On Good Friday morning his schedule slacked off, and he hustled over to Karen's new office in Old U. Her door was open, and he paused there, leaning against the frame, watching her. The space wasn't much: dingy, sparsely equipped—three pieces of gray metal furniture and an IBM electric typewriter. Her golden hair filled him with light.

She bent over a scatter of papers, her palms pressed against her temples. Her fingers arched outwards, holding a pen away from her cap. She was frowning.

"Headache?" he asked.

Her smile lightened his day. "Just a little bit, again," she said. "Maybe I need new glasses."

"How about a coffee break?"

She tossed her pen down. "Love it."

Her hair was swept back behind her ears and gathered with a twist of red yarn tied in a bow. He watched her straight shoulders, her supple body, the twin promises beneath her starched uniform. Her red rose wasn't pinned at all. She had just poked its short stem under the badge of her new identity, printed in gold letters on a field of black:

Karen Sondergaard, R.N.
Patient Representative

"How about tonight, Karen?" He followed her down the corridor. "Can you stand my cooking again?"

Karen stopped so suddenly that he kicked her foot. She turned to face him and his pulses pounded. At such close range her azure eyes were deep and immeasurable.

"I was afraid you'd never ask," she said. "Isn't it my turn?"

"Maybe. But who's counting?"

Their smiles matched in easy agreement. "I'd love to try your cooking again," she said.

They walked together down the dim hallway of Old U., but before they reached the shiny halls and bustling traffic of the new building, Karen halted again. She turned to Lance and took his hand and held it in both of hers. Her eyes searched his face.

"What is it, Karen?" he said. Her skin felt silky against his fingers.

"You make me happy, that's all. Thank you, Lance."

She squeezed his hand, and dropped it, and led the way into New U.

Lance straggled behind, his mind in tumult. God, she's beautiful! and I need two filets for tonight, and another bottle of red wine. She is almost as tall as I am. Do I have any more candles? What a marvelous set of muscles in a woman's pelvic sling!

He remembered dissecting them in freshman year, learning their intricate patterns as they weaved their cradles of support and constriction around those marvelous openings.

They reached the bright, trafficked hallway near ICU, and abruptly Karen stopped again. She pressed her hands against her temples.

"Lance, I do have a headache."

She had to be joking. He started to laugh. The oldest excuse of jaded wives sounded ludicrous in this time of ignited desire.

"You can't back out now, Karen. I've already planned the…"

"Lance…. Lanthe." Her voice slurred. "My…head…"

She looked like a person drowning in a pool. He seized her arm and put his hand to her face. Her expression turned blank. The light in her blue eyes went dark. Slowly she crumpled like a sack to the floor.

Lance panicked. He was in love. He couldn't understand. This couldn't happen to her; what was she doing?

On a different level, cool and professional, his heart racing, he fell into the protocol he practiced every year. Lance Rudd dropped to his knees beside Karen. He straightened her body on the floor. Check the Airway went the protocol; check the Breathing; check the Circulation; simple as A-B-C.

Her jaw was limp; he lifted it forward and opened her airway. He bent down, his face near her mouth, watching her chest. She made no respiratory movement, and he felt no breath against his ear. He pressed his fingers along her neck, and felt a pulse, strong and steady in her carotid artery. No cardiac arrest, not for this Viking queen.

He tilted her head back and lifted her jaw again. He placed his left hand over her beautiful eyes and compressed her nostrils between his thumb and forefinger. He bent down to her lovely mouth— oh mockery!—this wasn't what he wanted at all—and placed his mouth over hers. Was it a kiss of death, or of life? He exhaled strongly, forcing his own air into her lungs. He watched her chest move, rise easily to his breath, fall with his release. The curve of her breast taunted him, like a broken dream. He counted off the seconds in the prescribed routine to make twelve breaths per minute.

Marnie Bates rushed up beside him, her eyes at shock to see a white uniform in the role of victim. She translated smoothly into action. Within moments Lance heard the loudspeaker summoning "Dr. Blue to Intensive Care Unit." Five urgent repetitions.

An eternity passed for Lance in a nightmare he could not escape. His hands trembled. Karen made no sound, no movement. Her pupils dilated. But her heart beat on, and Lance supplied the precious breath. Marnie Bates returned and relieved Lance; she was as practiced as he in rescue breathing. And Lance heard the crash cart come rumbling around the corner.

Action restored his self-control. He took charge of the cart as a crowd of helpers began to assemble. He seized a laryngoscope, tore it from its wrapper, and knelt again at Karen's head. The long blade slid into her mouth, over the back of her tongue. He lifted its tip and opened her larynx to his view. Somebody held out an airway tube and he thrust it down her trachea. In a moment he had inflated its balloon cuff, connected the tube to a tank of oxygen and an Ambu bag. Now he had total control of her breathing.

A nurse anesthetist took over the rhythmic squeezing of the bag, and Lance stepped back. He was numb; he could only watch. The emergency team, its members running in from all directions at the code call, worked as one mind. Skilled and gentle hands lifted Karen's flaccid body to a litter. The procession moved off into ICU with Harvey Kanju marching alongside, shocked and solemn, already beginning his sober inventory: find a diagnosis which might allow someone, somehow, to bring Karen back.

Lance Rudd stood in the corridor, alone. He shook. He knotted his fingers together to stop their trembling. He glanced up the hall in one direction and stared down the other. In those corridors he knew so well he was lost, adrift in cold black disaster. The emergency cart stood canted and abandoned against the wall. Discarded wrappers and a spare endotracheal tube littered the floor. A flag of red lay among them. It was Karen's rose. Someone's foot had crushed it. The hot sweet memory of his desire for her echoed and welled up in his heart, and smashed against reality, for Lance Rudd knew that Karen Sondergaard was dead.

*   *   *

The old manse in Prairie Falls, where Karen Sondergaard grew up, was a tiny box of faded shingles. Above its narrow chimney of bare concrete blocks a spindly plume of gray smoke lost itself in the bare branches overhead. In the yard a stack of stove wood squared up at one end against the trunk of an elm tree, and dwindled toward the house in a long scatter of fractured bark and trampled snow. The handle of a splitting axe canted off from an unsplit log.

After Pastor died, Karen's mother had built a double door over her back step. It was just a snout made of stray boards, tarpaper and plastic, but its air-lock helped to keep the cold out when she carried in the wood. For the widow Sondergaard, Good Friday was no more sombre a day than any other.

Her back turned close to the stove, she sat at a thin-legged kitchen table and picked at a hard-boiled egg. She frowned in concentration, carefully keeping any bits of shell out of her potato salad. Logs in the stove burned down, settled, and thumped. Snow-melt from her heavy shoes trickled across the tilted floor and drained away under the door.

Thirty-nine years ago she had moved to this house, the bride of Pastor Haakon Sondergaard, who had accepted in that year both his new wife and his first call. The couple saw few challenges to their tenets. They settled down in austerity to the regularity of seasons through nineteen years, four children, and his final cancer. She lived on, unmindful of flies and ice, while her babies grew up and went their ways. She never considered whether she might be discontent.

She raised her eyes to the photos of her children, snapshots she had saved out of their letters and pasted on the wall. Erik in County Extension over to Duluth. Marlene and Lucia, married, satisfactorily as far as she knew, raising their little ones so far away—one in Arizona, one in California. They had to go and marry boys who went to the big State University, and now just see where their jobs took them. And finally Karen. Going to be an old maid, it looks like. A good girl, too; loves her nursing so.

She finished her meager lunch and went outside to throw egg shells to the chickens. When she climbed back into the kitchen, her telephone was ringing.

"Hullo?"

"Is this Mrs. Sondergaard?"

"It iss."

"Mrs. Sondergaard, my name is Marnie Bates. I'm a nurse at University Hospital, where Karen works."

"Ya."

"Mrs. Sondergaard, I'm sorry to tell you that Karen is sick. Something has happened to her, she collapsed, and we have her here in the Intensive Care Unit."

"I see."

The voice was gentle and patient.

"Do you understand what I said? Will you want to come to the hospital?"

She understood, all right. Life was about to deliver another disaster. Fear and panic churned inside her, but she pushed them down. She folded her feelings like wings, leaving no flutter outside. Like the tiny red blooms of lichen in the clefts and cracks of timeless granite, her emotions were not for display. She would deal with her feelings as she had always dealt with them: she would move impassively to do whatever it was that she must do.

"Mrs. Sondergaard, are you there?"

Of course she would go. There was nothing to keep her here. She could catch the bus to Minneapolis at two o'clock. She didn't know about connections, but they would be what they would be. If she could not catch a bus tonight, she would sleep in the depot.

"Mrs. Sondergaard?"

"Ya, I will come."

*   *   *

Father Kevin O'Leary rubbed his gimpy knee and gazed at the still shape of Karen Sondergaard, her lean body inert beneath a smooth white sheet. Her face was obscured by hoses and straps. Only her left arm was exposed, its pale skin pierced by a couple of needles, each connected to its tubing. He stood by the bed, chest high to his small form, and watched clear fluids drip relentlessly into small chambers under the two bottles that hung from a steel pole.

A twisting knot of protest rose in his throat, a knot he couldn't swallow down. Youth should never lie so still. On Holy Saturday morning, the darkest morning of the church's year, his mood matched the calendar.

Only her chest moved, heaving in passive rhythm to the quiet soughing of the ventilator.

The straps and hoses twisted Karen's nose and lips, reducing her face to a utility of connections. Her endotracheal tube sticking out of one nostril fitted itself by a Y-shaped connector to corrugated hoses that coiled like snakes across her pillow to hook up to a massive box beside her bed. Bellows and pumps, he supposed; gauges, valves, and switches. He understood the lines for oxygen and electricity that hung down from other connections overhead. But he didn't know what the red eyes meant. Only that electronic monitors watched over all and never looked away.

It all seemed so orderly, so completely under control. Even if all was lost.

He would not try to predict which way Karen would leave the ICU. Most patients made it "up to the floor." But it looked as if Karen would go the other way, down to the morgue. Whatever happened now, for her— for us all—it would eventually be the same anyway. On Holy Saturday, the words of Ash Wednesday echoed in his brain: "Remember, Man, that thou art dust…"

Young Nurse Bates came along with a syringe. He watched her squirt medication into one of the intravenous tubes and tap the drip chamber to rupture some bubbles. She waited until the fluid began to flow again in a sequence of orderly droplets, and then she pranced away.

Karen Sondergaard wasn't a prancer, he remembered. She had been graceful, but always very reserved with him. His collar, maybe. But he had seen her at work, her gentle hands converting an injection site into a badge of love. He knew ministry when he saw it.

He found a tiny wrinkle in Karen's sheet and tugged at it. He ached to bring the sacrament of healing to this child of God. He wanted to make its power bind her up and ease her passage, whichever way it was to be. Perhaps, like baptism, the sacrament could operate through desire, without the rite. Anyway, he figured, God didn't need it in order to do His will.

He fingered his rosary and lost himself in his supplication to Mary, "…pray for us sinners now and at the hour of our death, amen."

When he opened his eyes he was startled by the figure of a woman standing directly across from him. Her impassive gray eyes stared at him, at his Irish face, his Roman collar. They flicked down to his magic beads, trailing from his hand.

Her own hands were folded together at the waist, her elbows pinching a gray sweater-jacket against her narrow body. She was severely unadorned; only a gold band like a wire on one finger, and a face that wore its winters in craggy lines like battle scars.

Father O'Leary introduced himself. He guessed that this was Karen's mother?

"Ya."

Silence.

"She is a lovely girl, and a fine nurse. I'm sure you are proud of her."

"Ya, I vass."

Silence.

Father O'Leary tucked his rosary away quietly into his coat pocket. He shuffled his feet and his thoughts. How could he help?

"If you would be wanting me to do so, Mrs. Sondergaard, I could be in touch with Pastor Carlson. He comes here in case of need. Would that be helpful to you?"

Her face did not change. "Missouri," she said through closed lips.

"I beg your pardon?"

He could not remember when he had felt embarrassed in a conversation. Helpless, yes, God knew. But not flustered. What went on inside this granite lady?

"No, thank you."

Silence.

Well, she didn't need him! Rebuffed, he turned to leave. Her right hand descended to rest on Karen's knee. Her voice sounded strained.

"Mister?…uh, Father?"

He realized suddenly that she was more strange here than he. This was his hospital, after all, not hers; her daughter, not his. His stiff neck softened. He faced her from the foot of the bed, almost on her side.

"What can I offer you, Mrs. Sondergaard?"

"You don't like cremation."

Her bald statement was a question, her voice tilting up at the end. Father O'Leary fell back from it. He looked quickly at Karen, as if to shut her ears. He looked at the gray eyes boring into him. He groped for words.

"I don't prefer it, Mrs. Sondergaard, for a number of reasons. My church wishes to remind us all that we are to be rejoined, body and soul, when the kingdom comes. Why would you be asking me that?"

"If a person shouldn't cremate a body, a person shouldn't cut it all up either."

Again the flat statement, just enough rising tone to suggest she was asking, testing. He rested his hands on the bed, looked down at the blue veins under his papery skin. Why couldn't he know what to say? He never felt adequate as an instrument of the Holy Spirit. Surely no one had discussed autopsy with this woman, not with all Karen's machinery hooked up and running.

Then, suddenly, he knew the truth. Dr. Kanju must have been at her, anticipating a declaration of death. It was this newfangled donation of organs that she had on her mind. Now he understood her direction.

"It all depends on the reason, Mrs. Sondergaard. A good purpose may make it a proper thing, cutting it up or cremation or whatever. We are obliged to treat the body with respect, for it is the harbor of the human soul. But nothing we can do can make a problem for God. Whenever He wants to be putting the body and soul back together again, it's together they'll be!"

"Ya, maybe."

She frowned at her hard hands, resting on Karen's still form. Her lips formed a soundless word, then lost it and fell back in repose. Finally her thought struggled to speech. But her voice was muffled; her eyes were turned away.

"Who gets the heart, do you guess, in Heaven, if two people want it?"

Father O'Leary exhaled a long, slow breath. He was still groping.

"Well, now, that is a question, isn't it? And I'm a poor one to be trying its answer. But I have to be thinking that God made the rules, and He made us. So when he wants to restore bodies and souls, He'll be having all the parts He needs, whatever we might have done with them down here."

He watched her; he hoped to see some sign that he had helped. She stood rigid, her jaw set in a severe line. Her hands remained glued to Karen's knee.

Keep trying, O'Leary, he thought. Guide me, Holy Spirit, to the right words.

How about just saying it plain, straight out?

He moved a step closer and waited for her gray eyes to find his face. His snowy eyebrows knitted together; he gathered her into his heart.

"There are two things I want to tell you. Simple things. I hope they will help. The first is that God wants us to be raised up after death. And He sees to it—we don't. Your church says that, and so does mine. And that means you, and me. And Karen."

He dropped his right hand gently to rest on Karen's shin, a sympathetic inch from her mother's fingers.

"The other thing is that every major religious group in our country, even the Jehovah's Witness, has approved the idea of donating organs and tissues after death. No responsible opinion is opposed to the idea. Not one."

He had shot his arrows now. He knew nothing more to do. He shuffled his feet, worked his stiff knee in preparation for moving on.

"I'll be here again, Mrs. Sondergaard. I am praying for Karen. And I will for you, too, if you like?"

Her motherly hands rested still on Karen's knee. But her shoulders straightened as she turned to face the priest. Her eyes were moist; her lip trembled. Her voice was a hoarse whisper: "Ya, you bet."

*   *   *

Bitter. The coffee tasted as old as yesterday's, and bitter. Lance Rudd felt old and, since yesterday, bitter. He paced the doctors' lounge, cup in hand, but his tense steps gave him no release. There was no comfort in the leather chairs, and the TV set batting out the racket sounds of some junior tennis tournament down among the palm trees worked in vain: neither sight nor sound penetrated his sense. His mind resided down the hall, in ICU, hovering by the cold machines and the helpless body of Karen Sondergaard.

He dumped his coffee into the sink and crushed the styrofoam cup viciously in his hand. He balled it tight and slammed it at a receptacle. He missed. He didn't care.

Every quivering fiber drew him toward Karen's bedside. In the whole world only two places existed—there with her, and here in the bitter limbo where he was, wherever he was.

For he could not go to her. He was a transplant surgeon, and he was forbidden.

If he visited Karen, he would find her mother grieving and bewildered at the bedside. To her he would look no different from his colleagues attending Karen in all the welter of their sophisticated machinery. What would she believe if he next turned out to be wanting, not Karen, but Karen's heart, and eyes, and organs. Had he done less than he could for her daughter? When might he have begun to want her organs more than her life?

He understood the code; it was right. But he had never expected to desire what it forbade; he never dreamed that obedience to it would grind him to pieces.

Lance was acquainted with grief. He had fought his way through it for his father, for his mother, for his own diabetes. Grief was bad enough; suspicion or mistrust atop the grief would be unbearable.

He understood the code. But he wanted desperately to smash it.

"Lance, you look terrible. What can I do?"

Lance turned to the quiet voice of Dana Garrison. Her sleek dark head was bent over the coffee pot; her white coat stretched smoothly over her hips.

"Don't drink the coffee, Dana, it tastes like buffalo piss."

Her giggle died when she saw his face. She put the cup down and hurried to him.

"Lance, my friend, I'm sorry. Something is really wrong."

"It's Karen, Dana, haven't you heard?"

"Of course I have. She's my dear friend, and I feel dreadful. Harvey says she ruptured a cerebral aneurysm. And just two weeks ago we were all...."

Her voice dwindled away. Lance picked up her thought...

"Two thousand years is more like it. You took me to that party, and your friend Karen shot me right out of the saddle."

Dana's eyes grew wide.

"You don't mean...I mean...the immune and icy Dr. Rudd?...did you...?"

"Dana, I want to say this out loud to you, just once, so I can get it off my chest. And then we can forget about it. At least, you can."

"I'm listening, friend, and it's in confidence."

They looked about the lounge; they were alone. Lance spoke quietly.

"I just lost it over that girl. Maybe it was crazy to happen so fast; but I fell in love with her. Not fell; it was more like a crash. I've chased her as hard as I know how. And now this…catastrophe."

Dana's face was grave, her voice far away.

"So it can happen that way, all at once?"

She rested her hand on his arm. "It's a terrible up and down for you."

Lance struggled to control himself.

"Damn it, Dana, I want to be there with her. It isn't natural, to stay away like this. I've got to see her."

Dana's voice hardened. "You can't. Neither of us can. If it should come to organ donation…"

His dam broke at last.

"To hell with the organs. I'm going to see Karen. I've got to see what's happening to her."

His tension released in a drive for action. He pushed past her, his long strides unpent, his mind in neutral. But somehow Dana beat him to the door. She planted her slight body squarely in his way, and put the flat of her hand against the middle of his chest. He stopped as if he had run into a tree.

"Lance, you can't go. Listen to me. Give it up. Grieve. Hurt. Cry, Lance; but don't go!"

He towered over her as if he wanted to run her down. Then slowly he fell back against the arm of a chair; his long frame sagged.

"It's hard, Dana."

"Sure it's hard. Let's say how hard it is. Karen is probably dead; we're just waiting for the declaration. Tonight, maybe. Then it is over for Karen. But it is just beginning for Martin Stern, for a heart patient somewhere, for a couple of kidney patients. It is just beginning for you, Lance, you are the liver guy, the only one."

She pressed her hands on his shoulders and looked straight into his eyes.

"Let's say it all, all the hardest stuff. You are the one who has to harvest."

"I just want to see her, while she's still Karen."

His voice was like an echo; no fight remained. Dana's was tender, like a mother's croon.

"If you go in there, or if I do, Karen's mother wouldn't see a lover or a friend. She would see a transplant team drumming up business. She'd see vultures sitting in a tree."

Lance nodded, beaten. He slid back crosswise in the leather chair, his knees hooked across the arm. He wondered what there was in life, what there could ever be, that his career would not demand in sacrifice. There could be nothing harder than today.

He crossed the line; he made the gift. But some of his light went out, as if part of him had died.

*   *   *

"Do you remember Slim Gotch from Hopkins, Lotte?"

Talking to her was a charade, but Brovek clung to it. Gotch was one of the old names out of their training years, and sometimes, if he went back far enough into history, he could reach some remnant of her memory.

Lotte smiled in triumph.

"He wore bow ties and drove a convertible."

She pronounced it 'dwove.' His heart quickened. He watched her hands working the long needles, the yellow yarn.

In the fireplace the logs had burned down to thin glowing bones. He sat collapsed into the soft cushions of his leather chair.

"He's head of his department now," he said. "He's just been appointed to the American Board of Surgery. Do you remember the last time we saw him?"

"Who's that, Sandor?"

He sighed. He tapped the surgical journal that lay open on his lap, his finger thumping the glossy pages. He knew all the names listed there, announcements of new appointments, prestigious awards. They were men his own age, department heads like himself. But theirs were major departments—more patients, more research, more clout. He yearned for that kind of achievement.

His own department just was not vehicle enough. He didn't swing a big enough bat to earn the kind of national eminence that he breathed for. It was Slim Gotch who had told him so.

"You were considered for nomination, Sandy," he said. It was in San Francisco last March. The two met by chance with the happy handshakes they all repeated endlessly at their national meetings. Later they happened to occupy adjoining stools in the hotel coffee shop. Brovek tasted his bitterness afresh.

"I stood up for you," Slim had said. "But your department is pretty small, you know. It's too bad you can't put out some bigger numbers, maybe a few more papers. Your record is certainly good enough."

Good enough, but not big enough. That is what hurt.

He rested his head against the soft chair back and closed his eyes. He would have bigger numbers all right, in the new hospital. "It's my pleasure to introduce the moderator of our symposium, Dr. Sandor Brovek." He saw himself rising to the applause of his peers, maybe at the College, or the Society of University Surgeons.

He'd have another dozen residents in the program, maybe fifteen. Two or three would be assigned full time to the dog lab, another one to biochem. They would present their research papers at the Surgical Forums, Chicago, Atlantic City, wherever, and he'd sit and smile. Later he might overhear someone talking to Slim Gotch: "We keep hearing about Brovek's work; isn't he a friend of yours?" And Slim would gossip into the other's ear: "Not many people know about this, but I can tell you he did a number on Grover Iverson." "Got a check rein on him in the nick of time, is what I hear," the first one would whisper behind his hand.

Against his closed lids his wide-ranging transplant program rose up like the body of a pyramid, storeys high, full of activity, full of people. Grover

Iverson was tucked off over there in one well-behaved corner. At the top of the pyramid, his own academic position shone like a beacon.

Abruptly against his lids the structure twisted. He groaned aloud, his stomach churning, as the pyramid turned upside down, and came to balance on its pointy end, on Sandor Brovek, balanced on the outstretched palm of Martin Stern.

His eyes snapped open. He reached over and tossed a stick of birch into the fire.

"Where will you put your chips?" Potts had demanded.

And Brovek himself had said: "Which one of us must die?"

In his thoughts, worrying the problem every day like a dog with a rag doll, he had already murdered Stern a dozen times. But there was no donor then; it was all just smoke.

Not today.

Now he waited for the phone to ring—for his chips to be called in. A prime donor lay in his own hospital, shy only the formal declaration. And in a nearby ward lay an innocent Martin Stern, depending on Brovek's decision.

Lotte sat knitting, apparently content. The same Afghan had occupied her for weeks. She pulled off a new length of yellow yarn to feed her needles. The ball at her feet twitched on the dark Oriental, but against the nap of the rug the soft yarn couldn't roll away.

Again Brovek scanned the magazine lying open in his lap, the columns of names, appointments, honors, all the big guns making the grade. How could anyone expect him to vote for Martin Stern? Who was there to look out for Sandor Brovek, who in the whole wide world, except himself?

                    *   *   *

Fresh from a neat nephrectomy and a change into street clothes, Grover Iverson rounded the corner into Old U on the way to his office. Far down the corridor, in silhouette against the window, a man paced up and down.

Grover slowed. The set of the man's heavy shoulders and a sharp unease in his steps promised trouble.

Grover's fingers combed his mustache. He licked the bristly hairs, hoping the trouble was for someone else. He slid along on the soles of his loafers and almost slipped through his office door when the man spun around and called his name.

"Doctuh Iverson! I've been waitin' for you!"

Who the devil?

"I'm sorry. Do we have an appointment?"

Iverson groped in his memory. The man came near; he was expensively dressed—a new donor perhaps? Then the drawled words touched his memory file. Iverson flashed all his front teeth.

"Why, Mr. Buttner, what a surprise. Tell me how Deborah is getting along."

"Deborah is why I am here."

Buttner did not smile.

"I see. Well, let's step into my office and see if my secretary…"

"No." Buttner cut him off. "We are going into your private office and talk. Now."

Urgency or impatience Iverson was used to. Arrogance was something new, and it spelled trouble all right.

Three people sat in narrow chairs around his waiting room. His secretary pointed artificial eye lashes at her boss.

"Anyone inside, Beatrice?"

"No, sir, we're all just waiting for you."

He led Buttner into his carpeted inner sanctum and pointed him to a wooden chair of modern Scandinavian design. He lowered himself nervously into his own leather swivel chair in the shelter of his desk. He pinched up the trouser creases over his knees, and flicked his eyes at his adversary.

"Well, sir, I'm listening."

Forearms along the arm rests, hands dangling at the wrists, Buttner filled the chair with an air of confidence.

"You remember Deborah?"

"I do."

"She is home in Atlanta, fighting rejection of her graft. She is back on dialysis."

"I'm sorry." He wanted to say more, but prudence fenced him in. The initiative lay with Buttner.

"Deborah will not stay on dialysis. She wants to quit. She needs another kidney."

"That happens sometimes. It's still possible to be successful."

Buttner snapped his words. "They's two kinds of possible, Doctuh. One is in your realm, science—tissue matches and all that. The other is in the realm of chance—whether a suitable kidney goes to Deborah or some-wheres else."

Grover tried to read the signs. This was material they had covered already, before Deborah's first graft, and before Buttner's donation to the Iverson Foundation. But Buttner wasn't coming on as a supplicant; he was in the saddle. Iverson said nothing.

Buttner looked out of slitted lids, cold and still, as if waiting for Iverson to make a move. Iverson froze.

Finally Buttner spoke. "Tomorrow I fly to Riyadh. I'll be in the Middle East for several weeks. I can't ride shotgun for Deborah this time."

Iverson breathed deeper. This sounded like safe territory. He decided to test it.

"If Deborah returns to our care, we will do all we can for her."

Those narrow eyes fixed on him like a snake. "You will give her a kidney," he said.

"Last time you made a generous donation to my research foundation...."

"Not this time."

"You understand there is always a shortage of donor organs?"

"I do. But you will find a kidney for Deborah."

There was no supplication in the drawled words. The flat monotone was a decree. Or an ultimatum. Grover drew a line for defense.

"If it is possible, Mr. Buttner. There is always that 'if'."

Buttner drew a deep breath, hands clenched. The cold eyes bored in.

"I don't think you have the whole picture, Iverson." He rocked forward, the snake striking. "I have your balls in a choke chain; don't make me jerk on it."

Iverson fell back in his chair. His cremaster muscles crawled. He had read trouble in this man, and he was getting it in spades.

"I've got a plane waitin' and I'm gone. Deborah needs another kidney, and soon, and you are goin' to get it for her. You will put it in and you will get her well. There will be no rejection this time. You got all that?"

Iverson rubbed wet palms against his pant legs. He fought to keep his voice level.

"No one can prevent rejection in every case."

"I'm talkin' one case, Doctuh." He grinned wickedly. "One case, one choke chain."

Was this a bluff? Behind his hammering pulse Iverson felt a surge of anger. This guy wasn't Mafia standing there, not here in the Upper Midwest. What the hell was he talking about; what choke chain?

His anger made him rash. "Look, Buttner, unless you are breaking knee caps or something, you can't harm me. You're an anxious father with a sick daughter, and I'll do the best I can for her. Now go catch your airplane."

He opened a folder on his desk, but the characters danced and blurred before his eyes. Buttner rolled his bulk backwards, making the frail Scandinavian chair squeak. His voice was like honey.

"Why, Doctuh, you extorted money from me, don't you remember? You went and squeezed a desperate father for fifty grand before you'd help his little girl."

Iverson winced. "You made the proposal, Mr. Buttner. That gift was your own idea."

"And you accepted it. It's your dirty little secret, and any time I want I can pull up on your chain and tote you squealin' all the way around the yard."

Iverson scraped at his mustache. He had always figured this was the way his game would end. He reached for his last defense.

"Tote away. You'd be telling the whole world how you yourself cheated the system. That's not likely."

Buttner chuckled maliciously. "But they's one difference between us—I don't give a shit."

His chair thumped down on the carpet. "But the IRS will get mighty curious about that Foundation of yours. And you won't be professor any more. If that day comes, you'll be gone, Bubba, wiped."

It was true. Iverson crumpled.

"If we can get Deborah well, you won't—do this?" He couldn't repeat the imagery.

"Now you've got the picture, Doctuh. And don't forget the choke chain. I've got a very long reach."

At the door he turned back, one hand on the knob, one foot cocked up crosswise, a pose right out of Alfred Hitchcock.

"By the way, Doctuh. Do your colleagues sell organs too, or do you go solo?"

Iverson flared. "What the hell do you care?"

Buttner smiled. "I just wondered. If I have to jerk the chain, will you dangle out there all by yourself, or does the whole hospital come tumblin' down?"

Still grinning at Iverson, he gave the door knob a vicious twist. The door banged open and he strode out through an office full of startled faces.

"Thank you, Beatrice," he said.

*   *   *

Wilma Gale, R.N., piloted her five-year-old Subaru up to the gate-arm of the University Hospital parking lot. She lowered her window to insert her pass card, and felt the late morning sun on her arm, a warming spell that promised the arrival of spring. She inhaled the smells of moist earth, of frost coming out of the ground after five long months of ice. From somewhere nearby came the soft yodel of a mourning dove.

She let her round young body settle into the bucket seat. In her mirror she saw the smooth peach curves of her cheeks; only her smile-lines remained. Wilma believed in beautiful moments, and she accepted this one gratefully. It would balance the somber interview that lay ahead.

She spied an open slot and slipped the Subaru neatly into it. She dropped her keys and her parking card into her leather shoulder bag.

Interviews like this one always popped up on short notice, to pull her away from her electronic office into the dark tunnels of bereavement. She was here to solicit human organs, and if she ever felt ghoulish about her quest, she needed only to think of the computerized files back in her office: seventeen transplant centers clamoring for beating-heart cadaver organs; hundreds of human souls clinging to life with failing vital systems, praying for their names to be called. Until they lost their grasp and dropped out of her file. Wilma Gale was Director of ROPO, the Regional Organ Procurement Organization.

She never knew what she would come up against. Grief, inevitably. Often disbelief. Maybe anger. Survivors flashed their feelings from any-where in the whole human spectrum. She tried to start with the next of kin as they were centered in their own feelings, and then lead them to her goal. She thought of her work as urgent personal counseling in time of crisis. Not as solicitation.

She wore civilian clothes, a simple skirt of royal blue, a yellow blouse, and a matching blue bow at her throat. Neat, but informal. She never wore black nor any shade of red.

She checked the name she had written on her note pad. Her goal today was to win the donation of organs and tissues of the deceased—one Karen Sondergaard. Someone's signed consent would be her trophy for the day.

But Wilma Gale never forgot that she was first a nurse, a health professional. She cared equally about the next of kin—she read again—Astry
Sondergaard, mother. She wanted that signed consent to be freely given,
because that bereaved mother would forever live with its memory. In
Wilma's heart, her highest trophy was a double: that Astry Sondergaard
give life through her donation of Karen's organs, and also find, in the gift,
a healing for her own grief.

She walked across the asphalt lot, drawing long breaths of spring fragrance, and climbed the staff entrance into Old U.

She loved her job, at least the peak times when she made it all happen.
But she wondered about the dream she had had, twice in the past month.
She guarded a refrigerator full of harvested kidneys, each one washed clean
and tied up in a neat plastic bag. But hairy little imps in black clothing
kept sneaking behind her back to snatch kidneys and pitch them through
her office window into a dumpster down below. She lunged this way and
pushed that way and tried to drive them off, but they kept coming back,
and she woke up crying. She hoped she wasn't burning out.

She strode softly into the great cavern of ICU. She always expected
some kind of smell, and noticed the lack of it. She scouted down the
open-ended stalls, their still mounds of human flesh hidden under white
sheets, until she came to Karen's bed. The tangle of respiratory hoses
crawled from her face, and her ventilator clicked and groaned.

An old woman stood by the bedside, her still hands on Karen's knee.
Creases shadowed her leathery face, and her cheeks were sunken.

"Mrs. Sondergaard? I am Wilma Gale. I believe Dr. Kanju told you
about me. May we have a visit?"

The gray eyes were hooded, dull, as they rested on Wilma. The lips didn't
move. Wilma tried again.

"I'm sure you are tired, Mrs. Sondergaard. Will you come with me to
my office? We can sit quietly there, and I'll get you some coffee."

She waited for a response. In vain. She must engage this woman; maybe
talking was not to be the way.

"We will stay here." The voice was flat, the words final.

She was going to be a tough one, Wilma decided.

"Do you understand why I am here? Did Dr. Kanju tell you?"

"Ya."

"I am so sorry about all this. The people who knew your daughter were very fond of her. She was a good nurse."

She used the past tense purposely, and she watched for any response. She saw none.

"Do you expect any of your other children to come here to the hospital?"

"No. They are all too far away except Erik. He is only over to Duluth but his baby is sick, little Otto."

"Well, I guess you have talked to them on the telephone?"

"Ya."

"Do you understand what is happening to Karen?"

Wilma looked at the long shape under the sheets, moving passively to the action of the respirator. How could that flaccid body ever have come from that frigid woman across the bed? ever have nursed the breasts of that hollow chest? She looked up again to find the gray eyes waiting.

Astry Sondergaard said, "She is dead."

Flat again. Unemotional. Wilma was not prepared for such stoic realism. This person was going to be difficult, she thought for the second time. But her opening was plain and she pursued it.

"You are probably right. But the doctors have to be absolutely sure there is no chance at all for her to recover, before they will declare that she is dead."

"I know."

Her terse replies gave Wilma little to build with. She labored ahead.

"Modern medicine can do wonderful things for people. It can't restore our brain, of course; that's why Karen may be dead. But it can restore other organs for people, by transplanting good ones from people who die. People like Karen. Have you heard about organ transplants?"

"Of course. Karen was starting to teach about it."

"Yes, I know she was. So she must have thought well of transplant surgery. Did she ever talk to you about her own feelings on this, on giving organs after death?"

"She didn't know she was going to die."

"That's always the way, isn't it? We never expect the bad things."

Silence.

Wilma felt like a clumsy sailor who had spilled scant wind from a slack sail. Well, she would haul in the main sheet and try again.

"Mrs. Sondergaard, how do you yourself feel about organ donation? Karen's organs could mean new life to other people."

"No, I can't."

Wilma's heart sank. If she were to design the ideal case for organ harvest, Karen would be the pattern. Perfect in every way. But only with consent, freely given. She figured Astry Sondergaard was way ahead of her in this conversation, knew already that she would say No. Bad try, Wilma, somewhere you missed.

She said, "If that is your decision we will respect it. This is a very difficult time for you."

"I can't afford it."

Suddenly Wilma Gale began to understand this spartan woman and her hoarded words. Triviality just wasn't there for her. Her mind sat at the root of a question and worked only with what mattered. Everything else passed by unattended. The abundance of Wilma's own generosity welled up and flooded her heart with new respect for this hard-bitten survivor.

And her heart leapt with new hope as well. She heard the open door. She spoke tenderly, as to a bewildered child,

"Mrs. Sondergaard, whatever you decide about organ donation, yes or no, your expenses stop when Karen is dead. There is great expense for the surgical procedures that reclaim her organs. But you don't have to pay for any of it."

The silence this time was different. Astry Sondergaard rose up straight. She looked, as if for the first time, at the body of her daughter, at the beautiful face hidden and distorted behind its tubes, at the long limbs lying so limp. One golden tress had escaped from the tangle of attachments and lay in a curl by Karen's shoulder.

The old woman nodded her head slowly; two lonely tears lay in the corners of her eyes. She looked again at Wilma Gale.

"I didn't know that."

"Does it make a difference to you?"

"Ya. All the difference."

"Would you like to give us permission to save Karen's organs for other people?"

"Ya. She would like that."

The tears were gone; they had never reached her cheek.

"What about her brother and sisters?"

"Do they have to know?"

"Yes."

Silence. This time Wilma Gale relaxed. This time she rejoiced. She was going to win both trophies.

"Let me call them for you, Mrs. Sondergaard. We can go to my office, and I'll arrange a conference call. You can talk to all of them at the same time. You want to be sure they agree too, don't you think?"

"Ya, I suppose."

Wilma waited patiently now. She watched for any sign of a torrent beneath the ice. Karen's mother stood motionless beside the bed. Her leathery hands rested on the white sheet, her fingers open on Karen's knee. She gazed for long moments at Karen's face.

At last the old woman nodded once and stepped back. She folded her hands together at the waist, her elbows pinched close to her side. She looked directly into Wilma Gale's eyes, and her words came flat, without inflection.

"I wonder do you still have coffee in your office?"

* * *

Sandor Brovek's call was picked up after one ring, just as he would expect of Miss O'Hoolihan, even at home on a Saturday noon. He liked her dispatch. He sat perched on his leather swivel chair as if it were a starting gate, and pushed the papers aside to clear a spot on his desk.

"Mizzoh? Dr. Brovek here. I know it's Saturday…What's that?…Oh, sure, Happy Easter to you too, Mizzoh. But I'm probably going to spoil it for you. Look, we've got a big deal coming up today, a full box of new organs, and we'll need every bit of operating room capacity. I'd like to meet you there, and set up our plans. Can you come?…. Two o'clock is fine. I appreciate it."

He touched more buttons on his telephone, and the piping tones conjured up a new connection. He drummed his fingers in a rapid tattoo. He counted three rings, then four. Hospital phones were always slow. He remembered his college football games, waiting for kick-off, his body taut and ready.

"Operator? This is Dr. Brovek. I want you to deliver a message for me. Tell Dr. Lance Rudd to meet me in surgery at two o'clock…. No, I don't know if he's in or out or where. See if you can't find him somewhere, will you?…. Good, I'll count on that. Oh! Operator, make that a double. Same thing to Dr. Garrison…. No, I can't hang on while you page her; there's somebody ringing my doorbell. Just tell them both, okay?"

He settled the phone smoothly into its cradle and accelerated out of his chair. Lotte was standing in the front hall, her fingers knotted in front of her mouth. He slipped past her as gently as he could, while the bell rang again and he opened the door.

"Come in, Marnie. I'm sorry you had to wait. I was on the phone."

Marnie Bates looked smashing in street clothes. She stepped into the entryway, placed her soft hand in Brovek's paw, and dazzled him with a smile. Her radiance transfigured the dark hall The closed house stirred with her fresh scent and sap of spring. Brovek's blood rose. With Marnie here, maybe he wouldn't want to leave!

Hell, he thought wryly, if he didn't have to leave, she wouldn't be here.

Marnie's fragrance lingered in his nostrils as he turned to his troubled wife.

"Lotte, this is your friend Marnie Bates. She is going to stay with you while I am at the hospital."

Lotte's fingers loosed themselves and dropped from her mouth. Her slender shoulders uncringed, and she stood tall and composed. She extended a graceful hand to her friend, and smiled her patrician welcome.

Brovek took Marnie's overnight bag like a football under his arm and carried it ten yards into the guest room. He was intensely aware of her presence. Her light step beside him, her full bosom, the tiny waist she had cinched with a golden cord. He inhaled her fragrance and shuddered. He forced his mind to its business.

He showed her the facilities, and towels. He held her elbow lightly while he spoke softly to her large eyes, going down his check list.

"Marnie, I'm grateful for your coming on such short notice. I was desperate for a companion for Mrs. Brovek. Now, please call her Lotte; she likes that. You will find some steaks in the fridge, and whatever. Make yourself comfortable. If you have a good time, Lotte will."

"I'm sure we'll get along fine, Dr. B." She breathed her words; her lips pursed around the letter B like a caress.

"Lotte likes to knit and listen to music after dinner. But you'll have to start her off to bed around eleven. She may not think of it by herself."

Brovek reminded himself to make a proper farewell to Lotte. He reassured her with a kiss and the simplest possible message: "I'll be back, Lotte." He hoped the sentiment would linger even after the knowledge was gone.

Marnie followed him into the garage.

"You know where I'll be," he said. "God knows how long, though. You can call me if you have to."

"Oh, we'll do okay, Dr. B. She's a pretty lady."

"Yes, she is, my dear." Her lips were parted, and her eyes bright. He tumbled again to her fire. He took her hand. "And so are you. I wish I could stay right here."

Her hand rested in his. That elusive scent rose from her hair, and he wanted to put his face into it, breathe into her ear. His left hand crept around her and rested on the curve of her buttock.

She giggled. "Why, Dr. Brovek!" She looked directly into his eyes. "Maybe you'll ask me over some other time. I love listening to music."

Brovek dropped his hand. What he saw dancing in her eyes was nothing but mischief. His touch of lechery suddenly tasted of shame, and he did not like the flavor. He climbed into his car.

"I'll take good care of Mrs. Brovek," Marnie called through his window, as the garage door was rolling up. "I like to make people happy."

He jerked the black Lincoln into gear and backed to the street. He took his turn in the flow of traffic, and chafed at its pace.

He had made a mistake: one brief slip against his code, and against Lotte. Oh, she didn't know it, and never would. But he knew. He couldn't remember ever feeling this kind of pain before, this rotten feeling in his heart that he supposed was remorse.

Or fear. What kind of muck had he opened himself to? what gossip over hospital coffee cups? And what about Lotte, placed for uncountable hours in this woman's care?

"Take it easy, Brovek." He found himself climbing up the back of a Chevy ahead. He lifted his foot and coasted down until he could no longer read the Chevy's license number. He snapped his seat belt across his lap—he had forgotten that too. One wrong choice, he thought: one slip, and look at the troubles gather round. How long could good luck last?

God in heaven, he always needed good luck. His career was built on hard work, but good luck was the leaven in the dough. And he would need all the good luck he could get to smile on him today. A heart, two kidneys, a liver. The possibilities began to work in him. How would he assign his people? would they measure up to the load today? They had to handle the logistics of the harvest, the allocation of organs, the selection of patients. Forget Stern for now—he jammed that decision out of his way.

He itched with frustration. Some day he could plan something for the lungs and pancreas too. And maybe long bones. Why not? Transplants like those lay in the future, but not so far away. And if he had the capacity he would get the cases, he could do the research, he would have the clout to get grant money and to grow. It was a game of numbers—grow into glory or fall off the train. The whole thing hinged on St. Luke's. And there again, blocking the way, lay the figure of Martin Stern. Again he closed the door.

Today was today. The harvest would come first. Rudd and Garrison in the first operating room, taking all the organs they could save. First the heart. He would take a second room to transplant that. What a lottery prize that was going to be for someone: come in today and have your heart cut out! The kidneys would wait a day or two for all the tests that ROPO used to identify the most suitable recipients. Maybe the delay was what gave Iverson the chance to line up his money bags, the bastard.

But today, as frail and urgent as the heart, there was still the liver. Rudd would need another major room for that. Where would it go? He put no name to that patient either, and simply erased the question.

Four organs, three rooms, emergencies on Saturday! His old competitive juices came to a boil. Win or lose, he always loved the game, always gave it everything he had. His spirits rose; he would push his little kingdom to the max today! And any hospital center that could do a double transplant on a Saturday afternoon was good, wasn't it? Big enough, right?

Wrong. He groaned. Even with those notches on his gun, he was too small. He could never be more than a flash in the pan. "Brovek? Oh, yeah, he did a few cases back in '85, maybe '86 I think."

He merged into the freeway traffic, his foot tramping on the accelerator, his fingers clamped around the steering wheel.

Open heart surgery had already set the pattern: big centers thrive; the little guys lose their funding and fade away. And there he was, once again, face to face with Martin Stern.

Save Stern, stay small, fade away. For God's sake, how could he choose to do that?

He nearly missed his turn-off. He braked hard, rubber squealing. Behind him an air horn blasted. He jerked the Lincoln onto the exit ramp and a loaded semi roared past in a crash of sound.

He pulled down to exit speed, sweat on his forehead, hands shaking. So far his luck had held, but how much more could he use up before it was gone?

He had hoped Stern would die before a liver donor came along, and Stern didn't. Was that bad luck? No. He couldn't call a man's death good luck. To be good, luck had to be good for everybody. That was the kind of luck he believed in, the kind that went with his hard work in surgery. And he had a conviction about it: good luck grew out of good ethics. He knew his duty to Stern; he saw it as plain as the lane lines painted on the street.

He clicked his parking card in and out of the slot, and zoomed his Lincoln by a skillful inch under the rising gate arm. He steered into his reserved stall and went directly to the surgery suite.

He could see Mizzoh through the glass walls of her tiny office, that cubicle of glass tucked in at the center of her domain. She wore a green cotton scrub suit and paper hood. In twenty years Brovek had never seen her dressed up, and he wondered if she wore an outfit like this even to sleep in.

He banged his way into the office and pulled a chair to the front of Mizzoh's desk. Lance Rudd stood in the corner. He looked haggard, as if he hadn't slept much last night. Unusual for the impeccable Dr. Rudd. Garrison slipped in as he sat down, her flat-heeled shoes passing soundlessly in front of his eyes. She went to stand alongside Rudd.

Okay. Here were his players, and it was game time. Time for the pep talk in the locker room.

"Opportunity knocks for us, boys and girls," he said. "We have the best cadaver donor we could hope for, and we can harvest a whole hatful of organs."

They all stiffened. Nobody spoke. Mizzoh shot a glance at Garrison. Rudd was a ramrod. They stared at him like an enemy alien.

He'd forgotten the dead person was staff; maybe they knew her. Okay, it was a bad start; he couldn't quit because they were tender.

"Rudd, I want you to take charge of the harvest. We ought to get a heart and two good kidneys, as well as the liver. You see to that. Garrison can help you. Okay?

"Okay, Chief."

His flat response surprised Brovek. Today was Rudd's greatest surgical opportunity, and he sounded grim.

"Then we have to overlap in a second major room, Mizzoh, to start the heart for the top name on our waiting list. I'll do that, if you have the crew. Can do?"

Mizzoh hardly looked up. "So far we're okay, Dr. B."

So far? What was the matter with these guys? He swept his eyes over them all. This was challenge day; where was their spit? He picked Mizzoh's yellow pencil from the desk and twisted it in his fingers.

"The kidneys will just go on the machine for storage, but the liver will have to find a home today. That's a third room and crew, Mizzoh, to start during the harvest. How about that?

"Now we're getting thin. It's a holiday week-end. Some of my best nurses are away. Rooms 3 and 4 are okay; but 2 is getting that new surgical light—the one you ordered. That room is out of service. The other rooms are pretty small...."

Brovek grunted, a deep guttural rumble. When he built the new plant, he would do all these cases and more without a ripple. And for damn sure without all this reluctance. He began to resent it.

"Dr. Brovek?"

Was Dr. Garrison going to weasel too? He scowled.

"Your plans sound good to me, sir, but I haven't heard you mention ROPO. They will have some interest in these organs too, won't they?"

His scowl deepened. He didn't like the attitudes in his locker room before this big game. They ought to be loaded for action, turned on to their chances today. What the hell was wrong?

"We have the body, Dr. Garrison. We have the control. We'll use ROPO if we can't handle all the organs right here."

Rudd erupted from his torpor, leaning forward from his corner, eyes intense.

"Chief, the first priority about these organs today is that they survive. ROPO is the way to find the best candidates."

Brovek's anger rose up into his neck; he could feel it swell. Rudd talked like a bureaucrat, not a surgeon. The professor spat out his words in a flat stream.

"But those 'best candidates' may be anywhere, Rudd, in Iowa or Wisconsin. Hours away. That's important too."

Mizzoh attacked his other flank. "ROPO may be a good thought. If the heart or the liver could be shipped, we'd be in better shape here. To do both we'll have to stretch things tight for several hours. I need some leeway in case another emergency happens along."

Damn. His anger seethed under his black scowl. He was giving his engines a call for full speed ahead, and they were all farting. Consider ROPO. Holler for help. Settle for less. By God, he was ready for full capacity, more rooms, bigger crews. More spine in his doctors. Damn. He was the only one here with enough guts to go for broke. What was their trouble anyway?

The pencil in his hands snapped like a piece of glass.

Hold it, Brovek; it's three against one. Your head is stuck in expansion; they are tuned in to the limits we have today.

He tilted his chair back on two legs, deliberately precarious and unstable. He scowled at them, and watched them measure his balance.

"Okay." he barked. "Call Wilma Gale and see if she knows anything."

"She is waiting outside, Dr. Brovek. I asked her to stay a minute, just in case."

"Ain't that dandy, Dr. Garrison. Why don't you go and ask her in here then, just in case."

He banged his chair down. He stood up and paced the tiny office. One step brought him to the wall. When he turned he bumped into Rudd. Another turn and he banged Mizzoh's desk. He felt like a bear on a bicycle. He sat down again. He fixed a dark frown on Wilma Gale and rumbled in his chest.

His menace didn't come off. She sat there, hands folded, coolly professional, unmoved by his bluster.

In a calmer voice he said: "Ms. Gale, I would like you to find out what possibilities exist at other institutions within range for use of today's cadaver organs"—he shot a glance at Dr. Garrison—"just in case."

Gale's peach-like cheeks were unruffled.

"I checked the computer files already, Dr. Brovek, and made some calls. Mercy has a heart patient and they could be here by three-thirty for harvesting. They are standing by for a decision. North County has a liver patient. They will be here by five unless I call them off. By chance both candidates are type O blood, and so is your cadaver donor."

"And so is Martin Stern." Brovek's voice was harsh, and his words surprised himself. "And he is urgent."

After all his stalling and false hopes, the game was demanding his chips. He must decide at last where he would play them.

"Chief," Lance Rudd said, "Martin Stern is pretty far gone. He is just out of coma. His proteins are down. He is a high-risk candidate. At the very best he is border-line acceptable. The donor liver might have a better chance with the patient at North County."

Sandor Brovek stared at Rudd. Stern was Rudd's own patient. Liver transplants were still headlines; here was Rudd's opportunity to place his name among the trail-blazers of surgery. Why wouldn't he fight for Stern? for his own chance?

His eyes narrowed. Rudd couldn't know about St. Luke's and what rode on Stern's chances. Hell, he wouldn't much care if he did. There was no trace of guile in the drawn face and dark eyes. No, the temptation that Brovek felt was couched in himself alone, as it had been at lunch with Potts, as it had gnawed at his heart ever since. Turn Stern down; kill for St. Luke's.

It would be so easy. His own staff, Stern's own doctor, was voting No to Martin Stern. There was Brovek's escape route, his innocent, unassailable way to put Martin Stern out of the game. It was the murder plan he had flirted with from the beginning. He sank into a black study.

How deep into his life must duty cut? Was there a limit to what he owed Martin Stern? What would Lotte say, if she weren't reduced to baby-sitter status? His nostrils quivered with the remembered scent of Marnie Bates, and his hand burned where it had rested on her young buttock. The rear end of that Chevy loomed in his mind, his Lincoln smashing into it, as he flew against his windshield. What about luck? Why wasn't he lying on the freeway crushed under that semi? Where did healing come from?

His decision came as his decisions always came, with simple, surgical force; his chips came down, and he knew what he would do.

"Dr. Rudd, do you still have Mr. Stern in ICU?"

"Yes, sir, I do."

"You have not terminated active treatment?"

"No, we have not."

"Then he is still a candidate for liver transplant, correct?"

It was not a question; it was a decree.

But Garrison came at him again.

"Our heart patient is ideal, Dr. Brovek. She is not in the hospital, but she lives in town and she is ready. Another young woman with children, like Millicent Herold."

"I'm thinking of graft survival, Chief." Rudd again.

Brovek turned his ear impatiently. They would all have opinions, and he had to suffer them. Rudd went on.

"Best chances for success are for the heart to stay here, and the liver to go to North County."

How many times must he turn away from sin?

"Mizzoh, can we harvest and do both heart and liver today?"

Mizzoh spoke straight and tough: "One or the other, Dr. B. Try both and we'll bust the barrel."

"Lance?"

"Do the heart, Chief; it's getting too late for Martin Stern."

"Dr. Garrison?"

"Send out the liver, Dr. Brovek. The heart should be a shining success for you."

They could not know his agony, the thorns he had to swallow.

"Wilma?"

"Whatever you say goes, Dr. Brovek. I know Mr. Stern has been on your list for a very long time. But what about the doctors from North County? I'm not sure I can still catch them."

Brovek sat, fitting the broken ends of Mizzoh's pencil together, bending them apart again, turning them in his fingers. Suddenly he skittered them across the desk top.

"Okay," he said. "Enough talk. Here is how it is going to go."

He rose to his full height and leaned both of his big hands on Mizzoh's desk. He spat his words like a lash at each one in turn.

"Lance, you harvest. Start with the liver. Mercy can come and take the heart. I'll start Stern, and you finish putting in the graft. Dr. Garrison, you stay by Lance's side today. You'll be good help and you'll learn a lot. Mizzoh, marshal your players; we have a game to begin. Wilma, you do have the final consent, don't you?"

"Sure do, Dr. Brovek. But what about the people from North County? What can I tell them?"

Brovek took her elbow, shoved his face close to hers, and hissed through his teeth: "Tell them to come watch us do a damn fine liver transplant today, one that's going to work. Go tell them that."

He released her arm and she fled. Rudd pushed against his back, shoved him aside.

"Excuse me, Chief." His voice sounded choked. "If she's dead I can see her."

He disappeared. Dr. Garrison lingered in the doorway. She had something on her mind. She spoke quietly, but not casually.

"Dr. Brovek, I hope you will stick around today. This is a tough deal for Dr. Rudd, more than you know. He may need some back-up."

And she too was gone.

"What was that all about, Mizzoh?"

She shrugged. "Young folks, Dr. B. Who knows anything about young folks?"

And she strode out of her office.

Brovek sat down by himself. He felt lost, alone at the top. He had denied his staff, subverted their advice, and he had played his chips at last, against his own interest, on the side of ethics. Or was it superstition? He wondered. Could a man strive so hard to do right that he gets it all wrong?

*   *   *

Lance's long strides carried him straight from Brovek's obscene planning session to Karen's discreetly curtained bedside. Still tight with anger and frustration, he took in her lifeless form, her closed eyes, the jumble of tubes and wires weaving across the white sheet. He rested his hands lightly on her arm. Instead of the rescue tube he had placed yesterday, she wore a new endotracheal tube jammed through a nostril.

It was unfair. He wanted to scream, to tear away those hoses and wires, to take up her body in his arms, and just run away. An hour ago he could not have come to his beloved Karen. Now he was commanded to come, to take charge of her organs. Whatever parts of her still had a chance for life were his to maintain and to harvest. For two days he had suffered and grieved apart; now he was commanded to attend her, to ignore his feelings and go to work. The outrageous irony gave bones to his anger.

Mechanically he checked the litany of life support measures, useless now to Karen but providing the vital circulation to her solid organs. The respirator triggered mindlessly, moving Karen's chest up and down in a mockery of life. From under her sheet a plastic tubing drained golden urine into a bag—urine from the kidneys that he must preserve and garner for someone else. Along with her heart, liver, both eyes. Gifts that she was leaving for the world, priceless organs from the substance of Karen Sondergaard.

But they were not her sum! He remembered her happy smile, the flash of her perfect teeth, the hot promise of her generous mouth. She had been so much more than a collection of organs.

But only her solid organs were left alive, and their preservation was essential—the first link in the transplant chain. His management had to be just as correct, just as aggressive, as Harvey Kanju's had been. Adequate ventilation. Fluids and drugs to support blood pressure. To keep the kidneys working.

Lance forced his mind to the familiar disciplines of judgment. He checked the machines, the values, the tests, the monitors, and in the simple act of writing orders, he found a pinched comfort. There could be no more Karen here. Work time had come, and he must simply tend to an organ preparation.

A tiny Oriental orderly appeared with a litter and displaced Lance from Karen's side. Across the bed a nurse anesthetist disconnected the hoses from the ventilator and reconnected her portable self-contained oxygen system for transport. Other hands untangled the tubes and wires and rehung all the bottles and bags on the litter. Lance stood back and watched for the second time while expert gentle hands lifted Karen's body to a cart and rolled her away.

                    *   *   *

A Death Certificate:

Decedent:	*Karen Ann Sondergaard*
Date of Birth:	*27 May 1960*
Place of Birth:	

	(city or town)	*North Prairie*
	(county)	*Northland*
	(state)	*Minnesota*
	(country)	*USA*

Father's Name:	*Haakon Sondergaard*
Mother's Maiden Name:	*Astry Birgid Kjevne*
Cause of Death:	*subarachnoid hemorrhage*
due to:	*ruptured cerebral aneurysm*
Contributing Cause:	*none*
Other Disease:	*none*
Time of Death:	"When she hit the floor," he thought.

But he wrote:

1:05 pm, April 6, 1985

and signed his name:

(S) Harvey S. Kanju, M.D.

A Picture Postcard: *Dear Martin, Someone there named Father O'Leary has found me in Cancun. He thinks you are going to get your transplant. I hope so. My life is empty without you Martin. Please get well. I want to come back.*

Lila Mae

PS: The X on the picture is my room.

Two consent forms:

I,…(*name*) Astry Sondergaard…, hereby consent to the removal of organs and tissues from the body of my…(*relationship*) daughter…(*name*) Karen Sondergaard…for the purpose of medical treatments to unidentified other persons. I understand that such organs and tissues may not actually be used, or that such treatment may not be successful. I have received no material consideration nor promise of such consideration in exchange for this consent.

Organs and tissues to which this consent applies include: heart; liver; pancreas; kidneys; spleen; lymph nodes; connective tissue; skin; bone; eyes (*strike out any for which permission is withheld*) (None was stricken)

(S) Astry Sondergaard, mother

Witness: (S) Wilma Gale, RN

I, **Martin Stern** do hereby consent to an operation to be performed upon **myself** by **Dr. Lance Rudd and associates**. This operation is intended to remove my liver, a vital organ necessary to life, and to put in its place a liver transplanted from a cadaver donor. I understand that prolonged courses of medication will be necessary after the operation, possibly for the duration of my life, and that my cooperation in this follow-up care will be essential.

(S) Martin Stern

Witness: SuEllen Shafer, RN

A prayer by Father Kevin O'Leary"

"Divine Healer of the sick, Christ Jesus our Lord, without whose aid we can do nothing, look with favor upon those who perform these operations. Guide their minds and their hands that their work may be praiseworthy to You, and successful to those who suffer. In all things Thy will be done. Amen."

*   *   *

Through the window of the scrub room, Dana Garrison watched Mizzoh's surgical nurses transform the bare and cold Room Three into an operating theater. Myrna Bates laid out packages of supplies, while her crew in masks, gowns and gloves spread sterile drapes of green cotton over instrument tables and thumped down orderly racks of gleaming stainless steel instruments. Nurse anesthetists lifted Karen's body from a gurney and settled her gently into position on the operating table.

It could just as well have been me, Dana thought. Nobody is too young to die. Karen proves that. So did Danny Hovelund. And if I die, would they take my organs? God, they should. I'd want them to.

She watched the scurry of activity around Karen, assuring the artificial supports to ventilation and circulation that would keep Karen's solid organs alive for harvest.

Harvest? What a word! I wonder what Rusty will think about it, when I tell him I'd want my organs donated if...if the same thing happened to me.

She went to the scrub sink, lathered up her hands and arms in the warm brown suds, and went to work with the brush.

What a way for her and Rusty to carry on their love affair, she thought. Like, in bits and pieces. Finding little snatches of time. Talking over trays in the cafeteria. She was luckier than poor Karen, who finally fell in love and right away flamed out.

She took an orange stick and scraped under her nails and switched back to the scrub brush. One more time.

I wonder what old man Keaton thinks, when Rusty and I go smooching in his lecture hall. It has to be love, or I wouldn't keep calling him up and he wouldn't always run over here on a gnat's notice. But it's sure strange the way I shift gears into loving Rusty and then...yes, like right now...shift back into doctoring.

She stepped dripping into the operating room and dried her hands and arms on a sterile towel. With the nurses' help she thrust her arms into a sterile operating gown, and then her hands into her surgical gloves. At the table Pete spread wet, broad strokes of honey-brown antiseptic solution over Karen's exposed white flesh.

Shock and grief arose anew in Dana's throat, but she shoved her emotions down. She could have no margin here for softness or tears. She couldn't. Lance couldn't. She hoped that just this once he would obey her, and wait in the staff room until she called.

Pete and the scrub nurse draped sterile green sheets over the table, leaving a long central opening where Karen's chest and abdomen peeked through. Now the juniors approached the table beside Pete, resting their hands on the drape, in careful position to maintain sterility. Dana stepped into the surgeon's place.

How close we all live to the edge, she thought. And how little we believe it.

The operating light glared down on the surgical field. Dana probed the breast bone with her gloved fingers, gauging the incision. She ratcheted her mind down to the technical job before her, the shining scalpel that she held quietly in her hand. She drew it in a clean red line down the long midline of Karen's chest and belly. She cauterized bleeders and covered the edges with towels. It had to become just a routine incision now. Like a color plate in a surgical text. The harvest had begun, and Karen Sondergaard must disappear.

"Myrna," she said quietly, "you may notify Dr. Rudd that we are ready for him."

*   *   *

Lance watched the gurney carrying Karen's body until it left the ICU. Then he changed his clothes in the surgeons' dressing room and prowled into the staff lounge. Dana had ordered him to wait, and he was too numb not to obey. He snatched up the glass coffee pot and splashed hot brew into a styrofoam cup. A plate full of caramel rolls beckoned him, but after his years of diabetic discipline he hardly saw them. He looked over the roomful of empty leather chairs, chose one, held his coffee cup out to balance it and sank back crosswise, his legs hanging over the arm. Half buried in soft leather, he let his outrage boil.

The system asks too much. More than I can give. Screw it.

He blew a long breath across the steaming cup.

How am I supposed to ignore what's happened? How can I do my job with my guts in rebellion?

He jerked his frame around straight in the chair and hunched over the cup. The hot black coffee sloshed on his fingers.

I ought to just blow out of here. Dump this lousy world. Now-you-can't, now-you have-to? Screw it. I'll just kiss off. Never come back. Who in the hell would care? Nobody.

Sure as hell not whoever it was he heard rattling the coffee cups.

"Hey, Rudd," a harsh voice jumped at his ear. "Ain't that terrible about our nurse?"

Barney Popper's voice. Rudd groaned silently.

"She died, I heard. Kind of hits home when it's one of our own."

Rudd choked down an angry response. "Hits home, Barney, for sure."

"Well, hey, I get it. That's why you're suited up on a Saturday afternoon. Going to pluck a kidney or two?"

Rudd sat rigid and stared into his coffee. Today of all days, why did this buffoon come along?

"Right. We have a big job to do first. Then we'll implant today and maybe again tomorrow. Big job."

Barney poured coffee into his mouth with a whistling sound. His voice had bubbles in it.

"Boy, I got to hand it to you guys with your emergencies. I get 'em too, you know, C Sections and like that. But hell, I'll be done in an hour and go home again. You might as well be here for the weekend. And your patients are two-thirds dead, too. I don't see how you can do it."

His words hit Lance Rudd like a switch. He had braced himself against every kind of wind but warm. He looked at Popper, maybe really for the first time, where he stood before him, one foot stuck up on the arm of a chair, his bent knee pushing his belly away off center like a twisted penguin. He held half a doughnut in one hand; the other half bulged in his cheek.

Rudd set down his cup; his stomach churned; he fought down nausea. And yet the man's words were kind. His brown eyes were clear, even innocent.

Lance heard himself say, "Well, Barney, we just have to do it, no matter how tough it is. And hope the results justify the effort."

And there was his synthesis. His internal clamor subsided. We just have to do it. He could cope. For the first time in years he thought of the night he came home alone in a fog. He didn't know which way to turn, he was lost, and then the porch light came on over his own screen door. Everything came clear.

"It's life, Barney," he said again. "We just have to do it, no matter how tough it is."

The intercom clicked and buzzed. Myrna's voice crackled into the room.

"Dr. Rudd, we are ready for you in Room 3."

Rudd swung his legs and rose from his chair. "Okay, Myrna," he replied, And he thought, "I think I'm ready for you, too."

He picked his way around the munching Barney Popper.

"Thanks, Barney," he said.

Popper licked his fingers and smiled across his fist.

"Go get 'em, Tiger," he said.

*   *   *

Scrubbed, gowned, gloved, Lance elbowed his way to the center ring to continue the procedure Dana Garrison had started. Standard maneuvers they had done many times together in the last three months: split the sternum, open the abdominal wall, open the pericardium and cannulate the aortic arch.

The timing was critical, and should be perfect. The harvest team from Mercy was expected at any minute. Custom and practice reserved to them the harvest of the heart they would later implant. Lance checked the clock; he did not want to wait for them.

Smoothly he and Dana divided attachments that supported and suspended the abdominal organs. The spleen came out for further tissue-match tests with candidates for the kidneys. The two surgeons slid other cannulas into the lower aorta and its vein, the inferior vena cava. They placed a third cannula into the unique vein which carried intestinal blood not to the heart but to the liver. The portal vein was short but of large caliber, and critical to the liver's economy.

Lance looked again at the clock. Those guys should be here now. Carefully he passed blood-vessel clamps around the arteries and veins of the heart, and another clamp across the aorta at the diaphragm. Closure of this clamp and its partner on the inferior vena cava would effectively isolate the circulation to abdominal organs. It was time to proceed, and Lance was intense. Harvest of multiple organs was tricky; it was easy to work on one organ and injure another. To lose a key vessel was to lose the organ. To let it sit warm and bloodless meant it would die. Or even worse: it might be implanted and fail. The personhood of these organs flicked into his mind, and fed his intensity. These organs—Karen's organs—must survive.

"Myrna, is there any sign of the Mercy team?"

"Not yet, Dr. Rudd."

He wanted to holler at her. Where were they? How long? He steeled himself. Hollering never helped, even though other surgeons fell to it. Dumping his own tensions on Myrna would set everyone's nerves on edge.

The anesthesiologist raised her head above the drapes. "Her blood pressure is sagging a little, Lance. I'm pushing her volume, but she is getting weaker."

Protocol dictated first to isolate and cool down the abdominal organs, and next to remove the heart, before actual removal of the liver and kidneys. Those guys ought to be here.

"Myrna," he said quietly, "slip over into Dr. Brovek's room and see how he is coming along with Mr. Stern. Tell him we are having to wait for Mercy to get here."

He spoke to the students clustered in their sterile circle about the table. "Do you see the problem? If we proceed, we are starting ischemic time for the heart; if we wait, we may damage perfusion of the kidneys and liver. We have to balance our decision for the most good and the least harm."

Myrna returned. Her eyes were wide above her mask.

"Dr. Brovek said he is nearly ready for you and for the liver, Dr. Rudd. And he said for you to put the liver first. That's what he said: put the liver first."

"Okay, Myrna, thank you. We will proceed. Let's have the cold Collins solution."

His mood revived as he and Dana moved smoothly forward. They closed the clamps, isolating the liver and kidneys, and flooded those organs with ice-cold salt solution. They stopped the heart and flooded it also and packed it with ice. They divided its vessels and lifted it into sterile bags to be handed off to Myrna for more ice pack and then transport.

"Just like Hangarville, and Danny Hovelund," Dana said.

Lance glanced at her. "Except you did it all that day, took it out and tucked it in. You didn't have to wait for these Mercy guys. As it turns out, they're just delivery boys."

She grinned. "Or maybe girls, Dr. Rudd?"

Then, more soberly, she said, "I just hope they do their job on time."

They turned back to the liver, already flushed and cooled. There were several short and difficult veins draining from the liver into the vena cava just below the heart, inaccessible and too short to control. So they simply divided the cava above and below those veins, leaving them attached: this was the maneuver which made liver transplant possible. They looked again at the gateway to the liver, its undersurface with its triad of liver artery, portal vein, and bile duct. Each element was a vital link in the chain of success. These structures were easily divided.

"That ought to do it," Lance said. He cradled the detached liver in his two hands and teased it up from its great cavity under the dome of diaphragm. Up it came with a gentle sucking sound, and he held it for a skipped beat, watching it drip red stain onto the towels that Dana held beneath it. Carefully they settled it into a sterile basin of salt slush which Myrna took into custody.

"How long is it good for, like that?" a medical student wanted to know.

"Six or eight hours," Lance said, "so we're in good shape."

But his brow was furrowed. "What I worry about is the heart. We like to have that back in circulation within four hours or so, and that clock is running now."

The student's forehead wrinkled so hard that her eyes squinted nearly shut. Welcome to the hard world of truth, Lance thought.

They shelled the kidneys out of their beds of fat and stripped the ureters down on each side. Lance snipped quickly with his long scissors across aorta and cava again, and ureters. The brace of kidneys came out together, already flushed and cold, to be attached to a pump machine for preservation. Somewhere nearby, he supposed, two lucky souls likely to accept Karen's kidneys would be called by ROPO. At last their months or years of living in the strictures of dialysis would change.

Myrna spoke to Dr. Rudd. "Dr. Brovek is ready for you in Room 4. He will help you until Dr. Garrison gets there."

Lance rested his hands on the drapes. Half-empty body cavities gaped beneath them, the carnage of successful battle. He raised his eyes to Dana, and found hers already locked on him. They stood in silence. A student coughed and shuffled his feet.

Dana said, "Go ahead, Lance. I'll finish here. You can keep her liver alive, anyway."

Lance's voice was choked, nearly inaudible.

"Thanks, Dana, I'll see you next door."

*   *   *

With the care she would accord a huge and fragile egg, Dana Garrison lowered Martin Stern's new liver into the yawning red cave below his ribs. All the predetermined elements fell into place—the prepared space, the matching fittings to be coupled together, the latent power of life.

The symbolism struck her like a blow.

"Oh."

The sound escaped her lips in a low moan. Like a flash of lightning she saw her truth revealed. Transplant surgery! This was her destiny! The revelation set her to shivering. She bounced on her toes; her bones felt electrified. She quieted her trembling hands on the surgical drapes, but she could not hold still.

"You all right, Dana?" Lance looked up in curiosity, not alarm.

"Never better, Lance." She choked off her words. Her vision had always been a private mystery, and never far from her mind.

From eleventh grade at Hangarville High School she had taken a field trip with her classmates to an auto assembly plant in Kenosha. At the end of the tour, while her friends trooped off chattering to find the Coke machine, she had stood alone, rooted, absorbed in the process going on before her eyes. An automobile engine dangling from a conveyor chain had swung over her head and settled gently and precisely into the chassis moving below to receive it. The image had seized her that day, and had dwelt in her psyche with a power she did not understand. Ever after, in times of doubt or confusion, she could conjure up that vision. Through her ten years of devotion to medicine and surgery, always wondering if she were good enough to be there, she had kept counsel with that image of rectitude, of destiny. It became her test of judgment, her symbol of good karma. Based simply on her own faith in it. Now suddenly, she understood.

Lance needed to fit the donor and recipient ends of vena cava together so he could sew them. He needed her help, and she put her attention to the work. But her excitement was not to be denied.

"In its own way, this is beautiful, isn't it? Healthy tissues. Everything fits."

He chuckled. "Maybe I'll think so after it's all sewn in; right now it's hard work."

He placed a stitch, tied the fine threads in a skillful knot. Dana watched his slender fingers, quick and sure in their motions. He had a grace about his technique, a simplicity, that not all surgeons enjoyed.

His simple over-and-over suture ran between the two veins, bringing their edges smoothly together. She knew exactly how he meant it to look. Leakproof of course; also the two channels perfectly matched, so that blood would flow through without destructive turbulence.

While the other assistants held the wound open to Lance's vision, Dana worked to expose the exact area of his attention. It was a demanding task, elbow deep, deeper even than Martin Stern's backbones. The new liver had to lie in front of the vena cava which Lance was sewing. Her left hand tilted the liver forward so he could see; but she must not lift it enough to tear the new stitches. Her right hand held the thread lightly between thumb and forefinger to maintain tension on the suture line. "Not too tight, not too loose, but just right." Like familiar music heard with new ears, the old adage sounded fresh and sweet to her.

Lance was smooth and fast. His hand was light. His needle holder seemed to have a life of its own. Suture of the cava was soon complete and its clamps came off. Dana released the three-pound burden and let it settle into its new bed. She stretched her fingers, working the cramps out of her forearm. There were still three channels to go, two for blood and one for bile.

It was difficult surgery, delicate, full of hazard. She thought it was just one hell of a lot harder than implanting a heart or a kidney. But it was right for her. Liver transplant. This was what her old vision had been promising, all these mysterious years.

Her mind stretched ahead. What about her career, then? What would come next? Conviction settled on her with the power of a decision made. I'd never be happy in a place like Hangarville. I belong right here, in University Hospital. I'll help build the transplant program, and be the liver queen! All I need now is to earn the invitation.

Lance set up the portal vein union and started the suture line. This one was easier to get at, and the ends came together nicely. She followed his advancing stitch readily, keeping tension on the thread.

A vision of Rusty's dancing eyes popped into her mind, and her heart skipped. The picture came not from any of their recent stolen fragments of growing love, but from the night of their first kiss. Thank God for his sense of humor. Bozo could have been a disaster. Rusty was a foot taller than she, and she wondered what Bozo felt like to him, rattling on the belt at her waist, but vibrating significantly lower on Rusty's anatomy. She stifled a giggle.

But Bozo wasn't a disaster. She recalled his words floating after her down the hall, "I'll be back!" Her heart sang at the memory of his laughter. And their arranged meetings—they certainly weren't 'dates'—were times of—hey—what's wrong here?

Something had changed in Lance's suturing. A loss of rhythm. A feeling of imprecision.

She glanced at Rudd. He was staring at his work; a light layer of perspiration glistened below the rim of his cap. She watched the suture line advancing across the top of the portal vein. The needle holder was shaky, hesitant. It missed the needle point, stabbed at it again.

"Lance, are you okay?"

She spoke louder than she had intended. The other assistants snapped their eyes at her. But Lance didn't hear. He made no answer. His hand shook; he couldn't manage the needle holder.

She used her grand-rounds voice this time. "Dr. Rudd?"

No response. Something was going wrong here, and she didn't understand. But she had to act.

She took Rudd's hands in hers and lifted them away from the field. She took the needle holder and set it down on the drapes. Lance looked blankly at her, dumb.

"Myrna." Dr. Garrison took charge. "Call Dr. Brovek instantly to come in here stat. Then come back here yourself."

She fixed a burly young medical student in the intensity of her eyes, and spoke simply so she would not frighten him.

"I want you to break scrub, drop back, and help Dr. Rudd. He's ill and needs to sit down."

She watched panic arise in the young man's face. He wasn't ready yet to act out of pattern, act as a doctor, act alone. But her manner was stern and her direction plain. He moved. Rudd was docile. He retreated, and sat down on a stool in the corner of the room. The medical student hovered over him, helpless.

Dana nodded to her resident. "Pete, you and I have to stay on track here. We'll trade sides and keep at it."

She wanted to go to see to Lance, see what his trouble was. But her father's voice rolled out of memory: "There is no problem more urgent than the case you are operating on right now."

She crossed to the surgeon's side of the table and took up Lance's needle holder. She put Pete in position and readjusted the suture line. There was nothing here she did not know and understand. These structures had different names from those she had worked on before. But they were just blood vessels.

She completed the portal vein suture line, irrigated against air and clots, and carefully opened the clamps. Blood began to flow, Martin Stern's blood, into Martin Stern's new liver. The cells could breathe again, begin to live and not die. They still needed an artery.

The double doors blew open in a huge gust of air and Sandor Brovek sailed into the operating room. He saw Rudd sagging on the chair, nearly dropping to the floor. He knelt beside him, looked in his eyes, felt his brow, tested the pulse at his right wrist.

"Myrna!" he roared. "Orange juice! Candy! Whatever you have out there with sugar in it, get it in here. And you," he arrowed his voice into the anesthesia corner, "get an i.v. going here and pour some glucose into this poor bastard."

Then more gently he said, as if to himself, "Well now his secret is out."

Lance? Dana thought. Lance is diabetic? And yet her heart lifted from her spooky thought of the symmetrical deaths of lovers. An insulin reaction was a whole lot more scientific.

She was completing the hepatic artery suture when Sandor Brovek, in fresh gown and gloves, approached the table.

"Stay where you are, Dr. Garrison," he said. "I'll slip in next to Pete, and you show me what you have done."

There wasn't much she could show. The vena cava was invisible now. The liver filled its allotted compartment, like any liver. She pointed out the suture line in the portal vein. And now she removed the clamps from the hepatic artery. Fresh blood flowed through it, and the dark purple liver blushed red.

Brovek grunted. "Let's hook up the gut somewhere. Show me."

Dana was struck with the difference between these two teachers. Brovek's big hands were like spades. His broad fingers moved slowly. But his touch was soft and no motion was wasted.

They isolated a segment of small intestine to receive the bile duct from the grafted liver. Dana used a stapling machine for some of the repair, and the job was soon done. They inspected all areas, washed the belly out with salt solution, and were ready to close the incision.

"Dr. Garrison, I want to talk to you when you are finished here. I will be in my office, after I check on Dr. Rudd."

"I'm okay now, Chief."

Lance was standing behind Dana, behind the medical students, in his scrub suit, no gown. The edges of his face around the surgical mask were pale.

"Okay, that is, except for humiliated. I never had a bad reaction before."

Brovek gazed across Dana's shoulder, looking long at Lance Rudd. She had never seen his brown eyes so deep, nor heard his voice so gentle.

"Lance, let's go over to my office and find out what happened to that donor heart."

He stepped away, students and nurses scattering from his path. He shucked off his operating gown and surgical gloves, and rested his hand lightly on Rudd's shoulder. Dana watched them leave the room together, and heard Brovek's voice rumbling softly.

"Let's get something to eat, and then we'll wait for Dana in my office."

She turned back to her work, but her mind took flight, echoing Sandor Brovek's words. It was the first time he had ever called her Dana.

*   *   *

All through the late afternoon of Holy Saturday, Father Kevin O'Leary sat in his church hearing confessions. For him, this was the most solemn day in the calendar, the day after Christ's death, the day before His triumphant resurrection. The crucifix was suitably draped in penitential purple, and the tabernacle stood open, empty of the Lord's consecrated body. It seemed to Father O'Leary the most fitting of all days for reconciliation. He welcomed the penitents in his heart, and rejoiced in each absolution, each new beginning for a soul seeking God.

Sure, it was unfortunate that there were not so many seeking Him any more, at least not at St. Luke's. This poor dwindling old parish failed to tax his aging energy, even though he had no assistant any more.

Wearing his cassock and a stole, he sat in a folding chair by the altar rail. No one had come to him for nearly an hour. He wondered if people might be discouraged by making confession face to face. They had always had to trust their priest for silence; now they had to hope for amnesia besides.

He finished another decade of his rosary, and thought he might go home for a little bite of kidney pie before the vigil mass tonight. He decided he would wait just until that last sunbeam left the edge of the pews and started up the wall.

A youngish woman slipped silently into the folding chair facing him. He leaned forward, slipping the rosary into the pocket of his cassock.

"Good afternoon," he said, in a voice he hoped would melt any nervousness or fear.

"Bless me Father for I have sinned it is thirteen years since my last confession."

"That is a long time to be away, my daughter. And are you wanting now to come home again? to come back into the fullness of life in the church?"

"Oh, yes, Father, I just found out I do, I really do."

"Bless you for that. It's a big step, that is. All the saints will rejoice with you."

"I just want to kiss and make up, Father. So I can go to Mass like I used to."

He tried to warm her with his smile. If face-to-face offered any advantage, he would try to use it.

"Well, that's not exactly the way reconciliation works, but I guess it's got the idea well enough. Now, before I can open the door and welcome you back, you know, I have to examine any barriers in your life, and be sure you understand what you are doing."

The sunbeam crept across the pews, climbed the wall, and disappeared. The western windows changed to pink, and then to rose. His cheeks matched the windows; he hoped she could not see his startled eyes. But he would not call her wicked. Misguided surely, and embarrassingly honest. He decided she was sincere in wanting to find a better way for her life. He was relieved when her recital concluded.

"My daughter, what penance do you think is proper for you now? How can you show our forgiving Lord that you mean business after all this time?"

"Gee, Father, I don't know. It's been so long I don't know anything any more."

"Many people are confused, my child. The Church has passed through some feisty times the past two decades. Lots of things have changed. I wonder if you would think about taking formal instruction? You could catch up on us that way. Sort of like starting from scratch all over again."

"Okay, Father. I never really knew anything anyway. Sure, I'll do that."

Haltingly she struggled through her formula prayer, an act of contrition.

"And I absolve you, my daughter, to the extent of my ability and your need, in the name of the Father, and of the Son, and of the Holy Spirit, Amen. Go in peace."

"Thank you, Father."

He watched her go, pumping on spike heels, clattering the tiles of the empty church. Her long coat of dark mink blurred into the gloom. But her hair, nearly luminous in itself, threw back the colors of the votive lights until she passed into the street, and the heavy door closed behind her.

He stared into the unfocused darkness. Everything she said was sealed within his heart. But he was human, after all, man as well as priest. And he wondered to himself whether this newly reconciled child of God were not Mrs. Martin Stern.

*   *   *

Daylight faded to a couple of faint squares at Brovek's office windows. The two men sprawled unmoving in a couple of chairs, each lost in his own dark thoughts. Finally Brovek leaned forward and snapped on his lamp. Its green glass shade radiated artificial coziness, but Brovek felt more in tune with the uncozy mess on his desk. A pair of paper plates with crumpled paper napkins bore witness to his and Lance's foray into the coffee shop. Half a spear of pickle and some broken potato chips lay in a blood-red smear of ketchup. Lance tossed his tall wax-paper cup into the mess; its soda straw dripped a brown stain onto the blotter.

"That was my first malted milk in twenty years."

Lance's dull words were full of gloom. He slumped on the small of his back in the straight little chair for visitors which Brovek had chosen purposely to be uncomfortable. Brovek burped softly, dropped his own paper cup under the desk, where his waste basket was, sometimes.

"It was really my fault, Lance." His voice was low, as if the words seeped directly out of his meditation. "A harvest is a big job by itself. You should have had a chance to eat and catch up before the implant."

There was a long silence.

Lance sighed. "I was so intent on it I didn't pay attention. I thought I could bull through."

Brovek said nothing. Some things you had to bull through, and some things you couldn't. He had done his full share of bulling today, and was not at all sure he had pushed people in the right directions. Lotte and Marnie. Lance. Wilma Gale. Mercy Hospital and their heart patient. Too many decisions—not enough wisdom.

He hoisted his feet to the desk and leaned back. His heel pushed a paper plate and it teetered at the edge.

Quixotic is the word for the way I was today. Too damned intent on the purity of my own motives. I had an easy opportunity to condemn Stern and win St. Luke's, but I refused it. Good. That part is okay. I could never raise up a program of healing from a base of betrayal.

But why was I afraid to pass Stern over for normal, ordinary medical reasons? Real reasons? My whole crew advised it. Rudd, Garrison. Even Wilma Gale. But I couldn't. I rammed it through: get Stern his liver, no matter the cost. What was I trying to prove? Is there something inside I'm afraid of? Afraid even to look at?

Bull shit. Forget it.

I can't forget it. What about North County's liver patient? Did I pervert my trust there too? And our own heart patient for that matter. She's a young mother like Millie Herold. Who knows whether she'll survive long enough to get another chance? There's way too much here, more than a man can figure out.

Maybe Grover Iverson is right. Give up the moral and get practical.

He sat up again. A chunk of wax paper crunched under his foot, and he kicked at it.

He looked at Rudd.

He must be under anesthesia to roost so long in that terrible chair. He looks depressed as hell too, beaten, poor bastard. Probably wondering what will happen next.

He jumped at the sudden jangle of his telephone. The way the day had gone, he didn't want any more news. It jangled again, demanded his reaction. Lance leaned forward, his elbows on his knees as if he wanted to crawl into the phone.

"Wilma Gale?"

The whispered name sounded to Brovek more like an invocation than a question. Brovek wasn't so eager. The phone jangled again, relentless.

"Brovek here," he said, and nodded at Rudd. "Hello, Wilma, we are all ears here."

He cradled the instrument under his left ear. His face was impassive as if he were drawing no cards to a pat hand. He saw Dr. Garrison slip silently into the room, pull another chair up next to Rudd. He fiddled with a hangnail, bit it off. He knew he shouldn't—bad hygiene. He spat it out, and spoke into the phone.

"Thanks, Wilma…I know…We just have to keep trying."

He set the receiver quietly back on its cradle. Rudd and Garrison exchanged long looks. Her hand moved out to rest on Rudd's arm. 'Healing power can flow through that hand,' Potts had told him once. They were all going to need it; maybe Brovek most of all.

"Well, kids, here's the story. Mercy team was delayed, and by the time they implanted the heart it was just over six hours. They went ahead because everything else was so perfect. It started up okay, but it wasn't strong enough. They put in a balloon-assist. But the heart can't hack it, and they are going back now to take it out again. They'll try a Jarvik artificial heart, and hope for another donor."

The three shapes sat motionless around the green glass shade, matching darknesses. From the windows night fingered in and covered them like a shroud. Dana was the first to speak, her words so soft that Brovek could barely hear.

"The heart is more symbolic, Lance. But we can still hope for her liver, and tomorrow her two kidneys."

Brovek watched the two playing out some scene he didn't understand. Garrison's hand still rested on Rudd's arm, and now his hand covered hers.

"And her eyes and all that too, Dana. But it's not quite the same, is it? Somehow her heart seemed...."

Silence sustained his thought. The three sat in the gloom like a dumb-show. Then Dana changed the scene.

In a quick movement she patted Rudd's arm, took her hand away and stood up. She snapped on the ceiling light, and they all squinted in the sudden glare. With one sweep of her arm she funneled the debris from Brovek's desk into a wastebasket. Brovek reached down to contribute the paper cup from beneath his feet. She spun the basket into a corner and turned to meet their startled eyes.

"Now let's look at the positive side," she said. Her voice rang out in the small room. "We have a live patient with a new liver to take care of. And by Monday night our kidney guys should have two happy people freed up from dialysis so they can pee to their heart's content. Life goes on, and we have to grab hold of the pieces we can reach. Now, you two guys, quit drooping and start grabbing!"

Brovek grinned, caught up in her enthusiasm. He would like, for openers, to grab a fistful of her. By God, this was the spirit he needed in his new department, the spirit that reached for stars. Potts was right. He could forget that she was a woman; she was a surgeon!

His thought didn't set right, and he struggled with it. No, he could not forget that she was a woman. She was indelibly and warmly a woman. Okay. A woman AND a surgeon. Yes. He was content with that.

He looked at Rudd. His young associate, usually so immaculate and bright, was a mess. He sat in that terrible chair, with his shoulders hunched forward, staring at the floor. He looked like a buzzard. He had pulled off his cap and his hair stuck out like the horns of an owl.

"Lance," Brovek said, "it can't be the end of the world."

Rudd looked up with dull eyes, weary. His voice was mournful.

"Chief, you can't put up with a surgeon you can't count on. I think I have to resign. I'll go off somewhere and do something else."

Garrison's hand went to her mouth. She turned to Brovek, eyes wide.

Brovek's mind raced. He wanted no more failures today. Insulin reactions needed sugar, not suicide. Surgical prudence demanded safeguards, but not, certainly not, total abandonment. He tried a soft answer.

"You and I both knew there was a chance for this to happen. All right, it happened. Your secret is out. But nothing else is changed."

Rudd drooped even lower. "It could happen again tomorrow."

"Not with reasonable care. You worked here for nearly nine years, Lance, and it didn't happen."

Rudd remained unmoved. "Nine and a half, Chief, and then it did."

Brovek felt desperate. Lance was sinking as if he were in quicksand. Garrison was frozen on point.

"You are the best research mind in the medical school, Lance. After me, of course. You can't throw that away."

Rudd was unreachable. "That mind disappeared today, it just took a walk. I can't be any good to you now."

Brovek's mercurial anger sprang up behind his eyes; it furrowed his brow. He rose up over his desk, his hands splayed out across it; he towered over Lance Rudd. His collegial manner hadn't worked and now he was mad. His voice dropped into its deepest rumble.

"Dr. Rudd, you forget someone. You operated on Mr. Martin Stern today. In my department, that means you are going to bust your ass to get Martin Stern well again. Now hoist yourself out of that chair and go take care of your patient. The day that Stern walks out of here you come back in here and talk about what happens to you."

He bent over Rudd, spraying fire from his nostrils, settling fury on him like a thundercloud. Rudd stood up, furious, white in the face. He kicked his chair sideways and stormed out of the door.

"Dana," Brovek roared, "you better go along and make sure that Lancelot don't get lost."

Brovek followed her to the door and slammed it shut. He snapped off the ceiling light—he preferred the gloom. His angry explosion piled up all his guilts and his shoulders drooped. He crossed behind his desk and sat down. The green lamp shade glowed hypnotically, and he stared at it, waiting, waiting, for his confusion to release its grip.

Never had he felt so borne down in the loneliness of command. Even with inadequate data he alone had to make his decisions, enforce his decrees. And now today's chapter was over. Next came the inevitable reckoning when he must add up the score, compare the results he had intended to the results that he produced, and see how sadly they diverged.

And he had no one to share his burden. Oh, Lotte, he mourned, you were part of it once, and I need you still.

Sandor Brovek folded his heavy arms on the desk and rested his head on them. He closed his eyes. His shoulders rose and fell with his breathing. But he did not sleep. He could not weep. He would not pray. He let his mind run free.

*   *   *

Dana's exhausting day dragged to an end with a final circuit of ICU. The unit's harsh brilliance hurt her eyes. But the unit was quiet, with only the ordinary hum of machines and scraps of murmured conversation. She walked slowly around the perimeter of cubicles, pausing at each, checking the quiet forms under the sheets and eyeballing the monitors. She assessed the urine bags and suction bottles, each bearing its own message in the volume of returns, in their color and clarity. Despite her fatigue she felt the increasing clarity growing from her own self-confidence.

At 10:30 on Saturday night most of the patients were asleep. Stern was still unconscious, but he was stable. Rudd had gone—at home by now, she figured, licking his wounds.

She came to the nursing station and dialed a number on the telephone. Her tired spirit rose. Could a drooping flower revive in only the hope of rain?

"It's Dana."

"Dana? I don't know anybody named Dana."

"Oh, you're crazy. You know me—my name is Dana."

"The only Dana I know changed her name to Duck."

"She didn't change it, you beast. You drove her to it."

"I never drove her anywhere. She wouldn't come out of her cave."

"You flew her to Hangarville once, and almost killed her. No wonder she wants to stay in her cave…and she wants to see you here."

"When?"

"Now. Meet me in ICU and walk me home."

"Hold your breath."

Dana settled the phone into its cradle and stared into space. Her cave, he said. In a dream she had looked out of a dark cave over sun-bright green meadows while Rusty rode up on a white stallion. The horse pranced and floated in the air, just out of reach. When she tried to touch Rusty's hand, a tangle of monitor wires bound her arms. She tried to tear them away, one after another in agonizing slow motion, and when she ran outside the horse was gone, and she woke up, heart pounding. How long would a stallion stand, pawing and snorting, before he ran off forever?

"Where were you, Dr. Garrison, a million miles away?" The student nurse stood no taller than Dana. Her soft cheeks and baby lines suggested nineteen years of age, tops. She reached to the phone with her left hand, and a pinpoint diamond flashed from her ring finger. "May I use the phone?"

Dana lifted her hand from the instrument as if she had been caught in the cookie jar. She watched this student professional handle the telephone, poke a finger into the dial holes, cradle the handset against her cheek. This dimpled love-child probably had a ten-year head start over Dana's own time table. Probably an expert in somebody's bed.

She took her stethoscope from around her neck and folded it into the side pocket of her white coat. She walked slowly out of ICU, and Rusty was waiting.

He stood square and strong. His copper hair gleamed in the brightness of the corridor. Their hands met, and their lips brushed a comfortable greeting.

"What took you so long?" she whispered close to his ear.

He grinned. "Well, you see, I was riding over here on a white horse, and...."

Her fingers pressed against his lips.

"Don't even say it," she said. It was spooky how often their minds shared images. "I know what happened next. He didn't want to stop...."

Rusty looked deep into her eyes. "Duck, let's get out of sunshine alley here. There's got to be some place...."

Dana shook her head. Her own quarters were off limits. Here in the hospital, in her world, her total priority had to be her work. It was Bozo she slept with.

Yet every stolen hour with this man opened her heart more fully to his sunshine and his rain. She yearned to walk with him out of her cave and into another world. His world.

"Is it nice outside? Has spring arrived yet?"

"You poor wretch. You don't even know. Let's step out the front door and inhale the springtime."

She took his arm. "Visiting hours are over. Maybe there won't be anybody out there."

The street was empty. Parked cars lined the curbs, but all was dim and quiet. Dana slipped Bozo off her belt and squeezed him into the pocket with her stethoscope. That should keep him tamed. He could still speak if he wanted to; she could still hear him if she had to.

They sauntered down the steps, hand in hand. She breathed deep of the fresh night air, redolent of hidden flowers. Organ music filtered across the street through the closed doors of St. Luke's. The Mass of the Easter Vigil.

"Not counting the blizzard, Duck, this is the first breath of God's fresh air that you and I have ever drawn together."

"How can you not count that blizzard? I'll never forget it." She slipped her arm around his waist, and held him as they walked along. "Of course, I remember that day in a lot of other ways too."

"Name the way I want to hear you say."

She laughed, her voice like music.

"I met you, you big oaf! That would be number one for me even if it wasn't what you wanted to hear."

They wandered along in uncounted steps, feeling their liberation, knowing their captivity.

"Duck, this is neat. I like walking outdoors with you."

"Then why have you stopped?"

She knew the answer. She gave herself to his arms; she followed his lead like dancing. She slid her arms across his shoulders, and slipped one hand into his wiry hair, exulting in the toughness of it. She pulled him to her, her lips parted, her tongue eager. She felt his arousal; she could taste his urgency. And she knew her own.

It was time to stop the games. She wanted this man; she wanted every inch of him. She wanted his child. Her belly burned with desire, as if her womb opened in their kiss.

From across the street the opening doors of the old church released a burst of yellow light that slanted down the steps and across the pavement almost to their feet. A tumble of voices broke out, jubilant in Christendom's highest feast. "Happy Easter," they cried to each other. Leg shadows scissored the light beams into patterns on the street.

Rusty held her close. "Listen to all that," he said. "I want some of that joy for us too. Organ music, candles, the whole nine yards. When we can." He pressed her hard against him. "But I'm going nuts this way. I want you. What do you say?"

Her answer tumbled from her lips. "I say Yes, Rusty; every fiber of my body says Yes."

Her hands crept between them, against his chest.

"But not now, not tonight. I have duties waiting back there in my cave, and they are there tomorrow and the day and the night after that and for ten more weeks. Ten long, forever weeks. But then I will be sprung, and if you still want me, I will come to you with all my heart."

He gathered her hands in his, keeping her close, and brushed his chin on the top of her nose. His words came soft and slow, and very clear.

"I have waited thirty years to find you, Duck; in ten weeks you can't drive me away. For ten weeks I could stand on my head."

Abruptly his manner changed. "But," he said, moving away a few inches, "there's one trouble, Duck."

Here it comes, she thought. Ten weeks is too long. I'm driving him away.

But his strong hand planted itself firmly, possessively, on her buttocks and her heart eased. She allowed herself to be moved along toward the hospital door. His smile shone in the dark.

"What trouble, Rusty?"

"Standing on my head," he said, "is a tough way to take a cold shower!"

PART SEVEN

▼

EASTER

Uplifted by the Easter celebration at Our Lady of Peace, Horace Potts rose from his pew and genuflected before the tabernacle. Lingering incense from the thurible blended with the fragrance of spring bouquets. Row on row of white lilies lined the chancel steps, and rose in massed pyramids flanking the altar. He loved the joyful liturgy of the early mass, and the splendid music. Especially the trumpets. He drifted along with the crowd of worshipers, up the center aisle and out into the early morning sunshine.

He paused on the top step, and watched his fellow parishioners, sporty looking men in jackets and ties and their wives in spring hats and gay colors, most of them shooing children into shiny cars. Roaring off to egg hunts, he supposed, and family breakfast parties.

But he was, as he always was nowadays, alone. He settled his black Chesterfield about his shoulders, and squared his gray felt hat on his brow. He could easily forget his desperate illness of a few weeks ago, but the year-old loss of his Catherine lay always heavy on his heart. No downers today, he said to himself. It is too beautiful a morning.I'll try to enjoy the Easter mystery today, and live for tomorrow.

He strolled down the street to his blue Oldsmobile, wondering where he would go. Maybe drive downtown to University Hospital, catch some breakfast in the cafeteria. Maybe I'll see someone I know. And I can look around for a building site again. There isn't one I suppose, but I can play with it for a while.

When he came near Old U, he slowed to a crawl. Mixed smells of city and of spring, auto exhaust and dew-wet grass, wafted in through his opened window. He dawdled along, checking out the buildings on both sides. He matched them up, one by one, to the black boxes of Brovek's city map. He held each one catalogued in his mind, ranked according to its owner, its market value, its faults. Some were not suitable, and some were not possible. He counted them over, rejecting them all again, as he cruised around New U. The front door of St. Luke's was closed. Father O'Leary was to celebrate just one Easter mass, at ten. Imagine having but one single mass on an Easter morning. It was a telling manifestation of a tiny parish. He passed the shabby old rectory. Brovek was right: St. Luke's was the only possible site. Their building had to go right there.

He came to the small parking lot reserved for medical chiefs, and saw a black Lincoln parked there. Brovek's? Why wasn't he home with Lotte? Curious. He turned in to the lot and keyed the gate with the courtesy card that Brovek had given him after his coronary. He took a slot near the staff entrance, and entered the hospital.

Instead of going to the cafeteria, he walked through Old U, past Keaton, to the surgery department office. The door was unlocked. The reception area was silent and empty, the typewriters shrouded under black plastic covers. But the inner door to Brovek's office stood ajar. He tiptoed over and peered inside. He couldn't believe his eyes.

In the middle of the carpeted floor sat a waste basket mounded with squashed cups and broken styrofoam. It stank of old onions. Cushions from the Professor's couch lay scattered under the windows, along with a shoe and a scrunched-up pillow probably from a surgical cart. A tangled bath blanket filled the place of one missing cushion, and folded neatly over a chair he saw Brovek's coat and pants. The great man himself was standing in his wrinkled boxer shorts, gazing out the window, and urinating in the sink.

Potts thought he should retreat, but his dropped jaw nailed his feet to the floor. Brovek turned, saw him, and grinned.

"Good morning, Ho, I'm glad you weren't the cleaning lady."

"I don't know about that, Sandy. You need her pretty bad in here." He put his hat down on the Professor's desk and unbuttoned his coat.

Brovek splashed his hands under the tap.

"It's been a hell of a night, Ho, and I've made plans. You are just the guy I want to test them on. Happy Easter." For all his bulk, Brovek bounced on light feet, and the corners of his hand towel flew in patterns around his elbows.

Potts shook his head, trying to keep up. He dropped into Brovek's desk chair. It swung with him, spun toward the window, and he swiveled himself back to face Brovek. "What happened in here anyway?"

"Oh, all this mess? It's quite a story." Brovek rummaged in a desk drawer under Potts's elbow, and came up with a razor. He plastered suds over his face and scraped at his scrubby whiskers. "We had a day yesterday, Ho. We got ourselves a donor—heart, liver, the works. Yes sir, we had a day!"

Potts nodded. Good news for the program. Opportunity. Growth. But his brow furrowed, and he held his breath. His unanswered question erupted from wherever he had hidden it. How did Brovek play his hand? What did he decide about Stern?

"Not a perfect day. Rudd had a little trouble." Brovek splashed his face clean and wiped it with his towel. "And I'm second-guessing myself about some of it. But by God, Ho, it was a good day. We've got our first liver done. We've laid another cornerstone."

Potts measured out his careful words. "Before I celebrate, Sandy, I need to know about Martin Stern. Did you...did he...?"

"Maybe I did wrong there."

Potts sucked in his breath, and Brovek laughed. "No, Ho. Not what you think. Yes, I got Stern his liver. You knew all the time I'd do that."

Potts let out his breath in relief, and grinned. "If I'd known all the time you'd do that, I'd have been resting better. What was Rudd's trouble?"

"Shit happens. Too much work, not enough food. An insulin reaction wiped him out." Brovek sat down to pull on his pants, and jammed his foot into a shoe.

Potts rotated again in the swivel chair. He wondered if it would swing all the way around like his old piano stool. Too bad about Rudd.

"That could happen again, Sandy. What can you do to protect him? And his patients?"

Brovek stopped fiddling with his clothes, and spoke directly to his friend, the sass gone from his voice. "The first thing I have to do is get him to stay here. He resigned yesterday. Wanted to pack up and get out. I had to chew on him pretty hard before I could get him madder at me than he was at himself. But I made it, and he's got duties to do. He'll be okay I think."

Brovek looked about for his other shoe, couldn't find it, and shrugged. "But you're right. We can't ask him to perform for hours at a time without a chance to take care of himself. He has to be sheltered, and that's part of my plan."

He unfolded a clean shirt from a second desk drawer, and pulled it on. He tucked his shirt tail into his pants and stood before Potts, fastening the buttons.

"What is your plan?"

Brovek grinned. He drew in a monstrous breath that strained his buttons and stretched the fabric tight across his chest. "Expand, Horace. We expand!"

He let his breath go and grew serious. "There are opportunities all around us. Pancreas transplant for diabetes is what brought Rudd here in the first place. He is a first-rate investigator, and transplants for diabetes are just a matter of time—time and research. Why not right here? Why not Rudd? It's perfect!"

"St. Luke's again, hey? Everything hinges on that. How did it go with Stern?"

"Shit, it went fine. Rudd's spell could have wiped out Stern and his option. And given us our shot at St. Luke's. But your friend Garrison stepped in like she was born for it and finished things up. All I had to do was watch."

Potts retrieved the missing shoe from beneath the desk. "I'm glad of that, Dr. Brovek. I would hate to have things depend on a man who can't keep track of two shoes."

He pitched it at Brovek. He also came up with a broken soda straw that he held up, bent between his fingers. "You must have had some party in here last night," he said. "Things like this can start rumors."

Brovek laughed. He stepped into the shoe and jammed his heel inside.

"That's why you're not a surgeon, Horace. Here we are right at the part of the story you want to hear, and you fool around with a soda straw. A surgeon," he said, throwing his shoe strings into two graceful knots, "would go for the throat."

Potts was unimpressed. Brovek's powerful motions carried a taut energy that seemed to activate the air around him. Could too much energy be a fault? "A surgeon," Potts said softly, "might also go in right over his head." He stepped to the basket and dropped the straw safely inside it. "But I do want to know, Sandy. What about Dr. Garrison?"

"You were right about her, you were right all along. She is the best. She's got the balls, and she's as smooth as cream. If we get to expand, she belongs here with us."

Potts sat down again in the professorial chair and clapped his hands in pantomime applause.

"You will never be sorry, I'm sure of that. But I hate that damned 'if.' How are we going to get rid of it?"

Brovek faced the mirror and threw a loose Windsor into his tie. "*We* aren't going to get rid of it," he grinned, "*You* are!"

He snugged the knot and adjusted the tie ends as if they were the only two problems of his life. "I decided long ago I would work to give Stern his liver, and now I've done it. So now the whole deal is in your ball park. You deal with him."

Potts's eyes narrowed. The game had entered a new phase.

He ignored the professor's incredible self-satisfaction. Somewhere along the way, he himself, Horace Potts, would have to deal with Martin Stern. Nothing else would count. He must rethink the whole project in those terms.

Brovek babbled on. "He's got a four-to-one chance at getting well now. Give him another month or two to recover and he'll be your baby to deal with. Have you made a plan?"

Potts pondered. Somewhere inside of Martin Stern's needs he must find a key. Somewhere in his own mind he must find an answer that lay in hiding.

"No," he said, "I haven't any plan. But if you're going to get the bugger well, I guess I'd better go and figure one out."

He picked up his hat and waved it on his way to the door. "Have a happy day, Sandor. I think I'm going to take a little drive."

Maybe some day he would get to come back and try swiveling all the way around in the professor's chair.

*　　　　　*　　　　　*

Potts folded his Chesterfield over his arm and strolled to his car. The day was mild. Parked in the sun, his blue Olds had gathered in the heat. He put his hat and coat on the seat and rolled down the windows. He guessed he would drive around the hospital again; he didn't know what else to do; he was bankrupt of ideas.

So Brovek had made up his mind a long time ago! Had he really said that? The faker.

Potts shuddered. No. Brovek had wandered an uncertain path along the chisel edge of temptation. Martin Stern might have been sold for a lot more than thirty pieces of silver. But finally, when the chips came down, Brovek did right. Thank God.

So now it's my job, is it, to negotiate with Stern? To convert that aggressive developer into a willing seller. Not likely. What lever could change the man's mind? Money? Gratitude? Flattery? There's got to be an angle somewhere, the right button to push. But I haven't thought of it yet.

He found himself cruising the block behind the church. He didn't know these streets as well, their buildings standing between St. Luke's and the freeway. Pretty run down, most of them. They stood too far from the hospital to be of any use to him. He was wasting his gasoline.

And yet…. Somewhere there was an answer. His eyes narrowed…he needed to think everything through all over again. What was he overlooking?

*   *   *

"You look dreadful, Lance. Can't you get some rest?"

Lance glared at Dana. With her typical casual elegance she stood on the other side of the bed, her arms clutching Stern's chart against her breast. She had come up silently in the brightness of ICU, and found him here, his thighs pushed against the edge of Martin Stern's bed, staring at the hateful lump that lay inert under the sheet.

Why the hell shouldn't I look dreadful? All I've done for two long damn weeks is stand around this bedside. It's all Brovek will let me do, and he has to make me do even that. I don't give a shit about Stern. To hell with his precious liver. When he's well or dead I'm done. Kaput. Out of here.

But that isn't Dana's problem. I can't take it out on her.

He cocked his head toward the nurses' station to draw her away from the bedside. For her sake he adjusted his white coat to fit its limp fabric around his collar. His loafers still carried a pretty good shine. He didn't think he looked so bad. He forced a more pleasant expression to his face, and surprised himself at the frowning tension that released around his eyes.

"So how should I look?" he said. His voice was a low rasp. "I collapse in surgery, the boss bawls me out in his office, I check my patient five times a day and stand around between times, and it goes on and on. Come to think of it, you look pretty scrawny yourself." His tone softened; he wasn't the only one under stress. "How are you holding up, Dana?"

She smiled thinly. "A chief resident lives on the edge of exhaustion, you know that. I'm alive."

She looked alive, he thought: scrubbed cheeks, intelligent eyes, that elusive fragrance about her hair. Only a friend might notice the prominent bones of her face, the dark skin under her eyes. "You ought to put that boy friend on hold. He's hanging around here a lot."

Dana's cheeks colored, and she grinned quickly. "I'll consider your advice, Doctor. You say I should hold on to my boy friend?"

Yes. Lance changed his opinion. Hang on to him while you can.

He nodded, and took the chart from her hands. "You go on with your other patients. I'll wait for the lab results before I write Stern's orders."

"Thanks, Lance."

He watched her small figure go on about her considerable business.

Sure I can wait for the lab results. Why not? I've got nothing else to do. Nothing else to be. I've become a fraud, a hollow shell.

He returned to Stern's bedside. To Stern's body with its new liver, courtesy of Karen Sondergaard. To Stern himself, inert, unconscious under his sheet, inflating by machine, watering in and out through plastic tubing, struggling to live.

No credit to me, Martin, but you and I are struggling together. You're all I have left. You, that made me crap out in the OR. You destroyed me, you know that? I have nowhere to go but down, and I'd be gone now, if Brovek hadn't burned me. He rubbed my nose in your care, and I got so damn mad, I sat on my bed in Motherwell Arms and packed my suitcase.

A suit, a couple of shirts. I'd have blown out of here except for you. You're the one job I'm still mired in.

But maybe Brovek was right. Maybe the last few days are a good sign for me. I've started to sleep at night. Harvey Kanju has got me to controlling my blood sugar again. And just yesterday from somewhere inside I dredged up a decision about you, my only patient, that turned out absolutely right. And that felt good to me.

And so here I am, looking at you, Martin, and you need me bad. Something's going wrong, you're in trouble. You, or your lungs, or your precious liver. What's knocking you down? There are lots of possibilities. What's the right answer?

Despite his black mood, Lance's heart stirred. A conundrum of care always raised the stakes, and he had a history of responding to such calls, mustering extra energies and all his smarts to find the winning answers. And here came a hummer, right from Stern himself, and despite his depression, Lance warmed to it.

Stern's arm moved, and dragged his i.v. tubing across the sheet. Lance lifted the plastic so it wouldn't snag. After so many days and so much support, Stern's arm veins were mostly obliterated; a functioning i.v. needle was not a detail, it was a precious asset.

Lance pondered his patient. He knew how to proceed. He would go through his litany of suspicions, tests, exams; he would listen to his hunches, pray for inspiration, and by God come up with the answer.

There is more at stake here than just Martin Stern. If I can finish, after all, the surgical job I started, if I can bring under control the complicated chemistries churning away here? Hell, they're churning away in me too. If I can bring Stern through his trial, isn't there a shred of hope even for Lancelot Motherwell Rudd, M.D.?

*   *   *

After a three-hour-long by-pass procedure, Sandor Brovek raced into the surgeon's locker room and headed straight for the urinal. And there in front of him, blocking his way, stood Grover Iverson, backing up and turning around. They were two cocks in the same barnyard. In a comic dance that neither thought was funny they bobbed in unison one way and then the other, until Brovek snorted, dropped his scrub pants and bulled past Iverson to the fixture.

Iverson chortled. "A little urgency, Sandy? Are you starting to get up at night? Happens to everybody."

Brovek stepped out of the cotton bottoms, left them crumpled on the tiles and strode to his locker. If he did have to get up at night he sure as hell wouldn't tell Iverson. The bastard had claimed a kidney from the same donor as Stern's liver and put it in one of his out-of-town wealthies. In Brovek's surgical community Iverson was a putrid focus, an abscess that needed to be drained.

But Stern was still alive. Still in the way. Still held the key to St. Luke's. Brovek's throat tightened as he choked back his anger. At Iverson. At himself. He could have let Stern go. He struggled with his scrub shirt, trying to pull it off over his head. The damned thing was never big enough; it always got stuck coming over his shoulders.

He ignored Iverson, who stood at the mirror primping his fucking image. Brovek hauled his pants out of his locker and put them on, one leg at a time. He zipped up and sat down on the narrow plank bench to change his shoes.

And here came Iverson, a yard away, straddling the bench, shoving his face right at Brovek. He wore a white clinical coat and a bow tie. His slacks stretched over his knees without losing their crease. He pulled at his mustache.

"Sandor, I think you are right," he said.

Brovek masked his surprise. "About what?" he grunted.

"Putting all transplants in your department. We should have one policy for everybody."

Brovek held one shoe in each hand, his white surgical slipper with old red stains that long ago had turned brown, and a cordovan dress shoe that needed polish. He pulled the white shoe onto his foot.

"Quite a change, Iverson. What do you have in mind?"

Iverson swung his leg over the bench and walked again to the mirror. He fished in his pocket for a comb.

"Oh nothing, really. It's just time to evolve. You're into hearts, and now even livers. Lungs will be next. Donors are shared. It's time for a united transplant service."

It was too good to be true.

"Cut the bull shit, Iverson. A man doesn't give away a kingdom just because it's time. What's going on?"

Iverson wheeled on Brovek. His eyes burned.

"You don't have to know. Isn't my offer good enough for you?"

Brovek bent over his shoes, thinking hard. The offer matched his strategy; it was just what he was angling for. But it was too easy. What was the down side? Guilt by association? In bed with the enemy?

He got up and stood behind Iverson. From the mirror his own gray chest hairs taunted him. "Grover," he said softly, "I believe you have been selling kidneys. No proof. But that is untenable conduct. Do you agree to stop?"

Iverson's mustache twitched. "Stop?" he said. "Like stop beating my wife? I agree it would be untenable, and I'll never do it."

"Every kidney you put in will be assigned by ROPO, right?"

"Yes, of course. Okay."

A careless slur in his voice sounded almost desperate.

"Let me think a minute."

Brovek stepped to his locker, and pulled on his shirt. He walked to the mirror and began to tie his Paisley four-in-hand. "I'll want it in writing."

No hesitation. "Okay."

How far could he push this man?

"I want your letter of resignation, dated prior to whenever the Regents put your transplants under me."

Iverson flared. "Resign, hell, I'm not going to resign!"

In the mirror Brovek watched him scratch his mustache. "Before you come into my department I want a total break with the university. You can't drag your abscess in with you, nor the smell of it. This way, if it ever breaks out in public, you're already gone."

Iverson mouthed a word that sounded like 'Bubba'.

"What?"

"Never mind. You mean I don't actually resign?"

"If you're clean, you don't. But if a scandal comes along you already did. I'd have it in writing."

Iverson sank down on the bench.

"Okay. I guess I can trust you."

Brovek straightened his tie, smoothed it over his belly. Something still bothered. "What about you, Iverson. Can I trust you?"

"Sure you can."

"Is there a scandal in the wind? Is that what's blown you over?"

"Sandy, there isn't one I know of, and I hope to God there never is."

It was as close to a confession as Brovek needed. He watched with a cold heart as Iverson smoothed his white coat across his shoulders, flicked the lapel and left the room.

Brovek stood lost in thought. Had he done right? If Iverson's resignation was dated before the public knew there was a scandal, it would look like a cover-up. And he guessed it was. But Iverson was salvageable—a good operator, a decent scientific mind. And with his abuses stopped, the public need never know. No university could profit from the disgrace of its faculty.

His reverie exploded as the door burst open in his face. Barney Popper blew through it and braked to an emergency stop. He looked Brovek up and down and snorted.

"Hey, what's with you, Sandy?" He pointed at Brovek's feet, one clad in dirty white, the other in dingy brown. "Are you coming, or going?"

*   *   *

On the eighth day of May, Martin Stern woke up with an erection. For the first time since the other side of darkness, turgid power throbbed in his body. New strength in his muscles, new energy for his soul. His spirits soared. By God, he was going to get well after all!

Morning sun flooded his hospital room and warmed the blanket over his knees. If he could just get the damn window open, he'd bet he could hear birds sing. He threw back the sheet and climbed out of bed. He grinned as he picked up the plastic urinal from his bed table: here was another new skill of the last two days. The long tether that had drained his bladder for the past five weeks was gone. Master of the Universe, a man should not take simple gifts for granted.

His erection eased away as his bladder emptied, but his spirits remained aloft. He splashed cold water over his face and muffled himself with a fresh white towel. Bits of lint stuck in his dark stubbles, and he scratched at them with his fingernails. He threw the towel under the sink.

No more trays in bed, he decided. He backed his knees against the one soft chair in his room, and lowered himself into it.

Now for breakfast. My appetite is a new thrill, too. A man has to eat; where's my tray?

In his crowded private room, his knees nearly touched the corner of his bed. No wonder, with all the paraphernalia at the head of it, the hoses and fittings, the light switches, the drab beige curtain pulled back on its ceiling track around the bed. He eyed the heavy black cable lying across his pillow, the only good thing in the room, the TV controls.

He looked at the door, waiting for the thud of a nurse's foot, watching for the door to swing open and reveal her morning smile and his tray full of breakfast. Footsteps came near and passed on by. His stomach growled. He drummed his fingers on the chair arm.

The blackness of the past weeks washed again over his mind. The immutable artificial environment of ICU, no days, no nights, stagnant time measured only by the drop-drop-drop of fluids, the winking of monitors, the ministrations of nameless persons to his helpless body as he drifted in and out of consciousness. Ten weeks of blurred purgatory.

But that's over now! Today life has become manifest!

A soft bump against the door alerted him, and he watched it swing inward. But there was no smiling Nightingale face. It was Ben, the orderly, mooning his backside through the doorway, trailing a wheel chair.

Stern groaned. His trips with the tiny cashew-colored Hmong had been torture. Ben's wiry body struggled to control his load. The litter bounced on ramps and swayed around corners. Elevators jerked at every stop and start. Instinctively Stern spread his hands supportively over his belly.

Ben said nothing; his face, as always, stayed blank. He pivoted the wheel chair around to face Stern, locked the wheels, pointed to Stern and then the chair.

Nobody tells me, of course. I'm only the patient. So what's to argue? Ben can't speak English—or won't. But I get the message: no breakfast.

Stern climbed obediently into the chair and submitted his bare feet to a deft Asian blanket wrap. He watched his room recede as Ben backed him out through the door.

Now what? For the first time this morning I feel like maybe a real person, like a mensch; and suddenly they make me a pawn all over again? They think I have nothing to say?

At the nurses' station Ben padded over to the chart rack, pulled out a metal folder and dropped it softly into Stern's lap. He read the label: "Stern, M., Dr. Rudd."

If Ben can't talk, maybe he can read? But that nurse, she can talk. Nurses are always sitting there at that desk, always writing. Why don't they go take care of somebody?

He coughed out a summons for her attention.

"May a person ask what is happening to him this morning?"

Look at her, just a kid with freckles. I can read her thoughts like a floor plan. *Who is this guy?* she thinks. *He's not my patient. It's only seven-fifteen in the morning. I just came on duty.* They always fall back on that old line: *I just came on duty.*

Ah. Now the light comes to her face. It wasn't such a tough question after all, was it, honey?

"Oh, Mr. Stern," she said, "you are to go to Keaton Amphitheater for Grand Rounds today."

"What about breakfast?"

"We'll hold it for you, okay?"

Grump. So they could tell a person ahead of time. They could care maybe if a person was hungry? He knew what 'hold it for you' meant. Cream of wheat gone cold, with the milk on it gone warm. His appetite curdled. Go fight City Hall. He slumped back in his wheel chair and accepted Ben's silent push down the long hall.

They jilted into a creaking elevator and dropped two floors to emerge into a dim corridor. Old and shabby. Heating pipes running along under the ceiling. Probably has asbestos, too. Not like I'd build it, he thought. He rode passively as his chair rolled along the silent hall and stopped at a narrow door. Ben reached past his shoulder and pulled the door open. Sudden lights glared in Stern's eyes. Even squinting he couldn't see. Without ceremony he was shoved through the door.

Stern blinked and shaded his eyes.

Where am I? On a stage, for God's sake. I see theater seats rising up higher than I can focus, and a bunch of faces peering down at me. Who the hell are they? Young folks with solemn faces, straight mouths, eyes hidden by spectacles. If I'd had a chance I'd have worn my glasses. Then I could see. And I haven't even shaved yet. Shit.

He squinted and peered about for someone he could recognize. He spied Rudd a couple of rows up. And here came that lady doctor, Garrison. She walked right up to his chair.

"Good morning Mr. Stern."

Her voice suggested he didn't need to answer.

"This is a teaching conference of the surgery department. These are all doctors and nurses here to learn about your kind of problem, okay?"

Okay. He wished he got a nickel every time somebody said to him "okay." What it meant was "Just keep quiet and go along with the program."

But they should have let me know ahead of time. I could have worn my slippers, for God's sake.

Dr. Garrison turned to the multitudes, tapping her fingernail lightly against the metal cover of his chart. Her white coat fit smoothly across her shoulders, and draped over what he considered a very provocative rump. Her legs were neat enough; he wondered why a short girl like that wore flat heels. Maybe her feet hurt?

"This patient," she projected to the highest row, "developed sclerosing cholangitis about five years ago. The diagnosis was established with x-rays and biopsy at the time of surgery for gall stones. Medical trials of steroids were unsatisfactory. He got worse. In January of this year he was placed on the waiting list for liver transplantation."

He recalled that day in Rudd's office. It was his first inkling that he had any hope for recovery. That same day he threw a million bucks at the bishop that he couldn't refuse. The way a climber might throw a grappling hook across a crevasse to get a grip on the other side. And now maybe he would profit from the deal after all. Maybe he had found a new way to do business!

Dr. Garrison kept on talking.

"Adding a name to a waiting list is no guarantee of getting an organ. You see this patient now; he is getting well. But between New Year's and Easter he waited for a liver and grew sicker and sicker. He nearly died for lack of a donor."

Stern was entranced with center stage. She recited his woes, one after the other, and he nodded his head, remembering.

"We lost four opportunities for organs. One wasn't exactly lost, because ROPO placed the liver somewhere else. But it was lost for him. In February we had a suitable donor here, right in this hospital. Ideal situation. All the relatives agreed to donation, except one son. Blackball. No harvest. Heart, liver, kidneys, bone, skin, eyes all lost. Do you think we can be satisfied with this kind of consent process?"

Stern wanted to holler "No!", but he just jammed himself upright in his wheel chair and readjusted the blanket over his knees. His eyes were getting used to the light, and he could see people better. February, she said. Now it was May. If they had fixed him in February he could have wrecked the church by now, even dug foundations maybe.

The young lady doctor talks big, like she knows her apples. But she has a nice voice, low, and sexy.

"The other two cases were in community hospitals here in our own county. Both were good candidates for organ harvest. Can you guess why they were lost?"

Stern watched her, fascinated. Two cases?

"They were lost because nobody asked. Not to ask was a tragic waste of opportunity for patients like this one. I hope that some day soon hospitals will be required to develop formal procedures for seeking consent or be in trouble with their accreditation."

Serve them right, Stern thought, whatever accreditation means. Two cases right here in North County? One was enough to know about, I almost gave up after one, except for that priest. God of Jacob, why do they leave a critical thing like this to chance? What's wrong with people, they don't make a system that works? Harvest first, then ask, I say.

He listened on, in turmoil.

"Meantime this patient almost died. He developed hepatic failure and coma. He struggled out of that. But we had to decide if he wasn't too far gone for a transplant."

Too far gone? His old nightmare triggered out of its lair. The constant fears that had boiled in him through all those waiting weeks churned again in the pit of his stomach. But only as an echo.

Today I am safe. Laugh, Martin. If they'd learned it was me who beat them to St. Luke's, that's exactly what they would have said. "Too far gone, sorry, Mr. Stern." But they never found out! Here I sit, that's the proof of it. Tough luck, all you empire builders, you're too late now.

Where's Dr. Rudd? There, in the third row. Blessings on his house.

Hey, what's the lady doctor saying? Hell, I missed the operation! Listen up, Martin.

"...five weeks ago. He has had a tough convalescence."

Look who was saying it was tough! I'd like to tell them about tough.

"He stayed on the ventilator for fourteen days before we could wean him from it."

Fourteen years, more like it. Try it some time, lying in bed with a hose in your nose. You can't talk, the machine all the time blowing you up and down like a balloon day and night. Lila Mae came back in there somewhere and I couldn't even say hello. And weaning was worse, when they tried to take away the machine and I couldn't get enough air. Sometimes I just wished it was over with. I'd rather die than go on fighting. Except there was Lila Mae, sitting alongside, wanting me!

He looked at Dr. Garrison, standing there shorter than the first row of seats, still telling everybody about Martin Stern. He changed his mind; maybe he could do without so much attention. His stomach growled. God, how long since he'd been hungry? Wouldn't she ever quit talking?

"His next trouble was fever, and failure to thrive. Our problem was to distinguish between rejection of the graft and some kind of hidden infection. We checked for rejection by a series of percutaneous liver biopsies. Three of them. There was no evidence of rejection on microscopic examination."

That was when they stuck those big needles into me. I felt like the iron maiden. And it was five times, not three, if you count when they didn't get anything. Make it five times for the pin cushion, already.

"He was given antibiotics for herpes and for Pneumocystis. Finally sputum culture grew out Pneumocystis, and he responded well to a full course of trimethoprim. I remind you about Pneumocystis as an organism of opportunity in patients with deficiency in the immune system. It is cropping up in the new disease called AIDS, and transplant patients are at risk as well. This patient was immunosuppressed with Cyclosporin-A and prednisone, and he developed Pneumocystis pneumonia."

Stern grumbled to himself.

AIDS I don't have; why is she talking about AIDS? Pneumonia I had, and couldn't breathe. Pneumonia is bad enough without AIDS, God forbid.

"After his infection was controlled, his lung function recovered. We discontinued the ventilator and he began to eat. We withdrew artificial feedings three days ago. His incision is healing. He is up and around. His liver function tests are returning toward normal. We expect him to leave the hospital within a few days."

What good is it I sit here through all this. They should dress up a dummy like Martin Stern. Bring the dummy in, let the dummy sit here in the wheel chair. Or hire an actor to sit here. I could be eating breakfast now. Let the actor sit in front of all these faces.

"Are there any comments?"

He hitched at his blanket and it fell away from his feet. His bare toes stuck out; his bunions bulged. In the glare of lights he felt naked and diminished.

A voice from the seats asked something about bile; he didn't listen. Another voice answered. A deep rumble of a voice. Everybody turned to listen.

Deference. Stern knew it well, the tone given to him by architects and subcontractors. This had to be the Dr. Brovek he had heard about. The top boss. Stern located him easily, in the center of the front row. He didn't know Brovek was so big.

"Well, thank you for coming in, Mr. Stern." It was Garrison again. The silent Ben hovered behind her as if he were her magic genie.

So, Stern thought, you are through with my body now? You are going to cart me back to my room and spoon me full of cold cream of wheat, keep me like a thing in a zoo, and when you want me again for some other dumb thing you'll just send old Ben over to haul my body somewhere else? Nuts. You've forgotten somebody. Today Martin Stern is a mensch!

His face flushed. After weeks of misery he was back in the world, ready to make things happen. Anger spilled into his throat. Hot words jumped out. "Does a person get to say anything here?"

Garrison turned as if he had pinched her behind. He wished he had.

Now that he had claimed the floor, he didn't know what to say. But her open mouth with no words coming out goaded him on. He spoke past her to all the faces towering above him.

"I should thank you for my new shot at life. I know there are many of you who had a hand in my care, you should pardon the expression. I thank Dr. Rudd especially, who never stopped fighting to get me a new liver."

He squinted up at the tiers of faces. Their eyes seemed fixed on his dark stubble. His anger flared again. He searched out Rudd's face, turned all red. He was scowling.

How could a compliment be a bad thing? He looked at Brovek, who stared back at him like a problem on a chess board. Stern's instincts for negotiating jumped forward and took control of his mind. His impetuous words had plucked a hidden string with Rudd. He had sounded some kind of unexpected and alien alarm on the other team. Maybe he should pluck it again and see what happened. Rudd up? Try something down.

"So maybe a person should be grateful enough that bad things are forgotten."

He stopped again. Who would pick up the cue? Garrison was stalled. Rudd said nothing. Finally Dr. Brovek spoke.

"We would like to hear what you mean, Mr. Stern, if you would like to get it off your chest."

Well said. Stern admired the good ploy. Whatever the problem was, Brovek ducked it; it was still Stern's baby. Stern began to enjoy himself.

He pulled the blanket over his feet. Years of negotiating had taught him moderation; abrasion never won disciples. His voice dripped philosophical detachment.

"You see, it should be *me* you fight for, not my liver. It is a hard thing for a person to be sick. He gives up control, he entrusts his body to technicians. He has no choice. But you technicians—you have a choice. It becomes a bad thing if technicians take control of a body and forget that a person lives inside it."

He liked the way that came out. Even if they didn't respond, he was glad he said it. He would want to remember how he had told them.

He passed his hand over the stubble of his face, and thought of his missed breakfast. He watched Brovek. Nothing. Then Rudd. Aha. Rudd leaned forward, he was going to say something.

"Do you feel we have failed you in some way, Mr. Stern?"

Despite himself, Stern's feelings churned up and poured out.

"A miracle shouldn't be a failure, Dr. Rudd. But who gave me hope for a liver? Nobody in your program. Who called Lila Mae down in Mexico? Not you. Who kept reminding me I am a mensch? I should fight and not give up? A stranger, that's who. You made a miracle happen; an outsider made it possible."

Rudd's face screwed up, with lines all over it.

"Do you really believe, Mr. Stern, that without these—ah—motivational factors, you would have died?"

Martin Stern forgot negotiating. He forgot the rows of faces staring down at him. His surgeon became a target.

"Dr. Rudd, as God is my witness, I would have quit. Yes, died, God forbid. This is a hole in your program and you ought to fill it."

Oh, he had plucked something now! Rudd looked as if he were pole-axed. He rocked back in his seat, his mouth gaping, his eyes shooting fire.

Brovek's voice rumbled again, detached and cool. The pole-axe had missed the boss. "Thanks, Mr. Stern. We appreciate that patients have serious challenges to meet in situations like yours. There isn't much choice for them but to go along with the program."

Stern sat back. He'd gone far enough.But what was this? Dr. Rudd, sputtering, bouncing up right out of his chair.

He looked mad and he talked too loud. "Dr. Brovek," he said, "I don't think we can let it go at that. We have heard testimony here of a serious deficiency. I have heard the same opinion from—from someone else. I didn't believe it then. Now I do. If the program is deficient it is our job as physicians to correct it."

Sit down, Dr. Rudd, Stern thought, you'll get fired. Nobody talks to the boss like that, not in public. Stern peered at the boss.

Brovek surprised him. He looked like a cat with cream. He would look exactly like that if he had just drawn his fifth spade, and it was the ace, and he waited to push out his chips until everybody was watching.

"Very recently we started a program of this sort," he said. "under the direction of the late Miss Sondergaard. Perhaps it needs to be continued, with a physician in charge. We would need the right man, or, ah, woman."

He swiveled his great shoulders around until he faced square onto Dr. Rudd. His words drawled out as sticky as molasses. "Lancelot, if you feel strongly about this program, may I count on you?"

Stern was thrilled. He sensed a double message here, something in code hidden behind the simple facade. Fascinated, he turned his eyes back to Rudd.

The young surgeon was transformed. He sat down again, smiling. His frame draped itself across two seats, his long arms stretching over the backs of two more. He looked as if some great question had been lifted from his shoulders. Stern tried to puzzle it out. Rudd's gaze at Brovek was filled with—what?—affection? His words came out deliberate, arrow-straight at Brovek, as if they were the only two men in the room.

"Yes, Dr. Brovek," he said. "You may count on me."

Stern's juices surged. He hadn't had so much fun since the day he conned the bishop. He didn't understand what had happened here, but he knew, whatever it was, that he himself had made a difference. Maybe even a good difference. He would always remember how he spoke his piece. He had turned this freak show for doctors into a landmark morning. Today he was a mensch.

He lifted his palm jauntily toward the high seats. Caesar leaving the amphitheater. He smiled imperially at Ben. "You are my genie now," he commanded with his eyes. "Take me home."

In the dark hall he pushed his hands against the wheels, hurrying the chair ahead of the shuffling Ben. He jabbed the elevator button commanding the car to come. At the nurses' station he lifted the metal-jacketed chart from his lap and tossed it onto the desk with a clatter. Two nurses looked up, startled, the younger one choking back a cry of fright, her hand over her mouth.

"Hey, ladies," he laughed. "Martin Stern is back. Now, what about his breakfast!"

With a toss of his head he urged Ben on, back to his own room, his own chair and table.

Now, just let them bring me that cold cream of wheat, and I'll raise hell. A person ought to have bacon and eggs on a day like this.

▼

PART EIGHT

PENTECOST

To come late for surgery in Mizzoh's operating room would be a major offense, and Dana was about to be late. Struggling to stay civil, she kept her voice level for the junior resident who had screwed up her rounds.

"I make it a practice, Duane, to find the necessary x-rays every morning. Before my boss comes to see them."

She looked over the trio of medical students clustered behind Duane in the dimly lighted viewing room. They looked so young.

"If you have your films ready," she warned, "you can avoid getting your face full of wet feathers."

She flicked the switch impatiently, and four dark panels flickered into fluorescent brightness. Duane jammed the tardy films under the mounting clips and stood back. Dana bit her tongue.

A soft shadow hung like a bean in the middle of an empty left chest. Duane's intercostal tube was plainly visible, curled against the diaphragm. But it did not, as it should have done, suck out the air leaking from the collapsed lung. She had to help him adjust the tube, and she would be late to surgery.

"I've run into some trouble, Mizzoh. I'll be a half hour late."

She expected disapproval; Mizzoh's laugh over the phone surprised her.

"No problem, Dana. I just bumped you for Dr. Brovek's urgent carotid. He got one of the guys to assist him, so take your time."

Dana decompressed. She was grateful she hadn't chewed on poor Duane—his hand trembled when he put up those films. She remembered what her father used to say about fractured schedules: They're inevitable. But once in a blue moon the broken pieces will turn out to fit like a cut-out puzzle. If it happens, enjoy it.

"Let's go fix that chest tube, Duane. Come on, students."

In the surgical ward sunlight was just beginning to touch the dark windows. The spring morning made a lovely addition to her father's blue moon. She adjusted the chest tube to a flurry of bubbles in the suction bottle, and excused herself from the group.

In the nurses' dressing room she slipped into a fresh scrub suit, splashed her face and tugged at her hair with her pocket comb. With the bit of scent that lingered at the base of her neck, she entered the O.R. corridor feeling pretty spiffy. Until she looked down and saw her shoes. Those old friends had carried her through many battles, and they showed the wounds. Despite dozens of soap scrubs, blotches of rusty stain blossomed through her last layer of Shoe White. Well, these shoes would have to do, until July, and 'rusty' wasn't such a bad color....

"One of the guys," was that what Mizzoh had said? The old knot of uncertainty tightened in her throat. Why hadn't Brovek called her? She was his Chief Resident. She had scored triumphs in the past weeks—weren't they enough for the old chauvinist?

A deep voice that could only be Dr. Brovek's boomed out of Mizzoh's office.

"Dr. Garrison," it demanded. "I would like to speak to you for a moment. Can you come in here?"

She glanced through the window into her O.R., Room 2. The kind of case she would like to avoid. Lung cancer? Probably not, but there was a nodule in the lung that had to be identified. Pete was ready, standing beside the draped patient with his hand out for the scalpel. A junior resident and a student faced him across the table, waiting.

"Sure, Dr. Brovek. Just a sec."

She pushed the door ajar. "Pete," she said, "go ahead and start. Resect the sixth rib and I'll be there."

It was too much, having to crack the chest just to get at the lung for a sliver of tissue. Such major surgery simply to biopsy a lump offended her sense of proportion. She liked the new idea of probing about with biopsy needles in places once forbidden. If she had the authority, maybe she could avoid operations like this one.

"Good morning, Dr. Brovek. How can I help?"

He sat in his green scrub suit on Mizzoh's desk and dangled his legs. His broad hands rested on his thighs; they wore patterned lines of white powder. His vee neck sagged, and Dana could see the mat of curly hair that began abruptly at his collar line and covered his chest. She suppressed a giggle; she hadn't ever thought of a man's beard just growing out all the way down, so that he had to decide where to stop shaving.

"In another six weeks you'll be finished here," he said.

Her giggle died.

Her term as Chief Resident would end in six weeks, nothing new there. But today he had called in 'one of the guys' to help him, he hadn't called her. And now he said "finished." Like, gone?

She forced a smile. "Yes sir," she said, "the first of July."

The beginning of real life. Could she live her dream and stay on with Brovek, or would he shunt her off to find a job somewhere? And what about Rusty? The only thing certain about the first of July was that her life would change.

The thrill that had given her shivers during last month's liver transplant lived on; she felt its rightness every day, like a discovered destiny. But her future here was not her decision; it was Brovek's.

The great man's feet swung slowly in and out, his heels bumping the desk.

"I've had some inquiries about you," he said. "Dr. Bockmun at Hangarville is interested. I wonder what plans you are making for your future."

She steadied herself, folded her hands. Her fingers trembled. How could she say she had dreamed a lot, but hadn't made any plans?

"I've given all my attention to this job right now, I guess. I've thought about the future of course, but…I don't know…" She groped for words. "I've just sort of waited…you know…to see what would happen…. Here."

The last word slipped out unbidden. She felt her hot flush rise across her cheeks and forehead into the roots of her hair. She dropped to a chair, facing Brovek.

His eyes were dark; his voice seemed to tremble. "I'm not sure what our future is here at the University. If we're going to amount to anything, we need to expand. I don't know whether we can."

She gazed up at her chief. The hair at his temples pushed out from beneath his cap, gray, like the hair on his chest. She had never thought of his having problems beyond his patients and his research papers. This was a new dimension. No wonder his shoulders drooped. And everybody knew about his wife.

Dana said nothing.

"You know that I have to protect Lance," he went on. He slid forward and planted his feet on the floor. "I want him to switch to research—he's a good mind."

"I nearly died when he wanted to quit. He's too good for that."

Brovek nodded. "So we'll need to replace him with somebody on the clinical side, with students and patients and all. I'm tied up in the heart and lung cases."

Dana's heart pounded. Not an axe? Could it be a sword to anoint her shoulder? She stared at him, lips parted.

"I'll need somebody for livers," he said, "and whatever other organs we learn to transplant in the belly. Would you consider staying on?"

She jumped to her feet. She wanted to hug him, but she didn't dare. She stood stiff and awkward before him.

"That's what I want to do more than anything, Dr. Brovek!. I wouldn't consider anywhere else, if you want me to stay."

Mizzoh poked her head around the door jamb. "Pete's waiting for you in Room 2, Dr. Garrison. Are you coming?"

Brovek's total smile melted her. "I like that answer, Dana. Welcome aboard!"

His two great hands engulfed hers. All the caution flowed out of her limbs, and she floated on an impulsive energy of grace. She threw her arms around his shoulders and kissed him solidly on the cheek.

"Thanks, Dr. Brovek. You'll never be sorry!"

She turned a huge smile on a wide-eyed Miss O'Hoolihan. "Yes, I'm coming, Mizzoh. Tell Pete I'll scrub and be there in jig time. With bells on!"

*   *   *

Dana held the tip of the lower lobe while Pete applied the stapling machine and fired it to seat the tiny metal clips. She watched him cut off the bit of lung with its unknown lump. By the time the benign report came back from the lab, the lung closure was dry and airtight.

Dana stepped back from the table and stripped off her gown. She had a special celebratory move for her gloves. She pulled the right glove down by its cuff, turning it inside out and balling it in her left palm. Then she hooked her right thumb under the cuff of the left glove, pulled it inside out over the first glove, stretched it out like a sling shot, and let fire into a basket under the sink. Zingo. Brovek always did it after an especially good operation.

"Will you close the chest, Pete? I have a phone call to make."

Her words were honest; her appearance of nonchalance was pure deceit. She sauntered out of the surgical suite, pulling a white lab coat over her scrub suit. She listened for the bump as the double automatic doors swung shut behind her.

Abruptly she quickened her stride, leaned into her eagerness, nearly running, through Old U, straight to her own room and her secluded telephone. She had about one inch left to go when it jangled its own demand.

"Damn," she thought. But she said, "Hello?"

"Duck, I can't wait. I've got to tell you about this. Can you talk?"

The sound of his voice made her weak. She folded onto the edge of her narrow bed, holding the phone close to her lips.

"Rusty," she breathed. "It's happened again. I just ran over here to call you. I have something to tell, too."

"You go first."

"No, you called me first—by a second or two. You tell."

She heard his excitement in his rush of words. His dear voice pitched itself a couple of tones higher than his usual scratch.

"That guy in New York likes my story. He wants to publish it, and he wants to see more. Dana, I've got a chance!"

She imagined him at his desk in the apartment she had never seen, the sun streaming through a window over piles of papers and books, over his old Underwood with half a sheet of white bond sticking out the top, his feet propped alongside, his chair tipped back almost to collapse, and the phone pinched between his ear and his hunched shoulder. She wished she could walk in on him just like that.

"Of course you do, darling. I knew all those hours would pay off. You're a literary giant!"

His easy chuckle awakened her warmth and desire for him.

"No, Dana, no giant. But I'm alive. Now tell me your news, before you have to break for a commercial."

She couldn't keep the laughter hidden from her voice—she wished she could watch his face.

"I've been propositioned by a gentleman."

He missed a beat. She grinned; she had changed his pace.

"Come on, Duck," he said. "You wouldn't tell me that. If you had time to listen to propositions, I'd have taken you downtown on Easter Sunday."

She sobered. "And I'd have gone, too," she whispered. She paused, remembering. "But this one was different, lover. This gentleman was Dr. Brovek! He wants me to stay on here, join the staff, work in transplants. It's my dream of dreams, except when I dream of you. Assistant Professor of Surgery: how does that sound for starters?"

She wondered if that message would bring his feet down from his desk, and then she remembered she didn't even know where he was.

"I'm thrilled for you, Duck. What's the date today? We'll remember it to celebrate."

Dana kicked off her flat shoes and lay back against her pillow. She cradled the phone against her face.

"Today," she breathed into Rusty's imagined ear, "is the day we can plan. Where are you?"

"At home making love to my typewriter. What do you want to plan?"

"I don't know. Whatever. What do novelists plan with professors anyway?"

Her voice was husky. She wished he were here with her, in her forbidden bed.

"Escapades," he said. "They plan escapades with happy endings." His voice dropped to a murmur. "Let's plan one, Dana. Will you marry me?"

And now she missed a beat of her own. She felt as if she would float.

"Oh Rusty," she whispered; her voice gathered urgency. "You know I will. When? when? when?"

His irrepressible laugh bubbled in her ear.

"Well, you see, I've started this novel, and until I'm done with it I just can't do anything else."

Mercurial was what he was. He would never be dull. But he had shifted too far from her this time.

"Come on, you're teasing me. My time in prison is almost over, and Dr. Brovek says the first thing I should do is take two weeks off. What are you doing July first?"

Rusty turned serious. She knew how his green eyes would narrow, his wiry eyebrows squeeze together in a frown.

"I know an island in Florida. We can fly there, rent a cottage, comb the beach. No blizzards, I guarantee it. We'll leave on the third and be back for work on the fourteenth. The wedding can come before, or during, or after. You say, I'll be there. I love you, Duck."

"Oh, Russell, I love you too. And I want you. I want you now."

She curled up around the telephone, clasping her pillow against her body, hugging herself in excitement…. But hey? did he say the third?

"Did you say the third? What happens on the first?"

Rusty chuckled. "Well, Mrs. Doctor, I have a fantasy about that. On the first morning of July you will come creeping our of your cave to blink at the sunshine. And before you can gather your wits I shall scoop you up and drag you into my cave—I've got one too, you know. And there we shall lie in long-delayed and well-deserved delight."

Dana caressed the phone. Her nipples stood up. Her body begged to be touched. She murmured softly, urgently.

"If the way I feel right now is the way you felt on Easter, you should have had a hero badge. But it's only six more weeks, my love, and then….'

Rusty's voice was serious again, and vibrant.

"Dana, I mean every word. I love you. I want you. I want to marry you. I am mad for your body. Are you with me, all the way?"

She could not contain the jubilation that welled up in her heart. Her slender frame shivered, weightless. Her arms stretched upwards, toward the ceiling, toward the sky, and she crooned her song of joy to the lofted phone.

"Yes, Rusty, and yes I do, and once again, dear, yes I am, all the way."

*   *   *

Lance Rudd tried to gather himself before going in to see his next patient. All the shards of his shattered life were connected to that man, to Martin Stern. So it was with Stern that his reconstruction must begin. He rested his narrow behind on the corner of his desk and gazed into space.

If Brovek hadn't held me to the fire that day, I'd be out of here. Gone. But he did, and I still have a chance. I carried Stern through the valley of the shadows. That's something. And I have seen Karen's dream, that's something too. Old Brovek baited me with that like a hunk of raw meat. And I seized it.

Okay, Chief, you've got your boy. I'll take it on. But no bull shit. No more charades. Not even with Martin Stern.

Especially not with Martin Stern.

He squeezed his buttocks together, hard, and thrust his body up from the desk. His shin banged against a chair. Karen's chair. There she had sat and told him of her plans. There she had stood fast so he couldn't pass. Right here he had held her in their first impulsive embrace.

Strange. We never had a real chance to be together, to cut each other into our grooves. In some ways I don't miss her at all. But if I can redeem myself, it's because of her. Her spirit is part of me now, just like her liver working away in Martin Stern.

He rubbed his shin, flicked a blotch of dust from his loafer, and crossed the hall to examine Martin Stern.

He liked what he saw. Stern's jaundice was gone. His face was rounding out from his cortisone, but his belly was flat. It matched his gaunt and bony frame. A livid scar seared across the margin of his ribs.

"Well, Mr. Stern, you're back on the road to health. You've come full circle since last January, and most of the dangers are behind you now. You should continue to get better."

Stern grinned. He sat on the end of the examining table, a paper sheet spread over his lap. "So I just take the pills from now on and I live forever, is that it?"

Rudd returned his smile. Celebrations were easy.

"You know nothing is forever, and the pills are not automatic. It is absolutely essential for you to return here regularly for checkup and adjustment. You do understand that, don't you?"

"I have a bit of business around here for the next couple of years. I'll drop in."

Rudd let it go. Patients heard only what they could accept; he would reinforce the importance of follow-up treatment next time. But there was another nut to crack, and a tough one. His rehearsal hadn't helped. He wondered how to begin.

"I thank you for coming to the teaching conference last month. It may have seemed needless to you, but it helps students to see a real person. They get their fill of books."

"Probably I talked too much."

"No, I'm glad you spoke your piece. No one else could have said what you said."

"One thing was maybe too much, you didn't like. You got red when I bragged you up for finding my liver."

There it was, the can of worms he needed to open. Before he could start a fresh slate he must wipe the old one clean.

He pulled the desk chair around in front of him and threw his long leg over the back of it, his foot on the seat. He leaned on his knee, his face close to Stern's.

"Mr. Stern, these last months have been a difficult time, not only for you, but also for me. I want to tell you about two events. They both concern you, and what you understand of my work for you. The first thing is your surgery. I had a bad spell during your operation; I couldn't finish it. I want you to know that only the skill and dedication of Dr. Garrison and Dr. Brovek brought you safely through."

He watched Stern's face. The eyes were like steel; one cheek twitched. His lips moved silently, as if he were calculating.

Finally he said, "Thank God for them, then, Dr. Rudd. So you were not the only one to fight for me."

Rudd did not allow his eyes to waver from Stern's.

"I was not. In fact, Mr. Stern, the person you have to thank the most is Dr. Brovek himself."

Stern leaned back as if to release the compression between them.

"Dr. Brovek I haven't had the pleasure. I figure he was the big voice in the middle of the conference."

Rudd's small laugh cracked through his tension and disappeared.

"You've got it. He's the one, and he wants to meet you. I am to bring you to his office when we are through here."

He put the chair aside and stepped to the door to wait for Stern to dress. Stern grumbled.

"Maybe a person has plans? I could have appointments this afternoon."

"He was insistent, Mr. Stern. I hope you will come. I have no idea what he wants."

Stern crumpled up his paper sheet and pulled on his shorts and pants.

"I can tell you what he wants. A big donation is what he wants. Maybe to buy a decent gown that goes around a person not just half way. For that I might listen."

He stood, tucking in his shirt tail. "So, two events, you said? The second in some way was Dr. Brovek?"

His face turned to Rudd, solemn but open.

Rudd wanted to duck, to turn away. But he had to get it all washed out, every stain of his unhappy memory. He swallowed cotton. He leaned back on his own clammy hands against the door jamb, and spoke with painful clarity.

"The second was Dr. Brovek, yes. Some of us, Mr. Stern, myself included, thought you were pretty far gone for a transplant. We thought this liver should go…somewhere else. Dr. Brovek stood alone. He insisted that it should go to you, and he made it happen. He was right. I was not your champion, Mr. Stern. Dr. Brovek was."

He stopped. He felt exhausted. He watched Stern tie his shoes, and put a slow knot in his four-in-hand. His face made no expression at the mirror. Finally he turned to Rudd; his eyes were grave.

"Dr. Rudd," he said, "the truth is always good to tell, even if it is too much. You are a good man. Whatever your troubles are, may they lose their sting."

He pulled on his jacket, too big for him now, and smoothed its rough tweed lapels against his chest. He fastened one button over his flat belly and looked at Rudd like a doting uncle.

"Now I think I should meet this Dr. Brovek."

He motioned toward the door, palm up, like the gesture of a gracious host.

"After all," he said, "what have I got to lose?"

*   *   *

Usually Horace Potts thought of himself as plain vanilla, a number-cruncher with bad arteries. But here in Brovek's office his imagination was flashing. While Brovek sat like cargo in the chair behind his desk, Potts was tuning up for their meeting with Martin Stern.

Like a puzzled playwright he tinkered with the plot, twisted it one way and then another. When the curtain came down, St. Luke's Church must belong to him. For every trick the villain played, Potts set up a counter-ploy. And always his script came to the brink of defeat, and teetered there, and he would have to play his hidden ace. Would it work?

He had taken an enormous gamble, but the stakes were—well, the whole game, to win, or to lose. He brushed his moist brow with sticky hands.

It was almost curtain time, and he needed to set the stage. He wrestled two red leather chairs from the waiting room into Brovek's office, and shoved the shabby and miserable little visitor's chair into the corner by the door. Brovek watched, saying nothing.

One of the new chairs he placed at a slant before the professorial desk, intended for Martin Stern. Potts positioned himself in the other chair, facing the door, his back to the office windows. The afternoon sun warmed his shoulders; he tried not to drum his fingers on the chair's arm. But he couldn't keep still.

"Gratitude, Sandy? Do you think there's any help there?"

Brovek's bulk filled his own oversized swivel chair. His hands were folded on his clean desk top. A neat stack of rolled architectural drawings filled the space under the green shade of his desk lamp. They were the only evidence of any preparation on the professor's part.

"Only if he feels it," Brovek said. "I didn't see much gratitude when we brought him down to Grand Rounds last month."

"Maybe we're hitting him too soon."

Potts's body was all hard right angles in his chair; his fingers began to move.

"Catch the tear in his eye, Horace," Brovek said patiently. "Don't let it get out on the cheek."

Potts nodded. "Sure…. Well, we're committed to try him today anyhow. Our moment of truth, sort of."

His fingers drummed furiously, making puny thumps on the soft leather.

Brovek said, "Do you want to talk, or shall I?"

Potts looked gratefully at Brovek. Waiting was hardest; planning was more comfortable.

"You are the authority figure. He doesn't know me at all."

"Okay, I'll start. I'll put the problem to him. But he's a business man, and so are you. You may have to step in if there's a fight."

Potts stopped drumming and pointed a finger straight at Brovek's face.

"It must not come to a fight, Sandy. We would lose then for sure. Remember, we are the ones who want something. He has the upper hand here."

Brovek snarled. "What you mean is, we had his life in our hands and gave it to him free and clear. I went out on a fucking limb for that son of a bitch, and if he…"

He cut off his words and his anger and put on a welcoming smile. Lance Rudd tapped at the door frame, and through the open door Potts caught his first glimpse of Martin Stern. Medium height, too skinny for his clothes. Pallor under his dark complexion. His brown tweed suit and dull shoes belied the acumen that Potts knew to be standing there. He watched Stern's eyes flicking about the new arena. They took in Brovek, rising at his desk. They rested momentarily on the empty chair before the desk. They swept over to Potts, squinted against the light, focusing directly on their least known quantum, Potts's face. No one smiled.

Dr. Rudd led Stern into the room.

"I believe you met Dr. Brovek at conference," he said. "Dr. Brovek, this is Martin Stern."

Ritual handshakes. Brovek's voice was liquid.

"This is a more personal meeting than that one was. Mr. Stern, thank you for coming."

Stern sat down in the indicated chair. He spoke in stiff unrevealing monotones.

"More personal for you maybe. For me the other day was personal enough."

"Different perspectives, Mr. Stern." Brovek eased his frame down onto his chair. "You have been through a dramatic couple of months. I am very pleased you are making such a fine recovery."

They're fencing, Potts thought. Feeling each other out.

"It is a miracle. After five years of being sick, that didn't do my business any good. My thanks to Dr. Rudd."

Rudd sat down in the inquisitorial chair in the corner. He squirmed in discomfort. Potts, watching the drama unfold, saw a touch of color rising over Brovek's collar. But the Professor's voice rolled on like dark velvet.

"Dr. Rudd is a fine surgeon, and has done superb work for you. We are all proud of him. And of you."

Stern said nothing. He sat impassive. Brovek continued.

"Dr. Rudd would be the first to tell you that work like this cannot be done alone, that it represents the cooperation of a whole host of other people."

Stern leaned back in his chair and stared directly at Dr. Brovek. There was no trace of warmth.

"He told me that already."

The words of agreement sounded more like a challenge. Potts frowned. He was hearing the wrong kind of music. Brovek drove ahead, apparently unperturbed.

"Part of my job, Mr. Stern, is to develop the efforts of all these people into a coordinated program, so that people like you can be helped. Kidney transplants too. Hearts, and lungs. Some day we'll have pancreas transplants for diabetes. You will be interested to know that we are starting a research program on that subject, and Dr. Rudd will be in charge of it. When we can find the funds."

Rudd's head snapped up; he stopped squirming. Potts figured this was all news to Rudd. Brovek had sprung another of his private jokes, and now he went on without missing a beat.

"Development costs money, Mr. Stern, and takes space. Our transplant program here at University Hospital must grow. We have the opportunity to become a major national center for research and patient care. We can blaze the way to great things. But we need more money, and more space."

Stern didn't stir. He occupied his place like a redoubt, as if he sat behind glass. His eyes were hooded, his flat voice a ribbon of disinterest. "Everybody wants more money and more space. Join the race, you should pardon the expression."

Potts spot-checked Brovek for any sign of his mercurial temper. So far the big one seemed unperturbed. Potts relaxed a tad. No progress so far, but no trouble either.

Brovek said, "We have an expansion project in mind, Mr. Stern. This gentleman on your left is Mr. Horace Potts, a member of our Board, and the leader of our efforts to grow. I want you to meet him."

Potts stood up and extended his hand to Stern. Again the dark eyes rested on his face, measuring. Potts met his gaze, impassive. He too had played his share of commercial poker; he knew how to count cards.

Their hands met, momentarily. Stern stayed seated. Potts stood, hesitant, then retreated to his chair. This was a tough mark here, he thought. Martin Stern had seen them coming and he didn't want to play. Somehow Brovek would have to snare him into the game.

Brovek was silent. He stared at Stern.

Stern stared back.

Brovek blinked.

"It is our hope that after your adventures here at University Hospital you will feel some…ah…interest in our institution. We hope you too will want to see it grow so that we can help more people as we have helped you."

Next thing, Potts thought, Brovek would be on his knees. It was no good this way. They had to get Stern talking before his dead weight bore them down. He spoke into the void.

"I went through emergency surgery here a few months ago, Mr. Stern. I personally feel very grateful to this institution for saving my life. I suppose you may feel somewhat the same way."

Stern swung about to look again at Potts. His lip curled.

"Ain't that nice for you, Mr. Potts! So you know how I feel? Let me tell you what you know. I think my liver is a miracle. I am glad to get well. And for my worst enemy I wouldn't wish it to go through again. Auschwitz it wasn't, but the Riviera it wasn't either. So now I want to go away from here and forget it. Thanks for the memories."

Potts cheered inside: Stern was talking. He didn't care what he said if he just got off dead center.

Brovek spoke up again, his deep rumble claiming the small room for himself.

"Yes, you are certainly entitled to a change of scenery. The Riviera might be just the thing. But before you go I am hoping for some help from you."

Stern's dam had been cracked, and now the waters poured through.

"Dr. Brovek, in my wallet is my driver license. My date of birth is on it. It doesn't say yesterday. I figured you wanted to hit me up the minute Dr. Rudd said to come over here. You are talking to a sick man, sick for five years that didn't do my business any good. You are talking maybe to the wrong guy."

Brovek leaned forward in his chair. His arms splayed over the surface of his desk and he fingered the scrolls under the green lamp shade. Going for the throat, Potts thought. And maybe go in over his head?

"No, Mr. Stern," Brovek said intently, "you are the right guy. We are at a crossroads for our University. We can lead this nation in transplant surgery, or we can die on the vine. To lead, we have to build. We need your help."

Stern's back stiffened. His jaw thrust forward, and he glared at the professor.

"You are pushing me, Dr. Brovek. Pushing I don't like. I don't even have a bill for my miracle, and probably I need another miracle to pay for the first one."

He lurched to his feet. His chair skidded backward. But he leaned over Brovek's desk, his hands jammed down just inches from the scrolls. He hissed at Brovek, his words like projectiles.

"I don't want to be ungrateful. Also I don't want to be pushed. So don't ask me for your big donation. Leave me alone. Leave me go and get acquainted with my last dollar if I still have it."

He pushed up from the desk and wheeled toward the door. He pointed a bony finger at Lance Rudd's chest.

"Dr. Rudd, maybe you'd be so kind to show me out of here. I might get lost."

Rudd stood up, looking helpless. Brovek looked in despair at Potts. Potts licked his lips. His heart raced at the opportunity yawning before him. After a thousand rehearsals, now, finally, he was at center stage.

His words came out as slow and precise as a javelin pointed at Martin Stern's spine. "Mr. Stern, we don't want one dime from you."

He watched Stern's back, draped in that loose bag of dull tweed, moving to the exit. He saw it jerk, straighten, balance itself over braking feet. Slowly, slowly, it turned. Stern's dark eyes searched Potts's face in new appraisal.

Potts slid his chair to the corner of Brovek's desk. A shaft of sunlight through the window warmed his scalp. Like a theatrical spotlight. He turned his maximum bland smile on Martin Stern, and gestured an invitation to the other chair. Stern stood in neutral; he was still poised for flight. But not flying.

"I'll stand," he said.

Potts raced through a silent prayer that his script would play.

Aloud, he said, "It is absolutely vital to our institution that we expand. Dr. Brovek would be pleased to show you the conceptual drawings of our proposal. The thing is that we need to build it exactly on the site of old St. Luke's Church, which is property that belongs to you."

Now, at last, Potts saw the kind of response he had been probing for. Stern's eyes widened. His mouth dropped open. No sound came out. Then it closed again. His hands spread guardian fingers across his belly. He sank slowly into the second chair.

"You know that?" he whispered.

"Yes, we know."

"That old priest promised not to tell."

Potts smiled. "That old priest didn't tell. The bishop and I are old friends. He told me weeks and weeks ago."

Potts sat still. When the waters are moving, let them move. He had hit some kind of pay dirt. He watched Stern reshuffle his thoughts. Stern looked at Brovek.

"Weeks ago? You knew all the time?"

"Since February."

"Dr. Rudd told me he didn't fight for me—you did."

Brovek flicked his glance at Rudd, standing open-mouthed in the doorway.

"I'm afraid that is true, too," he said.

"And you knew?...You could have let me slip away," Stern said.

And then he brightened. His tone was conversational. "But you figured then somebody else would have the option, somebody could be worse."

Horace Potts reasserted his role.

"One million dollars cash for the option to Martin Stern personally, non-transferable. We know the terms. If you had died, the bishop would have kept your money and the land too. And then he would have sold it to us."

Stern slumped in his chair. His dingy shoes looked dull even in the sunlight. Potts pressed his advantage.

"We want to build specifically on the site of the church. We think your project is good too, but perhaps another site nearby would be even better."

Stern turned to Dr. Rudd.

"All the time, you knew?"

Rudd was bewildered. "I knew you, Mr. Stern. I have never heard about St. Luke's until right now." He shot a glance at Brovek. "Nor about pancreas research, either, for that matter."

Stern wasn't interested in research. He also turned to Brovek.

"But you knew," he said. "And you fought for my liver anyway. And now you ask me, hat in hand, to walk away from a million dollars, give up the best project I've had in five years. I don't think I understand you, Dr. Brovek."

"Nobody does, I guess," Brovek said. "Maybe I don't, myself."

Potts seized the floor. He must hold Stern to the main issue.

"Look, Mr. Stern, you don't have to give up your million dollars. Exercise your option and then sell us the land; you come out a wash."

Stern sharpened. He regarded Potts with new eyes, slitting with inter-est. He sat straight in his chair, feet tucked underneath, flight forgotten. He waded into Potts with music in his voice.

"Come out a wash, Mr. Potts? Washes are for losers. Winners like me build good projects and make money. Or if we back out for some good reason, we don't wash. We keep a little back, a little rub-off, just for the experience. Why should I listen to a wash?"

Potts the playwright took one careful scene at a time; he wanted no misplay.

"I've thought that through. If you insist on holding that property, we will just turn our plan around and build on the other side. That would leave your hotel to face our delivery entrance and loading docks. Your customers would have a very nice view of our dumpsters."

He had scored. Stern's face turned dark.

"Lord of hosts," Potts breathed, "don't let Brovek say anything!"

Potts sat impassive. He dared not look at the professor. With models they had turned their plan around at least five times; it couldn't work. Brovek knew it perfectly well, but Stern didn't.

Potts didn't want to test the Lord's injunction. He put on a kindly smile, and spoke again.

"On the other hand, if we build on the church site, we will have every desire to cooperate with you. There are many ways we can help each other. A tunnel between us, for example, for free passage back and forth in winter."

Stern grunted. His brows were knit, and all his lines turned downward.

"No, Potts," he said, "you're close. But it doesn't jell. If you get your site from me, then I have to scramble. I looked over all that property before, same as you did. Dogs, all dogs. Other sites would never pay. I've got my site, and that's that."

Now Potts did look at Brovek to hook him into his next speech: Don't miss this, Sandy; watch old Horace the playwright.

"Mr. Stern, think for a minute of a checkerboard. Move your project one square toward the freeway. That is an advantage for you. And we follow you one square. We build the new hospital on the church site, and you occupy the city block at our front door. Our architects can plan together for traffic flows. They could design the intervening space for a small park, with maybe a fountain. Doesn't that appeal to you?"

Stern's face was blank; his eyes revealed nothing. He would be grappling with new ground, Potts figured, trying to get the feel of it. He would need to pace off its dimensions behind the curtain of his mind.

He looked over at Brovek to share the brink. All their hopes and plans hung on this pinpoint moment of decision, the turning point of Potts's scenario. The dynamic professor was sunk in his chair, lips ajar, as if his own role were forgotten.

Stern cleared his throat. He shrugged, spreading his hands toward Potts.

"It could be worth considering, your suggestion. I know that block exactly behind St. Luke's. It would be a good site if you built across the street. I would have to see who owns it."

Potts pressed his hands on his knees. His chin pointed straight at Stern and his words poured out over it.

"As a matter of fact, Mr. Stern, we own it. Would you care to swap?"

He heard Brovek take in his breath, a short, sharp gasp. That was one response he wanted from his climax speech, and he smiled. But he kept his eyes fixed on Stern, watching for the other response he wanted, where the plot would at last unfold.

Stern gazed at Potts, his eyes wide and his mouth hanging open. Then he started to laugh, his shoulders shaking; he whooped in a happy roar like the sound of fences falling down.

"Look what happens," he gasped. "A person feels a little gratitude and right away he goes soft in the head."

His laughter evaporated like a mist, but it left creases around his eyes. He pushed back his chair and stepped over to Horace Potts. His fingers pointed to Potts's chest with an energy that kept him planted in the seat.

"You have maneuvered a sick man right into your trap," he said. "But it is a good-looking trap." His pointing fingers reshaped themselves into a hand. "One more condition, and I will shake hands on it."

Potts stood up, smiling. But he kept his own hand at his side.

"Tell me the condition."

Stern laughed again. "A little rub-off, Mr. Potts. Just something better for me than a wash."

Potts laughed too. "I think we can work that out, Mr. Stern, I surely do," He grasped Stern's hand in the age-old pledge of promises made.

But over Stern's shoulder he watched Brovek's face, mouth and eyes wide open, stunned. Show business, Potts told himself. Every person should have a little bit of show business in his life—even a plain vanilla business man. And maybe, he thought, grinning at Sandor Brovek, the curtain call is the best part.

▼

PART NINE

FOURTH OF JULY

As the Cessna cruised past St. Petersburg Beach, Dana marveled at the spidery bones of the new Skyway Bridge, still under construction. The huge bay at Sarasota passed by on the left, below her window; it looked like a pancake on a griddle. Then she could see only threads of roads and scattered buildings making their civilizing marks on the mangrove wilderness below.

In the blazing sunshine of the afternoon the shadow of their airplane raced along the water's edge, skimming the beach, dipping its shoreside wing at every tide creek and inlet. Dana watched her husband grinning in concentration, working the Cessna's shadow like a cursor in a computer game. Only five months ago this man had been a man unknown to her, a happenstance pilot, and she had entrusted her life to him. Now he was her dear husband. She hoped she had chosen the right course.

He was certainly masterful. On the first morning of her freedom she had stepped out of the hospital, blinking at the sunshine, just the way he said she would. And he swept her into his arms, nearly carried her to his car, and drove off with hardly a word. Her body stirred with the memory.

She rested her hand on his shoulder, and he winked and returned to his game.

But he had been gentle with her, sensitive to her consent. She found herself as eager as he, and their first days of exploration were joyous—shadowed only by the condition that she had laid on him before, on a Saturday afternoon in May. They were sitting alone together in their favorite spot at the top of Keaton Amphitheater.

"I mustn't get pregnant, darling," she had said. "Not right away."

"Okay, Duck, it'll just naturally take a while—fifteen minutes, maybe twenty."

She put her forefinger to his lips.

"Be serious, Rusty! You're signing on with me, remember: girl surgeon, brand new assistant professor."

Frowning, he lifted her hand away. "Masochist," he said. "Your ambition feeds on fatigue."

"Maybe so, but that's my first self. You know that. I can't give it away."

They sat quiet then, weighing the implications. She watched the dust motes dance in the light from the yellow windows. Before she went to parenting she needed to sink a tap root into Brovek's transplant service; her surgical career had to become real. She couldn't really see any problem.

Rusty had stirred, still frowning. "If you have to, Duck, you can keep the baby spigot turned off for a while. But don't lay it on me, okay? I won't be the timekeeper."

Okay. She accepted responsibility for her own fertility, and they never talked about means. She knew all about birth control—the methods were simple enough. But she wouldn't prescribe the pills for herself. She made her first appointment with Barney Popper.

The days of May surged by full of challenge, leaving her spent. The day and hour for Popper came and went while she repaired a ruptured artery. Twice she called his office after that without any answer, once on Wednesday afternoon and once after five o'clock. Her next appointment came in June. She sat down in his office with a 1984 Redbook, its

Christmas cover dog-eared and torn. She was thumbing through the ads when Bozo went off for a Doctor Blue, a cardiac arrest on Station 21. Without a backward look she loped off to the emergency. She was too damn busy to get back to Popper again, and she didn't worry about it much. There were always condoms; she had been sure Rusty would rather go that route than delay their escape.

Now, as she looked out at the Gulf of Mexico skimming by below, her brow furrowed; maybe she hadn't worried about it enough.

"There it is," Rusty said.

A narrow slab of island stretched a fragile barrier against the sea. A few cottages clustered on the sand, and near them a grassy slash across the brush represented the island's landing strip. Rusty buzzed it once to reconnoiter, and brought the Cessna around into the setting sun and set it down without a bounce.

"I'm getting better," he grinned. "Welcome to the garden of Eden, North Captiva island."

"Garden of Eden?" she thought, four days later. "The damned snake got here ahead of us."

She stabbed at the linoleum with a straw broom, steered a thin line of sand out through the screen door. "Come on, Rusty, I don't tell you how to run your airplane. Leave my fertility to me, I'll take care of it."

He put down the dish towel. "It's not exactly comparable. When we fly together, I don't make you wear a raincoat."

She giggled, but she saw his eyes were dark.

"It's temporary, you know."

"And meantime it's ugly. It turns me off."

"Wow! I couldn't tell!"

His jaw set. She had not seen him angry before.

"Besides, love," she said gently, "the method isn't the issue. Whether I get a baby or not is the point. I have a lot of things to think through. I have obligations at the University. I don't know how I could take care of a child."

Rusty took the broom from her hands and propped it against the counter. "Come on outside," he said.

They sat on the top step. It was still shaded from the morning sun, still wet with dew. They looked out over the sand dunes dotted with tufts of sea oats and clumps of cactus. The dunes fell away to a narrow beach, and the blue gulf beckoned beyond. He pointed to a flock of white ibis spreading their black-tipped wings in some common wisdom toward a secret destination. From behind the house came the coo of a mourning dove.

"I can be home a lot," Rusty said softly. "I want to do my writing at home, and we can hire somebody to cover—whoever—when I have to fly. It will work out."

A brown anole scurried across the step below them, stopping to puff out the orange fan of its throat. Its body gradually came to match the weathered wooden step.

"Rusty, my whole life has been surgery. I've never diluted it, and I could never give it up." She looked into his eyes. "But I mustn't dilute you either, and I get scared. Am I going to be enough wife for you?"

His green eyes swept over her; she counted off what he must see. Her thick hair curled and tangled in the humidity. Her face sunburned just short of blistering. Her small body perched beside him, her bare feet resting two steps higher than his. She searched for the clarity she loved in his face, the certainty of purpose. She couldn't find it.

"I need to check the airplane," he said. "We're supposed to have thunderstorms this afternoon."

Without another word he stood up and strode off down the short path to the beach, and then away along the water's edge. She watched his figure grow smaller until he left the shore, climbed through a thicket of sea grapes by the airstrip, and disappeared.

She couldn't see why it was such a big deal to him, but it was.

My work again. It gets in the way of every personal consideration, and it kept me from doing what I should have done. But is it so much I'm asking of my new husband? For just these few days?

She wandered down to the shore and waded into the water. She swam lazily a little way. The water was warm, and salty on the tongue, and made her eyes sting. Knee-deep in the gentle surf, she stripped off her shirt and shorts, turning her body to the sun. After a while she scrubbed herself with the wet shirt, and rung out the clothes and put them on again. She waded along the shore, chilled in the soft breeze and content to let the sun dry her and turn her warm again. Her skin felt stiff with the salt.

She came back to her starting place before their cottage, and stood there a long time. In their four days here they had not been apart until now.

The water lapped at her toes. The tide was starting in, the ripples rising gradually up the sand. Fresh ribbons of foam trailed across her feet like touches of velvet. The water touched Rusty's trail of footprints, the patterns of his straight toes, his high arch, sculpted in the soft sand. She fit her heel into one of the marks and wriggled her toes. They reached only to the ball of his foot.

"One flesh," she thought; "where are you, love?"

A wave washed past her, slithered further up the shingle before it receded. The water swept around her foot, tugging at the sand beneath. She lifted her foot, and the marks disappeared, the bare sand wiped as clean as a new slate.

She shivered. The beach was not just sand. It was a litter of dead things, like broken shells. They were the empty houses of departed creatures that crunched under her foot. A flock of sanderlings skittered in and out with the wavelets. Precious little birds, drilling their quick beaks into the sand and gulping down invisible bits of sand fleas. Suddenly she saw them as killer birds. Predators.

Okay, life is a cycle, I guess. We have a time to live and a time to die, just like the sand fleas and the shells. And the shore birds. This beach is full of life because it's full of predation and death. But this is my time to live, isn't it? To make love? To be in love?

Do the shells and the fleas think that way too?

Abruptly she turned her back to the sea. A few feet away, toward the dune, a sharp ledge ran lengthwise along the beach, a two-foot cliff where the sand had been sliced away in the last storm. A sabal palm still clung to the edge, its root hairs exposed and drying. More death and destruction. Another palm had fallen nearby. It lay there prostrate, its brown fronds half buried in the sand. She sat down on it, pensive, and stretched her brown legs out straight. Her heels dimpled the sand.

The sun burned on her skin. Her shadow lengthened behind her. Far away, over the horizon, clouds began to pile up, coiled masses of cumulus growing and coming on. Another day changing, she thought. Every day rotating away and never coming back. Little fish get eaten and sea shells die. Even the island washes away, sand drifting off, trees falling down. She did not look up when Rusty sat down beside her.

"Is the plane all right?"

"Yes," he said. "Are you?" His voice was gentle.

She did not respond. They watched an advancing cloud roil and blacken as it came on. It touched the sun, and its edge blazed like a fiery ribbon before it passed over the sun and hid it altogether.

Dana straightened, clasped her hands in her lap. "I think that I try to control too many things." She turned to face him. Against the dark sky his green eyes looked black. "Some things just happen. All by themselves. Whether I want them to or not."

"Can't argue that, Duck." He waited for her.

She turned back to face the sea. She carried a line of decision in the set of her shoulders, but her words still struggled to be born. They sat in silence, their toes digging the sand. The clouds came on in a towering black line over the water, and they felt the low rumble of distant thunder. A cool breeze touched her face.

"Maybe some things ought to happen without anybody being in charge. Do you think so?"

Rusty laughed. "One thing might happen if we stay here. That lightning could give us both a charge!"

He stood up, dusted his hands together and held them out to her. The first drops of warm rain splashed against her skin, and dimpled the sand at her feet.

"Maybe I don't care," she said. She kept her hands clasped around her knees. "Maybe I want to stay right here. Do you dare?"

His teeth flashed against the dark sky. "I dare anything you dare."

Her pulse pounded in her throat.

"Make love to me, Rusty. Right now. Right here. No raincoat. We need to give lightning a chance."

PART TEN

▼

ORDINARY TIME

In the farm fields around Hangarville, summer ended and autumn came, frost, and harvest moon. In the first days of November, the radio almanac predicted snow. Hjalmar Hovelund sniffed the cold air from the east, and believed it. He still had one field of standing corn, dry now and brown, and needing harvest. He hurried out before dawn to attack it ahead of the storm. By memory and by headlight he began steering his heavy combine up and down the rows. From high up in the heated cab he looked down on the brittle seven-foot stalks below, moving steadily into the maw of his machine. He watched its five long fingers threading themselves between the rows and listened past the roar of his engine to the level sounds of shattering stems and the rain of shelled corn into garner.

Twilight began to gather in the eastern sky. If he let his eyes adjust to it, as daylight came on, he could see clearly enough. He switched off his lights. At the end of the field he steered his big machine in a close turn to line up with new rows and start his journey back again.

A white-tailed deer broke out of cover in the heavy corn, waved its snowy flag and soared over three strands of barbed wire into his neighbor's field of stubble. He watched the young buck bound away, tossing its new spikes, until it disappeared into the willows by the creek.

He thought of Danny, and familiar unspeakable pain boiled up in his chest. Danny would have been in St. Paul now, his first quarter at Minnesota ag school. He had had his heart set on that.

And now his heart was beating for somebody else. Hjalmar found a vague comfort in that. At least it was something more to think about when he thought of Danny, when he slammed into the dead end of his hopes and dreams for his oldest boy.

He sighed, pulled the wheel around and moved his big machine back along the field. The sun reached across his shoulders to touch the stalks with gold.

The children would be off to school about now, the three that he had left. He imagined their nipped cheeks turning red in the cold, their breath rising in frosty plumes as they ran down the driveway to the main road.

The dead tassels awaited their destruction coming on. Black earth and mangled stems slipped by on his left side. Ahead, at the end of the standing rows, his pick-up was parked by the gate in the barbed wire fence. He decided he would finish this pass and go home for breakfast. Maybe the kids would still be standing by the mailbox, waiting for the bus.

*   *   *

In Keaton Amphitheater, the Chief Resident in Cardiovascular Surgery was sweating out a bad case before the glares and questions of the old S.O.B. Yes, sir, Pete said, he understood the gravity of a wound infection. No, sir, he didn't know where it came from. Yes, sir, he would be glad to look up infection rates since July, and report back next week.

The conference finally ended. Pete wiped his face with a white sleeve. He would have thought the old bastard would have been in a better mood, with his fucking ground-breaking party today. Fuck him.

*   *   *

Barney Popper fumed and stamped his feet. Mizzoh had made him start his hysterectomy at half past seven, and she knew damn well he preferred ten o'clock. Now it was after eleven, he'd just got out of the O.R. and the best sweet rolls were gone. The coffee tasted strong, and he couldn't find the sports page. He glanced at the news pages instead. The Big Three auto makers were rolling in profits, and the Dow closed over 1400 for the first time. It couldn't last.

Besides, he wanted to know about the surprise trade the Vikings made yesterday. He bulled his way around the room, checked a waste basket, and looked under a couple of chairs. No luck.

He banged open the door to the doctors' john. And there under the partition he could see Walter Pugh's gray slacks dropped down over Walter Pugh's black Windsor tips. He held his voice to a controlled roar.

"Damn it, Walter, let me have the paper when you're through in there, will you?"

Walter Pugh snickered in his reedy voice.

"That you, Barney? I'm not through with the paper yet. But I've read the newspaper. Do you want that?"

He snickered some more, and stuck the rolled-up sports section out under the marble partition, like a baton for the next runner in a relay.

*   *   *

At midday in Prairie Falls, the sun was warm, and her preparations for winter made heavy work. Astry Sondergaard was grateful to stop for lunch. She had spent all morning laying straw bales in careful rows against the base of her tiny house. Her muscles hurt and her back could hardly come straight as she climbed the tilted steps into her kitchen. She served up a small dollop of cottage cheese, and another of cold beans, and sat down at the table. She put her back to the narrow window, so that she could see to read. The envelope was tattered, and the folds on the letter paper were beginning to wear through. She could have recited the message from memory, but she held it up and read it again.

> "*Regional Organ Procurement Organization*
> "*Dear Mrs. Sondergaard,*
> "*We thank you again for the gift of life you made in the donation of tissues and organs in the case of your daughter, Karen. Because skin, bone and eyes are placed through tissue banking systems, we cannot report to you about individual recipients. We can tell you that your gift of these tissues makes it possible for burn patients to be saved, for bony fractures to be healed, and for blind persons to see.*
> "*Additionally we are pleased to report that your daughter's liver was successfully placed in an adult male at University Hospital who would otherwise have died. One kidney was successfully placed in a female patient at University Hospital. The other found a matching recipient in Kansas City, and was successfully grafted. Both of these patients are now well, and free from their previous need for chronic dialysis.*"

Astry Sondergaard stopped reading there. She wished she could find more solace in all that success. The donation had been a good thing for three people—more, actually. She read on, wishing the words would change.

> "*Unfortunately the transplantation of Karen's heart was unsuccessful. As you know, transplantation surgery is difficult and hazardous, both for the organs donated and for the patients receiving them.*
> "*We wish to thank you sincerely for your generous participation in these life-giving efforts.*
> "*Sincerely, (S) Wilma Gale, RN, Director.*"

Astry Sondergaard let the letter fall to the table beside her cold lunch plate. She stared into space. Somehow it had been Karen's heart that she hoped for, all the time.

*　　　　　　　*　　　　　　　*

"They have a beautiful day for the ground-breaking, don't they, Martin?"

Lila Mae Stern let her radiant platinum hair fall long and loose over her sable collar. She tossed her head so that the sunbeams danced in her brilliance. She placed her hand on her husband's arm and smiled at his clear eyes and virile features.

"You smile a lot, you know that, Lila Mae?"

His voice was gentle, as if he had discovered a butterfly. He placed his hand over hers, and together they strolled toward the patch of lawn between St. Luke's Church and the rectory. The one building was empty now, and the other soon would be.

Ceremonial shovels stood ready in an ornamental rack, and a dozen folding chairs formed a semicircle around them. There was a microphone on a lectern, and even a spinet piano with a three-legged stool set up on a four-by-eight panel of construction board lying on the grass.

Lila Mae's face was solemn. "I want to get involved with this new hospital, Martin. I'm so grateful to them, because I have you back. And have myself back, too. There must be something I can do to help—auxiliary, volunteer, I don't know. I mean, we are going to stay here for a while, aren't we?"

His arm slid around her waist. She warmed instantly to his strength. She looked into his face, her lips pursed, her eyes their most innocent.

"Baby," he said, "with God's help we are going to live here for quite a while. We have just a whole lot of building to do, you and I. And no better place to do it than right here."

*　　　　　　　*　　　　　　　*

Sandor Brovek lumbered across the street toward the knot of people gathering on the church lawn. For a change, he was on time. After the purgatory he had survived to reach this day, his jubilation tasted triply sweet.

He looked about for Lotte; Marnie was supposed to bring her. He nodded to a slender man with a cigarette, who looked familiar. The man stared at him a moment and turned away. His name didn't surface in Brovek's mind—hell, he wasn't trying to be a politician.

He stretched tall and craned his neck to look over the crowd. Their lives would be changed by this building of his, the grand vision which would arise on this grassy yard.

At the far fringe of the crowd he spied Owen Durshaw, out of his element. The Chairman of the Board of Regents, silver hair glinting in the sun. Durshaw stood alone, casting dubious glances at the makeshift facilities, the strange faces, the ectopic piano. Brovek decided a little bit of politics might be smart.

"We are honored to have you here, Mr. Chairman."

He grasped the limp hand and guided the old gentleman toward the podium.

"I'll entertain Mr. Durshaw, Dr. Brovek. I'm sure you have other responsibilities." Susannah Politon minced up to him on tiptoe. Her hair blazed in the sun light. Brovek wished her stiletto heels would punch into the turf—they'd probably pull her shoes off.

"Thank you, Madam." Brovek bowed to her back.

Through the crowd he saw Horace Potts, and waved. He chuckled. Potts's new suit—a charcoal pin-stripe—looked neat. Had his land deal taught him something about 'rub-offs'?

He saw Rudd over there, aloof and cool at the edge of things. His new assignment was the perfect challenge for his talent, with a lot less stress on his diabetes. Rudd would do well in research, given time.

He didn't recognize the young fellow standing beside Rudd, the one in a brown leather jacket. But look at Dana Garrison come up and take him by the arm! He must be her new husband!

Garrison is turning into a star. I hope she doesn't go and get pregnant right away. Do I see a special light in her eyes? She looks awfully matronly this afternoon, hanging on her husband's arm. Did Lotte look like that, all those many years ago?

He tried to remember.

"Hi, Dr. B!" A breathy voice spoke into his ear.

He turned instead to his wife. She had never lost her grace. Unchallenged, she could pass as royalty. "Hello, Lotte," he said.

And beside her, young, fragrant, close, stood Marnie Bates.

"Thank you again, Marnie, for pitching in for us," he replied. He held himself straight and put one hand on Lotte's arm. "This is a special day for me; I want Lotte to share it."

"Right on," Marnie said. "Me too."

*   *   *

Horace Potts strolled happily through the crowd and stood at the lectern. He listened in contentment to the babble of voices, his warm smile encompassing the world. His freshly shaved cheeks shone baby pink, and his new gray pinstripe suit draped him in dapper confidence.

I'm ready for this day, he thought, in more ways than people know. Public pleasure, private delight. Only Brovek knows what I did. And bless his heart he still doesn't quite understand. But I know this day is in a big way my own personal triumph. I won't claim the credit, but I'm content.

Tomorrow we start again. I'll glue my nose to the planning table, get ready for the inevitable crises while we're building. I've gone though it all before, from the ceremonial shovel to the ribbon-cutting somewhere far down the road. I guess I've missed it. It's good for an old bird like me to contribute one more time.

From the wobbly platform he looked out at the crowd. Nurses in white. Orderlies in green cotton skivvies. Brovek and his tragic Lotte. How fine she looked today, slim and regal. But she couldn't find her way home. His eye rested for a moment of appreciation on the ripe young figure beside Lotte—Marnie Bates, her baby sitter. They were getting to be a threesome, but that wasn't his business.

At the edge of the group he spied the newly-weds, Dr. Garrison and what's-his-name, Waters. Potts felt again his ridiculous pinch of hurt, that his virgin goddess could fall in love with someone else.

He caught the eye of Father O'Leary, and they nodded to each other. It was time to begin. Potts tapped the microphone. The speakers barked in response, and the people turned. Their voices straggled off, and he began to speak.

*   *   *

Jack Herold paced the edge of the yard, squinting against still another cigarette. This was a bunch of baloney. He had been through enough agony in the past year to last him all his life.

He nearly bumped into Dr. Brovek nodding his way through the crowd, looking for somebody. "He wouldn't remember me," Jack thought. "and I've had enough of him."

Left to himself, he would just stay home with his wife and kids and never stick his neck out. But this was Mil's day; how could he say No? She was so excited. If they wanted her to sing for their special event, why shouldn't she? She was singing better than she ever had.

His heart swelled at the sight of Francine, moving through the crowd, looking for him. Her budding womanhood shocked him; how could he not have noticed?

"Come on, Daddy," she said. "Mom and Eddy are over by the piano. Let's all be together."

He ground his cigarette into the grass.

Together? His eyes stung. Maybe he should feel excited about the new hospital, considering what they did for him in the old one.

*   *   *

After the invocation and some well-intoned words from Durshaw and Politon, Potts surprised the old priest with a second call to the microphone. Father O'Leary shuffled up to the lectern, grinning at the blur of faces, his eyebrows bobbing up and down like cottontails. He recognized Martin Stern, and tried to bring other familiar faces into focus. The warmth of his heart would surely guide his words.

"Maybe you thought the invocation would be enough out of me," he began. "But in a way I am kind of a principal in the event today. When the old wrecking ball comes rolling down the street, it's to pulverize the church and the residence I have served during the last thirty years. Is this a sad day for me? Sure, in a way it is.

"But ye know, these are just buildings. Man-made things. They were never important except for the people that used them to find salvation in this puzzling world. People are going other places now in their search for God. These old buildings and this old priest aren't so much needed any more.

"But just turn around now and look across the street. That's what I've been looking at out my window every day. It's a different kind of search that goes on over there, but it's a search for life just the same. And that place is getting bigger all the time, and it's about to swallow up this holy ground under our feet. The people that come to the new hospital will be searching for different answers, and the people that serve them will be different ministers. But just like before, the people will be the children of God. If you keep your eye on the people and not on the buildings, you'll see God's work still going on.

"But now I'm moving on. I thank you for your friendship and your love. May God bless ye, each and every one."

He stopped, his hands folded on the podium, his head bowed. His eyes blurred. He didn't want to say anything more, but he didn't know which way to go.

A woman's voice bugled out from the crowd—he thought it was Maureen O'Hoolihan. "What about you, Father, what are you going to do?"

Yes, it surely was Maureen, bless her loyal heart. He tried to pick her out in the crowd. She had asked a question he was excited to answer.

"Well, good fortune has smiled on me for sure. Cruise ships need a chaplain or two, and I'm off to the sea…. Different buildings again, do you see? The people stay the same."

Maureen sounded again. He found her round face hiding under a surgical cap, and he heard her tough love resounding in the Irish bray.

"You have to come back, Father. We need you around here."

He liked the response he could give here too. God had surely showered him with blessings. "Well, Maureen, when the new hospital comes along, I do hope to serve the people in it. I'll have a little apartment in the new hotel, too, where I can live out whatever days I have left. Thanks be to God!"

His words floated off to Ms. O'Hoolihan. His grateful eyes rested on Martin Stern.

*   *   *

The program ended with the Ave Maria of Gounod, sung in the clear soprano of Millicent Herold. As people drifted back to the hospital, Lance fell into step beside Wilma Gale. He jostled her with his elbow, and chuckled.

"Look at all those nickel-plated shovels, Wilma, and see who gets to take them home. Brovek had to figure out which end was the handle, and Stern shouldn't even try to lift one."

Wilma lengthened her stride to keep up with the tall man. Her full skirt billowed around her legs. "You're right. When the sweat work starts, the nickel-plate boys won't be in sight."

They stopped at the top of the broad steps that rose to the grand entrance of the hospital. Sunshine poured warmth over them, and they drank it in. Wilma pointed at the stone arch high above, and the golden words carved into it:

TEACHING—RESEARCH—CARING

"With the new program for patients, Dr. Rudd, all three of those are tied to your saddle bags. Dr. Brovek has really laid things on you."

"Long hours, but regular, Wilma. Perfect for an ambitious diabetic."

He wouldn't hide his disease any longer.

But now he harbored a different secret. A week ago he had passed 35, and according to his mother's will he was no longer frivolous. On that day, his lawyer and his banker passed cigars, the Motherwell Trust passed its sacred corpus into Lance Rudd's hands, and he had taken a chunk of it and given it away.

"Lance? You're a million miles from here."

Wilma frowned up at him, curious at his absence. He grinned at her; even in his thoughts he had been close to her.

"I'm sorry, Wilma." He sat down on the top step. "What do you think of your new job?"

"Too early to tell." She perched beside him. "I did ROPO long enough. I'm glad you hired me." She smoothed her skirt over her knees. "But the Patient Advocate thing really is a new job, Lance. Not just to me—it hasn't been done here at all. There's no manual of instruction, and no road map."

"So what's your approach going to be?"

She nodded. "Karen left her personal notes, and I have some ideas of my own. And your support is great. I didn't expect that from a doctor."

"I took a long time to be convinced."

The pain of it rose behind his eyes, the memory of Karen slashing at his blindness. 'A hole in your program and you need to fill it.'

Wilma's enthusiasm bubbled on. "I'm going to love the office and the new conference room. We'll have teaching aids, the whole smear. Who do you suppose the donor is?"

She searched his face, and he watched her eyes, clear and steady. She had all the guile of a new puppy. He probed deeper to see how she scratched.

"I think it's anonymous, Wilma. But remember—The Sondergaard Center is only the physical facility. An advocacy program will need vision and heart to amount to anything. Do you think you can handle it?"

"You bet, Lance. I can't wait."

The words tumbled from her lips. She patted his arm and whisked away.

He closed his eyes. A smile played around his lips. He tilted his face to the sun. In the crisp November air did he detect the faint but unmistakable fragrance of roses?

*   *   *

Rusty Waters dropped the cover over his old Underwood and sat back. He stretched his elbows high behind his neck and clasped his fingers together. Five o'clock. He promised himself again he would buy a word processor. Probably a Macintosh that had one of the new—what were they, mouses, or mice? Anyhow he planned to buy it with his first writer's check. He had the money spent four different ways in his mind, but he hadn't seen the color of it yet.

He strolled to the kitchenette and dropped the corpse of a chicken into a pot of water. He turned on the burner. He was chopping an onion when Dana came in, laughing. She brushed him with a kiss.

"Honey, what's that lovely new cologne you're wearing? I love it!"

Rusty thought he would never get used to this woman, his diminutive Titan with her dark eyes and flashing mind. Her wellspring of animal energy delighted him.

"Eau Nion," he said. "It's the latest thing down at Cub Foods."

He listened to the sounds of her settling in. She was humming, but he couldn't tell what the tune was. He heard her shoes drop to the floor of the closet. Water came on in the shower. He wiped his hands and went in to the bathroom.

"Gorgeous day for your ground-breaking, wasn't it." He had to holler over the rushing water.

"Sure was."

"What part did you like best?"

The ingenuous question was the first step of their dance, the game they played to share again a recent pleasure.

"You'll never guess."

Her voice was melody over the continuo of the shower.

He guessed. "Not your favorite Uncle Horace, then, that's too easy. What about the soprano? She was beautiful." He watched the shower door, the steam and the water blurring flesh-colored patterns on the glass.

"Better than that, Russell. Are you ready?"

The water stopped and the door opened. She stood before him, water dripping from her hair. It glistened on her round thighs, and on her turgid breasts and dark nipples. Her face shone in pure, child-like wonder.

"Rusty, she moved!" Her hands spread over her rounding belly, and she opened her trembling smile to her husband's eyes. "I felt her move."

Rusty could not speak. His love for this woman overwhelmed his senses. He fell to his knees, buried his face against her wet fur, and held her close. Then, without a word, he took her dripping into his arms. He carried her to their bed and he nestled her there gently, like feathers on feathers. His whole being filled with the vision of her soft body opening before him. His clothing drifted to the floor. He stood over her, silent, throbbing. Her limitless eyes locked into his own, calling him home. Weightless, he floated down upon her, entering, received, in wordless mutual celebration.

*   *   *

Sandor Brovek cleaned up the supper dishes and put them away. He went into the den with Lotte, the soft light dim against the wall of books, his CD machine playing at low volume, the fireplace dark. He tipped back in his recliner and let out a long sigh. Across his toes he gazed at the clean, chiseled lines of his wife's profile. She had lost count of her knits and purls weeks ago, but she never complained. In her fog she seemed as contented as a child.

It had to be natural for a man his age to respond to Marnie Bates. She brought youth and life into his house, like music into a museum. She was vital and warm in the sunlight this afternoon. Her smooth skin, firm over her slender arms, so soft in the vee of her blouse. How could he not respond? He'd be dead if he didn't.

The descending arpeggio of sevenths in the Mozart Clarinet Quintet was just too perfect. He snapped off the CD and decided to put Lotte to bed a bit early.

His response to Marnie didn't mean that he would do anything. God knew that was too easy! It was a fragile boundary that separated a fatherly gentleman from a horny old man.

He guided Lotte through her routines for bed. Dear Lotte. Her fires were cold in the ashes of her mind, and he could not exploit her body for his own desire.

He tried a cold shower, but his vision of Marnie Bates returned, Marnie in that exquisite moment of life, the full blush of ripening fertility. He must not dump his problem into her life.

The shower helped; he felt better. He slid into bed beside Lotte; she was already asleep. He turned out the light.

Moonlight threw dim shadows on the wall. Lotte's regular breathing played a soft counterpoint to his own pulse that murmured in his ear as it pressed against the pillow. His ceaseless pulse. It went on whether he paid attention or not. Like waves of the sea washing up on the shore. Like the problems for his department, endless challenges, running like a stream. Students. Research questions. New technology. And always, money.

The ceremony today was a milestone, a beginning. When he stood out there with that shovel on the rectory grass, he touched the future. His chance was coming now; no one could stop him. He would turn that stream of challenges into steps to glory.

The rest of the day was celebration, and the peak, he decided, was the music. The exalted phrases of Gounod. Millicent Herold radiant. Her lovely soprano spinning out the Ave Maria, '*nunc et in hora mortis nostrae*.' Now and at the hour of our death. Millicent Herold singing with breath he had given her through his transplant program, and yes, given her with his own hands. He heard her again, in his memory, her voice soaring over the sun-bright yard, clear and easy, as if it could go on forever.

About the Author

S.R.Maxeiner, Jr., M.D., spent his professional life in the disciplines of surgery, including study, teaching, and private practice. A Clinical Professor of Surgery at the University of Minnesota, he retired in 1987 to a life of writing, boating, and land preservation in the sanctuary island of Sanibel in southwest Florida.

9 780595 187072